To Karen -

a consider friend

Member of St. Pauls.

Enjoy! Jayce Lee McStoch

JUSTICE FOR JULIE

By

Joyce Lee McIntosh

ISBN 0-7414-6612-0

Printed in the United States of America

Published June 2011

INFINITY PUBLISHING
1094 New DeHaven Street, Suite 100
West Conshohocken, PA 19428-2713
Toll-free (877) BUY BOOK
Local Phone (610) 941-9999
Fax (610) 941-9959
Info@buybooksontheweb.com
www.buybooksontheweb.com

ACKNOWLEDGMENTS

Thanks to my fellow authors in Sun City Center Writers Group, especially our tireless moderator, Rosie Clifton and editor extraordinaire, Robert Mills. Your insightful critiques have been invaluable. Thanks also to Chris Lucka and Mary Lou Bugh of Mid-Michigan Writers, for their dedication to the world of writing.

On a personal note, heart-felt thanks to my friend, Patti Foster, my talented sister, Judith Winder Lowy, and my steady-as-a-rock husband, Jim McIntosh for being such tireless readers and for giving me their unending support.

ONE

Thirty-eight and dead tired, Lindsey Delaware closed her eyes and leaned back, sinking wearily into the soft gray leather of the limo's sleek interior. Absently, she reached out to the seat beside her, then choked back a sob as her hand closed on nothingness. "You should be here, Brian," she murmured, "and you, Jules." Thoughts of them tore at her heart as brutally as the raking talons of a bird of prey. And she knew with a sad certainty that their absence was fully her doing. *This is beyond insanity*, she thought. *I can't walk down the street without being surrounded by well-wishers— and yet I've never been so alone.*

January's cold sun glistened on the white exterior of the highly polished, heavily armored limo. As it drew to a smooth stop, Special Agent Kris Andrews exited hurriedly and, after a careful scan of their surroundings, opened Lindsey's door. Extending his hand, he helped her from the vehicle and in what was for him an unprecedented move, dropped playfully to one knee and kissed her hand as if he were her knight in shining armor. "Welcome to your castle, my lady," he said with exaggerated politeness, letting Lindsey know how pleased and excited he was for her.

Shaking off her reverie, Lindsey forced herself to join his antics. Tapping him lightly atop his thick crop of neatly trimmed, sandy hair, she responded with a smile, "You may rise, Oh Faithful One." At the precise moment he regained his footing Lindsey heard a slick, soft whine, followed by a sickening thud. Instantly, the young agent sank back to his knees, then fell face forward at her feet—leaving her fully exposed to the sniper's next shot.

Twenty years earlier: Eighteen, and filled with the abundant energy and optimism known only to the young, Lindsey Delaware strode across the long stage to accept her high school diploma, then turned to the podium to deliver her speech. Her eyes searched the crowd, coming to rest on the broad form and thicket of snow-white hair belonging to her father, U.S. Senator James Delaware. He was easy to spot. Of course it helped that he was waving both arms at her enthusiastically.

As Lindsey smiled in his direction, James grinned in return, then dropped his arms and nearly blushed at what was for him decidedly undignified behavior. But today was clearly an exception for the usually reserved senator. *Valedictorian,* James thought with pride as he watched Lindsey's captivating smile gather the attention of her audience. *The highest ranking student in Dover's graduating class of over five hundred!* He wiped away tears of joy and sadness as her clear, precise voice reached into the audience, easily filling the spacious auditorium.

"To our amazing parents," she began. "We brought you here today to thank you—and to tell you that you are about to be let off the hook. No longer do you have to scold us for eating junk food, for missing curfews, or forgetting our manners. You've done your job well, and now it's up to us, the Dover High graduating class of 1998, to shoulder the responsibilities you've carried for eighteen years." Her eyes settled on her classmates seated at the foot of the stage, in majestic rows of purple and gold. "Are we ready?" she called loudly. Like a pride of eager young lions released from their cages, the students rose from their seats in a unified roar of assent that echoed through the auditorium, along with whistles, high fives, and eager shouts of, "Bring it on!"

Lindsey smiled a moment as she watched them celebrate, then her demeanor grew serious. "Are we ready to give back what we were given?" she shouted over the noise of the raucous crowd. "To not only live by the standards we were taught, but to do even better? To make personal sacrifices in the name of equality and justice? Our parents taught us right from wrong—now it's our job to right the wrongs that are happening all around us!" The room went from joyful celebration to sudden stillness as the students settled back into their seats. "I've always admired the Israeli youth who volunteer two years of their lives in service to their country when they complete their schooling," she continued. "All of them, men and women alike, dedicate themselves to using their talents to strengthen their nation and secure their freedom. Are we ready to do the same?"

James joined in the enthusiastic applause rising in response to his daughter's challenge. Although she had not shared her commencement speech with him, the strength of her words and the commitment they held for fair play and equality were no surprise. She had such a love of justice—perhaps because it had been so brutally denied her and her mother. "If only your mother were here to see this, Lins," he whispered softly, then stopped abruptly, replacing his regret with a small prayer of gratitude. It was a miracle he still had Lindsey.

TWO

A cold wind and a dusting of snow blew due west of Boston across the Charles River and swirled onto the campus of Harvard University. It was February 1999. Bill Clinton, a self-styled "New Democrat," was cruising through his second term in office with the highest approval rating of any president since WW II. But the country was growing weary· of his questionable moral behavior, and despite his popularity he was facing the dire prospect of being the first American president to be impeached since Andrew Johnson.

Lindsey had been raised during the Reagan years and she and her father, both staunch Republicans, were looking forward to the fall election. The Texas Republican, George W. Bush, was gearing up to knock Clinton's vice president, Al Gore, out of the presidential contest, and Lindsey and her father had high hopes that the country would soon be led by a conservative Republican once again. But at this particular moment, politics was the last thing on Lindsey's mind. She was deeply engrossed in a thick textbook dealing with the history of criminal law, while munching on a slab of pizza dripping with extra sauce and cheese.

Julie, Lindsey's Harvard roommate, helped herself to a third slice from the box as she eyed Lindsey pensively across their small dorm room. "It's not fair, you know." Lindsey looked at her questioningly. "Not fair that someone so damn smart is so disgustingly gorgeous!"

4

"So you'd prefer me to be dumb and ugly?"

"Maybe," Julie replied with a teasing smile, but Lindsey detected a ring of truth in her response.

"Julie Trent—I think you're half serious!"

"Well, think about it, Lins. What chance do I have with any of these handsome hunks on campus once they get a good look at my sexy roommate?"

Lindsey visibly retreated from her words. "You don't really know me, Julie, or you wouldn't say that . . . believe me, I'm no competition."

It was an odd set of circumstances that had brought the two young women together. Upon graduating from high school, Lindsey had captured a highly prized Harvard scholarship that provided a virtual free ride, covering all costs of tuition, room, and board. Knowing her father could well afford to pay for her college education many times over, Lindsey's sense of fair play kicked in. She insisted James sponsor another deserving student from the Dover graduating class who would jump at the chance to attend the Ivy League university, but could ill afford its exorbitant fees. After careful screening, Julie Trent had been the fortunate choice.

With a high school graduating class as large as theirs, Lindsey and Julie, who had socialized in different circles, barely knew each other. But when James and Lindsey first met with Julie and her parents, the two eighteen-year-olds took an instant liking to each other and although there was no expectation that they would room together, they both agreed it would be a good match.

They were well into their first year at Harvard and had never had a serious disagreement, but at this moment Julie wanted to kick herself when she saw the look of hurt on Lindsey's ashen face. "Hey, I was only teasing, Lins," she said earnestly, and felt absolutely miserable as she watched unbidden tears fill Lindsey's somber gray eyes. She had always admired Lindsey's great good looks from afar while in high school, and had been astonished to find that Lindsey's air of casual elegance was not the least bit affected. She was the kindest person Julie had ever met, as well as the smartest.

Julie reached out and took Lindsey's hand. "Seriously . . . it was just a joke. I *love* having you for a roommate, and it's okay that you ace all your exams and look like a movie star."

Lindsey snuffed back her tears and pushed her hair away from her face, shaking her head. "We have to talk, Jules. I should have told you sooner, I guess, but it's something I don't like to get into if I don't have to."

"Good grief! What is it, Lins? I can't imagine you having any deep, dark secrets."

"Well, it is deep and pretty dark, at least for me." She hesitated as she looked into Julie's concerned eyes. "I'm sure you heard about the accident a couple of years ago . . . the one that took my mother's life?"

Julie nodded. "I guess everyone at Dover High knew about it, Lindsey, and how terrible it was for you and your dad. It must have been so hard to come back to school."

With an effort, Lindsey pushed away the painful memory, then took both of Julie's hands in her own. "What few people know, Julie, and what I seldom talk about is how bad my injuries were when that drunken idiot slammed his car into Mom and me. There was nothing the doctors could do to help my mother. And they—they had to perform radical surgery on me to stop the bleeding. They saved my life . . . but I'll never be able to have children."

Julie drew back in shock. "Oh God, Lins," she gasped. "I'm so sorry."

"Yah, me too." Lindsey's tears were flowing freely now and Julie wrapped her in a comforting hug, sharing in her sadness. "I know a lot of women are happy with their careers, Jules, and don't even want kids—but I'm not one of them. Maybe it's because I was cheated out of the chance to be a mom, and because I see how much it hurts Dad. Jeez, it's so unfair, you know? He'd have been a wonderful grandfather." Lindsey pulled away and tried to collect herself. "And that, dear friend, is why I won't be competing with you in the dating scene. That deep, dark secret is one of the first things I have to get into if a guy starts to get halfway serious."

Out of equal parts concern and curiosity, Julie went on-line to look through the archives of the *Dover Post*, finding the articles from two years earlier that dealt with Lindsey's accident. Julie was infuriated to learn that the man responsible for the senseless travesty had been driving under a suspended license *and* had seven previous convictions for drunk driving. Apparently, through the efforts of a well-paid, zealous attorney and a too-lenient judge, the man had never been jailed for more than a few weeks after each DUI. Then as if it were his God-given right, he would return to being the dangerous drunk behind the wheel—until he'd blown through a red light and struck Lindsey and her mom as they crossed the busy intersection. Too late, he was convicted of vehicular homicide and given a twenty-year sentence for ripping away the life of Lindsey's mother. *And the lives of Lindsey's unborn children,* Julie thought sadly to herself.

Later, Julie admitted to Lindsey that she had read the details of the horrific accident. "I don't know how you got through that, Lins, without going ballistic. I'd have wanted to kill the guy."

Lindsey admitted that, at age sixteen, it had been a difficult struggle for her to leave the devastation behind and go on with her life. "But Dad was a big help, along with extensive grief therapy. And I knew it was what Mom would have wanted. So now I just focus on my dream to finish school, become a lawyer, and serve as a public defender."

"And I know you're going to be terrific, Lins."

"I hope so. But Dad keeps insisting that I would go much further in my law career as a prosecutor."

"No way, Lins. I know you. Prosecution just isn't part of your nature—despite the unfair hand you were dealt."

*   *   *

Their time at Harvard seemed to ebb and flow—sometimes dragging endlessly through the sheer drudgery of monotonous classes, and at other times accelerating at the speed of light when a challenging professor set their imaginations on fire. Lindsey was majoring in pre-law, while Julie focused on the humanities. Julie often told Lindsey that when they finally graduated from Harvard and entered their chosen careers, she seriously envisioned herself as a renowned psychotherapist and Lindsey as a famous, hot-shot attorney.

The two females made for an attention-getting contrast on campus. Lindsey was strikingly tall with a long, willowy body and shoulder length ash-blonde hair that she wore caught back in a thin suede band, or left to fall in silky waves around her classic, ivory-skinned face. Her serious gray eyes held a hint of blue, and when she smiled, men and women alike found her beauty captivating. Julie, who envied her roommate's stunning good looks, seemed oblivious to the fact that she was just as attractive in her own way. Of medium build with choppy brown hair and a pixie smile, her large, dark-brown eyes and generous mouth easily caught the attention of watchful young males. She was rarely at rest, her curvaceous body exuding a graceful energy that had most men wondering what it would be like to capture her in a romantic embrace.

Ironically, even though hands down they were two of the best looking women on campus, neither of them ventured seriously into the Harvard singles scene. Julie, despite her often stated interest in handsome male hunks, seemed to shy away from most dating opportunities, while Lindsey directed every ounce of energy into her studies. She loved the law passionately, and the fascination it held for her seemed to satisfy all her needs, including the need for male attention.

"Sublimation!" Julie proclaimed one afternoon, lifting her head from the pages of her *Intro to Psych* textbook and pointing an accusing finger in Lindsey's direction. They were sprawled comfortably on several stuffed, multicolored pillows littering the floor of their dorm room, and had been quietly studying until Julie's sudden declaration.

"Why are you pointing at me like that, Julie Trent, and what on earth does sublimation have to do with me?"

"It's what you're doing—I knew Freud had a word for it! You're transforming all your sexual energies into nonsexual activities!"

"Get outta here," Lindsey grumbled. "You and your psychology mumbo-jumbo. It's so . . . esoteric—not concrete like the law. And you can't prove any of Freud's theories. They're simply not—scientific."

"Can too," Julie protested, her chin in the air. "Just look at you, Lins. You're a perfect Freudian example of sublimation. Listen to this: 'One with few sexual outlets who diverts sexual inclinations into passionately creative work of the highest order.' That's you! Why, from what I've heard, even your profs say no one on campus can hold a candle to your creativity in the classroom—or your passionate love of justice."

"Let me see that," Lindsey scowled, reaching for the textbook. Scanning the pages, she quickly found what she was looking for. "Aha! See? It says right here: 'Just how the human mind diverts instinctual, sexual energies into the pursuit of art or science is unresolved.'" She slammed the book shut and handed it back. "Can't prove it, Jules, so it doesn't exist—and it has nothing to do with me."

With a knowing smile, Julie silently reopened the book. *Does too*, she said to herself quietly, then with a contented sigh snuggled down and burrowed deeper into the mysterious workings of the human mind.

*   *   *

It was near the end of their sophomore year, with George W. settling into a highly contested presidency, when a very excited Julie announced that she had just been invited to the Delta Chi Delta frat party.

"And you're going?" Lindsey asked in surprise.

"No, *we're* going, girlfriend! You *and* me." Lindsey vehemently shook her head in disagreement. "Common, Lins, it's gonna be the highlight of the year. The Delts are known for their wild parties and Jonas—isn't that a great name?—anyway, he's in my Human Sexuality class, and he invited me and said to bring you along. It's not really a date—I don't think. They're just asking a lot of women to come for the fun." She looked at Lindsey critically. "You know—F-U-N? That thing we never have time for?"

Despite her reluctance, the following Friday night Lindsey found herself at the frat house, submerged in a sea of partying students who were sloshing drinks on the Delt's much used furniture and carelessly grinding out cigarette butts on the oak plank floor. Lindsey was downing her fourth Bud Lite, about three more than she'd ever had at one sitting before, and wondered why Julie was still nursing her first. They'd promised each other to relax and blend into the happy throng. No point in doing this if they didn't do it right.

As she felt the warm buzz of alcohol flood her system, Lindsey looked around with a sloppy smile. She had to admit, there were some gorgeous looking guys in the crowd, especially Jonas. His loose dark hair hung to his shoulders and glistened handsomely in the overhead lighting. At this minute Julie was leaning into him and talking loudly so she could be heard above the crowd noise and the pulsing beat of the 'Frat Brats,' a popular on-campus, hard-rock band. Giving up, Jonas took her hand along with Lindsey's and pulled them out onto the veranda. "Couldn't hear a thing in there, sweetface," he grinned at Julie. "So tell me again why we haven't seen you two around our social milieu before."

Jonas continued holding Julie's hand and she laughed with obvious pleasure. "It's all Lindsey's fault," she confided. "For the past two years she's confused *doing* great with *feeling* great, and I, fool that I am, went along with it."

Lindsey sputtered in protest. "Not true, Jules." She glared at her through a haze of alcohol.

"Aha," Jonas said with the superior smile of a psych major. "You're one of those foolish women who think the pure sense of academic accomplishment can take the place of mad, passionate sex." As Lindsey shook her head in denial, Jonas eyed her speculatively. "Okay, let's put it to the test, shall we . . . a pop quiz?" Without waiting for an answer he asked, "Since coming to good old Harv,' how many guys have you dated?" She stared at him silently. "Okay . . . how many times have you partied 'til dawn?" No answer. "Had a hangover? Smoked pot?"

Lindsey was beginning to feel foolish along with feeling slightly tipsy, and she quickly covered it with anger. "I know how to party, thank you, Jonas!"

"Is that so?" Reaching into his jacket, he drew out a sorry looking, hand-rolled joint of marijuana. With a teasing smirk, he lit it and held it out to her. Lindsey backed away, the heavy sweet aroma mixing with the effects of the alcohol she'd consumed. "Show me, pretty girl. Prove to me you know how to party."

Julie reached out and took his arm. "Don't, Jonas. We've never . . . we don't—"

He shook his head in disbelief. "Never?" He took a step closer to Lindsey and stared into her gray eyes, misty with the effects of alcohol. "Daddy's girl, right? You promised him you'd never smoke pot and never get laid. Beautiful woman like you? How sad is that?"

In defiance, Lindsey snatched the joint from his hand, sucked in a mouthful and inhaled deeply. Coughing furiously, she handed it back to him. "There, satisfied?" she rasped.

He grinned happily and tried to hand the joint to Julie, who was wearing a look of absolute fear. "C'mon sweetheart, Jonas likes to share his weed with beautiful women." She backed away, shaking her head and looking at the smoking joint as if it were a writhing snake about to attack.

Lindsey, feeling the effects now of both alcohol and marijuana, laughed gaily at Julie's reluctance. "Now who's being a sublimating goody two-shoes?" she teased. "Take a hit, Jules. This party was your idea, after all."

"No . . . not this." To his surprise, Jonas saw tears on Julie's cheeks and taking his thumb, gently wiped them away. Then he leaned down and pressed his forehead seductively against hers. "Do it for me, Baby," he whispered, then took a hit and blew the smoke tantalizingly in her ear. "Just for me." He held it to her lips and watched carefully as she reluctantly took a small puff. "There now, that wasn't so bad, was it?" He took another deep draw for himself, holding the smoke in his lungs for several long seconds before exhaling, then handed the joint back to Lindsey. "Go for it, Lindsey," he encouraged as she took her second hit.

Lindsey seemed to handle this one better and nodded in appreciation as she passed it back to Julie. "It gets better, Jules. Try it again." Julie protested weakly, but Jonas urged her on. Within minutes, the three had smoked the joint down to a nub, and Jonas fished a clip out of his pocket to hold what was left so they could finish off the last few dregs.

As the warm breeze of May stirred around them, the two young women were now flying high on pot. Jonas watched with interest. Julie's look of abject terror had dissolved into something more contented and dream-like, and he smiled knowingly, fairly certain she'd be back for more. Lindsey, on the other hand, seemed to be having an adverse reaction to the warm air, cold beer, and high-grade Mexican pot. She wore little make-up, and her normally appealing complexion had taken on a greenish hue. Jonas snickered knowingly as he watched her hands begin to shake, sweat forming on her brow. In a panic, she reached for Julie as her stomach wrenched, then roiled viciously.

"Whoa, girl," Jonas exclaimed as Lindsey violently ejected the contents of her unhappy stomach onto her Reeboks. Jonas grabbed her by the arm and steered her off the porch onto the lawn where she promptly threw up again. "Think we should get your friend home and tucked in for the night, Julie." He looked at her with a charming smile. "Then you and I can finish what we've started—you'll love it, I promise."

THREE

Settling down with her laptop, Lindsey idly scanned through the current listing of job opportunities found on *Legal Jobs.Com*. Her father, always the pragmatist, strongly advised that before beginning her final year at Harvard, she immerse herself in a summer job—one that would provide a blast of realism as to what it really means to be a public defender. Not too subtly, he was trying to steer her in the direction of working on the prosecutorial side of the law, and even though she had a year of course work to complete before applying to law school, he was insistent that she work for a time under the auspices of a municipal court judge.

"Municipal Court Bailiff—safe and boring," Lindsey grumbled into the cell phone propped under one ear as she read the job description appearing on her screen. "Listen to this, Jules. I'd be arranging Judge Skow's personal schedule, keeping his court docket in order, and making sure he had all the necessary legal reports needed to make judicial decisions."

"Sounds good," Julie responded in a sleepy voice, trying to wake from a long afternoon nap that had been interrupted by Lindsey's call.

"But jeez, Jules, municipal court jobs deal only with tame misdemeanor offenders. I can see it now. This Judge Skow character will be meting out blind justice to irate parking ticket offenders, clueless mentally ill bag ladies, and scared shitless teenage shoplifters."

"Doesn't sound real exciting," Julie agreed, smothering a yawn.

"Oh well," Lindsey sighed as she jotted down the phone number. "At least it'll give me some courtroom experience.

But as she continued to scroll down, her eye caught something of much greater interest. She sat at full alert. "Hey Jules, this one sounds more like it. *'Raver County Adult Probation (RCAP) now interviewing qualified applicants to manage small caseload. Temporary position.'* That would be way cool, Julie! County probation officers deal with felons coming through the Court of Common Pleas. It's far more serious stuff than municipal court misdemeanors."

"And this serious stuff is what you're looking for?" Julie asked skeptically.

"Sure. I'd be working with a caseload of convicted felons who would have been on their way to prison except for a benevolent judge who granted them probation." She paused a moment, thinking of her mother. "Or more likely, they avoided prison through the efforts of an expensive defense attorney. Grand Theft, Felonious Assault, Breaking & Entering, Drug Trafficking, Attempted Rape—"

"Whoopee! Sounds like you hit the bottom of the barrel—just what you wanted," Julie teased.

Lindsey ignored her. *"And* I'll be out in the community, face-to-face with the offenders—not stuck in some stuffy courtroom all summer!" Her excitement was growing by the minute. "I'm calling them right now, Jules . . . ah, sorry I woke you."

"S'okay. Not sleepy now, just hungry. Call me later, girlfriend."

Immediately after ending her call with Julie, Lindsey dialed the listed number for RCAP, crossing her fingers that the position had not yet been filled.

Two days later, an enthusiastic Lindsey Delaware drove her silver Sebring convertible along I-95 to an interview just over the state line in Raver County. Working in the heavily populated county seat over a hundred miles from her home in Dover would require her moving there for the summer, if she got the job. It had been explained during her initial phone call that the current RCAP officer was on maternity leave and if hired, Lindsey would be handling her caseload until September. Perfect! Just in time to begin her Harvard senior year in the fall.

She found a parking spot a few blocks from the probation office and nervously walked the bustling streets toward what she hoped would become invaluable training in her chosen field of criminal law. She was dressed in a trim gray suit interwoven with threads of blue that accented the hint of azure in her eyes, and she strode smartly along the city sidewalks in gray, low-heeled pumps. She had smoothed her glistening hair away from her face into a soft twist at the base of her neck and, even though it was a gloriously warm day for May, had driven with the top up on her convertible to stay neat as a pin. She was as ready as she could get.

Lindsey had shared her good news about the interview with Julie, but had not yet said a word to her father.

"Why ever not?" Julie had questioned. "Your dad's cool, Lins. He'd never try to stand in your way."

"No, he wouldn't. Oh, he'd scowl and grumble at first about my reckless decision, but in the end he'd put aside his protective misgivings and start pulling strings to get me the job. But I'm determined to do this on my own, Jules. It's time I carve out my own future without Senator James Delaware smoothing the way."

Of course, Lindsey sighed as she continued her brisk walk to the interview, oblivious to the admiring stares she was garnering—anyone answering to the name of Delaware in this part of the country would find it nearly impossible to remain anonymous or avoid preferential treatment. Her home state derived its name from one of her very own forefathers, the 3rd Baron De La Warr, and over the years the Delaware lineage had done so well in state politics that it was now virtually impossible to differentiate the state from the Delaware family.

Lindsey had seriously considered applying under an assumed name—Julie's to be precise—but ditched that idea when it hit her that using an alias was a ploy used by those who operated on the wrong side of the law—not something a smart probation officer would do! She decided she'd just have to make light of her illustrious ancestry if it came up during her interview.

It turned out to be a long, grueling day—much more demanding than Lindsey had anticipated. After checking in promptly at 9:45 a.m., she was handed a five-page exam by a well-dressed, attractive but unsmiling brunette working behind the front desk. "Take the hallway stairs to the basement classroom," she instructed, barely giving Lindsey a glance. "Elevator's out of order."

At the foot of the long, metal staircase, Lindsey found a tattered GED sign taped to the door of a musty, windowless room. Stepping in, she saw that the long narrow classroom contained several haphazard rows of uncomfortably small, scarred school desks. With effort, Lindsey squeezed her long frame into one of the few remaining seats. She had been told that today's group of applicants was only one of several— over two hundred had applied for the job. *Who would have thought there was this much interest in becoming a temporary county probation officer?* she wondered. Even full-time, the job paid barely $30,000 a year even though it required an extensive education.

Although Lindsey, as a rule, sailed through written exams, this one held some surprises. After three pages of mostly ethical questions—"Would you hire one of your probation clients to work on your car? He is a mechanic by trade and in need of work to support his large family." "Would you advise a distraught probation client facing a divorce to seek pastoral counseling?"—there followed several scenarios describing defendants and their criminal behavior. The question asked after each example was, "What sentence would you recommend the court impose on this defendant? Explain your reasoning."

Two hours later, Lindsey returned the completed exam to the disinterested brunette at the front desk. "Not exactly a test you can study for," Lindsey mumbled. The woman sniffed and told her to check back after lunch to see if her score warranted taking the next step—a personal interview. Lindsey hadn't a clue as to how well or how poorly she had done, so after a hurried lunch that settled in her stomach like a hot jalapeño, she returned once again to the probation office, where she was pleased to learn that her interview was scheduled for two o'clock that same afternoon.

As with the written exam, Lindsey found she was ill prepared for what followed. At the appropriate time, she was led by Stephanie (the brunette had finally decided to divulge her name) to a conference room for what Lindsey expected would be a one-on-one interview. Instead, she was faced with a room full of at least a dozen conservatively dressed men and women. As she stared in stunned silence, a tall, darkly handsome man stood from the long conference table and introduced himself as Royce White, director of RCAP. He gave her a friendly handshake, then indicated an empty chair at the head of the table. As she seated herself, the others began introducing themselves as either probation supervisors or Raver County Court of Common Pleas officials.

Before she was barely settled, the officious-looking group began plying her with a barrage of questions that delved into counseling theories, interracial biases, supervision styles, communication skills and finally, her personal understanding of criminal justice. Was it to punish or to rehabilitate? Lindsey stumbled through her replies and forty minutes later, just when she thankfully thought the interview had come to an end, one of the female supervisors, Samantha, addressed her abruptly.

"I'm curious, Ms. Delaware. How on earth did you manage to score so highly on our written exam?" She eyed Lindsey suspiciously, as if she had somehow acquired prior knowledge of the test questions. The audacity of the woman's challenging remark left Lindsey speechless, and she could only stare at the woman open-mouthed until Royce stepped in and smoothed over the tense moment.

"I want to compliment you, Lindsey, on your superior writing skills. And I think what Sam meant to say was that you were right on target with your sentencing recommendations, which is remarkable for someone with no prior courtroom experience." Samantha snorted at his comment as if it lent credence to her suspicions.

That was too much for Lindsey. She rose and stared the woman down. "I strongly believe in fairness and justice," she stated slowly and clearly, "for the victim most certainly, but also for those people caught up in circumstances that make it difficult to walk the fine line of civil obedience. Perhaps that had something to do with my performance on the exam!" With that she turned, shook the director's hand, and thanked him for his time. The room was silent as she shut the door firmly behind her.

Driving back to Dover following the interview, Lindsey lowered the top of her Sebring and sped Southeast along the interstate as she mentally replayed her disastrous performance. Not only had she acted a complete failure, she now looked like one. Her suit was wrinkled, her hair had fallen loose and was whipping around her face, and she had rubbed off what little makeup she had worn. She dreaded telling Julie about the whole affair, but knew she'd feel better after unloading on her. Thank goodness she hadn't said anything to her father!

Julie, rather than returning home to her parents for the summer, had found a no-brainer, part-time job at a local bakery and was staying with Lindsey and James. She had her own room in the Delaware home and preferred being there even though her parents lived only a few minutes across town. Lindsey could understand Julie not wanting to be around her mother. The few times Lindsey had met her, she seemed a distant, almost bitterly cold woman. Julie's dad, however, was just the opposite. Outgoing and likable, Mr. Trent was just plain fun to be around. The talented band director at a local high school, he was very popular with staff and students alike. Whenever Lindsey mentioned the striking difference between the two, Julie brushed it off and simply changed the subject. She made it clear, without actually saying so, that any discussion of her parents was off limits.

When Lindsey reached home, she went straight to Julie's room, tapped lightly, then opened the door. Julie, stretched out on her bed with a movie magazine, turned her head and looked at Lindsey expectantly. Then, taking in her disheveled appearance and glum expression, she offered a sympathetic, "Uh, oh—not so good, huh? What on earth happened?" Julie couldn't fathom Lindsey blowing a job interview. "They disqualify you because of your dad? That could work against you, I guess."

"His name never came up." Lindsey sank onto Julie's bed, lowering her head into her hands and rubbing them discouragingly against her face. "But it was a pure disaster, Jules. And the worst of it is, even if I were offered a 'do over,' I don't think I could handle the stupid thing any better."

"Lins, I refuse to believe that! I'm sure you impressed the heck out of them! You're just underestimating yourself— I bet you blew everyone else out of the water, and you'll be the last applicant still afloat."

Lindsey shook her head morosely and rose from the bed. "You should have been there, Jules . . . well, there's no hope for it. I might as well give up now and apply for one of those darn municipal court jobs." As she grumbled, she wandered over to Julie's desk and absently picked up a current grade transcript that had been thrown carelessly aside. Lindsey gasped. "Jules! What the heck? Your GPA is down to 2.5! If it drops any lower you'll be put on academic probation!"

Julie scurried off the bed and grabbed the transcript out of Lindsey's hand, glaring at her as she tore it in two and tossed it in her wastebasket. "There's more to life than getting good grades," Julie said defensively.

"Like Jonas?" I know you spend most of your free time with him—but I assumed you were keeping up with your classes." Lindsey took her by the shoulders and shook her in frustration. "What's going on Jules? You've changed. You seem so . . . so lackadaisical since you started seeing him, almost too much so. Nothing seems to bother you. You sleep in late, then you wander around in a daze, eating everything in sight . . . if that's love, please spare me!"

Julie shrugged and threw herself back onto her bed, fluffing the pillow under her head and closing her eyes as if preparing for a nap. "Julie, listen to me!" Lindsey said sharply. "You had a 4-point average your first two years here. Most kids mess up when they're freshmen, not juniors."

Julie opened her eyes and stared at the ceiling. "What can I say—I'm a late bloomer."

"You're not blooming—you're wilting!"

Julie chuckled and patted her tummy. "How can you say that? I've gained 15 pounds since meeting Jonas."

Lindsey, sensing she was losing the battle, took a deep breath and regrouped. "Are you happy?" she asked quietly.

"Never more so."

Lindsey didn't doubt her words. "Tell you what, Jules, if you keep your grades up until we graduate, I'll make sure you and Jonas have the best wedding ever."

Julie cut her a hard glance, started to speak, then changed her mind and said resignedly, "I never said Jonas would marry me, Lindsey." With that, she turned away and buried herself deeply in her pillow. Lindsey stared in stunned disbelief for a full minute before giving up and leaving Julie to her nap. *Today has been a nightmare*, she thought as she silently pulled the door closed behind her. *Between my rotten job interview, and then discovering Julie's sacrificing herself for that jerk Jonas, it runs a close second to the worst day of my life!*

The phone call came two days later. As if shell shocked, Lindsey remained helplessly silent as Royce White enthusiastically congratulated her and asked if she could report the next morning at eight to start her training. "I know I'm rushing you, Lindsey—you have to find housing here, and all. But the probation officer, p.o., you're filling in for left two weeks ago and her caseload desperately needs attention . . . Lindsey? Are you there?"

"Mr. White? You—you're offering me the job? I . . . I thought, after the interview . . ."

"It's Royce . . . and you did outstandingly well," he laughed. "The officers always give applicants a rough time— it's a test to see how well they can handle the stress of dealing with—shall we say, a large number of less than cooperative probation clients."

Somehow Lindsey doubted that Samantha had simply been testing her. Even so, she politely accepted the position, assured Royce she'd see him first thing in the morning, and quietly ended the call—then screamed exuberantly at the top of her lungs. Her father came running up the stairs from his study, his face an ashen white. "Good Lord, Lindsey! What on earth—?"

She threw herself in his arms and hugged him. "Nothing's wrong, Dad. Everything's wonderful, in fact. I just landed a great job for the summer—all on my own. And I know I'm going to love it . . . as much as you'll hate it."

FOUR

Lindsey threw enough clothes in the back of her Sebring to get her through a week of work at RCAP, then took off for Raver before sunrise. She reached the probation office with time to spare, but her heart skipped a beat as she took in what in her nervousness, she had failed to notice before. The windows lining the narrow three-story brick building were badly in need of a good washing, while the worn steps leading to the doorway were littered with empty paper cups and a scrunched-up McDonald's bag. The large entrance door had shed most of its green paint and was paneled over with plywood where several panes of glass were missing. As she stepped inside the building she saw that the elevator, doors wide open, was still out of order—and had no doubt been so for some time. It was littered with old papers and something suspiciously wet in a back corner. At that moment she vowed never to invite her father to RCAP!

When Lindsey reached the front desk, Stephanie eyed her sullenly as she handed her a folder full of blank employment forms. "Fill these out," she said sternly, "then I'll take you to see Mr. White." Twenty minutes later, Stephanie walked Lindsey to Royce White's office, knocked loudly, then opened the door and left Lindsey standing.

Royce waved her in and pointed to a chair at the side of his desk as he continued talking on his phone. When he finished he gave her a warm smile, rose from his large metal desk and went to a file cabinet where an ancient Mr. Coffee machine perched on top. He filled two Styrofoam cups with some of the hot, strong brew and handed her one. "Hope you like it black—it's all we've got to offer. We're lucky to have this, I guess. As you can see by our surroundings, the taxpayers aren't putting much funding into our county justice system at the moment. When I started here eight years ago, Lindsey, our county probation officers were among the highest paid in the state . . . now we're the lowest." He laughed softly. "Nothing to do with my management skills, I can assure you."

Royce spent the next few minutes giving Lindsey a brief history of his background—retired military, master's degree with a strong emphasis on counseling, and fifteen years in criminal justice. His dark skin was smooth and ageless— only his slightly balding gray hair gave away his age.

"I like to think I made director of RCAP on my own merits, Lindsey, but you'll meet several supervisors here who were passed over and think otherwise. They're convinced I was given the job because I'm African American, and there's nothing I can do to change their minds." He smiled at her openly. "I guess you'll have to make up your own mind in the short time you'll be here. Actually, you and I are in the same fix, I think. A lot of the staff here will assume you were given this job because of your father."

Lindsey's head shot up. "I . . . I was hoping—you knew then? *Is* that why I was hired?"

"Not at all. If anything, the officers were much rougher on you during the interview because of your background. But despite that, you managed to convince them that you were the best candidate for the job."

"Still . . . I was hoping I could just fit in here without anyone noticing."

He laughed long and hard. "Lindsey, that's about as likely as me fitting in here without anyone noticing I'm black!"

Minutes later, Royce walked Lindsey down a long, dusty hall to meet Denise, the p.o. who had agreed to take over Lindsey's training. Like Stephanie at the front desk, Denise was smartly dressed and attractive, but was a petite blonde and far more friendly. She put Lindsey at ease immediately, her large blue eyes and long lashes painting an appealing picture. "I hear your interview was pretty tough."

"How did you know?" Lindsey asked.

"Girl, there are no secrets around this place. Working in the court system is like living in a soap opera. But let me tell you, if you think that interview was rough, wait until I fill you in on everything a p.o. has to do!"

The small caseload mentioned in the on-line ad turned out to be eighty-six strong, mostly men, with a smattering of twenty or so women. Denise warned her that the few women Lindsey would be working with would give her as much grief as all the guys put together. "The women offenders were used to a free ride—a few days in jail and then back home. Judges were reluctant to impose longer sentences because most of them have kids at home with no one to care for them, so they just got a slap on the wrist. Not anymore! Times have changed. Now it's all about punishment as a deterrent and sending the kids off to Children's Services."

"Is it working? I mean the prison sentences. Are the women less likely to re-offend?"

Denise shrugged. "Hard to tell. They rarely complete their Conditions of Probation successfully, so they're sent back to prison because of their failure to follow through with the judge's orders."

"Conditions of Probation?"

"It's like a contract you have each new client read and sign: 'No new offenses, report to your p.o. twice a month, drop urines for drug testing every week, get a job or enroll in GED classes, pay off your fines, court costs, and any restitution imposed by the judge—or go back to jail.' It'd be pretty easy for you and me, but almost impossible for a lot of them. Most have no transportation, no reliable babysitters, and very little money. I tell you, sometimes I feel like a tyrant lecturing them about having to follow through better. But if they don't, I have to take them back to court on a P.V.—that's a Probation Violation, and they have to explain to the judge . . . well, you'll find out."

By the end of the day, Lindsey had "found out" more than she wanted to know, and was trying to assimilate all of it before dealing with the fifteen clients that were scheduled to see her beginning at nine the very next morning.

*　　*　　*

Julie found Jonas sitting on his deck watching the fast flowing Charles River make its way downstream. On the far west side of Cambridge, he had a magnificent view of the water and was only a short drive from the university. Today, she had driven from Dover through several hours of crushingly heavy traffic to see him.

"Hey, Babe," he greeted her. "Staying for the weekend?" A late afternoon breeze moved through his long dark hair as he motioned her to a deck chair beside him. He smiled lazily as he lit up a joint and handed it to her.

She fell wearily into the canvas chair, tipped back her head, and closed her eyes as she drew in a deep hit of the drug. "Maybe . . . probably," she replied as she handed it back to him. "But, Jonas, I've got to stop this—the weed, I mean. My life is a mess! I tell myself I'm going to get my act together—study hard and get my body back in shape—and then I just don't remember to do it. It's so hard to concentrate sometimes . . . heck, I made about seven wrong turns on my way here just because I couldn't stay focused."

He looked at her seriously. "Going off reefer—that's a hard thing to do, Jules."

"But I have to, Jonas! I had to sign up for summer classes to retake Calculus and Statistics. I got a 'D' in one and a 'C' in the other. They're killing my GPA and I have to get them off my transcript—but I know I'm going to have trouble keeping up."

"Maybe not, Babe. Stand up a minute."

Puzzled, she rose slowly from her seat. His eyes traveled up her body, examining her as if she were a contestant in a beauty pageant. "Yah, I think you're ready."

"Ready for what? Jonas, you're making me nervous."

He chuckled and pulled her into his lap. "I've got something that's going to make you feel better than new, Babe, and I think you can handle it. Not only will it give you all the energy you need, it's going to give you a high that'll send you to the moon." He reached deep into his jeans, drew out a small plastic bag, and shook out a tan-colored rock about the size of his little fingernail.

"Jonas! Is that what I think it is?"

He nodded his head sagely, then nuzzled her ear. "It's called a lot of things—electric Kool-Aid, candy sugar, glo, nuggets, Roxanne. But what it is, Jules, is 'crack.' Crack cocaine, and it's the answer to all your problems, trust me."

She started to argue, fear clouding her face. But Jonas reassured her as if he were instructing a small child. "I know all the trash you've heard about crack, but you'll do fine with it as long as you're careful—as long as you control how much you use, it can't control you." He held the small piece of crack up to the fading sun. "In this little piece of rock, Jules, I see an 'A' in both your classes with energy to spare. Besides, it's an appetite suppressant, so," he patted her slightly bulging tummy, "it'll take care of this little problem too."

*   *   *

Her second day on the job, the financial straits of RCAP became even more apparent as Lindsey viewed the bleakness of what was to be her private office. Stephanie had led her to two temporary, eight-foot-high panels standing on braces and upholstered in dusty gray burlap. The panels had been pushed against an end wall in an open area of the large, first-floor room that housed all eighteen probation officers. There was about seven feet between the panels, just enough space to cram in a small green metal desk, an upholstered office chair, and a bent-up folding chair for clients. *So much for privacy*, Lindsey thought with dismay as she settled carefully into her chair, which had lost one of its wheels. "Well, at least it holds me okay," she grumbled. When she brushed the left plastic armrest with her hand, it fell to the floor. Reaching down to retrieve it, she discovered that the floor under her desk was gritty from weeks—months?—of not seeing a broom or vacuum.

She shook her head in resignation. The only bright spot that saved her office from being truly terrible was the small, plate glass window on the end wall. Dirty, yes, but it had an actual view of an old hickory tree that seemed to be home to several squirrels and an array of birds.

Denise stepped into Lindsey's makeshift office and laughed at her dismay. "I knew you'd be shocked. Nothing but the best for county probation officers! I didn't have the heart to show it to you yesterday, but you being the newest p.o. means you get stuck with the crummiest office."

"That's fair, I guess—but can't RCAP afford a cleaning service at least?" She used an index finger to scrape a layer of dust off the phone on her desk.

"We have one . . . but they only get paid to clean the bathrooms and empty the wastebaskets—any other cleaning is left up to the personal efforts of each p.o., depending on their individual standards of cleanliness . . . you can borrow my broom and bottle of 409 anytime you want."

Lindsey found it disconcerting to begin working directly with clients after only one day of training, but Royce and Denise had both assured her she'd be fine. "The clients are going to like you, Lindsey," Denise told her, "and letting them know you're committed to helping them stay in the judge's good graces will establish a bond with them. That's what being a good p.o. is all about."

Lindsey jumped when her desk phone gave a sudden sharp ring. Sourpuss Stephanie, the nickname Lindsey had assigned to the woman at the front desk, informed her that Jamie Jeffers, her nine a.m. client, had arrived. Lindsey had scanned through his file earlier that morning and learned that he was thirty-two and had three drug abuse convictions—she had no idea what to expect.

Jamie was small, nearly a foot shorter than Lindsey. And even though the May weather had turned muggy, he was dressed warmly in a tan, tattered, and stained Carhart jacket. Baggy black jeans and unlaced work boots completed his outfit. Lindsey thought it was doubtful that his thinning, light-brown hair had ever seen a professional barber. Instead, it had been roughly cut with scissors to hang loosely over his ears and forehead. As she led him to her cubicle—she refused to dignify it by calling it an office—his vague blue eyes darted from object to object, never settling in one place for long. Lindsey motioned him to the folding chair where he sat, leaned forward, and clasped his hands between his knees. He looked at her expectantly, a non-threatening grin on his elfin face. She liked him immediately.

Opening his file, she read aloud his Conditions of Probation, just to make sure they both knew what his judge expected. Then they chatted for awhile, mostly about how he was getting along. Once he seemed relaxed with her, she decided it was time to get down to business. "Jamie, it's good that you haven't been arrested on any new charges, but Judge Dowling wants you to drop a urine at the rehab center once a week for testing, and you should be working on your GED." When she looked at him for his reply, she saw that his attention had been drawn to the tree outside her grubby window.

"Squirrels," he said simply, nodding at one sitting perkily on a low-slung branch. "I like squirrels." He cocked an eyebrow at her. "Did you know my parents were squirrels? Raised me in a tree just like that one." He nodded once again toward the window. Lindsey was speechless as Jamie continued speaking matter-of-factly, as if he'd just described the day's weather. "Ma and Pa were good to me, being squirrels and all. Taught me that I was sent here to destroy evil"—he leaned forward in his chair—"and you're evil," he said menacingly.

"Jamie!" Lindsey bolted from her chair. He was smiling at her innocently again. If he was mentally disturbed, Lindsey reasoned, and there seemed to be little doubt of that, the wisest thing to do was to ignore his crazy comments— she hoped. "I . . . I'm walking you downstairs. We're going to get you enrolled in GED classes here." He went with her willingly. They were halfway down the metal stairs when she noticed a trail of yellow urine escaping his pant's leg and dripping down the steps in a steady stream. "Jamie! What are you doing?" she screamed.

He shrugged sheepishly. "I can't help it . . . you're so pretty . . . you got me too excited—"

Lindsey burst into Denise's office, thankful to find her alone. "I can't do this!" She was breathing heavily; her normally light, clear face mottled a bright red.

Denise started to laugh, then stopped. "You're serious!"

Lindsey gave her a drip-by-drip account of what had just happened, at which point Denise resumed her boisterous laughter, tears sliding down her face.

"Denise, I mean it! I'm quitting before Royce fires me. Half the staircase is dripping with Jamie's urine, and I'm the one responsible—"

Wiping tears from her cheeks with the back of her hand, Denise rose from her desk and put an arm across Lindsey's slumping shoulders. "You're not quitting and you're not getting fired—but you're right, you *are* responsible. Come with me. I'll show you where we keep the mop for occasions like this. And look at it this way; you're already through the worst of what can happen to a new p.o.—probably."

Lindsey's next two clients failed to keep their appointments. Denise had warned her that a DNR—"Did Not Report" was both a bane and a blessing for probation officers because she now had to contact the clients by phone or mail to reschedule, but she also had a free hour to dedicate to brushing up on her caseload. Raver County's Common Pleas Court boasted eight judges, and each judge had their own idea as to how probationers should perform in the community. Some judges wanted a memo from the p.o. if the client disregarded even one of their conditions, while others were far more lenient—and one judge didn't want to hear a word unless one of his probationers was arrested for a new offense. Fine for them, Lindsey grumbled, but it played havoc with the probation officers who had to keep it all straight.

As she reviewed Jane's case files, the p.o. she was filling in for, she was dismayed to find that many of Jane's clients had not been seen for two months or more. If Lindsey couldn't track them down soon, she'd have to ask the court to issue a warrant for their arrest. She spent her lunch hour sending out warning letters with a deadline of ten days to respond. Then she discovered that one of her male clients had been scheduled to meet with her at seven on Friday evening, even though the office closed at five. And it looked as if he reported regularly, so she'd have to stick around to see if he showed.

Mystified, she traipsed back to Denise's office carrying several of the files. "Me again," she apologized as she took the chair across from her. "I thought you said Jane is a top-notch p.o., Denise, but her caseload is a mess! It looks like she's lost track of twenty or thirty clients."

"Jane's a friend of mine, Lindsey, and she's very conscientious. I can't believe—here, let me see those files." After a few minutes of silent perusal, Denise closed the last file and blew out a long, exasperated breath. "Looks like a clear case of 'dumping,' Lindsey. You're right, you've got a real mess on your hands."

"Dumping? I don't understand . . ."

"These bad cases are all transfers from other officers. Evidently, a few of the sleazebags here went through their caseloads, transferred a bunch of shit to you, and no doubt took some of your best clients in exchange. Pretty rotten thing to do, but don't worry. I'll go to Royce and we'll get it straightened out."

"No—you can't do that, Denise." Lindsey slumped in her chair. "It's because they know who I am, isn't it? *The* Lindsey Delaware? They figure I was handed the job on a silver platter and they're out to prove I can't handle it."

"Probably," Denise said reluctantly. "But we can't just let it pass. I have to let Royce know, Lindsey."

"Fine! If you have to tell him, go ahead. But tell him I'm okay with the way things are. I don't need or want him to step in to rescue me. I'm used to it, Denise. I've had to prove myself to others since day one, and I'm stronger for it."

Denise gave her an understanding smile. "I don't doubt that for one minute—well, hop to it, girl. You've got some serious work to do before we can start having lunches together. Too bad the county doesn't pay overtime. All we get is yelled at by the judges if we mess up."

When Friday came, a worried Denise apologized for the umpteenth time for not being able to stick around until seven to see if Lindsey's late client came in. "I hate leaving you here alone, Lindsey—you tried to reach the guy to change the time, right?"

"He doesn't have a phone, Denise, and even if I'd sent a letter, there's no guarantee he would have gotten it in time." She looked at Denise with more assurance than she felt. "Don't worry. What's the worst that could happen?"

Denise stared at her speechlessly until Lindsey broke out in laughter.

At five, the staff began exiting the building as rapidly as if the fire alarm had sounded, eager to begin their weekends. Denise gave her a guilty wave goodbye as Lindsey settled down at her desk, poring over files to familiarize herself with her eighty-six clients. The probation officers were given an alphabetic printout each morning, listing everyone who had been arrested in the county the previous day. Each sheet had four columns of names and was typically six or seven pages long. If any of her clients were on the seemingly endless list, she was to immediately notify the judge who had granted probation to the offender. Lindsey found it to be a daunting task.

As she worked, she tried to ignore the creepy quietness that settled around her—she'd never known the probation office to be so empty or still. Fortunately, her client arrived a few minutes early and as she interviewed him, it seemed he was trying hard to stay out of trouble. He had paid a few dollars on his court costs and had attended two AA meetings since his last visit. He explained that he was looking for work, but most employers weren't interested when they learned he had a criminal record.

"So you're not working?" Lindsey asked. "I thought you might have a job that made it necessary for you to come in this late." When he assured her that he could report anytime she liked, and added he had wondered himself why his appointment had been made so late, Lindsey knew that this had been another attempt to convince her that she didn't belong at RCAP.

When she left the building, locking it securely behind her, she uttered a heartfelt, "Thank you, God," for having gotten through what had been a very scary time for her. Lindsey resolved to never let anyone put her in that situation again. She was unaware that Royce watched from his second floor window until she was safely in her car, parked a short distance down the street. Then, with a nod of approval he turned out his light and headed for home.

*　　*　　*

By the following Monday morning, Lindsey felt she was starting to get a handle on things. Denise had insisted on taking some of the problem cases from her and transferred some "sweet" ones to her in their place. "The only problem you'll have with the clients I'm transferring to you, Lindsey, is they'll be pissed that I'm not their p.o. any longer, but you'll work through that in no time."

The hot sun was streaming into her cubicle through her sparkling clean window, and she pushed back from her desk to admire the view. She'd come in early this morning to Windex it inside and out, and to scatter some peanuts and birdseed on the windowsill. She was actually going to have time to take her lunch hour and was looking forward to getting out of the building at noon with Denise. A leisurely walk and a Greek salad at Zerba's seemed to be in order. She reached for her phone to dial Denise's extension just as it shrilled its unpleasant ring.

"Judge Kent wants to know where the Joel Bateman report is!" the voice demanded. "The hearing's scheduled for Wednesday afternoon."

"Report?" Lindsey asked weakly, correctly assuming that it was Judge Kent's bailiff bellowing so rudely in her ear.

"The P.V. report," he said curtly. "The judge should have had it a week ago!"

P.V.? Searching through all the alphabet soup that had been thrown at her the last several days, Lindsey finally tumbled to its meaning. "Probation Violation." Something was terribly wrong here. Evidently one of her clients had violated the conditions of his probation and was in danger of being sent back to prison—and she didn't know a thing about it. "I'll get right on it," Lindsey promised to dead air as the bailiff slammed down his phone.

A moment later, Denise stepped into Lindsey's cubicle. "Ready for lunch? Uh, oh." She stared at Lindsey, who was sitting with head bowed and briskly rubbing her face in what appeared to be an act of desperation. "Now what?"

Lindsey raised her head and looked at her bleakly. "I think I'm in deep shit this time, Denise. How long does it take to write a P.V.?" She repeated the bailiff's urgent demand, watching with sinking heart while Denise's blue eyes widened in a face turning two shades whiter.

"Oh, crap, Lindsey! Forget what I said about Jamie's pissing on the stairs being the worst that could happen—*this* is the absolute worst! We're talking at least a five-page report here! If Bateman's re-offended, you have to get a copy of the arrest report, write up the circumstances of the offense, get a statement from the victim, a statement from Bateman—he's probably locked up in the county jail—and then you have to write your conclusion and sentencing recommendation. That's really what the judge is waiting for—your recommendation. Ninety percent of the time, the judges follow our decisions . . . that way, if there's any ruckus from the public about the sentence being too lenient or too harsh, the judge wiggles off the hook by saying he simply adhered to the probation officer's recommendation."

"You . . . you mean I have to decide whether this Bateman character goes back to prison or not? My, God, Denise, I've never met the man!"

Denise shrugged. "Yah—well, that's why they pay us the big bucks, Lindsey. Come on woman, we've got us some serious work to do."

The report became a joint priority effort for Lindsey and Denise. Whenever either of them had a free moment or a DNR, they worked on the report. For Lindsey, it seemed an excruciating task to track down all the information that was needed. For starters, Bateman's file was nowhere to be found. A frantic search was launched and Front Desk Stephanie, who had warmed up to Lindsey after observing all her tribulations, discovered that it had been misfiled under the 'F's . . . no doubt another deliberate attempt to fluster the resented interloper. Then Denise sent Lindsey to the Safety Building to pick up a copy of Bateman's arrest report. "Show them your badge so you don't have to wait in line," she instructed. The day Lindsey was hired she was given a shiny blue and gold badge enclosed in a black leather case that read, "Raver County Adult Probation." This would be her first opportunity to put it to use.

Feeling somewhat guilty for cutting through the throng of people hovering in the narrow hallway at the Safety Building, Lindsey elbowed her way to the counter and held up her badge for the officer to see. He was harried, overweight, and sweating. He ignored her for a minute or two, then stopped and stared at the badge. "Don't mean shit to me," he growled. "Take a number." Forty-five minutes later her number was called. This time a different officer, short, pudgy, and female, waited on her. When Lindsey told her what she needed, the officer rummaged through several file drawers, found the report, and ran off a copy. As she handed it to Lindsey she said, "Next time just show us your badge and you won't have to wait in line." Lindsey glared at the swarthy-faced fat guy who stood behind his co-worker, smiling smugly. Gritting her teeth, she thanked the female officer, knowing a complaint would get her nowhere—but she'd be damned if she'd ever take a number again!

Reading the arrest report, Lindsey learned that Bateman had picked up a Domestic Violence charge. At her first opportunity, she called the victim listed in the report who vehemently stated she wanted Bateman's "dumb ass" put away for the rest of his unnatural life!

Lindsey felt trapped at her desk, seeing client after client and praying for a DNR so she could get to the county jail and meet Bateman in person for his statement. Denise had briefed her on the procedure for getting into the jail. "Just tell the big guy in the glass booth who you want to see and show him your badge."

"Yah, right." Lindsey could already see trouble coming.

The county jail was located a short three blocks from the probation office, straight down Lincoln Avenue. Lindsey walked the distance quickly and stared up at the eight-story, gray-stoned edifice, the top six floors showing long rows of narrow, barred windows. Crossing her fingers that things would go smoothly, she climbed the worn stone steps that lined the front of the building and walked through a set of heavy glass doors. Twenty or so people were milling around the large foyer, some dressed in suits and others looking hopelessly shabby.

Lindsey walked directly to the square glass booth where a uniformed, overstuffed sheriff's deputy lounged on a four-legged stool, using a sawed-off broomstick to punch a series of buttons on an overhead panel. It was his effortless way of controlling the floor-to-ceiling barred gate that let people into the inner workings of the jail, and of operating the elevator that would take them to the upper floors that housed the inmates. *Is everyone in corrections overweight?* she wondered as she reached into her handbag, took out her badge and held it up to the glass for the deputy to see. He scowled and shook his three chins. "Where you going with that?" he asked through a small circular opening, pointing at her handbag. She stared at him blankly.

"Can't take ladies' purses inside."

"But . . . but officer," she sputtered. "You just let several men through who were carrying large briefcases."

He shook his head as if she should know better. "Brief-cases, yah, but no purses."

"Oh, Christ!" she said in disbelief, looking around helplessly. "I don't suppose you can keep it for me while I see my probation client?"

He snarled without replying, then motioned her away, looking to the next person in line.

With as much dignity as she could muster, Lindsey strode from the building, then broke into a run back to her office. When she reached her cubicle she threw her bag in a drawer, grabbed a pen and yellow pad and headed back out to the street. She stopped when her feet hit the pavement, slapped her forehead and turned back to retrieve her badge from her handbag. Then, taking a deep breath, she headed back to jail.

Lindsey sat across from Joel Bateman in a small interview room on the sixth floor of the jail. He wore an orange jumpsuit, left unsnapped to his navel, and white crew sox with brown rubber sandals. He gave her an evaluating once-over when she introduced herself as his p.o. "I need your statement, Joel, about the fight with your girlfriend. Tell me whatever you want Judge Kent to know." He stared at her silently as he took a deep draw on his unfiltered cigarette.. She could read the mistrust in his dark, deep-set eyes. "The arrest report makes you out as a real jerk," she warned, "and I think you'd want him to hear your side of the story."

"Yah? Think he's gonna believe anything I have to say?" He dropped his half-finished cigarette onto the gray concrete floor and crushed it with his sandaled foot. Then conceding that she held his future in her hands, he looked at her squarely and began describing the events that had led to his arrest. He maintained that his girlfriend blew up at him because she thought he'd screwed her girlfriend. "She told me she was going to call my p.o. and tell her I was smoking dope again." Joel dropped his head and stared at the cigarette butt on the floor. "She was gonna say I switched someone else's urine for mine whenever I took a piss test and that's the only reason my piss comes up clean. When she headed for the phone, I lost it. I called her a bitch and ripped the phone out of the wall. She ran to the neighbors, told them I was trying to choke her with the phone cord—which I wasn't. But they believed I was trying to kill her, so they called the cops." He looked at Lindsey sadly. "I swear I didn't lay a hand on her. I could'a run, but I waited for the cops to tell them what really happened. That didn't do no good. As soon as they found out I was already on probation on a drug charge, they snapped the cuffs on me. I've been sittin' in this stinking jail for three months, waiting for my case to come up."

"So you didn't try to choke her?" He shook his head. "And you weren't using?"

"No! And that's the God's honest truth."

"So you're completely innocent of everything your girlfriend accused you of?"

"Well, not exactly," he said with a small smile. "I *was* screwing her girlfriend."

By eleven o'clock Wednesday morning, Lindsey held the finished report in her hand; seven pages of single-spaced text along with a blue cover page stamped "Confidential!" She had struggled long and hard with her recommendation. If Bateman was guilty of his girlfriend's accusations, he should be sent to prison to finish out his original sentence of one to three years for drug abuse, and be given additional time for the domestic violence charge. But even though she had not met him in the best of circumstances, she found she was inclined to believe him—especially when she learned that his urine had tested clean at the time of his arrest. If his girlfriend was just being vindictive, Lindsey could find little value in sending him to prison for the next several years, forcing the state taxpayers to pay roughly $30,000 a year for the cost of his confinement. She opted instead for continued probation with the added condition that he enroll in, and successfully complete, anger management classes. Lindsey was pleased when Denise commented that Judge Kent would be more than pleased with her recommendation and with the overall quality of her first P.V. report. "But you better walk it over to the courthouse right now and hand it to the bailiff personally, Lindsey. Judge Kent's court convenes at two p.m."

The Raver County courthouse was adjacent to the county jail, but a great deal more impressive. A massive structure of white marble, its Federal Revival style touted a gold-leaf dome and tall white columns with the U.S. and state flags flying atop the six-story building. Lindsey checked the directory as she stepped inside, located Judge Kent's courtroom on the 3rd floor and opted for the wide staircase rather than waiting for the elevator. Out of breath from the long climb, she pushed open the double wooden doors and stepped into the hushed elegance of a high-ceilinged, blue-carpeted room with dim lighting and dark wood trimmed in white. She felt like she was in church.

The bailiff stood at his desk rifling through a stack of papers and raised his head when she approached. Just as she began explaining who she was, the judge entered from his chambers, black robes flowing as he strode toward his bench: "Judge Kent . . . sir," she said politely, "I've brought the Joel Bateman report. I apologize for not having it to you sooner."

He approached her with an icy glare that froze her to the spot and snatched it from her hand. "Apology not accepted!" he bellowed. "I don't have time to read it!"

FIVE

Lindsey parked her silver Sebring in the circular drive, cut the engine, and rushed inside. "Anyone home?" she called hopefully. Julie was staying with Jonas for the summer in Cambridge to retake some classes, but like Lindsey, she drove back to Dover each weekend to the Delaware household. Lindsey couldn't wait to tell her everything that had transpired during the past week.

With a delighted squeal at the sound of Lindsey's voice, Julie came hurtling down the sweeping stairs that curved from the floor above. They gave each other a hard hug, after which Julie started asking questions non-stop. Lindsey couldn't believe the difference in her friend over the past few weeks. No longer sluggish and overweight, Julie seemed to be bounding with energy. She told Lindsey she was doing great in her summer classes, was much more on top of things, and felt wonderfully alert and energized.

They each grabbed a diet Pepsi from the fridge, while Julie gave a disinterested "no thanks" to Lindsey's suggestion that they have some chips along with the soda. Then they went into the den to relax, waiting for Lindsey's father to arrive for their customary Friday evening meal together. Lindsey began recounting the recent events at RCAP while Julie, eyes widened, gasped in disbelief. "You were set up in so many nasty ways, Lins," she said angrily.

"How can people be so devious? Are you going to tell your dad?"

"You bet—as long as he promises not to get involved. I think I'm through the worst of it. And this should prove to everyone, including Dad, that I can handle tough situations on my own."

Later that night, Julie took a solitary walk through the spreading lawns of the Delaware estate, enjoying the sweet fragrance of the artfully decorated gardens. Partly out of respect for Lindsey's father, but mostly out of fear of being caught, she never used inside the Delaware home. So she had come to know the outdoor landscaping intimately well. She lit her joint and drew in heavily. The crack she'd used earlier on one of her frequent walks had her so wired, she needed a few hits of marijuana to calm her down or she'd never get to sleep. Fortunately, Jonas always gave her enough of what she needed to get her through the weekend.

She was so thankful he had come into her life. He treated her with nothing but kindness and affection and demanded little in return. She smiled as she pictured him sitting casually on his deck in canvas shorts and scruffy sandals. He had an aura of uncomplicated contentment that made her feel safe and secure. She adored him—he was her hero. More importantly, the drugs he gave her made that horrid, ugly part of her go away.

*   *   *

Six weeks into the job, P. O. Lindsey Delaware felt like an old pro, confident that little could faze her. It hadn't taken her long to spot the con artists and manipulators on her caseload. They watched her through hooded eyes, warily trying to determine exactly what it was she wanted to hear when they reported for their twice-monthly visits. And she'd learned to confront those who swore that their kids, angry wife, dog, etc., had lost, stolen, or destroyed all their Alcoholics Anonymous slips. So, they had nothing to verify their attendance at their court-ordered AA meetings. Her favorite shady character, though, had been the man who called late the day of his scheduled visit and tearfully asked to be excused as his mother had "passed" and he had to attend her funeral. That might have worked, but unfortunately for him Lindsey had read through his file and found that his mother had allegedly "passed" six months previously when Jane had been his p.o. Trying to hold back her amusement, she sternly lectured him that unless his mother had been miraculously resurrected, he could no longer use the occasion of her death as an excuse. From now on he'd be required to bring in a memorial card from the funeral home to verify his story.

Even though these few seedy characters stood out, they were not representative of her caseload. Several of her clients were mentally ill and should have been under psychiatric care rather than being caught up in the criminal justice system. By far the most, at least eighty percent, were clients who had run afoul of the law because of addiction to drugs or alcohol. They didn't seem to Lindsey to be strongly entrenched in a life of crime, and she was inclined to believe that once they got control of their addiction problems they would lead law-abiding lives.

Ironically, most of Lindsey's problems on the job came from the "right" side of the law. Her last scary episode had occurred two weeks earlier when a burly corrections officer had literally chased her out of the jail—although she was certain she'd done nothing to deserve his anger. She had been admitted into the first floor booking area to interview Roy Brice, one of her probation clients who had just gotten himself rearrested on a D.W.I. charge. The booking area was always a madhouse, and after taking Roy's tearful statement (he was looking at five-to-fifteen on his original grand theft charge if his probation was revoked) she was unable to locate the officer who had brought Roy into the tiny interview room. Giving up, she walked Roy back to the oversized booking cell that held nearly a dozen men, all of whom were waiting to be processed and taken upstairs to regular cells. She motioned to an officer standing near the cell and told him that she had finished with Roy. She was nearly out of the building when the first officer came barreling after her, red-faced and steaming. He was incensed that she had not returned the prisoner directly to him and he was not about to listen to her rational explanation. She felt fortunate that she escaped the jail before he could lay hands on her.

While she disliked going into the county jail, Lindsey very much enjoyed sitting in the various courtrooms to absorb all that she could about the judiciary process. Denise had told her to set an hour a week aside to observe court proceedings and familiarize herself with each of the eight county judges. Much of what she saw dismayed her, and she vowed that if she were ever to become a public defender, she'd treat her clients with the respect they deserved but were rarely given. Most often, shortly before the bailiff called out a defendant's name at an initial arraignment hearing, the public defense attorney would breeze into the courtroom, seek out his client whom he had never met, and whisper loudly, "Are you working? Got anything good I can tell the judge to make him go easy on you?" It was generally understood that, unless it was a first-degree felony charge, the defendant would plead guilty and hope for the best. At less than fifty dollars an hour, the public defender was loath to spend time arguing against the prosecutor's case.

Today Lindsey was observing Judge Clark as he sat high on his bench overlooking the crowded courtroom. He was a handsome, middle-aged man of medium build with sleek blond hair that contrasted nicely with his black robes and fashionable rimless glasses. Standing before him was an attorney and a man of about fifty who was dressed in an ill-fitting suit and a tight, embroidered cap. "Mr. Atkins!" the judge snarled at the attorney. "Advise the defendant to remove his hat in my courtroom."

Atkins conferred briefly with his client and then said apologetically, "I'm sorry, Your Honor, but my client wears his head covering for religious purposes."

Judge Clark bellowed. "Well, you can inform your client that in this courtroom *I'm* God. And I'm telling him to take off the hat!" He rapped his gavel sharply. As if on command, an overhead water sprinkler burst open, spilling a heavy stream of water directly onto the judge, knocking off his glasses and thoroughly drenching him. The spectators seated in the galley gasped in unison, the defendant gave a wise, smiling nod, and the judge, dripping a trail of water, fled to his chambers like the proverbial rat deserting a sinking ship.

Lindsey was grinning from ear to ear when she returned to the office and found Denise at the coffee machine. "Well, did you learn anything helpful in court today, Lindsey?" she asked.

"Definitely. I learned that our esteemed judges who rule from on high aren't infallible," she laughed, and proceeded to tell Denise what had transpired.

"Well, it won't take long for that story to spread through the court system," Denise laughed. "Our soap opera continues."

Denise had recently filled Lindsey in on the story behind gorgeous, Front Desk Stephanie. It seems Stephanie had considered herself a happily married woman until the birth of her third child. Then she began putting on weight, then lots of weight, and the once slim, trim brunette her husband had married eventually evolved into a two-hundred-and-thirty pound hulk! Disgusted, her husband finally gave Stephanie an ultimatum. Unless she took off all the extra weight, they were looking at a divorce. He hadn't married a fat woman, by God, and didn't intend to stay married to one.

Stephanie was devastated. Even though she worked full time, she knew she was a good wife and a great mom to their three kids. She loved her husband more than she could put into words . . . and she had thought he felt the same. Hurt and desperate, she nearly starved herself getting off the weight, knowing full well that if their roles had been reversed, she would never have considered leaving her husband and destroying their family.

So now her husband had his fashion-model wife back—and a disillusioned, angry Stephanie played the role to the hilt. She not only flirted openly with every male who looked at her, she flaunted the fact that she was willing, able, and available. She engaged in one flagrant affair after another, proving to both her husband and herself that she was a highly desirable woman. "And isn't it just amazing," Denise said with a sad shake of her head, "that sick husband of hers would divorce a fat wife, but not a cheating one."

*   *   *

Breaking all speed limits, Lindsey maneuvered her car in and out of Friday afternoon traffic on the crowded freeway in a panic to reach home. She was scared and angry—mostly scared. Thanks to today's in-house training at the probation office, she had learned more than she wanted to know about the effects of marijuana abuse—and they fit Julie to a 'T.' There was no doubt left in her mind that Julie's sliding grades and expanding weight had been due to the use of pot! Lindsey dealt her steering wheel a hard smack as she recalled the night she had encouraged—no, bullied Julie into taking her first hit of marijuana. Stupidly, Lindsey had thought it ended there, but obviously she'd been wrong.

Arriving home, she flew up the stairs to Julie's room and walked in unannounced. Julie looked at her in surprise. "Hey, what's up?"

Lindsey walked directly to her and took her by the shoulders. "I want you to look me in the eye, Julie Trent, and tell me you're not using pot."

"Whoa! Where'd that come from?"

"Just level with me, dammit!"

Julie backed away and laughed nervously. "You know, your dad is not going to like that extensive vocabulary of cuss words you've started using since working at Probation."

"Quit stalling, Jules . . . please, be honest with me."

Julie threw up her hands in surrender. "Okay, okay. I did get into using pot pretty heavy. But not now . . . you've seen how much better I'm doing."

"But how, Julie, how did you let this happen? After that first time, I never thought—"

Julie sighed and sank onto her bed. "Yah. That first time . . . you were so sick, you thought you were going to die. But me? I thought I'd died and gone to heaven!"

"I—I don't understand. Why, Julie? Why would it affect you like that?"

"I can only tell you that when I use . . . used pot, I felt— like something missing in me had suddenly been filled. I felt whole—and wonderful—and clean."

"Clean?" Lindsey shook her head. "I—I still don't get it, Jules."

"I can't explain, Lindsey. That's just how it is."

"You're still using, aren't you? You and Jonas." Julie refused to look at her. "Julie! You have to get Jonas and that marijuana crap out of your life!"

Julie buried her head in her hands and started sobbing. "I don't think I can live without it, Lins. At least until I finish these two classes. It's helping me now, see? I only have one more week and then my finals. After that I'll quit, I promise."

She raised her head and looked at Lindsey imploringly. "And Jonas isn't the bad guy you think he is. He's helped me more than you can know, and he doesn't ask for anything in return. He—he doesn't even ask for sex, Lindsey."

Lindsey looked puzzled. "But I just assumed . . . why not, for heaven's sake? He's a great-looking guy and I know you care about him."

"It's—it's because of something that happened . . . when I was a kid. The thought of sex—it makes me feel as sick as you felt when you took your first hit off that joint. But Jonas—he's okay with it. He just says he'll wait until I'm ready."

"Oh, Jules!" Lindsey hugged her. "What a pair we make . . . I can't have kids and you can't have sex."

"But I'd trade with you, Lins. I'd trade in a heartbeat." She started laughing then, wiping at her tears. "'Cause if I can't have sex, I can't have kids either!"

The fact that Julie wouldn't talk about whatever had happened to her as a child that made her feel so rotten about herself bothered Lindsey almost as much as Julie's admission to using pot. But during breakfast the next morning Julie acted as if they'd never had the conversation, and gaily made plans for a movie and dinner out for the two of them. "But first," she said with a heavy sigh, "I have to drive over to my parents' and get some things. Jonas has this great pool and I need my swimming gear and some summer clothes—in fact, I doubt that I'll ever be moving back home, so I may as well clear out everything." Lindsey looked at her in surprise as Julie reached across the table and took her hand. "Jonas asked me to move in with him, Lindsey."

"I see. So, is this your way of telling me we won't be rooming together this fall?"

Julie gave her hand a squeeze, then returned to eating her breakfast. "Right . . . but we'll still do lots of stuff together, Lins, I promise. Jonas is out a lot, so I'll be on your campus doorstep more often than not."

Lindsey looked at her knowingly. "Probably not a good idea for me to hang with you at Jonas's—too much "stuff" around?"

Julie ignored her comment, sending the strong message that it wasn't a topic for discussion. Instead, she turned the conversation back to her parents. "Will you go with me, Lins? Help me move the rest of my things out?"

"Serve as buffer between you and your parents, you mean, right?"

"You're very perceptive, today, Lins. Is all this insight a result of dealing one-on-one with criminals every day?"

"I keep telling you, Jules, it's the legal system that's opened my eyes, not my probation clients."

They arrived at Julie's home shortly after lunch. She spoke briefly to her parents, then went directly to her room to begin packing while Lindsey remained behind to visit a while. Rosalind Trent watched Lindsey through careful, green eyes. She was a pale, thin woman, tall, with a noticeably long, thickly veined neck. Lindsey could imagine that prominent throat producing shrill, angry screams directed at Julie. *Why ever would Larry Trent marry a harsh woman like her?* Lindsey wondered. Larry smiled as he motioned Lindsey to a chair, his shirt sleeves rolled to the elbows, exposing strong, sinewy arms. He was a muscular, broad-shouldered man, with friendly brown eyes and graying, dark brown hair.

As the three of them sat in comfortable stuffed chairs in the living room, Rosalind tolerated playing "nice mom" for a few minutes, then excused herself to return to some pressing business in the kitchen. Larry stood to watch his wife leave, then shook his head sadly, eyes moving in the direction of Julie's room. "I hate to see my little girl leave us, Lindsey. You have no idea how much I miss her when she's not around." Lindsey thought she saw a glimmer of tears in his eyes. "But the way things are between her and her mother, I doubt that she'll be coming to see us very often—not that she does now." He looked at Lindsey hopelessly. "Once Julie became a teenager, I found I had to walk a tightrope between the two of them, you know? Trying not to take sides. I guess I didn't do a very good job of it, but it's been so hard all these years trying to keep our family on an even keel."

His tears were flowing freely now and Lindsey took his hand in understanding. He was the exact opposite of Julie's cold-as-a-fish mother. "If it's any comfort, Mr. Trent, Julie has never said a mean word about either of you."

To her dismay, this seemed to release a torrent of emotions that he must have been holding back for years. He buried his head on her shoulder and sobbing, wrapped his arms around her waist. "Jesus, my little girl! She grew up so fast, Lindsey." Not knowing what else to do, Lindsey patted him on the back sympathetically waiting for him to regain control as he cried his heart out on her shoulder.

"Get your hands off her, you filthy creep!" Screaming at the top of her lungs, Julie flew into the room. "Lindsey! Get away from him!"

Click—click . . . like the tumblers on a lock, the pieces fell into place, opening a long-locked door to the terrible truth. *Dear God*, Lindsey thought. *It was Julie's own father who had hurt her!* Lindsey stumbled away from him. *No wonder the thought of sex made Julie feel like throwing up! No wonder she couldn't bring herself to talk about it!*

Larry glared at Julie, his face twisted in fury. "What the hell's wrong with you?" he bellowed as she pulled Lindsey down the hall away from him and into her room.

"I've got to get out of here, Lins." She was breathing in hard rasps, nearly choking. Then she pointed to a few cartons packed and sitting on her bed. "Help me carry these out to the car. The rest of my shit can just stay here and rot—along with the two of them."

Julie was shaking too badly to drive. She rested her head on the back of her seat, eyes closed, as Lindsey backed out of the driveway. Driving silently down the quiet neighborhood street, Lindsey had no idea what to say. But when Julie began crying softly, Lindsey reached over and took her hand. "Jules, you're okay now—he can't touch you ever again."

"But I'm not okay, Lindsey," she shuddered. "I'll *always* feel his hands on me—inside me. Every time he came into my room he said it was because he loved me, but there was no love in him, Lins, only a sick kind of lust."

Now Lindsey began crying along with her friend. She couldn't imagine what it had been like for her. "I'm so sorry, Julie. Someone should shoot the bastard—or castrate him!" Then a sudden thought struck her. "Jules!" she cried in disbelief. "Through all that commotion, your mother never left the kitchen!"

"Yah, well that's no surprise." Julie sat up and rifled through her handbag for a Kleenex. Roughly wiping away her tears, she stared straight ahead and began talking in a monotone. "It started when I was nine. I felt so ashamed, so *awful*. I couldn't work up the courage to say anything to Mom for a long time, until I was nearly twelve." Julie thought back to that terrible day. "She slapped me in the face

. . . so hard, Lindsey—everything went black for a minute. Then she screamed at me. Screamed that I was lying. That he was my *father* and I was never to talk about him like that— ever! But she knew—she knew I was telling the truth, because the next day when I came home from school there was a bottle of pills sitting on my bedroom dresser . . . birth control pills. A concerned mother's gift to her sexually active twelve-year-old daughter. So it went on—for a long time. He—he taught me how to please him, Lindsey, how to tease—how to be his little whore—!"

"Aww, Jules . . . no." Lindsey wept bitterly at what had been done to her friend. "What's wrong with him? How could he do that to a child? His own child!"

Julie took a deep breath. It felt so good to finally let it all out. "When I turned fourteen, I bought this wicked, long-bladed knife from some hood hanging out at our school. I put it under my pillow. The next time Dad came into my room I didn't say a word. I just drew it out and held it up for him to see. He backed out of the room and never bothered me again." She gave a short laugh. "And every time Saint Rosalind changes my bedding, she puts it right back under my pillow . . . it's still there. Thank God, I won't be needing it anymore."

They drove in silence for several minutes toward Lindsey's home. Then Julie spoke softly, "What just happened, Lins? I know it was bad for you—bad in so many ways. But for me? It helped so much to finally get it out in the open."

Lindsey glanced at her, then gripped the steering wheel hard, knowing she had to ask. "Did talking about it help as much as smoking weed does, Julie?"

Julie hesitated only a moment. "No . . . not as much." *Not nearly as much*, she admitted to herself. "But I have to give it up. I know that."

"But how can you do that living with Jonas?"

Julie felt herself growing irritated. "I'll work it out, okay? You have to trust me on this, Lindsey."

SIX

Denise had an open door whenever Lindsey needed to talk. And today she desperately needed to talk. Without revealing Julie's identity, she gave Denise a thorough rundown of everything that had transpired over the weekend. "I'm so worried about her, Denise. I get it that when she uses pot, it chases away her nightmares, but I also see what it's costing her."

"And you think she's been using drugs for about a year, right?"

"Just marijuana, right."

A year on pot and hanging with junkies, I wouldn't bet on it, Denise thought to herself. "So, are you getting her into rehab?"

"Rehab! No. I don't think it's that serious. She's sure she can stop using on her own . . . she asked me to trust her and I do."

"Lindsey, whenever an addict says 'trust me,' you're about to be blindsided."

"But she's not an addict, Denise. It's just pot, for heaven's sake. I'm thinking more about getting her into psychotherapy . . . to work through what her parents did to her."

56

Denise shook her head. "Most therapists won't touch someone who's abusing drugs, Lindsey. They think it's a waste of time. Look, you've been here long enough to know what drugs can do to a person. You're losing your objectivity over this friend of yours."

Downcast, Lindsey returned to her cubicle. As much as she relied on Denise's judgment, she just didn't think using marijuana was something you had to go into drug rehabilitation for. But she didn't doubt for a minute the addictive powers of hard drugs—coke, crack, meth; now those were serious drugs. One of her favorite clients, Betty, came to mind. A forty-five year old RN, she got hooked on the codeine contained in a non-prescription cough syrup. She had violated state law by going to several different drug stores and purchasing more of the cough syrup than was legally allowed during a given time period. Betty abused the codeine-laced cough syrup to the point that, not only could she no longer perform her nursing duties, she couldn't even think clearly enough to help her young son with his fourth-grade math! After several months, a pharmacist tumbled to what Betty was doing and she was arrested for abuse of a controlled substance. She lost her RN license, served six months in the county jail, and was then ordered to serve a five-year probation term.

Betty was undoubtedly one of the kindest and most caring persons Lindsey had ever met. But even though she had been clean for three years now, there was no way she'd ever get her nursing license back. She struggled to support herself and her son with a low-paying retail job and devoted all her spare time to him and to her fellow members of Cocaine Anonymous, a twelve-step recovery program similar to AA. Drug abusers had established CA as their own recovery program because they were not always welcomed into AA. Alcohol, after all, does not carry the stigma of being an illegal drug. So it was somewhat understandable that AA members did not feel comfortable sharing their meetings with court-ordered, drug-abusing criminals.

Lindsey didn't understand why she was so protectively drawn to her clients, but the simple truth was—she was. And she believed she'd be a better public defender for it—as long as she could spot the cons, the serious criminals, the sociopaths. They lived to take from others, and didn't care whom they hurt in the process. *They're the ones who should be filling up our prisons,* she thought ruefully, *not people like Betty, or squirrelly Jamie, or most of the people on my caseload.*

She thought of Jed, the sixty-year-old man convicted of welfare fraud. He was guilty of illegally cashing his deceased father's last welfare check. "I knew it was wrong when I done it," Jed told her with chagrin. "But that old devil temptation got the best of me that time." He shook his head with remorse. "I spent six months in the county jail, have to find some way to pay the money back to Welfare, and I owe the judge more in fines and court costs than what the damn check was worth in the first place!"

As a rule, Jed was very conscientious about keeping his appointments, so Lindsey was not surprised when he reported to her office during a raging thunderstorm. What did surprise her was that he'd walked through the downpour without a coat or umbrella. His clothes were literally soaked, and as he sat at her desk she watched the water drip from his white, curly hair and from the stubble of whiskers on his chin. He hadn't called to change his appointment because he didn't have a phone. He also didn't have a car, and had no one to give him a ride, so he'd walked.

When they finished, Lindsey refused to let him walk back to his home in the relentless rain, even though he'd assured her it wasn't too far. It was her lunch hour so, breaking all rules, she convinced the old man to let her drive him home. Once outside he ran with her to her car, then stopped dead cold when he saw the classic Sebring and the spotlessly clean seats.

"Not too far" turned out to be at least thirty city blocks. "Jed! Do you mean to tell me you walk all this way every time you come to see me?" He shrugged as if it was of no importance and directed her to turn right at the next street. As she drove through the rain, deep into the inner city, she could only pray she'd remember how to get back to her office.

Denise collapsed in her chair when Lindsey told her what she'd done. "Sweet Jesus, Lindsey, you don't *know* the man. He could have robbed you—hurt you!"

"I wasn't frightened for one moment, Denise, except for possibly getting lost in that part of town. Besides, you know as well as I do that if he'd had the money for a good defense attorney instead of a public defender, he'd have gotten off with a slap on the wrists instead of handcuffs."

"Well, damn! That's our system, Lindsey. And you've got to promise me not to do anything that dumb again, okay?"

"I can promise you this, Denise. I'm not making that poor old man walk all that way here every other week . . . I told him I'm reducing his reporting requirements to once a month."

"Well, that must have made his day."

"Actually, he seemed a little disappointed."

Denise stared at her, then said with fake agitation, "Do you have any more confessions before I get out of this chair?"

Lindsey thought a moment. "You mean like getting warm hugs from Ben, my six-foot-four, three-hundred-pound, built-like-a-football-player client who's got a murder rap on his record? And one from Angie, who hadn't bathed in three weeks because she'd been living in her car?"

"Hugs!" Denise sank deeper into her chair. "Lindsey, you know we can't do that!"

"I didn't initiate it, Denise. Believe me, it's the last thing I wanted or expected. But I managed to find a room for homeless women at the 'Sparrow's Nest' for Angie, and she was so excited, she threw her arms around me and started to cry . . . it wasn't that bad actually, as long as I held my breath."

"Ohh-kay. Now tell me about Ben the murderer. We're supposed to have only *non-violent* felony offenders on our caseloads, so how on earth did that happen?"

"Thankfully, I didn't know about Ben's murder conviction until *after* the big hug. He's done so well on probation, I told him I'd send a request to his judge for early termination. When Ben realized he'd be totally 'off paper' he gave me a huge bear hug that nearly squished the breath out of me. It wasn't until I was going back through his file to do the termination paperwork that I found the old murder charge. He'd served fifteen years, and then was released on some kind of technicality. I got him on a passing bad checks charge that he picked up several years after his release from prison."

Denise was looking at Lindsey in stunned silence, then shook her head in resignation. "Go—get out." She flapped her hands at her. "But if you engage in anymore off-the-wall antics . . . I don't want to hear about it, understand? And for God's sake, don't let Royce find out!"

Lindsey saluted her with a smile and a "Yes, boss," and returned to her desk. She knew her "antics" paled in comparison to probation's ongoing soap opera. Just the day before Bill, one of the few probation supervisors who opted to carry a weapon, exited the men's john holding his small

.38 at arms length, dripping water everywhere. "It fell in the crapper!" he lamented. "The damn holster slid off my belt just as I was taking a squat." 'Could happen to anyone' was the general consensus after the roar of laughter died, but Lindsey was of the mind that only Bill would be dumb enough to announce his *faux pas* to his entire department of co-workers.

Lindsey tugged at her small casement window and when it screeched open a crack, she pushed out a few peanuts to the waiting squirrels. Her time here was moving too fast. It was already mid-July, and as difficult as the job was, she was going to miss being a p.o. Even her father had adjusted to her temporary role and enjoyed the stories she came home with each weekend. He had served many years as a State Appellate Court judge before becoming a senator, and was not surprised by the courtroom dramas she encountered.

"The whole system is flawed, Dad," she argued whenever he tried to defend the injustices she saw. "Last week a guy appeared in Judge Bauer's court on a drug trafficking charge after he'd been caught up in a sting operation. His lawyer explained that the defendant had recently lost his job and answered an employment ad in the *Daily Independent.* The undercover cop told him there'd been a lot of applicants, but if he could bring him some high quality 'grass,' he could guarantee him a good paying job.

"This guy had a clean record, Dad, but he had a family to support and was desperate for work. So he asked around, made a buy, and took it to the cop . . . who promptly placed him under arrest. His attorney argued that this simply wasn't fair, but Judge Bauer slammed his gavel and shouted, 'No one ever said the law is fair!' But it should be, Dad, it should be." She was nearly in tears.

"Now, Lindsey," her father patted her hand. "You don't know the whole story. The judge probably had some information that shed a whole different light on the case."

"I hope you're right, Dad," she said with a snuffle. "But I doubt it."

"Don't be such a skeptic, Lindsey. I rubbed shoulders with countless judges during my time on the bench, and the majority of them work hard to keep their biases out of the courtroom."

"That's not what I see, Dad. You should have witnessed Judge Kent's performance last week when he sent an eighteen-year-old kid to prison for five years for grand theft auto."

Her father looked at her with a puzzled expression. "That's the law, Lindsey."

She shook her head in disagreement. "But this kid was just a passenger in the car when the cops pulled it over. His friend was driving it and had picked him up minutes before to give him a ride. He swore he didn't know the car was stolen, and had nothing to do with the theft. But the judge just glared at him with such anger, I think the kid stopped breathing for a minute. Then Kent ducked under his bench and came up holding a rearview mirror. 'See this, Mister?' he bellowed at the kid. 'This is all that's left of my mother's car that was stolen last month. From now on you better pick your friends more carefully!' How can he get away with things like that, Dad?"

"How do you know that young man was telling the truth, Lindsey? Besides, I'm sure he'll be out on probation shortly and then—and then the judge was right. He'll have to choose his friends more carefully."

"Yah, and try to find a job with a felony conviction on his record."

Lindsey still felt angry and frustrated whenever she thought of the conversation with her father, and she had to shake it off or else it would color her entire day. She gathered up a pen and notebook and crammed them in her new briefcase, one that was acceptable to "Mr. Fatso in the Booth," who decided just what could and could not be taken into the jail. She reminded herself to try to go easy on him. When she'd complained to Denise about the plethora of rude, grossly overweight correction officers she kept encountering, Denise explained that most of them were on one kind of disability or another and assigned to light duty. "They're disgruntled cops, Lindsey, who'd rather be out on the streets playing 'cops and robbers.' Instead they're stuck inside filing reports and pushing elevator buttons."

I just wish they'd keep their disgruntled-ness to themselves, Lindsey grumbled to herself as she walked the short distance to the jail. *Maybe I can get in and out of there today without being ridiculed or assaulted.*

The thick aroma of fried bologna assaulted her as she stepped off the elevator onto the third floor. It didn't matter what was being carted to each floor for breakfast, lunch, or dinner; it always smelled the same. Lindsey swallowed hard at the thought of eating every meal from a metal tray of bland, barely heated food.

All the women incarcerated in the county jail were housed on this floor unless they needed medical attention. Lindsey waited in the closet-sized interview room for Sue White to be brought in. She had spotted Sue's name on the daily arrest report that morning, shortly before Sue called from the jail asking to be seen. Now she slouched across from Lindsey on one of the two metal folding chairs that took up most of the floor space in the windowless, cement-block room. She nervously brushed back strands of lifeless brown hair that had fallen into her face and seemed reluctant to speak.

"I don't usually get calls from the jail, Sue. Most of my clients hope I won't find out that they've been arrested so they can avoid a probation violation."

"Yah, well . . . I'm in a jam, see. I—" she started crying. "That cop—Detective Nowak? He's got my fiancé, Johnny, locked-up in here for robbery. But I'm his alibi, see? John was with me that night, I swear. But Nowak says I'm a liar, and that if I don't testify against John he'll slap me with an accessory to robbery charge." Sue was shaking now, crying hard as she wiped her nose with the sleeve of her orange jumpsuit. "I got three kids, Miss Delaware, and Nowak says they'll go into foster care if I go to prison." She looked at Lindsey frantically. "I don't want to hurt Johnny, but what else can I do?"

"You're in here now on a shoplifting charge?"

"Yah, and I'll cop to that. I got busted trying to walk out of K-Mart with some school clothes for Angie, my youngest. It's only a misdemeanor and I won't get much time out of it—but a robbery charge? They could send me away for a long time!" She stood and began pacing in the small room, but three steps each way was all she could manage. "My kids are with a babysitter right now, but I got nobody to keep them for me if . . ." She couldn't finish.

Lindsey had no way of knowing if Sue was being honest with her, but she was aware of Nowak's reputation. He had a higher arrest and conviction rate than any other detective on the force, which had earned him a great deal of respect. She had also taken one of his self-defense classes early in her training and when he learned she was a p.o., he'd actually growled at her. "You're one of those do-gooders who get the dirt-bags back out on the street after we risk our necks locking 'em up." She hadn't known how to reply then, but she knew what to say to Sue now.

"Susan, sit down and listen to me." As they sat knee to knee, Lindsey took both of her client's hands in her own and looked directly in her eyes. "You beg, borrow, or steal—no, scratch that." She started over. "You sell whatever you own and borrow whatever more you need so you and John can hire the best attorney in Raver County." Sue started to shake her head. "I'm dead serious here. It's the only chance you have of staying at home with your kids. You do it for them."

As Lindsey rode the elevator back to the ground floor, she toyed with the idea of using her own substantial funds to help Sue and John, but knew she would be violating one of the basic laws of ethics if she did. "Dual Relationships." They were so easy to step into, but so often went devilishly wrong . . . they were anathema to all caring professionals.

Just as Lindsey thought she was getting out of jail unscathed, a uniformed arm reached out to stop her. The nameplate above his badge read "Deputy Wolff," and he spoke brusquely, as if it were a great bother. "Hey, we got a 'sicko' on the second floor. Bobby Griese? Judge Kent wants somebody from probation to see him."

The jail's medical unit was located on the second floor. Most of the medical problems found there dealt with mental illness, and such was the case with Bobby Griese. As the corrections officer led her to Bobby's cell he told her he wasn't going to take them to an interview room—he wasn't even going to open the cell door, as they'd had too much trouble getting him inside. The cell was basically a metal, ten-by-ten, windowless cage. Its solid steel door had a small slit at eye level and allowed Lindsey to observe Bobby lying on his cot, hands locked behind his head and staring silently at the low ceiling.

"The judge wants to know if we should transport him to the 'funny farm,'" the c.o. said.

"I can't determine that," Lindsey protested. "I'm not a psychiatrist, for heaven's sake."

"He just wants you to talk to the guy and see what you think."

Knowing it would cost the jail megabucks for a psychiatric evaluation, Lindsey quickly tumbled as to why she was being instructed to interview the inmate. The judge wanted a free opinion before going to the expense of hiring a psychiatrist to come into the jail.

After the c.o. left her standing outside the cell, Lindsey spoke softly to Bobby through the small opening in the door. "I hear you're not doing so well today, Bobby." At the sound of her voice, Bobby bolted from his cot as if it were on fire and charged the door, banging it repeatedly with his fists. She backed away, thankful that the heavy steel door stood between them.

"Who gave you the right to say I'm not doing well?" Bobby screamed, then began slamming his head against the hard metal.

Lindsey felt helpless as he continued to abuse himself. "I'm sorry, Bobby. You're right, I shouldn't have said that. I'm leaving now . . . I'm sorry I bothered you." The banging stopped as she walked away and hurried back to the c.o. in his glass control booth. "That poor man needs serious help," she told him. "He's definitely mentally ill—probably paranoid schizophrenic."

"Naw, he ain't crazy," the c.o. sneered. "He fried his brains on drugs a long time ago. Probably find 'em in the bottom of a crack pipe," he laughed nastily.

"He needs to be seen by a psychiatrist," she asserted angrily, "and you can take that straight to the judge."

*   *   *

Jonas met Julie on his front porch and with a happy hug, swung her off her feet. "How did you do, Baby?"

"How do you think?" She gave him a smart-alecky smile. "I aced the suckers!" With the taking of her final exams, summer classes had finally ended—and she still had the entire glorious month of August to play with until her senior year started in early September. Going inside, she flopped down on the overstuffed living room couch and watched with chagrin as her hands began to shake. "Took four hours to get through the bastards, though." She drew a shaky breath. "I had a good hit just before I left the house this morning, but I could really use another one right now."

Jonas was watching her contemplatively, and seemed in no hurry to act on her request. She looked at him expectantly. "Hey, I'm seriously 'jonesing' here," she laughed shortly. "I'll be climbing your walls in a minute."

To her surprise, he sat down on the couch beside her and took her hands. "We've got to talk, Jules."

"Sure," she agreed easily. "But get the stuff first and we can talk after, okay?"

"Jules . . . I can't."

"Can't?" Her voice wavered; he had never refused her before. "What's wrong, Jonas?"

"I can't keep supplying you, Baby. I waited until your exams were over to tell you this, but I'm tapped out." He looked at her with what seemed to be deep remorse.

"Jonas! Why didn't you say something? I just thought— with you being a big time dealer and all—"

"I'm not exactly big time, Jules, and crack and pot don't grow on trees . . . well I guess technically pot does, but I gotta pay for what we use."

"Of course—sure! I'm so sorry, Jonas. I just wasn't thinking. I'll get a job right away. I'll pay you back—pay for what I use." She thought a moment. "I have no idea what we're talking here. A couple hundred a week?" He shook his head slowly. "Three hundred?"

"More like three hundred a day, Jules."

She lunged from the couch. "A day? Three hundred a day? Jonas, that's impossible! That's, that's—"

"About ten grand a month," he nodded matter-of-factly. He was exaggerating the cost of what she routinely used each week, but figured it wasn't likely she'd catch on.

"My, God!" She sank back down beside him and buried her head in her hands. "I've got to quit using, Jonas . . . please help me!"

"That's gonna pretty tough, if not impossible, Baby, as deep as you're into the shit." He could read the desperation in her eyes. "But hey, what about your rich friends, the Delawares? They're rolling in money, and I'll bet Lindsey could get her old man to spring for what you owe, and then we'll see what happens from there."

"No! Absolutely not, Jonas! I don't want them to know anything about this."

"Well, there is another way." He laughed softly, enjoying the moment immensely. He'd waited over a year for this. "Women, especially good-looking women like you, have a real advantage over us guys, Jules. All you have to do is spread your pretty little legs." She stared at him in stunned disbelief. "Sex for drugs, Julie—all the dope you want and it won't cost you a thing."

She delivered a stinging slap to his face. "Are you crazy? Sell myself? I can't—you *know* I can't. If I could be with anyone, Jonas, it would be you, but I can't. And you promised . . . promised to wait until I was ready!"

His sultry eyes traveled over her ripe, curvaceous body. "Jules . . . you're ready."

"No, damn you!"

He smiled benevolently, knowing her fear of being with a man would soon be dominated by her need for drugs. And he could see she was already hurting, her entire body shaking now as she pressed her hands against the cramps assaulting her belly, aching for the drugs only he could give her. A wave of God-like power surged through him, filling him with desire for her seductively tempting body. He took her in his arms and spoke softly to her. "An addict's gotta do what she's gotta do, Jules. A hundred bucks a pop—four or five tricks a day, won't take you long to get back on your feet—so to speak." He laughed at his own sick humor. Then he pushed her away. "I gotta go to the can, Babe. Be right back." He raised an eyebrow and joked—"Don't go anywhere."

He watched her from the dim hallway with grim satisfaction. The instant he'd left the room she pulled the cushions from the couch, searching desperately for an errant piece of crack. Finding none, she scrambled to her knees and ran her hand under the couch—typical behavior of a junkie who was crashing. He snickered as he watched her frantic search, knowing it would be fruitless, as he'd vacuumed carefully just that morning. After enjoying the show a few minutes, he strode back into the room and pulled her to her feet. "Aww, Baby, you don't have to do that." She looked at him hopefully, but he shook his head. "No more freebies, Jules. He brushed a kiss across her trembling lips. "But look, you know I care about you so . . . maybe it'll be easier if you start with me. You know I won't hurt you." He hummed softly as he looked into her fearful eyes. "You can show me some of those tricks your dad taught you . . . Gawd, Jules, the johns will be knocking down my door to have a piece of you." He thought a moment then laughed raucously. "A piece of Jules for a piece of rock—how's that sound, Babe?"

With every ounce of strength she could summon, she pushed him away, screaming foul oaths that would impress a brazen female warrior. "Never, Jonas, you sonofabitch! Never!" He reached for her but she slapped his hand away. "I don't want you and I don't want your damn drugs." She snatched up her handbag and ran from the house, praying that she could drive the endless miles to Lindsey without collapsing into a convulsive fit.

It was late. James had already locked up when he heard someone, a woman, pleading and pounding at the front door. "What the heck?" he muttered. Pulling back a side curtain, he saw Julie standing on the wide veranda, crying hysterically. He quickly opened the door and putting an arm across her shoulders, ushered her in. "What on earth is wrong, child?" He looked at her with concern. "Are you ill?"

"Lindsey," she moaned. "I have to see Lindsey."

"She's in her room, Julie. Go on up . . . I hope she can help," he added to himself as he watched her half run, half stumble up the stairs.

Without pausing to knock, Julie burst into Lindsey's room. The long drive from Cambridge had seemed to take weeks instead of hours, and with the state she was in, she couldn't believe she'd made it safely. When Lindsey turned and took in Julie's tearful, disheveled state, she reacted with frightened alarm and demanded to know what was wrong— but Julie couldn't think where to begin. They stared at each other, neither knowing what to say until nature solved Julie's dilemma. "Need . . . bathroom," she managed to squeak out as her stomach jolted and wrenched viciously.

When she returned, Lindsey motioned her to a chair, took one look at her sweaty, pale face marked with violet shadows of fatigue under her eyes, and went to retrieve a wet cloth to place on her forehead. "Mom used to do this for me whenever I was sick," Jules. It always seemed to help."

Julie took the cloth from her hand and looked at her plaintively. "It's not going to help what's wrong with me, Lins. I . . . I need your help to get into detox." Lindsey stepped away, then sank like a rock onto her bed. "It's more than just marijuana," Julie admitted. "It's—cocaine too, Lins. I didn't know how deep I was getting into it—and now it's too late to stop without medical help. I . . . I don't have any insurance, so I can't go to a hospital . . . and I have no idea how to get into an indigent drug program, but I thought—because of your job you'd know."

Lindsey's head was spinning—reeling with guilt for getting her friend started on this path, with remorse for not recognizing the seriousness of the problem, with anger at the unfairness of something so evil ensnaring Julie in its deadly trap. But none of this emotional turmoil was going to help now. It was a time for action, not emotions, not recriminations. "No . . . no insurance, Julie? But you're still in school. Surely your parents have kept you on their family health policy—"

"They dropped me like a bad seed once you knew—once their dirty little secret was out," she said harshly. She rose from her chair and began pacing the room, too restless to sit still. Her arms burned like fire and she scratched at them futilely, distracted only by the recurring pains in her stomach. "I—I know the county has places where people can go for help, even if they don't have insurance or money." She looked at Lindsey with desperation. "I just need to get through the next few days, Lindsey, and then I'll be okay. Can you help me?"

Lindsey stood and reached for Julie, stopping her pacing and enveloping her in her arms. "You need more than detox, Julie. You need in-house treatment, at least thirty days of drug rehab once you've detoxed. The county has a free drug treatment center, a pretty good one, but Dad and I are going to see that you get the best. There's a private drug rehabilitation facility on the outskirts of Dover. Their success rate with addicts . . . with cocaine addiction, is one of the highest in the country."

"Lindsey, no!" Julie backed away. "I can't tell your dad. It was hard enough telling you!"

"We'll do it together, Jules. He'll understand, and he'll want to help."

Julie looked at her with worried eyes. "Did . . . did you tell him about my situation at home?"

"I wouldn't do that without asking you first, Jules, but I think he needs to know everything if we're going to ask for his help. You're the psychology major, but I think what your parents did to you has a great deal to do with what's going on now."

Telling James was as awful as Julie anticipated, but he made it as easy for her as he could. The three of them sat in his study and he listened intently, without interruption. When she finished her sordid story, he simply stood and motioned her to him. Then he embraced her warmly and told her he'd make the phone call to 'New Beginnings' while she went to her room to pack for a month's stay at the facility.

Julie clutched the railing and, with Lindsey at her side, slowly climbed the wide staircase to the room James had made available to her years earlier. Julie was hurting and shaking too badly to do her packing, so Lindsey began sorting through the clothing in her closet and dresser. Then Lindsey carefully folded and packed several pair of jeans and cotton tops, along with some socks, underwear, and personal items. She had just closed and zipped the bag when James called up the stairs that everything was set.

"I'm going with you, Jules," Lindsey said with a quick hug. "Dad will drive."

Julie looked at her sadly. "He hates me now, doesn't he, Lindsey?"

"Hates you? Julie Trent! How can you think that? Couldn't you see that Dad feels nothing but sympathy for you—for all that you've gone through?"

Julie bowed her head. "You saw sympathy, Lindsey—I saw disgust."

SEVEN

Once Julie was safely ensconced in "New Beginnings," Lindsey enthusiastically continued her mission to absorb all that she could glean from the legal system, and the people caught up in it. She was learning more than she ever hoped to know, and despite the unpleasant rocky patches she frequently fell into, she knew she would miss her role as a county probation officer. She was wrapping up her final week at RCAP and was pleased to know that many of her clients would miss her as well.

The young client she was about to see was a blatant exception, however. Randal, a deeply freckled, red-haired, twenty-two-year-old with a piss-poor attitude enjoyed pushing Lindsey hard. Typically, he would skip several appointments before showing up unannounced, always wearing a black sleeveless shirt and blue jeans that fell far short of his ankles. His graying sox bagged over his high-top tennis shoes which were frayed all the way through to his toes, and she had come to dread the smug sneer on his all-too-cocky face. Several times he had reported to her office just as she was on the verge of requesting a warrant for his arrest, always shrugging off the fact that he had failed to follow through with any of his court-ordered conditions. Having had enough, she complained to Denise about his arrogant behavior and told her she had decided to take him back to court on a technical violation for non-compliance.

But Denise advised her to make him sit through a meeting with Royce before giving up on him—and that was just about to happen.

Neither Lindsey nor Randal knew what to expect as Royce directed them to seats in his office. He had arranged a chair close to his own for the misbehaving reprobate, and had placed Lindsey several feet away, letting Randal know that he now was dealing one-on-one with the Director of Raver County Adult Probation. Royce began the conversation in a slow, low tone, speaking quietly to the young man who finally seemed to be paying close attention. Royce reviewed all the requirements Judge Kopf had set forth and asked Randal if he understood these were the things he needed to be engaged in to stay out of jail. Randal nodded his head but shrugged complacently when Royce asked him if he was complying. Royce leaned forward and stared directly into Randal's now-worried face. "Are you physically handicapped, Randal?" he asked sternly.

"Wha—handicapped? No, no sir, I'm not," he answered .with confusion.

"I see . . . mentally retarded?"

"No," Randal asserted.

"Well . . . then I guess there's no reason why you can't follow through with what's expected of you, is there?"

Randal bowed his head and whispered a miserable, "No."

"I'm pleased we're in agreement, Randal." Royce took Randal's hand and shook it hard, as if he were congratulating him on some marvelous achievement. "Now, I happen to know Ms. Delaware is a very capable, very patient probation officer, but if you step over the line again, I've instructed her to let me know immediately . . . and I personally will place a call to Judge Kopf and let him know we've washed our hands of you. I would think you'd rather be sitting in anger management classes than in jail, correct?"

After the meeting, Lindsey told Denise how impressed she had been with Royce's performance. "He knew exactly how to get through to that kid, and I actually believe Randal's going to shape up, although at first I think he was a little put off when he discovered Royce is African American." She hesitated, then continued. "Denise—I get it that kids like Randal have a hard time accepting blacks in positions of authority, but I just don't understand the resentment some of the staff here has toward Royce. Several times they've gone out of their way to let me know how inadequate he is. They make crass jokes about his stupidity and drop comments with nasty smiles about there being only one reason why he got the job . . . is all their animosity just about race, or is there more to it?"

"I don't know of anyone in this department who has the dedication and know-how to accomplish everything Royce has since coming here, Lindsey. He convinced our public school system to give us our own GED teacher here on site, and then he went out and found the desks and supplies—he laid the carpet in that room with his own hands, for crying out loud! And he's the reason we have weekly AA and CA meetings here—it wasn't easy to get them to come downtown and open their meetings up to our 'criminals.' So yah, it is just about race, and there's nothing you, or I, or Royce can do to change it."

When Lindsey returned to her tiny cubicle she pushed away her frustration and began studying the current arrest report. During the past four months, her caseload had grown at an alarming rate; it was easy to miss the names of any of her clients who might have been arrested the previous day. There seemed to be a steady stream of new offenders directed to Probation by the eight county judges, and even though the probation officers worked in rotation taking on new clients, she always gained far more than she could close out each week.

Finding no familiar names other than the notorious Lottie Dick, who faithfully lived up to her name by being arrested for prostitution every other day (the cops called her 'Lick-a-Dick') Lindsey tossed the arrest report aside and, while waiting for her next client, turned her attention to the three insistent squirrels on her window ledge begging to be fed. As she appeased their hunger with some stale saltines, she began reminiscing about some of the many men and women she had worked with over the past four months. While Randal would no doubt stand out as one of the most difficult, Gavin would always be the most poignant. It was difficult to keep him out of her mind. He had been convicted on several counts of drug trafficking and since he had a prior felony offense, he had been looking at a harsh sentence. But through the efforts of a talented, well-paid attorney, Gavin was granted probation.

As a rule, Lindsey had a hard time maintaining her sense of fair play when working with drug dealers, but when she first met Gavin Rhodes she couldn't help but be impressed. Unlike many of her youthful clients, he was thankful the judge had granted him five years probation rather than ordering him to spend the next several years in prison. Clearly, Gavin was very different from the likes of Randal. A tall, handsome male of African American descent, Gavin dressed carefully and spoke politely during his visits. But what struck Lindsey most was her discovery that he had been an outstanding athlete and an honors student all four years of high school. On his first visit, they established an easy rapport by talking football, her favorite sport. After a few minutes of speculating about which teams would make it to the next Super Bowl, he raised his eyebrows and queried, "Do you really like the game, Ms. Delaware, or are you just putting me on?"

She laughed and asked, "Would you be convinced if I told you my favorite player was Bo Jackson, until his career with the Raiders ended prematurely due to a degenerative hip disorder?" Gavin sat back in his chair, clearly impressed, and before the visit ended he began talking to her about his current employment frustrations.

He was working in a men's clothing store at little more than minimum wage, and had no hope of finding anything better because of his criminal record. "I won't lie to you, Ms. Delaware, I was heavy into selling dope . . .and now, shit!" He looked at her apologetically. "Sorry, Ma'am."

She waved him on. "I've heard much worse, Gavin, I can assure you."

"What I make in a day," he continued, then shook his head, "I was making twenty times that when I was dealing.. Huh—I felt like such a big shot, walking around with a wad of hundred dollar bills in my pocket. If you deal and don't use the stuff, there's no limit to how much you rake in."

"It must be hard walking away from that kind of money; but Gavin, you know the detectives are watching you now, and if you go back to selling . . ."

"I don't want any part of prison, Ms. Delaware, and I was sick of watching what the drugs did to the kids I sold to—but the money, it's not just about me. I set my folks up in a really nice house and now there's no way I can keep making the payments. And my girlfriend—the best we can do is a night out at McDonald's when I used to give her anything she wanted—jewelry, clothes, fur coats, a nice car."

It was clear that Gavin had gotten himself in a real dilemma, caught between the legal system and the demands of his family and friends. "I know of only one way out for you, Gavin." He looked at her with perplexity. "The only way you can honestly make a decent living is to get a college education. You have to know you're capable of that, don't you?"

"I've thought about it," he admitted.

That was all Lindsey needed to hear. On each successive visit she enthusiastically described the excitement of college life that awaited Gavin and encouraged him to enroll in the nearby state university. Once he was accepted and registered for classes, she would consider her short career at RCAP a tremendous success.

But something was clearly wrong. Weeks went by without Gavin receiving a reply to his application. "Gavin!" Lindsey finally proclaimed with frustration. "You should have heard back long ago. What's going on?"

He sat silently staring at the scuffed, wooden floor, then slowly raised his head and gave her a hard look. "You really want to know? My girlfriend tore it up, that's what. She doesn't want me hanging around a bunch of college chicks, get it? And my friends from the Hood? They used to look up to me. I was head honcho, and now I'm the butt of all their jokes. They ask me if I think I'm some sort of smart ass— talking about college, and if I think I'm too good to hang with the likes of them!" His dark brown eyes filled with frustration as he rose to leave. "All I have left is my reputation, Ms. Delaware, and I'm not going out on a limb for anyone and lose that too!"

"I'm . . . I'm sorry Gavin, I didn't realize—"

"Yah, well . . . I guess college was more your dream than mine, anyway." The truth of his words struck hard as he left her sitting forlornly at her desk.

Lindsey wasn't really surprised when his lawyer called a week later. Gavin Rhodes had been arrested across the Delaware state line with twenty liters of cocaine in the trunk of his car. "It's his third trafficking offense, Ms. Delaware.

No way out of it—he's looking at a mandatory twenty years to life."

Lindsey choked back the lump in her throat. Gavin was a hard lesson learned, and even though Denise assured her that the end result would have been the same, she vowed never again to take control of another's life, no matter how good her intentions.

The office was sizzling with the news that Gloria Whiting, one of Raver County's four illustrious commissioners, was paying a visit to the probation department over the lunch hour to make a plea for United Way. The commissioners, along with the county judges, were responsible for the probation department budget and made all decisions regarding its welfare and operation. Denise warned Lindsey that Gloria was not in good standing with the probation officers at the moment. They would begrudgingly attend her presentation, but the reception would be less than enthusiastic. Denise went on to explain that six months earlier, in the midst of an ongoing budget crunch, the commissioners had eliminated all work-related mileage for county employees. "The problem is we have a high risk unit here, Lindsey, one that Royce wrote a state grant for. The grant pays the full salaries of every p.o. working in the unit, so cost wise it's a freebie for the county."

Lindsey nodded in acknowledgement. "They're the probation officers who get all the bad boys, the high risk clients who are likely to re-offend, right?"

"Right, and they're the officers who carry the .38's"

"Like, Drop-It-in-the-Toilet-Bill," Lindsey interjected with a laugh.

Denise ignored her comment. "The thing is, Lindsey, they carry because the grant requires them to make home visits to check up on some pretty dangerous characters in really bad parts of town. Since the state pays their wages, the county agreed to pick up the tab for mileage, but when the commissioners eliminated that perk, the probation officers in the unit were told they'd have to pay out of their own pockets for car expenses."

"And since there haven't been any pay raises here for the past two years, I can see why that caused some animosity."

"That's not the worst of it, Lindsey. The commissioners are county employees too, see? So that means they can't get reimbursed for mileage either."

"Seems only fair," Lindsey said.

"Well, fairness has nothing to do with it, it seems. Because somehow the commissioners managed to find the money in our strapped county budget to buy four county vehicles for their personal use. And we're not talking compact Fords or Chevys, mind you, but top-of-the-line Lincoln Town Cars complete with stereo systems and wraparound seats. And since the limos are owned by the county, the commissioners don't have to put a personal penny into maintenance or mileage."

Denise chuckled as she watched Lindsey's face turn red, angered at the blatant injustice. "I knew that would get your dander up, kiddo. But everyone here values their job, not withstanding the ridiculously low pay, so you won't hear them utter a word of dissension when Gloria gives us her little motivational speech . . . and you won't either, understand?"

It was clear that Gloria Whiting was the kind of woman who thrived on being the center of attention. Dressed in a spiffy designer pants outfit of black and red silk, she was adorned with glittering jewelry and heavy makeup. The overall effect fairly screamed that here was an in-control, flamboyant woman that you didn't want to mess with. "You'd think she was dressed for dinner at the Ritz rather than lunch at Probation," Denise whispered in Lindsey's ear. The officers were seated on metal folding chairs in the basement meeting room, lined up like obedient tin soldiers, listening with polite but intense dislike to the words of their general.

Lindsey had to admit, Gloria was a great communicator. Even though she'd been forewarned and fully prepared to dislike the woman, Lindsey found Gloria's plea for United Way contributions to be heartfelt and effective. "Everyone sitting here," Gloria concluded emphatically, "knows that as county employees we work harder, smarter, and more effectively than city employees. So I'm challenging this department to not only meet but exceed the city probation officers' pledges to United Way this coming year." She was not oblivious to the several gasps and moans that escaped her audience. "I know, I know," she said, holding up her hands. "They have us outnumbered by twenty or so officers, but I'm certain that we can do better then they, because we're far more dedicated to what we do." As she gathered up her papers she smiled broadly at the scattered applause, and with a brief nod to Royce, escaped the room to go on to other more important activities.

The officers sat in stunned silence for several moments, then erupted into loud dissension. "The nerve of that woman," one of the officers fairly yelled at Royce. He shrugged and nodded his head in agreement, but said nothing as he left the room, knowing any derogatory statements about Gloria and her parting words would get back to her immediately.

"What's going on?" Lindsey questioned Denise, who was clenching her teeth as well as her fists. "Am I missing something here?"

Denise drew in a deep breath in an effort to calm herself. "I can't believe it, Lindsey! Challenging us to contribute more than the city officers? She has to know they make ten to fifteen thousand a year more than we do!"

"More?" Lindsey was shocked. "But they work with misdemeanor offenders, not hard-core felons. And I know their caseloads are a lot larger than ours, but they only see their clients once every three months, not every two weeks like we do!"

"It's simple, Lindsey . . . all city workers are unionized. If they don't get fair pay and regular increases, they go out on strike. At one time we were all on the same pay scale, but they've outdistanced us greatly over the years."

"Then—then why don't the county employees unionize, Denise? That seems to be the obvious answer."

"Don't think we haven't tried. But whenever we attempt to organize, the commissioners go screaming to the judges that we're about to bankrupt the county. Then the judges get all riled up and start making phone calls to the union execs, telling them to back off or else, and everything ends up at a standstill. And when we dare to complain, the judges blame the commissioners and the commissioners blame the judges, and there you have it."

"But then, why on earth don't the county probation officers go for the city jobs whenever one's available?"

"Well now, we can't have that, can we? Think of the drain that would put on the county probation department if all their well-trained officers jumped ship and went over to the city at every opportunity? And that's why there's a tacit agreement between the two . . . the city won't hire any probation officers away from the county, no matter how qualified they are."

It was Friday, Lindsey's last day at RCAP. She rapped on Royce's door and when he ushered her in with a large smile, she reluctantly handed him her badge. "Ahh, it's that time, is it?" he said softly. "We'll hate to see you go, Lindsey. You've been like a breath of fresh air blowing through the department."

She smiled at the kindness of his words, then spoke hesitantly. "Royce . . . I almost feel like I should apologize for the behavior of some of the probation officers here."

He eyed her speculatively. "No need for that, Lindsey." After studying her silently for a moment, he decided to continue. "The feelings of racism run deep, I'm afraid, and it's instilled from one generation to the next." He shook his head. "I made sergeant before I retired from the Army, and I often think of the young recruit who spoke to me of his initial reluctance to be part of my unit. 'My Daddy taught me to never take orders from a black man, Sarge, so this has been a real hard thing for me to do.' He had tears in his eyes, Lindsey, and I knew he was still in a quandary about it."

"But Royce, how do you know who you can trust? I've seen too many officers here who treat you like a long-lost friend, but then stab you in the back at every opportunity."

Royce chuckled and nodded his head. "You shouldn't worry about it, Lindsey. We 'black folks' have a built-in radar system. We pretty much know who we can trust and who we can't—we'd never have gotten as far as we have without it."

As Lindsey busily worked at cleaning out her desk, Denise rapped on one of her free-standing walls and jokingly asked if she could come in. "You're already in, Denise," Lindsey laughed, "so have a seat."

"I don't want your time here to end on a sour note, Lindsey," Denise said as she settled onto the metal chair reserved for clients. "I know some . . . a lot of the experiences you've had have given you an unrealistic opinion of the people who work in our legal system."

Lindsey cocked her head. "I wouldn't say that 'unrealistic' is the best way to put it, Denise—how about . . . jaundiced, or toxic?"

"Ouch! That bad, huh? Well, we're going to fix that tonight before you head back to Dover. Two of our 'best in blue' are going to pick us up right after work and drive us to the F.O.P. spaghetti supper fundraiser."

"F.O.P? Oh yah, Fraternal Order of Police . . . two cops? You sure they want me to come along? I'm afraid their opinion of me is just about as toxic as mine is of them."

"Naw, these are two of the good guys, Lindsey. They're serious, well-trained, disciplined officers . . . and neither of them ever chased you out of the jail—as far as I know."

The uniformed officers arrived promptly at 5 o'clock in a shiny black van equipped with siren and police radio. They sat at the curb while Denise and Lindsey piled into the rear passenger seat. After swift introductions, the driver pulled out into traffic and stomped hard on the gas. The wheels screeched loudly on the pavement until they reached a traffic light half a block away. "Damn!" the officer complained as the light went from caution to red and he had to slam on his brakes. As he sat impatiently drumming his fingers on the steering wheel, his partner turned up the volume on the police radio and then reached under the passenger seat, bringing out two cold beers. Popping the tops, he handed one to the driver and they each managed to swallow several large gulps before the light changed—at which point the driver once more began speeding haphazardly through the city traffic. "Privilege of the uniform, right?" he said, glancing at his partner with a smug smile.

"Privilege of the uniform," he agreed.

Lindsey looked at Denise with a mixture of disbelief and horror, but her friend was not in a talking mood. She had lowered her head into her hands and was shaking it in silent resignation.

*　　　*　　　*

Julie finished straightening the small bed in her solitary room at New Beginnings, just as the authoritarian voice on the loudspeaker announced breakfast was hot and ready in the dining room. Well, scrambled eggs were not exactly what she was hungry for, she grumbled as she fought back the relentless craving for crack, but they would have to do.

Although thankful to be in the private facility, Julie was beginning to resent not having any free time to herself, even though she had been told a tight regimen was absolutely necessary for her and the other fourteen women in the well-run facility. Busy addicts had less time to dream, plot, and scheme about getting high. So it was out of bed at six-thirty, with thirty minutes to shower, dress, and spruce up her room before breakfast. Then the women were directed to the gym for thirty minutes of vigorous physical exercise, followed by two hours of group therapy, a CA meeting, cleaning or kitchen duty, and finally lunch. The afternoon schedule was just as demanding with more exercise, more group therapy, more cleaning duties, an hour of individual therapy with a real-live psychologist, dinner, and an evening AA meeting before the exhausted women fell into bed.

Even though rehab was distressingly hectic, it was a breeze compared to the first few days of detox that had been hellish for Julie. Unable to keep anything down, she needed close medical attention to control the cramping, shaking, dehydration, and rapidly fluctuating heart rate caused by her withdrawal from marijuana, cocaine, and crack. Now at least she could eat without throwing up, but as she slowly regained her physical strength, the psychological withdrawal from the drugs began to play havoc with her emotions. She learned that withdrawal was not only a physical thing, but a state of mind; an encompassing blanket of excruciating pain as well as an absence of peace and well-being. When Julie had first started using, the mental barriers she had created in childhood to protect her from the worst of her nightmares had evaporated. And as the terrible memories of every evil thing her father had done to her came flooding back, she thought she would surely drown in shame. Only by continually escaping into the haze of marijuana and cocaine was she able to stay afloat.

Thus, Julie's life prior to rehab had become a balancing act—using just the right drug in just the right amount at just the right time to help her through the day. When depressed, she used. When happy, she used. And now, faced with her current dilemma of not being able to hold her sickening memories at bay, her only thought was to seek relief in using. If it weren't for Dr. Lyle Grey, her psychologist at New Beginnings, she was certain she would have relapsed days ago. And even in a highly regulated rehab facility like New Beginnings, there was always a way to make it happen. One of the women in group had put it succinctly. "I'd sniff bicycle seats if I thought it would make me high!"

Julie met with Dr. Grey in his private office for one hour each afternoon. He had such an easy, non-threatening way about him that she soon found herself telling him about Jonas and how the drugs he supplied had insinuated themselves into her life—and the life Jonas was hoping to push her into. Lyle nodded his head knowingly, his straight brown hair falling into serious brown eyes. As he pushed his hair aside he spoke softly. "It was what he had planned for you right from the beginning, Julie. Thank God you were strong enough to walk away and find your way here . . . too many young women don't. You see them on the streets every day, barely scraping by on what their pimps dole out, and so hooked on drugs they don't really care how badly they're being used or what happens next, as long as they get their next fix."

It was Sunday, a day free of all structured activities except for the usual morning CA and evening AA meeting. And it was visitor's day. Julie had not been allowed visitors during her first fourteen days at the facility, as was the rule for all new residents, but today she had survived the long wait and Lindsey had promised to come as soon as visiting hours started. Julie had kept her abreast of the goings-on at the facility through a daily phone call, but could hardly wait to see her in person.

Lindsey was the first to arrive. With a welcoming squeal of excitement, Julie gave her a long, hard hug while the staff and residents who were scattered about the visitor's lounge smiled to see their open display of affection. After a short tour of the facility, Julie took Lindsey's hand and pulled her to a small table in the lounge where they could enjoy coffee with fresh baked cookies and a private conversation. Despite their frequent phone calls they talked non-stop now, as if they had gone years without speaking, reminiscing about the classes they had already completed at Harvard and speculating about the new semester about to begin. When Lindsey grew serious and asked her friend if she felt ready to face the stiff requirements of her senior year, Julie assured her that everything was going far better with her recovery than she had ever hoped, and added that her sessions with Dr. Grey were largely responsible for the progress she was making. "Of course, Lyle wouldn't want me to say that . . . 'I'm responsible for my own recovery,' he'd say in that serious, soft voice of his . . . oh gosh, I wish you could meet him, Lins. I know you'd understand. He's just what the doctor ordered . . . so to speak."

Before they knew it, the two hours allowed for visiting had evaporated like mist into a sunny day. "Oh, hell, Lindsey. This is shit! You have to leave and we were just the 'F' getting started."

"Jules! Your language is as bad as mine, and you don't have the excuse of working at Probation."

"It's who I hang with, Lindsey. This might be a high-class rehab facility, but it's filled with low-class druggies."

When she met with Dr. Grey the following afternoon, Julie enthusiastically told him about Lindsey's visit. "She's coming again next Sunday, Lyle, and I'd love to have the two of you meet. She's stuck with me through all this drug crap when a lot of non-using friends would have turned tail and run."

He nodded thoughtfully and gave her his easy smile. "I'm guessing you two know everything there is to know about each other, right?"

"Of course. It's that kind of friendship. We share everything."

"Even what you haven't shared with me?" He stared at her intently. Her mouth fell open as she looked at him, speechless. "What is it that's driving all the craziness, Julie? What took you from being a really great kid, an exemplary student, into the sick world of drugs?" He could sense the growing anger in her silence, but he continued pushing. "You've told me all about the drugs and how they make you feel, but we haven't even scratched the surface, have we?" He paused, but she refused to speak. "If you don't get it out, Julie, I can't believe you'll stay clean once you leave here." More silence. "It's really great that you were able to talk to Lindsey, that you were able to open that door with her, but now you've got to trust me. We've got to dig deeper—"

Julie stared at him with utter disbelief. "Did she tell you? She didn't—she wouldn't!"

He held up his hand to stop her. "No, of course not. But I'm not new at this, Julie. I've learned to look behind the smoke screens addicts hide behind to protect themselves . . . and you do realize that you've just admitted that there *is* something you've kept hidden. Something only Lindsey knows?"

Julie left her seat and began pacing the small office. "Dammit . . . I can't. I don't want to talk about it, Lyle. It's history. It's not a part of my life anymore."

"Wrong, Julie. It's so much a part of your life, it defines who you are."

She sank back into her chair and began sobbing, covering her face with her hands. "God, is it that obvious? Can you tell just by looking at me? Am I that hideous, Lyle?"

She looked like a small wounded animal huddled in her chair, and every part of Lyle Grey ached to reach out to her. To pull her into his arms and comfort her—but he could help her only with his carefully thought out words. "Hideous? You're one of the most beautiful women I know, Julie, both inside and out. And our work here together is to help you see that—to believe that."

She looked at him out of desperate eyes. "You know what I want right now?"

He nodded his head understandingly. "You want to use. A pipe full of crack, or a snort of cocaine would make it all go away . . . but only for a little while, Julie. You know that better than I. But if you choose to use instead of being honest with me, where will that get you?"

Her next week of therapy was grueling. As she slowly pulled all the festering ugliness from that dark place deep within her psyche and reluctantly laid it out for Lyle to see, she told him she'd never worked so hard in her life. "This is tougher than sitting through a three-hour stats exam," she complained bitterly as Lyle insisted she describe not only the sick things her father had done to her but, more importantly, what she was thinking and feeling as she lived through each act of molestation.

"That bad, huh? Well, knowing how most psychology students hate statistics, I guess we'd better quit for the day."

"Thank, God!" Julie breathed a sigh of relief.

"But Julie . . . one more thing. I want you to think seriously about reporting this to the authorities."

"Lyle! No! Drag all this out into the public? Never! Besides, as much as I hate what he did to me, he's still my father. It would ruin him—and my mother! How can you think I'd ever do such a thing?"

"Because your father teaches music in a high school, Julie. Because too many impressionable teenage girls are exposed to him every year. And because child molesters typically have hundreds of victims over their lifetime."

"Child molester? No—it was just me! He never touched another child—"

"How can you be so sure, Julie? How can you be certain he's not doing exactly that to some other vulnerable young girl?" Julie covered her ears to shut out his accusations. "I have to report him, Julie. You don't have to bring charges, or even talk to the police, but I have to alert them to the possibility. They have to keep an eye on him—investigate!"

"Dear God," Julie moaned. "Will there never be an end to this?"

Lyle leaned across to her and took her hands in his. "It's part of the healing process, Julie. And I'll be here to help you through." He tilted her chin up and looked in her tearful, sorrowful eyes. "You know, as bad as all this is, some day you're going to be one heck of a therapist in your own right—you'll have so much experience to draw on, so much insight to help others."

"Gee, thanks," she said morosely as she wiped at her tears. "That helps a lot."

"Maybe not right now, but it will someday. Trust me, Julie."

It was a muggy Wednesday afternoon that signaled Julie's last few days of treatment at New Beginnings. Friday would mark her twenty-eighth day of sobriety and her last day of therapy with Lyle. She sat in his small, book-lined office and watched as he hurriedly jotted some notes in the case file opened on his desk, waiting for him to start their session. He had seemed somewhat distracted—even remote, during their last few meetings and she surmised he was as bothered as she that they would no longer be working together. He had told her just yesterday that he planned to refer her to another psychologist in Cambridge somewhere near the Harvard campus, but she was not about to let that happen. She couldn't imagine walking away from the work they had started together—from everything he had come to mean to her—and starting over with someone new.

He closed the file, put down his pen, and looked at her across his desk, smiling at her briefly. "Well, I guess it's time we get started," he said almost reluctantly as he moved to the large, comfortable chair facing hers.

"Before we do, I have something I'd like to discuss," she interjected. "It's terribly important to me and my sobriety that we keep working together, Lyle, at least for several more months, and I'm certain Mr. Delaware will loan me the money for weekly sessions with you. Since I drive back to Dover from Harvard practically every weekend, I could see you here late on Friday afternoons if you can fit me into your schedule." She leaned back with a happy smile, confident that he would be as pleased as she with the suggestion.

But instead, he lowered his eyes and shook his head. He was silent for several moments, then spoke carefully. "Julie, you've taken a lot of psychology classes . . . so you're aware of 'transference' and how it works in psychotherapy?"

She looked at him, not understanding where he was going with this. "Of course. Transference develops in many client/therapist relationships. The client reacts to the therapist as if he is the person in her life who she has major issues with. She can safely get all her negative emotions out, dump them on the therapist, and then they work through them until her issues are resolved. It's called 'catharsis' and it's a *good* thing. So what's the problem?"

"Yes, transference is good . . . but not counter-transference." he stared at her intently.

"Lyle—you don't, you've never said . . ."

"I have feelings for you, Julie. Strong feelings."

"Lyle! *Stop* . . . you know you can't say that. It's not allowed—"

"It's too late, Julie. I've lost my objectivity and that will soon be disastrous for both of us." He hesitated, then continued on. "I've talked to one of my co-workers about this and she agrees . . . I *have* to refer you to someone else."

"You—you care about me so you're sending me away? That doesn't make any sense! We're two intelligent people, Lyle. We'll know how keep our sessions strictly profes-sional. We've been doing it for a month, for heaven's sake!"

"Julie, no! How can I challenge you to take risks, confront you when you're being obstinate, when all I want to do is hold you close and keep you safe?"

"All right—all right." Julie spoke slowly. "So I'll see a new therapist, and you and I can start seeing each other— nonprofessionally." She looked at him hopefully. "I'd really like that, Lyle."

"You've taken the ethics classes, Julie. You know the rules."

"I don't want to hear your damn rules, Lyle." She folded her arms and glared at him.

"Two years, Julie. We have to wait two years before we start dating . . . and even then the Ethics Board frowns on it."

She rose slowly, tears streaming down her pale, angry face. "Damn you, Lyle! Damn you to hell!" She stormed out of his office, slamming the door loudly behind her.

There were no locks on the door to her room, so she shoved a chair tightly under the knob and dared anyone to try to enter. Then she sulked . . . for hours. She refused to come out for the evening meal, or the AA meeting, or for Lyle when he pounded loudly on her door, pleading with her to talk to him. When he finally threatened to break the door down to make sure she was all right, she pulled the chair away and flung open the door, but still refused to come out. She marched to her bed and sat down decisively, crossing her arms.

"Julie," Lyle begged from the doorway. "Don't do this. Don't throw away everything we've accomplished so far."

"*Me? You're* the one who's throwing *me* away because of your precious ethics!" She sighed deeply, "Oh, what the hell. I should be used to it by now. Julie's convenient and disposable, so everyone gets to use her and then ditch her."

She looked at him sadly. "Just go away, Lyle. I'm too tired to argue anymore."

She was still sitting motionless on her bed when the evening lights dimmed down, leaving only small security lights glowing in the hallway. She was so angry—and scared. After hours of trying to decide what to do, it seemed to her that she really had only two choices—stay clean, which meant living and sleeping with the constant image of her father in her bed, or do whatever the hell she had to do to get the drugs that took it all away. Because being clean and sober without Lyle meant dealing with the bad stuff all alone. She wasn't strong enough to fight the memories so long repressed—reliving the nightmare of her father in her bed. No! Better to score, to pop pills, to float away on a cloud of drunkenness. . .

She looked at her small, darkened room. She didn't have to stay here. She wasn't locked in. All she had to do was call Lindsey to come for her. She cautiously stepped into the hall and quietly walked to the pay phone in the lobby. She stared at it for several long minutes. But when she inserted the coins and dialed, it wasn't Lindsey she called.

The car arrived shortly after daybreak. Julie, waiting on the porch steps, threw her bag in the back seat and settled silently beside the driver. A long time friend of Jonas's, he gave her a welcoming nod and began the long drive back to Cambridge. Once they were on the interstate, he reached into his shirt pocket, extracted a joint, and lit it one-handed with a small lighter. "Here," he said handing it to her. "Jonas thought you'd be needing this."

She didn't let herself think for even a second about what she was about to do. This was the path she had decided on and there was little point in changing her mind now. The first hit took her halfway to heaven. How she had missed this.

Another hit and she was filled with a deep sense of peace and non-caring . . . everything was going to be okay now.

By the time she reached Jonas's home, she was more than pleasantly buzzed. He was waiting for her and opened the screen door with a grin. "Well, well. The prodigal druggie returns—like a worker bee to the honey pot, right Julie?" She smiled dreamily through a blurry haze as he took her bag and led her up the stairs, his arm around her waist. "You can use my room to freshen up in, Babe—there's a new chick using your old room right now."

Reality began to set in. "I see . . . it didn't take long to replace me."

"Things move fast in our world, Jules." He ushered her into his plush bedroom that sported an unmade, kingsize bed and, setting her bag on the floor, gave her a quick hug. "Now, just wait here for a while. I'm gonna make a quick call to a guy, Romero, who's just been dying to f—to meet you." Now reality hit her full force. With a malicious smile Jonas watched her shiver, knowing it had nothing to do with the cold air she'd left outside. "What?" he said. "You knew what you were coming back to."

"I—I know . . . but, Jonas, I don't think I can go through with it."

"Shit!" he said explosively. "Look, I'll make it easy for you—but just this one time, okay?" He shoved her across the room to an unobtrusive, glass-topped table. Reaching underneath, he popped open a small hidden drawer and withdrew a square glassine baggy filled with white powder. Her mouth began to water as he spread two lines of coke on the glass surface. Stepping back, he said, "All yours, Baby. This should put you in the mood." Seconds later, she felt as if she hadn't a care in the world. All she wanted to do was sleep forever. "Hey," Jonas shook her roughly to be sure he had her attention. "You just snorted more in ten seconds than

Romero's going to give us for a whole hour with you." He shook his head with disgust. "Oh well, that's the life of an addict, right?—another day dumber and deeper in debt. So be nice to this guy, okay? We owe him a lot of cash. And, Jules, he's kinda particular, so you have to put on a good show . . . you know, all the sex stuff you did with your old man? Act like you're aching for him—beg for it, plead with him to fuck you . . . and you will, Jules. Believe me," he smiled a twisted grin, "if you want a steady supply of the good stuff, you will."

EIGHT

The private phone in the Delaware household rang sharply at nine a.m. Lindsey rushed to her father's study from the kitchen where she had been enjoying a leisurely breakfast, and grabbed it on the third ring. Calls on this line were usually for her father, but James had gone to his Dover law office early that morning to catch up on several cases before the Senate resumed sessions in a few days. She was surprised when the male voice asked for her, and even more taken aback when the caller identified himself as Lyle Grey, Julie's psychologist.

"Good news, I hope," Lindsey said apprehensively, alarmed by the rushed quality of Dr. Grey's voice.

"I'm afraid not, Ms. Delaware, unless you can tell me Julie is with you."

Lindsey sank into the black leather chair next to her father's desk and grasped the phone tightly. "Here? Why would she be here? She won't finish your program until Saturday."

Being careful to not violate the strict rules of confidentiality, Lyle told Lindsey as much as he could about Julie's early morning flight. Sick at heart, Lindsey told him she'd call Julie's parents, although she had little expectation of her being with them, and then she'd call Jonas, where she desperately prayed she had not gone.

Julie's mother answered the phone and was outraged that Lindsey had called. "Why would she be here? Aren't you aware what she has done to us? Her *father* is being investigated because of her lying mouth, and is likely to lose his job. When you find her you can tell her for us that she is never to enter our home again—do you understand?"

Lindsey hung up the phone without uttering another word and reluctantly dialed Jonas in Cambridge. When his recorder picked up she left a brief message, asking only that he call her. He responded almost immediately; obviously he was screening his calls. When she asked if Julie was there, he sounded surprised. "Jules? Haven't seen her," he lied easily. "Isn't she in that fancy rehab place down in Dover?"

Lindsey could think of no other person that Julie would go to in distress. With a burning throat, she held back her tears as she called her father at his office and told him what was happening. "It's not unusual for young adults to fail at rehab the first time around, Lindsey," he said reassuringly. "Some have to go three or four times before it finally takes—but I know how worried you are. You should probably call the hospitals, and I'll have a talk with the boys at the Dover Police Station. They'll check around and keep an eye out for her—it's going to be all right, Lindsey."

But it wasn't all right. Weeks went by with no word from Julie. Reluctantly, Lindsey returned to Harvard without her friend and tried to immerse herself in her studies, but her concentration was constantly interrupted by thoughts of Julie's whereabouts. Not only did she not know where she was, Lindsey had no idea whether she was dead or alive. She slept restlessly, bizarre dreams of her mother and Julie intertwining in macabre dances of drunken drivers, drugs, and death.

Lindsey managed to obtain a medical exemption from classes for Julie, so her college career would not be damaged if . . . when she returned, but Lindsey felt hopelessly frustrated, unable to help her friend in any other way.

When the shock of the 9/11 terrorist attack struck, the ensuing death and destruction added to Lindsey's anxiety. Somehow her worries about Julie became entwined with that terrible tragedy, and by the time finals week arrived at the end of the first semester, she gave up much hope of ever hearing from Julie again.

*   *   *

Julie was freezing. Jonas had made her walk several long blocks in the gray December cold, not willing to drive her or spring for the cost of a cab. She was to pick up a "package" from the Cambridge address he had given her, warning her she would find her butt in jail if she was found with it in her possession. She gritted her teeth in anger. As much as she had once loved Jonas, she now hated him. In fact, she had put him right up there with her father on the hate scale.

As she rushed toward her destination, carefully maneuvering the broken slabs of concrete that formed a haphazard city sidewalk, she wrapped her short coat around her for what little warmth it provided. The cold burned like fire. Her thin legs, dressed in nothing but black net stockings with spiked heels, were fully exposed to the cold below her leather miniskirt.

There were scores of abandoned houses in this part of town, and when Julie finally reached the crack house on its deserted street, the only sign of life were weeds growing in the cracked driveway. She stood on the porch, breathlessly shuffling from foot to foot in the chilly air, waiting for someone named Hank to answer her sharp raps on the heavy wooden door. After several minutes, a voice yelled at her from inside, telling her to go the hell away. When she yelled back that Jonas had sent her, the door opened slightly and a very tall, very large man poked his bald, dark head through the opening, carefully scanning the street in both directions. Finally, satisfied that she was alone, the man grabbed her arm and pulled her into the house.

The rooms on either side of the hall were dark and devoid of furniture. Old newspapers littered the floors. Julie looked nervously at the barren surroundings and the stranger staring down at her. "Are you Hank?" she asked apprehensively. He nodded once then, still holding her arm, moved her further down the hall to a closed door. He opened it with a key and pushed her inside. The room was unusually large, as a wall had been knocked out to increase its size, and was dark as night, as crack users had a heightened sensitivity to light and sound. The windows were covered with black plastic garbage bags to keep out the light—and the prying eyes of any unwanted observers. At first all Julie could make out was the glowing end of joints being smoked and eerie faces, like death masks, illuminated by the sudden flash of flame hovering over crack pipes. Once her eyes adjusted to the gloom, Julie could see that there were a dozen or more people in the room, all in various stages of a narcotic haze. The heavy air reeked of a potpourri of weed, crack, sweat, and sex. And on the floor in one corner of the room a small stack of needles were available for those who preferred shooting up with heroin.

Several of the women were barebreasted and seemingly oblivious to the eager hands that pawed them while they stared stonily into space. Another was engaged in heavy sex, the man grunting and groaning while several more stood in line waiting to take his place. *What am I doing here?* Julie screamed to herself. This was her first encounter with what went on in these places, and she swore it would be the last.

"Wait here," Hank instructed, and disappeared from the room. Minutes later he returned with what looked like a misshapen loaf of bread, tightly wrapped in brown paper and tied with heavy twine. "Where's the cash?" he demanded, then smiled nastily, aware of her uneasiness.

Julie pulled out the thick, sealed envelope that Jonas had stuffed into her bra and handed it over. "It's all there," she told Hank. Jonas trusted her with large sums of money simply because he'd spelled out in gory detail what he'd do to her if she ever dipped her fingers where they didn't belong.

Hank counted it carefully and nodded in agreement, handing her the package. With a sigh of relief, she shoved it under her coat and turned to leave, but Hank reached out and grabbed her arm. "Wait a minute, sweetheart. The cash was only part of it. Jonas told me how good you are with big men like me. You're part of the deal . . . didn't he tell you?" Hank growled as she started to back away, then pushed her hard against the wall. "I'll make it easy for you, girlie. All you have to do is get down and suck my 'gun.'"

Knowing there was no way out, Julie sank numbly to her knees, wanting only to get the ordeal over with. But as she fumbled with his fly, he laughed uproariously and slapped her hands away. "Not that gun, stupid cunt—this one!" He pulled a six-inch thick-barreled Glock from his waist band and pressed it against her cheek. "Go on, sweetheart. Open up. Show big Hank how much you like sucking on his gun."

She cringed as he pushed the weapon against her lips, forcing them open. And as the barrel slid into her mouth she prayed—prayed that Hank would pull the damn trigger.

*　　*　　*

Finals are over at last, Lindsey told herself as she carried the last of her belongings to her car before setting out for Dover. Wiped-out from a two-hour Philosophy of Law exam earlier that morning, she nonetheless felt as if a huge weight had been lifted as she considered everything she'd studied, written, turned in, and taken during the past several days. Eager to leave campus and start the long drive home, she was in the act of trying to stuff a large cardboard box into the small trunk of her convertible when her cell phone rang. She was tempted to let the call go into voicemail, but reluctantly grabbed her backpack off the front seat, dug out the phone, and flipped it open. "What?" she answered, more sharply than she'd intended.

There was a long silence. "Lins?"

Lindsey clutched the phone as if it were a life-line and she a drowning woman. "Oh my God! Julie!" She let out a joyous sob. "Where are you? Talk to me. Don't hang up—"

Julie spoke wearily into the phone. "I'm not going anywhere, Lins—God, it's so good to hear your voice." A hacking cough wracked her lungs. When she recovered she said reluctantly, "I—I need your help again, Lins. But this is the *last* time, I swear. I'm going to do it right this time. If I don't I won't make it, Lins. I can't go on like this. Can—can you come get me?"

Lindsey banged impatiently on the steering wheel of her Sebring as she sat in what looked like a moving parking lot. The Cambridge traffic crept slowly, like a mass of mindless turtles, making the drive across town seem unending. Long minutes after her call, Lindsey drove slowly along a narrow city street, looking for Julie. The directions she'd given had taken Lindsey into a terrible part of town, and she couldn't wait to get Julie safely in her car and back home to Dover. A cold wind swirled an array of dead leaves and trash along the sidewalks and gutters, adding to the gloom of the neighborhood and discouraging everyone but the most diligent from being out.

Lindsey was halfway down the block when, glancing in her rearview mirror, she saw the young hooker she had just passed waving at her frantically. Puzzled, Lindsey frowned—then slammed on her brakes and sat there, motionless. It couldn't be—but it was. Julie came running up to the car and then stood waiting in the cold, arms crossed, while Lindsey reached across the seat and unlocked the passenger door.

As Julie slid numbly into the car, Lindsey stared in dismay at her drawn features. She had lost a good twenty pounds and her once beautiful complexion was now a pasty gray, accentuating the dark lavender shadows beneath her eyes and her pale, hollowed-out cheeks. "I . . . I'm sorry, Julie. I didn't recognize you. Your clothes—jeez, Jules, what's happened to you. You're dressed like a . . ."

Julie gave a short laugh. "Like a high-priced call girl? Well, I *am* a call girl, Lins—one of the best, I'm told." She turned her head and looked her friend in the eye. "Do you still want to help me, Lins? I'll understand if you tell me to get lost."

Lindsey didn't hesitate, overwhelmed with guilt for the part she'd played in Julie's tragic downfall. She reached over and clasped a freezing hand. "Of course I'll help you, Jules. I promise. Any time, any place, anything you need, I'll be there for you. I swear it!"

As they drove along the darkening interstate toward Dover, Lindsey glanced at her friend curled beside her in a protective ball, already shivering from the early effects of drug withdrawal. Breaking the silence, she said, "Jules, it's time to come back now—back to who you were before you got into all this mess."

Julie looked at her skeptically. "Do you really believe that who I used to be is who I truly am, Lindsey?" She shook her head with disgust. "You always see the good in people, Lins, no matter what. How do you do that?"

"Lindsey shrugged. "Don't know—but it's a good thing, isn't it?"

"But you only see in me what you *want* to see, what you remember before the drugs. But it's too late, Lins. I blew my chance when I left rehab. It didn't work for me, face it. I'm just a broken junkie that can't be fixed. For your sake, you should just give up on me."

"No, Julie! It didn't work because the system is broken, not you! And I won't give up. I can't. I love you as if you were my own sister. Remember all the great times we had together? We can get that back, Jules, I know we can."

"Do you know what I remember most, Lindsey? The rush I got the first time I used."

"Oh, Jules, don't—"

"Don't you get it yet, Lindsey? As much as you love me, that's how much I love getting high! Once I started using, I could never really be . . . be *with* you. I was always jonesing, looking for my next fix." She looked sadly at her friend. "You and I have been on a mission since that night we used, you know? My mission has been to keep using until I can find that first glorious rush again, and yours has been to stop me—neither one of us has been successful, have we?"

Tears blurred Lindsey's eyes. "Julie, I'm so sorry. If I hadn't pushed you into smoking pot that night with Jonas—"

"Lindsey! For heavens sake, stop it! If I hadn't discovered drugs with you it would have been with someone else. I was an addict waiting to happen." Lindsey shook her head in disagreement. "Look, with my *first* hit I became an addict in training—now I have a PhD in addiction. You just helped me find what I'm good at." She was silent a moment, then choked back a sob. "Shit! I'm such a goddamn hopeless addict! So stop blaming yourself, Lindsey. It's my fault! My own fault! My own damn fault! I'm the one who screwed up my life . . . on second thought, it was my father who screwed me!"

U.S. Senator Delaware sat in his study leisurely reading the *Washington Post,* one of several papers delivered daily to his home in Dover. He sighed contentedly, sinking low in his too comfortable leather chair, cracked with age, so old now it conformed perfectly to the lines of his large frame. He reached for the humidor on the corner of his desk and took out one of his favored, five-year-old Dominican wrapped, Cuban leaf cigars. He breathed in its heavy aroma appreciatively before lighting up, then slowly drew in on the long, fat cylinder of tightly packed tobacco. He chuckled as he blew out a satisfying puff. This was one of the few things he and Lindsey disagreed about. Not so much the health hazard, although that did bother her, but mostly the principle of the thing. He had put his foot down when she brought home that foreign-made BMW a few years ago, insisting that she take it back and get an American made vehicle instead. But when it came to his cigars, the commitment to "American made" went right out the window. As far as he was concerned, the Dominican Republic ran smoke rings around everyone else when it came to making good cigars— notwithstanding that they grew Cuban tobacco seeds to accomplish it. He indulged now, knowing it would be his last cigar for awhile. He never allowed himself to smoke while Lindsey was home, and he expected her to arrive any minute. He'd finagled his way out of the office early to surprise her and was looking forward to spending as much time with her as he could manage.

Harvard Law! She had been accepted and was already registered for fall classes. He was so darned proud of her, more and more each day as she continued her journey into becoming an amazingly smart, pleasingly social, very attractive young woman—well, he thought so anyway. He frowned then. As usual, when he marveled at Lindsey's accomplishments his thoughts turned to Julie and the tragic turn her life had taken.

Just as he was beginning to wonder what was taking her so long, he heard Lindsey at the front door. Giving a satisfied chuckle, he put out his cigar and carefully waved the smoke away before hurrying to meet her. He gasped with shock when he saw both her and Julie standing in the hallway, Lindsey helping her out of some kind of flimsy coat. "Julie! My God, child, is it really you?" He rushed to give her a welcoming hug, but stopped abruptly as she flinched and backed away from him.

"I'm so sorry, Mr. Delaware. I know I let you down . . ."

"Nonsense, Julie, I'll hear none of that. It's just a huge relief knowing you're all right. And why so formal? You've called me James for years . . . actually, I'd be so pleased if you'd call me Dad like Lindsey does." He looked at her earnestly and held out his hands to the tragically thin young girl who was dressed so crudely and shaking like a leaf. "Please, Julie?"

With a sob, she ran to him and threw herself in his arms, craving the warmth and protection he offered so freely. But after a few moments she gathered what strength she had left and backed away once more. "I'm so . . . so filthy. You don't want—" She looked at Lindsey imploringly. "I need to bathe, Lins . . . for hours . . . in a hot tub." She smiled sadly at James. "I'll never figure out how to repay you . . . Dad. But I promise I'll try."

He waved away her concern. "Do you want me to call New Beginnings, Julie? I'm certain they'll be more than happy to have you back."

"No!—I know what it cost you before, and I can't let you do that again. But there's a county facility in Dover for indigents . . . the ARC?"

James nodded his head knowingly. "Addiction Recovery Center. They have a good reputation . . . but Julie, you don't have to go there. They don't have the—the amenities that New Beginnings can offer."

"I *do* have to go there, Dad. I have to do it right this time. I don't have a penny to my name and that's where indigent addicts go. But it helps so much knowing you and Lindsey haven't given up on me."

Lindsey took Julie's hand and led her to the stairs. "Let's get you that hot bath, Jules. You're shaking like a leaf."

"It's not from the cold, Lins," Julie said through chattering teeth. "And it's going to get a lot worse before it gets better."

Once she was immersed in the hot bath with bubbles up to her chin, she called to Lindsey and asked her to sit with her while she tried to soak away some of the grime that infested her body inside and out. Lindsey sat quietly on a chair, watching her friend suffer through the beginnings of withdrawal, and listened while Julie "confessed" to all that had happened over the past several months. She started with her first encounter with Romero, one of hundreds of "johns" she succumbed to so Jonas would give her a roof over her head and a daily supply of drugs, pills, and alcohol. "Jonas was determined to keep me fully in his control, Lindsey, and he did just that by insisting I start shooting heroin."

"Sweet Jesus, Jules . . . you didn't?"

She nodded her head sadly. "He locked me in his room and made me go without any drugs for three days—I was so sick, Lins—and finally I gave in. He showed me how to inject it, then laughed when he saw how hard the stuff hit me . . . I swear I'm such an addict, Lindsey, I could get high on a handful of daffodils without even trying!"

She took Lindsey through every sickening detail of her drug-addicted life and ended with today's grim experience in the crack house. When she told her how badly she wanted Hank to end it all for her, Lindsey was so angry she couldn't contain herself. "I can't stand to think what that jerk has done to you, Jules. I swear, if I had a gun I'd shoot the bastard!"

Julie smiled bleakly and asked through chattering teeth, "Who? My father or Jonas?"

"Both of them!"

"I guess I haven't had much luck with the men in my life . . . or mothers either. You are so lucky to have a father like James . . ." She grabbed for the plastic container Lindsey held for her and retched. "How did all this happen, Lins? I slid into hell so effortlessly . . . and now it seems nearly impossible to find my way out."

"You'll make it, Jules. I know you will! You and I are strong women . . . we're alike in so many important ways."

"No! You're nothing like me! You can't imagine slithering through human slime just to get high . . . I've always wanted it so bad, Lins—needed it! And no matter what disgusting thing I did, afterwards, when Jonas shared a line of coke with me or I shot up with heroin, what I had just done meant nothing—nothing like the rush of power and elation that comes with that fast, hard hit of narcotics."

The bath water had cooled by now and Julie was shaking uncontrollably. "Will—will you pack whatever warm clothes you can find in my room, Lins, while I dry off?" She waited until Lindsey left the room, ashamed of her skeletal form. Wrapping herself in a thick towel, she went to her room where Lindsey had laid out jeans, a blue cotton shirt, a navy pullover sweater, and a pair of warm woolen socks. After she dressed and slid into a pair of loafers, she went to find Lindsey in her own room. "I haven't felt this wonderful since I left rehab," she commented, then clutched her stomach as it wrenched with pain. "Well, almost," she corrected.

Lindsey had the phone book out and lying open. "I found the number for that rehab place—the ARC. Do you want to make the call?"

"If I can stop shaking long enough." After three abortive attempts at punching in the number, she finally succeeded and with a sigh of relief, leaned back in the desk chair while the call went through. She hit the speaker phone button so Lindsey could hear the conversation . . . and because she wasn't sure she could hold onto the receiver much longer.

After the seventh ring the phone was answered by an authoritarian voice saying, 'You have reached the ARC . . . please hold. Your call will be answered in the order received.' Julie and Lindsey both moaned. Several minutes later, after listening to a badly scratched recording of *"On a Clear Day,"* Julie made a hurried trip to the bathroom and back before her call was finally answered by a woman who sounded rushed and impatient. "The ARC. Who's calling?" When Julie gave her name and her reason for calling, the woman sighed. "Look, our beds are full . . . Julie is it? The best I can do is add your name to our list. Call every morning at nine to check in, and as soon as we have a bed available you can come in for an Intake Interview."

Julie gasped in disbelief, then with a sob pushed away from the phone and rushed once again into the bathroom.

Lindsey spoke into the phone in desperation. "Please! You have to help her. She's really sick!"

"All addicts are sick and need help, Miss," the woman responded. "If you're worried about her, take her to the County Clinic where she can detox. Just make sure she calls in here every day or her name comes off the list." The dial tone hummed loudly as the woman hung-up.

When Julie, pale as a corpse, returned from the bathroom, Lindsey held out her arms and hugged her tightly. Julie chattered through clenched teeth, "Looks like my d— day is ending as badly as it s—started. Isn't it a shame," she gave a short laugh, "now that I'm f—finally ready for rehab, they're not ready for me."

"No! That's not how this is going to end! I'm not going to watch you suffer like this, Jules. Wait here while I go talk to Dad."

As Lindsey descended the stairs calling for her father, Julie was certain of only two things—she would *not* take any more money from the Delawares—and she would *never* go back to Jonas! With quiet resolve, she returned to her room and gathered up the navy blue peacoat and duffel bag of clothing Lindsey had packed for her. Then slipping the warm coat on and her loafers off, she crept silently down the long, carpeted staircase. When a sickening wave of dizziness overtook her halfway down, she clutched her shoes and bag to her chest and sat down abruptly, waiting for her head to clear. When she slowly got up again, she had barely enough strength to make it outside to the garden . . . but make it she would! Because there, beneath a stone bench in a carefully concealed, water-tight container, her secret stash of drugs had lain hidden for months.

As she huddled on the icy bench, her panting breath visible on the cold night air, Julie opened the square plastic box and removed the butane lighter, thinking her day would truly come to a tragic end if the thing didn't work. It ignited on the third try and she hurriedly lit one of the joints, knowing the soothing effect of marijuana would calm her heaving stomach. Minutes later, feeling somewhat better, she carefully lifted the clay pipe out of the box and a small gray rock of cocaine. A hit of crack would take the edge off the effects of her heroin withdrawal, then she would hitch a ride to the back streets of downtown Dover. And even though she would still have a deadly craving for the potent drug of heroin, this was as good as it was going to get. "Weed and crack are going to get you off heroin, Jules," she cried into the cold night air—"and I'll die before I ever start using it again . . . because I'll surely die if I do.

NINE

Harvard Law was everything Lindsey had hoped for—challenging classes with great professors and an opportunity to balance the lopsided view of corrections and the law that she had acquired during her four-month stint as a county probation officer. *And*, she was dating. Roland Brice, a fellow first-year law student had attached himself to her the day she dropped twenty pages of notes while rushing to her next class. He was not quite as tall as she, nor nearly as bright, but was cute, with curly brown hair and light brown .eyes, and was easy to be with. And even though she would have preferred a more casual friendship, there was something to be said for releasing pent-up sexual tension with someone you liked and trusted. But striving for fairness and a clear understanding, she frequently reminded him that what they had was not serious—and never would be.

He didn't seem to mind and readily agreed with her whenever she brought the subject up. What he didn't tell her was that over time he was confident his agreeable, easygoing personality would grow on her and she'd change her mind. He also neglected to tell her about the conversation he'd had with one of their male classmates who, when he discovered Rollie was dating Lindsey Delaware, nearly went ballistic.

"You're kidding me, Brice! My God! She's every man's wet dream!"

"Yah," Rollie agreed, "she's gorgeous, brilliant, and rich. What more could a guy ask for?"

"What more could you ask for? You mean you don't know?" He looked at him in mock horror. "Everyone on campus knows she can't have kids, stupid!"

Rollie frowned at him. "And that's supposed to be a plus?"

"Think about it, man. Sex whenever you want it with no condoms and no chance of a paternity suit! That's the best sex any randy-assed, horny male could ask for!"

Actually, Rollie had been disappointed. Since she hadn't insisted on using any kind of birth control, he'd hoped that he could get Lindsey pregnant with his kid and then she'd have to agree to marry him. Now he'd have to rely solely on his charm and subtle persuasiveness.

The Harvard Henchmen, all six dressed in tight black pants and tunics of sleek black silk, jacked up the volume on their battery of speakers and shook the large student union auditorium with vibrating waves of hard rock. Lindsey swore she could feel the music as much as hear it. The punch that Rollie was bringing her after each dance was undoubtedly spiked, and Lindsey reminded herself to stick to her limit. And inevitably, whenever drugs or alcohol were involved, her thoughts turned to Julie. It had been over a year now since her last disappearance on that cold December night, and Lindsey had run out of ideas as to how to find her. Whenever she had free time, she would leave campus in her small silver Sebring and cruise the back streets of Cambridge where known prostitutes and addicts hung out. Then she would circle the area around the crack house where she had found Julie before. And on several occasions she had dropped in on Jonas unannounced, hoping against hope to find her there. But each time she barged in and loudly called out for her, Jonas was adamant that he had no idea where she was. "That bitch owes me big time, Lindsey, and I want to be the first to know when you find her."

"Fat chance of that," Lindsey said scathingly. And once she was convinced Julie was indeed nowhere around him, she called the nearest police precinct and alerted them to the large amount of drugs Jonas was dealing throughout his exclusive neighborhood from his prestigious, colonial-style house. As far as she knew, he was at this minute sitting in the Cambridge county jail awaiting his pretrial hearing. Good riddance, Lindsey told herself. She had learned that Jonas was one of those perpetual students who never bothered to graduate. His only interest in college was the plush drug market and hard cash he harvested from the Harvard students.

Rollie interrupted her train of thought. "Enjoying yourself, Lindsey? Band's pretty good for local guys, don't you think?" She nodded enthusiastically. She had promised herself to enjoy the social aspects of law school as well as the academics, and not bury herself in her books as before. It had been a good decision. While she continued to excel in her classes, she was less compulsive about her studies and often allowed herself the luxury of campus social and political events.

Taking a small sip from the glass of vodka that contained but a hint of fruit punch, her eyes wandered casually over the dance floor, then stopped abruptly when they encountered a smashing dark blue Dolce & Gabbana suit, which the wearer filled out handsomely. With more than a little interest, her curious gray eyes took in the man's measure. Lindsey was tall, but he was far taller. He stood at least a head above the intimate group he was conversing with, his authoritative stance commanding their attention. *Handsome doesn't begin to describe his good looks,* she thought breathlessly. *He's at least six-foot-four of pure masculinity and screaming with obvious sex appeal.* His dark copper hair was thick and neatly trimmed, and while his square jaw and the set of his mouth told her he could be stubborn as well as determined, it was his widely set, midnight-blue eyes that dominated his strong face.

As if sensing her eyes on him, he looked quizzically in her direction, then taking in her tall stature and alluring figure, smiled. It was a slow, incredibly warm and sexy smile—and nearly knocked her off her feet. She found it impossible to look away and smiled in return as delicious shivers swept through her, her pulse thrumming heatedly. *I always thought love at first sight was a fantasy,* she thought with amazement, *but this might be it! Correction—this is* lust *at first sight!* The heat he was generating as he continued to smile was reaching deep into parts of her that no man had ever set on fire. Without taking her eyes off him, she grasped Rollie's arm and asked over the loud roar of music, "Who *is* that man staring at us?"

Rollie had noticed her intense interest, and feeling more than a little threatened, he took Lindsey's arm and led her back onto the dance floor. "It's *you* he's staring at, Lindsey, not *us* . . . he's a hot-shot attorney from D.C.—Brian Winchester. He has a doctor's degree in law and lectures here sometimes . . . *and*," he added heatedly as he pulled her close and urged her into the rhythm of the slow dance now playing, "he's sexually warped."

"He's impotent?" The fire consuming her body slid into deep regret.

"Hell, no! Just the opposite. He's insatiable. The word is that Winchester uses women like one of those disposable blowup dolls—talk about sexual insanity!"

"But—he looks so, so . . . omigod, Rollie, he's gorgeous."

"Yah—right. But watch it, Lindsey. He's like the fresh fruit you get at the super market—tempting on the outside but rotten to the core inside!"

With a soft sigh of resignation, she settled into Rollie's arms and swayed to the music, wishing he were a little taller so she could rest her head on his shoulder. And as they danced, she glanced once again in the direction of what she now thought of as forbidden fruit, but was disappointed to find the alluring man had disappeared.

"Shit!" Rollie snarled. She drew back and looked at him in surprise just as an arm clad in dark blue reached from behind her and tapped him on the shoulder.

"Mind if I cut in, young man? I have something to discuss with the lovely woman you're dancing with."

Rollie glared at him, then backed away reluctantly. Lindsey turned slowly and instantly found herself engulfed in the strong embrace of Dr. Brian Winchester. He grinned at her with warm blue eyes—and she was at once hopelessly captured by the seductive face looking into hers. "Provocatively sexual" floated through her mind as the sensation of being locked in step with the man's enticing body adeptly wakened pent-up longings she hadn't known existed . . . and his smile suggested he knew she'd never had feelings like this. Embarrassed, she hastily looked away—but like a moth flirting with a flame, she couldn't help but wonder how close she could get to this man without getting burned.

Pushing caution aside, she thought only of how wonderful it was to dance with a man taller than she . . . and what harm could one dance do, after all? As he moved her effortlessly to the soft beat of the music, she struggled to make light conversation, but found she was frustratingly tongue-tied. For *Pete's sake, I'm behaving like a doting teenager,* she told herself derisively, feeling as if she had no command over her actions whatsoever.

As the tempo of the dance quickened, Dr. Winchester pulled her closer, and although his arms held her no tighter than Rollie's had, she felt herself melt into the heat of his body like she'd never done with any other man. He leaned down and put his lips against her ear, causing her to take a deep breath. "Have you signed up for my *Art of Plea Bargaining* seminar, Lindsey?" he asked softly.

"I—no. Should I? I mean, I will—"

His quiet laugh was low and masculine. "No, please don't. I make it a strict rule to never date my students." She drew back, her gray eyes looking at him with a startled expression. His appealing laugh sounded once again as he drew her even more tightly. "Yes, I know you're Lindsey Delaware, and that you're an amazingly bright law student, and that yes, we are definitely dating—unless you have a strong objection."

Rollie's words of warning ebbed away like the receding notes of a siren's call as she rested her head on Brian's shoulder and breathed in his enticing scent, then struggled to gain an equal footing with him "I can't think of an objection at the moment, Counselor . . . but I'll let you know the instant I do."

"Spoken like a true lawyer in training," he nodded with amusement, holding onto her waist when the music ended. As Rollie approached, Brian's clear blue eyes warned him away, and Lindsey found herself still wrapped in his arms when the next dance began.

*   *   *

Brian just couldn't figure Lindsey out. Since he started romancing her nearly two weeks before, she'd let him get only so close, then she'd back off like a frightened kitten, practically hissing at him with claws extended. Kissing her was great, but when his hands began to wander, yearning for the touch of her naked skin, she invariably unglued her lips from his, arched away, and brought their evening to an abrupt close with a light, "Good night, Counselor. I had a lovely time."

It's not like she's never been with a man, he thought with frustration. It was common knowledge that she and that Roland character had been intimate for months. How many times had he overheard conversations among his students speculating on how a "nonentity" like Rollie Brice had been able to entice Lindsey Delaware into his bed?

"It's probably because of her problem," one of the co-eds had mewed cattily. "She has to settle for whoever will have her." Brian had no idea what Lindsey's "problem" was, but he couldn't imagine anything horrible enough to keep him away from her.

*   *   *

"I should have known! I'm such an idiot," Lindsey screamed at Brian. Jonas had walked away with no more than a slap on the wrist, even though Lindsey had done everything she could to ensure a stiff sentence. Upon learning of his arrest, she had provided the county prosecutor with everything she knew about his drug involvement, and even volunteered to testify. But Jonas, with years of successful wheeling and dealing behind him, had more ill-gotten money stashed away than a slick Bernie Madoff; and the top-notch attorney he acquired artfully painted him as a hopelessly naive college student.

"Jonas," his attorney pleaded, "is just a young kid who had the misfortune of falling in love with and yes, admittedly using drugs with Julie Trent, a long-time friend of the wealthy, influential James Delaware family. Amazingly," his attorney argued, "Ms. Trent managed to disappear at the exact time of Jonas's arrest, thus avoiding prosecution herself, and now the Delaware family is blaming Jonas for her disappearance and all *her* wrongdoings—*and they want revenge!"*

After this carefully constructed opening statement by the defense, the prosecutor reluctantly informed Lindsey that her testimony against Jonas would now seem purely vindictive, and with no other evidence than the few drugs found in his home at the time of his arrest and no prior offenses, he was given a suspended sentence with credit for time served (six hours in Booking while waiting for his attorney to bail him out), and two years probation.

As Lindsey sputtered her anger and frustration to Brian as he was driving her home from the sentencing hearing, he empathized fully but could only advise her to try to let it go. "Jonas has a rap sheet now, Lindsey, and rest assured the cops will be watching him. They don't like the fact that he got off so easily any more than you do. He'll slip up sooner or later and they'll nail him to the wall the second time around. Until then, try to put it to rest."

She was working hard on that, and thought she had started to come to terms with the unfairness of it all, until she left class a few days later and found four slashed tires on her aging but treasured convertible. If there was any doubt who was responsible, it was resolved by the warning etched deeply in the silver finish along the entire length of one side of the car. *Back off Bitch! Paybacks Are Hell!* It was signed with a large capital *J.* But as Brian pointed out, it proved nothing—"J" could stand for Julie just as well as Jonas.

*   *   *

One month into their relationship, Brian was so frustrated with Lindsey's continued elusiveness he decided to hash it out with her, even if it meant losing her. "What the hell's wrong, Lindsey?" he swore the next time she pushed him away after a particularly hot, breathless kiss. "Bad breath? B.O.? Or are you just the world's consummate tease?" He shoved himself off her living room couch where they had been romantically entwined for the past half-hour while listening to a Streisand C.D., and stared down at her.

Lindsey knew she could avoid the issue no longer, even if it meant losing him. It wasn't fair to either of them to let him take her to the gates of heaven only to have her slam them shut. She drew a deep breath. It was time to let him know about her fear of pushing him into sexual hyper-drive. "It's . . . it's your reputation that scares me off, Brian." Her voice was barely a whisper.

"My what? You mean just because I'm a well-known attorney? Why should that be a problem? Look, I'm not much older than you, Lindsey, but I got real lucky when I started my practice a couple years ago. I picked up a controversial case that no other D.C. lawyer wanted to touch, and the publicity was astounding when things went my way."

Lindsey recalled the case. A prominent Washington newsman, Devon Shore, was arrested for killing his wife, Melanie, and their three young children in a murderous rage, then burning their two-story colonial to the ground, destroying all evidence. The prosecutor had an iron-clad case against Devon, or so everyone thought. But during the trial Brian was able to raise enough doubt to unsettle the jury, and in the end they were unable to reach a unanimous verdict. A hung jury meant not only the expense of a new trial, but the horrifying possibility that Devon would get off scot-free.

At that point everyone in D.C. despised Brian Winchester as passionately as they hated the villainous Devon Shore. But during *voir dire*, the selection of a new jury, staggering evidence came to light that pointed the finger of guilt in another direction—at Devon's brother, Mike. The muffled voice of an anonymous caller informed the D.C. Police that

Mike had always had more than brotherly intentions toward Melanie Shore, *and* that he had lied about being in New York at the time of the murders. With a possible motive and his once solid alibi blown to pieces, the D.C. cops skewered Mike with relentless pressure. His ultimate breakdown and tearful confession cleared Devon of all guilt—and Brian was suddenly a hero.

Lindsey shook her head emphatically. "Of course it's not your legal reputation that worries me, Brian. I admire your skills as an attorney, and what you did for Devon Shore was nothing short of miraculous. It's . . ." she swallowed hard, "it's your reputation with women that frightens me."

"My what?! Women as in plural? Just how many women do you think I've had?"

"It's not the number, Brian. It's more the—the intensity."

He looked at her blankly. "Now you've lost me, Lindsey. What on earth are you talking about?"

Lindsey closed her eyes and scrubbed a hand over her face, reluctant to repeat the ugly accusation Roland had made about Brian's sexual prowess. But there was no backing out now, so taking a deep breath, she plunged ahead. "I—I was warned that . . . that you're like a sexual machine with no 'off button'. Once you get going—well, you're endurance is legendary and you have no mercy on your partner."

Brian's blank stare widened into one of incredulity. "My God! What a bunch of horse shit! I mean, the macho part of me wishes some of that were true, but unfortunately I'm just like every other guy I know. I hang in there long enough to give me and my partner a pretty good time, but then I require a definite breather, along with a hot shower and something really fattening to eat before I can possibly entertain the thought of a second sexual go-round." He thought a moment, then eyed her with a frown. "Who on earth fed you that line of bull, Lindsey?"

She shrugged. "It doesn't really matter." She paused, thinking of all the time they'd wasted because of Roland's apparently malicious lie, then her gray eyes twinkled with mischief. "Besides, just as soon as you show me what your brand of lovemaking is *really* like, I'll give the reprobate a graphic update and make sure he regrets his evil little game."

Brian gave a hearty laugh, then picked her up and swung her in a tight circle. "Well, if lovemaking is what you have in mind, I can definitely help you out there . . . and I promise, even though it sounds tempting, you won't for an instant feel like I'm some kind of insatiable sexual robot."

Lindsey couldn't have asked for a sexier, yet warmly tender lover than Brian turned out to be, and even though her repertoire of men was exceedingly limited, she doubted a better lover could be found. He had slowly undressed her in the dim light of her bedroom, then lowered her gently onto the bed. She felt herself melting into the hard strength of his body as he carefully caressed her and softly spoke her name to reassure her. "Lindsey, I've dreamt of this since the first time I saw you, but I'll stop anytime you say the word."

"Bri," she breathed huskily, twisting her fingers into his hair. "All these weeks you don't know—how much I've wanted this."

"Oh I most certainly do, sweetheart," he moaned. "Any more self-inflicted abstinence and I would have been walking around with a permanent hard-on."

Her laugh was silenced with a surprised utterance of joy as he swiftly entered her, filling her with a hot, hot, pulsing beat that matched her own. Then he waited, willing her to set the pace . . . and she found she must, slowly at first, then moving to a heated, rapid thrusting as the fire he had lit urged her on. Roland had been so, so wrong. She was not a mere sex object—Brian treasured her for the woman she was. She knew by the sweet touch of his mouth on hers, the feel of his gentle hands erotically stroking her breasts, the sensation of his throbbing sex deep inside the core of her being. As she cried out his name and begged him for more he quickly began matching her movements, riding her as fiercely as she rode him, and together they followed their pounding emotions to the height of ecstasy, reaching their climax in perfect harmony.

"Oh my," Brian breathed heavily, then simply collapsed his body onto hers, fully sated.

As Lindsey wrapped herself securely against him, she knew their first sexual encounter had been more than wonderful—it had been magical. And even though it was way too early in the game, she was certain that love had found them.

After a few minutes of quietly lying together, Brian nuzzled her ear and asked softly, "Lindsey? You okay?"

"Umhum. Wonderfully okay."

"Good, because . . . I don't believe this . . . and I don't want to scare you off, but I think I can skip the shower and the fattening stuff and get right into round two."

She responded with a soft, delicious laugh and began moving her hips against him in a slow, sensual rhythm, encouraging his growing erection. She pulled his face to hers and delved her tongue deep into his mouth, taking his breath away. "Don't worry about scaring me off, Bri," she sighed, ending the hot kiss. "We have to make up for all the time we've lost, and by my count we're at least thirty rounds behind."

TEN

Wiping briskly at the scuff on her new tennis shoes, Julie vowed never to wear four-inch stilettos again. Her now comfortably recovering feet were firmly entrenched on solid ground, no longer walking the streets as a high-class hooker, and she fully intended to keep them right where they belonged. The reception phone shrilled loudly and she answered on the first ring in a friendly, reassuring voice. "Addiction Recovery Center. Can I help you?" She had completed her six-week training period at ARC, and this was her first day on the phones. She vowed no one would receive a harried brushoff on her shift, no matter how hectic things might be at the center.

The caller on the other end of the line was sobbing hysterically. The voice was that of a young female, but Julie could understand little of what she was whimpering into the phone. She tried to calm the woman, then gripped the phone tightly as she realized she was listening to garbled threats of suicide. She motioned frantically for Jackie, her supervisor, and covered the mouthpiece as she explained what was going on. Jackie shook her head. "We don't do suicide," she said firmly. "Try to get the caller's address and then call it in to 911."

Julie was shaking by the end of the call. She'd managed to get an address, but the distraught woman had hung up as soon as she realized Julie was reporting her location. Julie looked pleadingly at Jackie. "How will I know what happened?"

"You won't. That's part of the job, Julie. Doing the best you can, then praying everything goes well." Jackie hesitated. "You might want to keep an eye on the news to see if anything is mentioned that could relate to the call." She gave Julie a reassuring pat on the shoulder. "Problem is, the stress can be real hard to take. Our phone staff burn out pretty quick and either leave or try to move into a different slot here."

And that was exactly what Julie intended to do. She had called Lyle Grey at New Beginnings as soon as she nailed the job at ARC and reestablished contact. She revealed as much as she was comfortable with about her recent past, and was pleased to report to him that she was four months into her recovery—no drugs, no alcohol for 120 days. And even though she had not completed her psychology degree at Harvard, when she told Lyle what she hoped to do he assured her that she had taken enough psych and substance abuse classes to get her into his private training program. It was designed to teach recovering addicts how to counsel men and women who were trying to break their habits, and he had taken her on as soon as he had an opening.

Julie knew she didn't have nearly enough clean time behind her to be counseling other addicts, but by the time she finished Lyle's classes she hoped she would be ready. And that's when she planned to call Lindsey. She had put her friend through so much agony already; Julie vowed to stay out of Lindsey's life until she was certain that she had her own life in order—as certain as any addict could be. So many times she had picked up the phone, to let Lins know she was free of Jonas's vile clutches and was surviving on her own. But she had to be more than just surviving. When she called Lindsey it would be to tell her she was sane, sober, and supporting herself by helping other addicts. That day couldn't come soon enough, but come it would. She had lived far too long with an overabundance of self-loathing.

*   *   *

Law school had flown by as quickly as a kid on a skateboard, and with her degree in hand, Lindsey looked expectantly toward her future with Brian. He had mentioned more than once that she would make a terrific addition to his law practice in D.C., and now that her head was cleared of tort law, precedents, briefs, and exams she could fill it with dreams of when they would marry and where they would live. They had been together exclusively since clearing up Rollie's crude exaggeration of Brian's sexual prowess, and Lindsey had concluded she'd never find a man more compatible with her sometimes too serious temperament— let alone one who was as charmingly handsome, brilliantly competent, and genuinely compassionate as he.

This evening he was treating her to an exclusive dinner in the Bar Room, hidden away on the second floor of The Harvard Barrister, a private club frequented by successful attorneys. Brian kept a suite of rooms there for his use whenever he was in Cambridge teaching, or visiting Lindsey, and he had promised to pick her up this evening around eight.

Trusting that tonight would be the perfect night for the long anticipated marriage proposal, Lindsey took a lingering shower in her small apartment near Harvard Square where she had stayed during all three years of law school. Then, with little time to spare, she slipped into a sexy, black evening dress that accentuated her long, graceful curves, and set it off with the emerald necklace and dangling earrings her father had given her last Christmas. The brilliant green stones provided a perfect contrast to her gray-hued eyes and long ash-blonde hair that she had fashioned into a French twist for tonight's occasion.

Brian proclaimed her to be a knockout when he arrived at her door, and she laughed when she saw he was sporting a dark green string tie with his custom-tailored black tux. "People will think we coordinate our evening attire, Brian, both showing up in black and green."

"It'll just give them something more to talk about, I guess. You know they can't keep their eyes off us when we go out." He gave a deep mocking sigh. "But then, we're such a stunningly handsome couple, who can blame them?"

They laughed and joked throughout their meal, trying to remain oblivious to the admiring glances of other diners sitting nearby. As they reminisced about some of the memorable times they had shared while she was still in law school, Lindsey couldn't resist reminding Brian of their first ski outing in Vermont.

"You dragged me out of bed at the crack of dawn so we could be the first skiers at the top of the mountain," she recalled. He had raced her down the long, steep slopes designed for expert skiers, then rushed her to the lift to do it again—and again, and again. By lunch time, out of breath and hopeful that Brian would agree they had skied enough downhill runs to justify the outrageous cost of their lift tickets, Lindsey suggested they go back to the lodge to collapse. Pretending reluctance, he'd agreed to return to their room on the condition she give him a full body massage to relieve his aching muscles *and* be a willing participant in whatever else that may lead to. What it led to was hot sex in a warm shower that left them exhausted as well as completely satisfied.

The next morning she had talked Brian into a leisurely breakfast, during which she suggested a quiet afternoon of cross-country skiing in lieu of another day of punishing downhill.

"I don't know anything about it, Lins," he'd protested. "Isn't that what pansies do when they're too freaked out to ski the mountain?"

"Wait and see," she said with a knowing smile. After renting x-country skis, boots, and poles from the Nordic Center at the foot of the mountain, Lindsey started out at a fast pace with Brian following glumly behind. The trail had been freshly groomed and led into a covey of thick pines towering overhead. The only sound the couple made was the swish of their skis gliding across the snow, and as the trail wound slowly up the mountainside, Lindsey hoped Brian would find the activity as peacefully exhilarating as she did. "Watch for deer, Bri," she'd called over her shoulder, "and wild turkey. They're beautiful and something you'll never see when you're racing downhill."

After climbing steadily for a mile or so, they came to their first downhill slope. "About time," Brian grumbled, sweating profusely. "We're finally going to get some action."

"Brian, wait!" Lindsey cautioned as he skied around her and started down the steep hill. He had made it nearly halfway down, gathering considerable speed when his skis hit a small rise and, flailing in the air like a wounded duck, he landed in a huge drift. Raising his head to glare at her, he spit out a mouthful of snow. "These damn skis don't have metal edges! How're you supposed to stop?"

Lindsey skied down the hill and stopped gracefully at his side by turning both skis sideways and digging them into the snow. "Kinda like that," she said matter-of-factly.

"Showoff," he groused. "Now tell me, now that I'm buried in the snow, how am I'm supposed to get up on these things. They gotta be half the length of a football field!"

After a short lesson, Brian was up and ready to whiz down the rest of the hill. Lindsey had told him he could sidestep down if it got too steep, but he stubbornly skied his way down, falling two more times on the way. And just as he was gliding comfortably again on level ground, he saw a large hill looming ahead that, somehow or other, he was expected to climb.

"Okay, so now what, Lindsey? Do they have a ski lift around here?" He looked at her suspiciously.

"Well, not exactly, but we do have a couple of options," she said seriously, even though she felt like rolling in the snow while laughing hysterically. "You can get a running start and ski up—but I think this hill is too steep for that. Or, you can herringbone up." She set about showing him how to place the tip of one ski at a sharp right angle and then bring up the other at a sharp left, creating a nice herringbone pattern in the snow as she made her way up. "Just be careful that you don't cross the tails of your skis behind you," she called back, "or you'll be in serious trouble."

"Now she tells me," she heard him sputter as he added a few frustrated cuss words while once again picking himself up out of the snow. But suddenly, he was speeding up the hill, passing her by and standing at the top, smiling down at her with a triumphant grin, declaring himself to be "king-of-the-hill" as she made her way slowly to his side.

"Brian . . . how did you do that?"

"I chose option number three," he gloated, skis resting on his shoulder. "Take your skis off and run up."

He tackled her then and rolled her into a thick snow bank at the side of the trail. "How about kicking *your* skis off and having wild, hot sex with me in the snow? That's something else you don't see when doing downhill."

"Hah! Do you really think I'm going to lay bare-ass naked in this freezing stuff?"

"You can have the top," he laughed as he rolled her over, then swore profusely. "Damn, I just discovered one more thing I hate about cross-country—I'm trapped behind endless layers of boxer shorts, long underwear, and ski pants!"

Only after some time had passed could Brian laugh as wholeheartedly as Lindsey over memories of their cross-country misadventure, and then only after she had sworn to never put him through the ordeal again.

Now, growing suddenly serious, he reached across their small table and took her hand in his. He held it lovingly as they finished the last of their wine. "Dessert here or my place?"

"Your place, definitely," she smiled, but wondered why he hadn't mentioned their future during the lovely romantic dinner.

When they reached his suite on the third floor, he barely had time to kick the door shut before pulling her into his arms and smothering her with passionate kisses. Pausing for a breath, he stood back and ran his wildly blue eyes over her slender body, his face filling with desire. "God, Lins, how can you look so incredibly innocent and so tantalizingly sexy all at the same time?"

Holding back her own desire, Lindsey put her hands on his strong shoulders and held him at bay. "Wait, Brian. Don't you think we should talk first?"

"Talk? Uh-uhh," he hummed, pulling her close again. "It's time for dessert, remember?"

She slipped away. "I'm serious, Brian. I've finished school, I have my law degree, I passed the bar exam . . . I need to know about us."

"Ahh, you women," he laughed, "always so practical even at the most romantic times."

"Bri . . . please."

"Okay, let's get comfy in bed and I'll tell you what I see for us." He pulled her toward his bedroom, but she shook loose and settled resolutely on his living room couch.

"I think this will be safer for now, lover boy. You know you have the ability to make all serious thought seep from my mind like warm pudding when you have me in your bed."

Disappointed, he sighed as he sank down beside her. "Okay, you win—but I've got us on a time limit. Ten minutes and we're heading for the bedroom." He pulled her in his arms and rested her head against his shoulder. Then he breathed seductively in her ear. "Maybe a little foreplay here on the couch isn't such a bad idea anyway." He used one hand to loosen his tie and undo the first few buttons of his pleated formal shirt as the other slid to her breast and stroked it suggestively through the filmy material of her evening dress.

She pushed his hand away. "You're using up our ten minutes, Brian . . ." then had second thoughts and snuggled closer. Perhaps this was his way of leading up to the proposal.

"Okay, Lins," he kissed her softly on her moist lips and smiled into her silver gray eyes. "Let me tell you what I've been thinking . . . I'm hoping you'll join me in D.C. as a full partner!" He beamed at his generous offer. "Just as soon as you're ready to buckle down, you can start the hard work of practicing law with me—and I've found a small townhouse near my office that we can share. If it doesn't meet your approval, we'll look for something else—of course, you'll want to keep a small place of your own for appearance sake."

"Appearance sake!" She sprang from the couch and glared at him, folding her arms with a show of great dignity. "Brian Winchester! Your arrogance is amazing. Do you really think I'd be content living with you as your mistress? Good Lord, I'm nearly twenty-five! I want to share a *real* home with you . . . a real *life*."

He scowled, trying to make her understand. "I don't mean forever, Lindsey. But right now our careers have to come first. You're just getting started, and even though the Devon Shore case put me in the spotlight, that notoriety will fade quickly. It's going to take a lot of hard work and total dedication to get to the top of our field—so we have to put marriage on the back burner for now, sweetheart, until Winchester and Delaware is the first name that comes to mind when a big case hits the legal system." He reached for her hand and pulled her back into his arms. "But there's no reason the romance has to go out of our relationship, sweetheart. I couldn't stand that. I don't think anyone could have better sex that we do. And eventually we can have it all, if you'll only be patient for awhile—a successful practice, marriage, a family—."

Suddenly, the color drained from Lindsey's face as reality hit her full force. "Oh—my—God!" she gasped. "It's not about our careers, is it? It's about our not being able to have kids." She buried her face in her hands, then straightened and looked at him pleadingly. "But—you never mentioned . . . I—I assumed you were okay with it." She stared at him then, hurt and angry. "Why, Brian? Why didn't you say something long ago? Afraid all that good sex would come to a streaking halt?"

"What the hell are you talking about? I'm not even ready for marriage yet, let alone starting a family . . . and what on earth do you mean? Why won't we have kids when we're ready?"

Lindsey looked at him in disbelief. "Come off it, Brian. How could you not know, when it's been the hottest topic on campus ever since someone leaked the news about the accident that took my mother's life and robbed me of any hope of having children of my own? 'Poor Lindsey Delaware—a great looker but a real loser when it comes to being a mom.'"

Brian stared at her. Those comments about "Lindsey's problem" finally made sense. He was stunned. "Lindsey, I swear to God, I never knew! It may have been common gossip on campus, but no one mentioned it to me—I'm just a visiting professor, remember? . . . And I can't believe *you* never said anything! Is that why you're pushing for marriage? What—were you going to tell me I'd never be a father once the ring was safely on your finger?"

She rose unsteadily to her feet and backed away, edging toward the door. "I can't believe this is happening. Brian! I *always* make certain that people who matter to me *know!*" She looked at him with desperation. "Dear God . . . except for you. I can't . . . I was so sure you knew—I thought you were being kind, not putting me through the ordeal of talking about my inability to have children, knowing how terribly hard . . ." She bowed her head, unable to shake off a deep sense of shame. But years of pent-up anger came to her rescue, replacing the shame with rage. Glaring at Brian, she spoke with bitterness. "But it's what every man wants, isn't it? Heirs to carry on the family name?" She picked up her small black clutch where it had fallen to the floor during their passionate entrance just minutes ago. "Well I'm sorry, Brian . . . I'll never be able to give you that." She choked back her sobs as she stepped into the hall and closed his door behind her. Blinded by tears, she resolutely made her way to the elevator that would take her out of the building and away from her dreams.

Dumbfounded, Brian sat motionless, trying to make sense of what had just transpired. But after a few heart-stopping minutes he realized the woman of his dreams was leaving him, and he rushed from his room to stop her. When he made it to the outside entrance, he saw her standing at the curb flagging down a cab. He wanted so badly to rush to her side and pull her into his arms, promising marriage and whatever else she wanted or needed to stay with him. But the reality of her parting words struck him like a stun gun to the heart, rooting him to the spot as if he were made of stone, unable to move or speak. Dear God, if he married Lindsey he'd never have the son he'd always envisioned; a son who looked like him, who learned from him, who excelled in school and sports, and who grew into the man who would follow in his own footsteps. And he'd dreamed of having a daughter. A real beauty who was as smart and charming as her brother . . . and who looked just like Lindsey. He stood there numbly, realizing that his dreams for a family would never be realized—not if he married Lindsey.

He watched her get in the cab. She never looked back. Didn't see him staring after her. Didn't see the conflicted grief on his face. And even if she had, it wouldn't have changed a thing.

It was well after midnight, but she had to make the call. "Dad? Daddy? Did I wake you? It's Lins."

"Well, of course it's you," James yawned sleepily. "Who else would be calling me Daddy except my own daughter?" There was a long pause as he came more fully awake. "But you haven't called me Daddy in years . . . what's wrong, Lindsey? Have you heard from Julie? Is it bad news?" His hand tightened on the phone as he realized she was crying.

"It's bad news all right, but not about Julie—Dad, Brian and I just had a major breakup. I want to—I need to come home and . . . can I work for you, Dad? Do you have room for me in your practice?"

"Oh my dear, darling daughter! Nothing would make me happier—but I'm so sorry about you and Brian. I just assumed you would be working with him."

"You and me both, Dad, but—that's not going to happen." She was crying so hard now, it was difficult for her to get her words out. "Oh, Daddy. I thought he knew about me—but he said he didn't, and . . . and I could see in the way he looked at me that it was more than he bargained for . . . or less, I guess."

"The bastard! Well . . . he's not the man I thought he was, Lindsey, and he certainly doesn't deserve you. Doesn't he realize most men would give their right arm to have you?"

"Yah," she laughed dejectedly. "Their right arm, but not their first-born child."

"Lindsey, stop that! I won't have you feeling sorry for yourself. Damn! I could throttle that man. Don't let him make you feel rotten over something you'd come to terms with years ago!" There was a long pause before he spoke again. "We Delawares are a strong lot, Lindsey. Take a day or two to recover from this, then pack up and join me in Dover, just as soon as you're ready to put that shiny new law degree of yours to work."

ELEVEN

The hectic flurry of packing and moving from her small apartment in Cambridge to Dover, then unpacking and settling once again into her childhood home and the office her father had given her, was a blessing. James didn't try to hide his elation that his daughter was joining him in his firm, and had immediately had the sign on the front of his Dover office repainted. In a handsome blue and gold it now proclaimed, "Delaware & Delaware; Attorneys at Law." Both Lindsey and James held back tears as they stood on the walkway, admiring the sign's pleasing appearance. But James's tears were those of pride, while Lindsey's were those of sadness. She couldn't help but think that once her father retired the sign would again be repainted. There would be no other offspring to continue on in the firm—it would revert simply to "Delaware" once again.

By staying incredibly busy, Lindsey found she was able to chase away the hollow ache in the pit of her stomach during most of each day, but it nearly consumed her as she lay alone in bed at night. *For heaven's sake, get a grip, woman*, she told herself angrily, punching her pillow as she tried to shape it into a more comforting cushion. *Damn thing's soaked with tears; I should just trade it in on a new one.* "Brian," she cried bitterly into the darkness, "I so hope you're suffering as much as I am!" How many sleepless nights had it been since she'd run from him at his club in

Cambridge? Too many—more than he was worth. She could only pray that practicing law with her father would eventually be stimulating enough to take away the emptiness that haunted her both day and night. What was it Brian had said? It would take a lot of hard work and total dedication to get to the top? Well, if that's what he wanted, she was about to give him a run for his money.

Since both Lindsey and James enjoyed cooking, they had fallen into the habit of preparing their evening meal together and eating in on most weeknights. And although James tried to get her to go out on weekends and renew old acquaintances, so far Lindsey was resistant, content to stay at home to read or watch old movies while he went out alone. Tonight, she was busy pan-frying salmon fillets in parsley and olive oil for their Thursday night dinner when she heard James answer the phone in his study. A few minutes later he came to her in the kitchen. "It's for you, Lindsey." He spoke in a serious tone while trying to hide an excited grin. "I'll take over here."

Good Lord, is it Brian? Lindsey wondered as she hurriedly wiped her hands and walked into the study. What would she say? She still loved the man, yes, but could she overlook how he had treated her? She hated how her voice trembled when she spoke into the phone. "H—hello?"

"Hi, Lins. Bet you totally gave up on me, huh?"

Lindsey's heart skipped a beat. "Julie? Julie Trent! My God, is it really you?" Julie laughed on the other end of the line. "Damn you, Jules! I don't know whether to cry for joy or cuss you out for all the grief you've caused me!"

"Well, while you're trying to decide, can we make plans to have dinner? We have a lot of catching up to do."

"Yes! Of course! But where on earth are you? I scoured every corner of Harvard Square and the city of Cambridge looking for you, but you were nowhere to be found!"

"That's because I was right here in Dover, getting clean and sober. I knew I couldn't do that if I was anywhere near Jonas . . . but look, I'm calling from work so I have to make this short. How about tomorrow at seven? Wendy's on Court Street—I'm buying, and a burger at Wendy's is about all I can afford." Her laugh was light and filled with happiness.

"Julie, I'm a full-fledged attorney now. I can afford to take us to a really nice—"

"Absolutely not! It's time I started paying you back for everything you and James tried to do for me over the years— and besides, you could *always* afford to take us anywhere we wanted to go. But things are different now, and you're just going to have to get used to my style of generosity . . . and Wendy's."

"Okay—Wendy's is good . . . I like Wendy's." They were giggling delightedly as they ended their call with promises to meet the following evening.

Lindsey was half fearful that she wouldn't recognize her old friend. Julie had been so thin and frail when she last saw her—what, more than four years ago now?—and she could only imagine what she'd been through since then. But the Julie who was waiting for her at the small corner table in Wendy's was beaming at her with a healthy glow. She was dressed casually in jeans and a white cotton shirt that she filled out appealingly—and her excited, girlish smile made Lindsey's heart sing. She unconsciously let out a sigh of relief as she sat across from Julie, grabbed for her hand, and held it tightly.

"What? Surprised you, didn't I? Thought I'd look twice my age, with no teeth and wisps of thin gray hair?"

Lindsey didn't know how to respond, as that's pretty nearly what she'd been expecting. "Sort of . . ." she admitted reluctantly.

"Well, that's exactly where I was headed, so don't feel bad. I appreciate the honesty . . . and the obvious fact that you think I'm gorgeous once again."

Her smile became serious. "And I'll be honest with you, Lins. If I hadn't gotten away from drugs, I wouldn't be here today. I'd be locked up in some institution . . . or dead. That's what's at the end of the line for junkies like me if they stay on the ride too long. Thank God, I jumped off . . . and it's mostly because of you that I did, Lindsey. Knowing how much you and your dad cared about me—loved me, gave me the courage to run from the hell of addiction into the hell of detox and finally into the tough, but wonderful world of recovery."

"Jules—I didn't do . . ."

"Shh. You always took the blame for my addiction, now it's time you took some credit for saving my ass! And you better let go of my hand," she laughed, pulling away. "People are starting to wonder."

"I guess I'm afraid to let go, Jules. Afraid you'll disappear again."

"Never again, Lindsey. I've got too much going for me here." She proceeded to tell her about her job at ARC as a full-fledged drug counselor, and that she had finally enrolled for her last year of classes at Harvard. "And the absolute best news, Lins; other than having three years, four months, twenty-two days, and"—she checked her watch—"six hours of clean time; is that Lyle and I are dating—well, more than that, we're lovers actually. He helped me through all that bad stuff about my father—and it doesn't bother him too much about all the johns I did for drugs when Jonas put me out on the streets."

"Lyle sounds like a pretty special guy, Jules."

"Special is an understatement, Lins." She leaned closer and whispered, "Because the high I get from doing it with Lyle is better than the high I got from doing it with drugs—well, almost."

They were still laughing uproariously as they went through the long line and carried their food trays back to the table. Julie eyed Lindsey's chicken salad and diet root beer with disdain, proudly pointing to her double-decker cheeseburger, Frosty shake, and fries. "I can get away with all these fat, sugary calories, Lins, because I still have a little weight to put on."

"Well, you keep eating like that and by December you can get a job playing Santa Claus."

"True," Julie agreed with a grin, then grew serious as she looked closely at her friend. "Lins, you're face says you're really happy to see me, but there's a lot of sadness in those gray eyes of yours. Fess up—what's going on that you're not telling me?"

Lindsey sighed deeply and started at the beginning, filling Julie in on all the highs and lows of her failed relationship with Brian Winchester. By the time she had finished, Julie was holding both of Lindsey's hands as if *she* would never let go. "I'm so sorry, Lins. You were always so worried that the kid thing would ruin things for you, and I was always so certain it wouldn't. I'd love to give that macho jerk a piece of my mind and a kick in the n—but I never even met the guy."

"You don't know how I wish I could say that, Jules. Hey! Enough of this—we're celebrating, remember? How about another yummy chocolate shake while I get a refill on my diet soda? Then we'll make plans for you and Lyle to come to dinner. I make a mean pasta salad and Dad will be elated to see how well you're doing."

"Yuk to the pasta salad . . . but it'll be really great seeing your dad again."

*   *   *

This was when it caught up with him. He was fine during the day, buried in his law office. But home alone after work, that was the pits. At a loss as how to make things right with Lindsey, Brian had let days slide into weeks, and weeks into months, and now he feared he'd let way too much time go by. She was no doubt convinced by now that he was a royal ass—but damn, just because he'd acted like one didn't mean he was one . . . did it?

He caught a glimpse of his reflection in the mirror as he paced his lonely bedroom. Looking closer, he didn't like what he saw staring back at him. The dark shadows under his heavy lidded blue eyes made it obvious he wasn't sleeping nights. Plus, he was long overdue for a haircut—and Christ, he must have forgotten to shave this morning! He was really going over the edge. He wondered if Lindsey looked as beat as he did . . . naw, she never looked anything but beautiful.

"You gotta get your act together, buddy," he spoke to the man in the mirror. "You've either got to see her and get this resolved or . . ." Or what? Do what he had been doing practically every night since she left—lose himself in a three-hour therapy session with Kenny, his local bartender? Kenny was a great listener. Only problem was, he rarely gave anything back in the way of a reply. This defect didn't bother Brian overmuch, however, because while Kenny wasn't exactly a great conversationalist, he seemed to understand how much Brian was hurting—and for Gawd's sake, he didn't want that put into words anyway.

He took his regular seat at the bar. Brian liked Monday nights best because most of the guys sat away from the bar, wrapped up in whatever football game was playing on the large-screen TV at the back of the room. They paid no attention to his one-sided dialogue with Kenny. As Brian once again rehashed the fateful night he'd lost Lindsey, Kenny, white hair and mustache neatly trimmed, studiously polished a shot glass and nodded in sympathy. Periodically, he held the spotless glass to the light, gave it another swipe with his bar towel, then set it down in front of Brian, who would signal for another shot.

That part of the ritual fulfilled, Brian held the amber liquid to the light, nodded his approval, and downed the burning whiskey in one quick swallow. "Wow," he shook his head. "That's enough to make a grown man cry."

"No, man . . . that's enough to *keep* you from crying."

Brian looked at Kenny with amazement. "Wha . . . did you say something, Kenny?"

"The whiskey, bro. It numbs the pain so you don't have to deal with it. Bet your old man taught you that real men don't cry, right?"

"You're damn right! Well, Winchester men anyway."

"Too bad. A five minute gut wrenching crying jag when a guy is hurting can do wonders—makes him want to fix the problem so he doesn't have to keep feeling like crap. . . it's bad for my business, though."

Brian was speechless as Kenny continued. "So, how long have you lived with this, man? Two, three months?" Brian nodded glumly. "Well, seems to me this Lindsey of yours, she's lived with not being able to have a kid since forever. But you, you can just walk away from it, can't you—and looks to me that's just what you're doing. But think about it, man. She can't. She's stuck with it, isn't she?"

"So you're telling me to quit feeling sorry for myself?"

"Whatever, man."

"But we'll never have a family, Kenny. And I never realized how much I wanted kids until she dropped her bombshell."

"It's called ADOPTION, Brian. Ever hear of it?"

"But—they wouldn't really be mine . . ."

"Yah, they would—if you wanted them bad enough . . . enough to be a real dad."

*　　*　　*

It was six the next morning when Brian called Nancy, his "what-would-I-do-without-her?" secretary, getting her out of bed. Without explanation, he instructed her to cancel his appointments for the day. Next he hurriedly showered and shaved, ate a donut on the way to the barber shop, then impatiently navigated busy U.S. 50 east from D.C.onto U.S. 13 which took him into downtown Dover and to Lindsey's law office—a ninety-five mile, two-hour trip that seemed like twenty. He considered it a good omen when he found a metered spot directly in front of the colonial style building, then bolted inside like Rambo on a mission, determined to set things right and make up for all the time they'd wasted.

The slightly plump, middle-aged receptionist jumped up just in time to insert herself between him and Lindsey's closed door. "And you are?" she asked, flashing her concern with hard, dark eyes.

"Just let her know Brian's here," he said impatiently, "I guarantee, she'll want to see me." But even though he used his most persuasive techniques to convince her that he had to see Lindsey immediately on an urgent personal matter, the woman stood her ground. She motioned him to a comfortable looking, navy leather chair and told him he'd have to wait, as Ms. Delaware was presently with a client. Not used to being on the waiting end of a law office, Brian scowled but did as he was told.

As he tried to restrain himself on the edge of his seat, he couldn't help but admire the sedate ambiance of Lindsey's waiting room. Decorated in various hues of blue with off-white accents, it spoke of affluence without being ostentatious, and was definitely more feminine than any law office he'd seen.

During the months they had been apart, Brian had followed Lindsey's career by subscribing to the daily Dover newspaper and reading the *Court News*. He was aware that she and her father handled a large percentage of cases that came before the bench in Dover's Common Pleas Court, and he couldn't help but wonder, had she joined him in his D.C. practice, how successful they would have been as a team. He was certain that under his careful eye, he could guide her to the pinnacle of success he strived for.

After what seemed like an eternity but was actually just a few minutes, Lindsey's door opened and a gray-haired, slightly stooped man exited. Brian jumped to his feet and rushed into the room before the flustered receptionist could stop him.

Lindsey was stunned. "I tried to stop him, Ms. Delaware," the receptionist huffed as she followed him in, "but he paid me no never mind and barged right in."

"It's okay, Beverly," Lindsey said without taking her eyes off him. "Tell my next client I'll be a few minutes."

Beverly sniffed her disapproval loudly as she backed out of the room, closing the door sharply behind her.

Brian smiled broadly as his eyes traveled yearningly over Lindsey's tall, slender form. She was dressed in a tailored, light-blue business suit that really set off her sexy gray eyes—and he couldn't get enough of her. She looked so damn appealing, he just wanted to scoop her up in his arms and . . . oh, what the hell, he decided as he crossed behind her desk and did just that, adding a quick kiss for good measure.

"Brian Winchester! What on earth do you think you're doing?"

He brushed back her hair and nestled his lips against the softness of her oh-so-enticing neck, breathing in her heady scent. She tried to pull away, but he held her close, wanting to make her understand that no other woman could fascinate or captivate him as she did. "Oh, Lins, you don't know how much I've missed you."

Finally freeing herself, she stepped back and straightened her clothing. "Do you really think you can just waltz in here and pick up where we left off?"

"Just listen to me, Lins. After you left, when I thought about what happened, I knew—I knew you hadn't been trying to hide anything from me. That's just not something you would do . . . so we can, we *can* pick up where we left off." He reached for her again but she backed away. "Look, you said you wanted to get married, so I'm accepting your proposal, Lindsey. Let's go for it!"

"Stop right there, Brian!" She swiped her hand through the air, cutting him off. "You come barging into my office unannounced, uninvited, insult me—"

"Insult you?"

"You just don't get it, do you? You are *so* acting like a lawyer—and we all know what a great lawyer you are—talking over people, ignoring their feelings, doing whatever it takes to win . . . but that's not conducive to a loving relationship, Brian."

"Lindsey, I don't—"

"Oh, but you do—when something's important to you. Other times you can be kind, considerate . . . loving." A lump formed in her throat. "Okay, okay." She ran a hand through her hair, gathering her thoughts. "You're right. I proposed to you once. Now I'm going to do it again. I propose that we go on as before . . . a sexual relationship without strings, without marriage. Of course, it will have to be kept 'under the covers,' so to speak, for propriety's sake. Can't sully our reputations now, can we?" He looked at her with dismay. "That's what you wanted, isn't it?"

"Come off it, Lindsey! I admit I was way out of line assuming you'd live with me without any promise of marriage—and that it took me way too long to come to terms with us not being able to have kids. But I'm here now, practically on my knees—" She looked at him askance. "Which is no doubt where you think I should be," he added as his anger grew.

"I don't know what I think, Brian. Maybe we need more time . . . Look, my client's waiting. Please, just leave now." There was a deep sadness in her voice.

He shook his head helplessly, then threw his hands in the air and left her standing there. When he reached his car, he banged his fist on the hood. "Christ!" he exploded. "I acted like an ass again!" Morosely, he climbed into his car and drove his sorry ass home.

After that disastrous encounter, Brian persistently called Lindsey, apologizing earnestly and acknowledging his culpability in their breakup. "I should have proposed that night, Lindsey. I pretty much knew that's what you were expecting, and I don't know what on earth I was waiting for. And when you told me about—about the kid thing, I should have wrapped you in my arms and tried to take some of the hurt away. That's what I want to do now, Lins, if you'll give me the chance."

Finally, Lindsey cautiously agreed to try dating once again. But on the three occasions they went out, both Lindsey and Brian remained leery of saying the wrong thing or of being hurt once again. So they danced around anything serious, avoiding the risk of connection in either the bedroom or in discussions of their future together. And just when Lindsey was nearly convinced that things might work out for them this time around, she received a newspaper clipping in her morning mail that knocked her off her feet. It was a recent article from the society page of a D.C. paper. The accompanying black-and-white photo depicted a smiling, elegantly dressed Brian Winchester holding an equally smiling, elegantly dressed female, Adriane Woodridge, on his arm.

Lindsey's phone rang. She answered absently, her eyes locked on what she held in her hand.

"Lindsey?"

"Brian," she replied flatly, wiping at the gathering tears in her eyes with the hand that held the photo.

"Lins, I need to tell you . . . before you see it in the paper—to explain."

"Too late, Brian. Some kind-hearted soul sent me the photo. I'm looking at it as we speak . . . I must say you have good taste. This Adriane of yours is really quite lovely." He could hear the pain in her voice.

"Jesus! Now don't jump to conclusions, sweetheart. Adriane's just a bored socialite who fancies herself as a news reporter. She asked me to escort her to the annual Press Corps Ball here in D.C. It doesn't mean anything . . . *she* doesn't mean anything."

"I see . . . and is this the first time you served as an escort for the lovely Adriane, Brian?"

There was a long hesitation before he mumbled reluctantly, "What the hell, you'd find out anyway. I've seen her a few times. She's so damn persistent . . . that sounds pretty lame, doesn't it?"

"It sounds like something I don't want to get involved in, Brian. You are obviously very important to Adriane—important enough for her to make certain I'm aware of your relationship—I assume she's the one who sent the clipping."

"Lindsey! We don't *have* a relationship! And yes, Adriane probably sent the clipping when she found out you and I are back together. I told her I wouldn't be seeing her again. Besides, she was just someone to take out to dinner once in a while, that's *all*."

"One more non-relationship, Brian? Maybe you'd better work on what you've got going with her. Lord knows *we* aren't going anywhere." Brian continued to argue in his defense until suddenly Lindsey screamed into the phone, "Damn you to hell, Brian! I won't let you do this to me again. It's over, okay? Go play with your little socialite and leave me alone." She slammed the receiver down so hard her hand stung. "God knows Adriane can give you what I can't," she said with a bitter sadness. Then she lowered her head into her hands and cried her heart out.

Beverly rose from her desk and quietly shut Lindsey's door without interruption, her heart going out to the sweet young thing. She had never trusted that man. Not since that day he charged into the office like some lion king of the legal system, stalking the poor little lamb in her law office.

TWELVE

Julie and Lyle were doing their best to help Lindsey through the desolation of her most recent breakup with Brian. It was tough for Julie to witness how hard Brian's playing around had hit her friend. "Scumbag!" she snarled. "I know some really mean gooks who would love messing him up a little—if it'd make you feel better, Lins."

"Hey, watch it, sweetie pie," Lyle cut in. "You're soon to be a Harvard grad—don't want to mess that up just for the sake of a little revenge."

"I'm done messing up my life, thank you," Julie smiled at him with love in her eyes.

Lindsey laughed and reached for her friend's arm. "What would I do without you, Jules, you and Lyle? You two can cheer me up even when I'm wallowing in a sea of self-pity." Lindsey was sitting at the kitchen table in Lyle's small Dover home, where he had prepared a home-cooked spaghetti dinner, and even without the customary glass of red wine, the meal was scrumptious.

During dinner, in an effort to forget about "scumbag Brian" for a while, Lindsey regaled Lyle with stories of her days as a probation officer. Julie had heard them all when Lindsey was living through them, but enjoyed the retelling and Lyle's reactions. "My favorite is the squirrelly guy,

Jamie, who pissed down three flights of stairs," Julie laughed uproariously. "Wish I could've been there."

"Not for the cleanup, you wouldn't," Lindsey assured her..

Following their meal and the joint effort of straightening up the kitchen, the three ambled into Lyle's small den where they had spent many productive evenings "soul searching," hoping to avoid repeating the mistakes that had caused each of them so much heartache in the past.

Tonight, Julie took the lead. She was working hard to uncover the beginnings of her addictive past and was cutting herself no slack in the ownership department. "It wasn't drugs I was abusing, it was my life! And I knew—knew what drugs and alcohol would do to me—that they'd take over my life if I gave them the slightest chance."

She thought back to her first encounter with alcohol. "I was invited to a don't-tell-your-parents beer party when I was a sophomore in high school. Never drank before. Thought I was so cool. I had three or four beers . . . woke up hours later in a nasty puddle of my own vomit not knowing where I was—hardly knew *who* I was! Anything could have happened to me while I was passed out. Scared the shit out of me!"

"That's why you were so reluctant to use pot that night with Jonas," Lindsey said guiltily. "If only I hadn't pushed you—"

"I wish you'd get over that, Lins. Jonas had my number even then. He'd have romanced me into using sooner or later, with or without your help . . . that's what I'm trying to tell you, I *knew* what I was doing! I can't blame anyone but myself for my addiction . . . not Jonas, not my mother, not even my father . . ."

Lyle reached over to where she sat in one of his soft, cushiony chairs and squeezed her hand reassuringly, then dug into some sad, scary moments from his own abusive childhood. He ended vowing his resolve to never, ever physically harm another human being—especially those he loved. "I'm convinced I will never act on the violence my father instilled in me, Jules, even though we psychologists put a lot of stock in the notion that our pasts determine our adult behavior."

Julie shook her head. "If I thought what happened to us when we were kids dictates who we are today, you and I are seriously screwed!"

Lindsey sighed deeply. "After all the horrors you two went through as kids, you still have yourselves together far better than I do. Me? I think of myself as a hollowed-out shell pretending to be a woman."

"Lindsey Delaware!" Julie exploded. "I could just shake you! You're so much more than that." She looked at her friend in disbelief. "Is that the way you see every woman who can't have kids?"

Lindsey hung her head. "No, I guess not . . . maybe."

Lyle rose from his chair and went to the couch to sit beside Lindsey. He took her hand in his and held it comfortingly. "Didn't you have any counseling after what happened to you and your mom, Lins? You must have—that was way too traumatic to deal with on your own."

"I had some grief therapy, and Dad. We talked a lot. I guess we both thought that was enough. He kept assuring me that despite what had happened, I was still a beautiful young woman . . . and I kept thinking, yah Dad, maybe on the outside, but inside I'm an ugly mess." Her tears were flowing steadily now, and Lyle pulled a pristine white hanky from his shirt pocket.

"I always carry one of these," he smiled softly as he wiped the tears away. "Seems like I have a habit of making people cry." He raised her chin and looked her in the eyes. "Seriously, Lindsey, Jules is right. You're so much more than you give yourself credit for." He hesitated, then spoke earnestly. "I hope you'll take me seriously now, because as Dr. Grey I'm telling you that you need to see someone professionally. You obviously never worked through that horrible time—it's just like it happened yesterday, isn't it?"

She nodded her head, relieved that he seemed to understand her torment, and agreed to his setting up an appointment with a therapist friend of his. Then, having had enough of gut-wrenching seriousness for a while, the threesome decided it was time to turn their discussion to happier events.

"Are you just loving being a hot-shot attorney, Lins?" Julie teased. "I knew you'd be one of the best, and it looks like the city of Dover agrees with me. You're in the news all the time. And I can't tell you what a blast it is to turn on TV and see you looking back at me!"

"Keeps me busy—and that's good, I guess. Less time to think about you-know-who. Oh, and now Dad wants me to get involved in party politics! Wants me to work on the election board and run for the district chairman spot. I keep telling him I'm only twenty-six, and that people have probably had enough of the Delaware family in politics all these years. But he just reminds me about the Kennedy clan on the Democrat's side. He says it'll soon be time for me to climb aboard that proverbial Republican elephant and ride on into Congress."

Julie looked skeptical. "I don't doubt that you'd make a wonderful Congresswoman, Lins, but I worry about you being tough enough. You're too nice . . . don't you think those nasty politicians would just eat you alive?"

"Not after Brian Winchester!" Lindsey set her shoulders and raised her chin. "I learned a lot from that man, Julie, and I'll never let anyone walk over me again!"

*　　*　　*

Lindsey spent the next two years engulfed in her practice, making her mark in local politics, and avoiding eligible men at all costs. After two years of therapy she could honestly say she felt better about herself. Her therapist, Anita Lopez, had helped her through the grieving process for not only her mother, but for the children she would never have. Even so, there was no way on earth she would ever again expose herself to the pain of falling in love. And, as if needing to remind herself just how painful that could be, she dedicated herself to following Brian and Adriane's courtship in the society pages, waiting with certain dread for the day they would announce their impending marriage.

As was their custom on sunny summer days, she and Julie were jogging in Dover's city park after finishing their day's work. As was also the custom, Julie persistently voiced her concerns about Lindsey's decision to remain single. "I'm not meant to have a family, Jules, so—what was the psych term you used . . . diversion? I'm diverting my maternal instincts into creating a fantastically fulfilling professional life."

"Sublimation, Lins," Julie corrected, chugging down some tepid water from the plastic bottle she carried, "but it means pretty much the same thing. But, hey. Just because you can't have kids of your own doesn't mean you shouldn't marry and adopt. You'll be a wonderful mom. That's what Lyle wants to do."

"What—be a wonderful mom?"

"Yah, right . . . no silly, adopt."

Lindsey stopped running and, hands on knees, lowered her head to breathe in some badly needed air. Julie circled back and, stopping short, did the same. Once she caught her breath, she said seriously, "I'm not the healthiest person around since using heavy-duty drugs all those years, and Lord only knows what they might have done to my reproductive gene pool. Safer to adopt, I think—if the agencies are kind enough to trust a recovering addict."

James was so excited he could feel his heart thumping. He couldn't have asked for better news. Cassidy, the Republican Congressman was retiring at the end of his term. His seat as Delaware's single at large representative in the U.S. House of Representatives would be up for grabs at the 2008 election. With a little arm twisting, James was certain he could get him to endorse Lindsey as his replacement, and that would go a long way in getting her elected . . . that and the Delaware name.

Lindsey's reaction was just what he'd expected. "No, Dad! Absolutely not! I'm not ready for Congress—especially the U.S. Congress! I barely know what I'm doing as our district's party chair. Besides, no one will vote for a twenty-eight-year-old Republican female in this state—even if she is a Delaware."

James laughed heartedly. "You let me worry about getting the vote out, young lady. Just concern yourself with what you want to accomplish next term as the youngest female member in the House of Representatives."

And as usual, when it came to politics James Delaware was never wrong. When the ballots were counted on a cold November Tuesday, Lindsey had won hands down over a much older and more experienced male opponent who had not campaigned nearly as hard as she, believing Lindsey didn't have a ghost of a chance against him. "Well now, isn't that just something?" her father sighed with satisfaction when the results were announced. "Now we have a Delaware in both the Senate and the House."

"Well, I promise you one thing, Dad. For years the American people have been advocating for the world of politics to change. But every American leader who has promised to make those changes has failed to do so. I fully intend to do better!"

James smiled broadly and with a nod of agreement said, "Mom would be so proud."

Lindsey's first order of business after taking her Congressional seat in January 2009 had been the selection of a top-notch staff, and as she made her choices she didn't have to suffer a twinge of guilt about possible accusations of cronyism. Her list of close friends was extremely short and consisted primarily of Julie and Lyle, neither of whom had any interest in a political appointment. Anita, her therapist, was always pointing out how, despite Lindsey's outward persona of friendliness, she kept herself closed-in, unwilling to let anyone, male or female, too close. Lindsey had to admit this situation proved Anita's point, as well as proving Julie's theory that if you're not careful, your past can definitely take charge of who you become. But the flip side of not having an army of friends was that she was able to hire a bevy of very talented, very capable people without her judgment being clouded by misguided loyalties. Except for Beverly, Lindsey's law office receptionist now elevated to personal assistant, none of her new staff had any prior connection to either Lindsey or her father.

Today, she was tackling her second order of business as she drove the short, congested miles from Dover to Smyrna, where Delaware's State Correctional Center housed over

2,500 male offenders. Memories of her days at probation were often marred by thoughts of Gavin Rhodes, the young, reluctant drug dealer who was now living out a possible life sentence behind concrete walls. She had written him several times after his incarceration, and even though he had never replied, his wasted life chewed away at her piece of mind like the sharp teeth of a prison rat. When she reached the prison and parked her aging convertible in the visitor's lot, she had to admit she was hoping to accomplish a small miracle. Knowing the legal system as well as anyone by now, she was aware her chances were pretty slim. Her only hope was that by using the Delaware name and the fact that she was a newly elected Congresswoman, she could pull the miracle off.

Forewarned of her arrival, Lindsey was met in the visitor's area by Deputy Jones, one of the facility's two deputy wardens. He graced her with a nervous smile, unsure of the purpose of her visit. He was confident that Delaware ran one of the most progressive, efficient, correctional systems in the country, but one could never second guess these politicians—especially the female variety, who were known to get their skirts in a twisted snit over trivial things like high-caloric diets and low personal hygiene . . . it was a prison, for Chrissake!

He relaxed a little when she told him she'd come to see an inmate—Gavin Rhodes. Then he gave her a hard second look. "Yah, you're the one, all right."

"I beg your pardon?"

"He's got your pictures plastered on the wall of his cell. Keeps a scrapbook with news clippings too, or so I'm told." Lindsey tried not to show her surprise. "I don't think you're on his visitor's log, though. You know, not just anybody can come in here." He caught himself. "Sorry, Congresswoman Delaware. We, ah, we run tight security here, and even though you have clearance to check out our facility as long as you're with a c.o., prisoners are off limits unless they have you on their list."

"I'm aware of that, Deputy Jones, but I spoke to Warden West personally just yesterday and he assured me everything would be arranged."

The deputy shrugged and turned away, ordering her to follow him to the small room where he already knew Gavin would be waiting. *Just trying to give her a hard time,* he smiled to himself. *Didn't work though,* he had to admit.

Gavin stood when she entered the cement block, five-by-six-foot visitation room. He was classified as medium risk, so personal contact was allowed, but Lindsey was well aware of the observation room behind the mirrored glass facing her. She was prepared for the physical changes that Gavin would have incurred during his several years behind bars—or so she thought. But the young inmate could easily read her shocked disbelief as she stared at the stranger who greeted her. "Yah, it's me, all right," he reassured her with a rueful laugh. "Prison rehabilitation brings about all kinds of changes."

When she'd last seen him nearly seven years earlier he looked like he'd stepped off the pages of Ebony. Regal in posture, tall and slender with thick, curly dark hair, intelligent brown eyes, and golden brown skin, he had radiated the ideal image of a charismatic African American male. And the heart-stopper that iced everything had been a beaming warm and friendly smile that attracted people like moths to a flame. But that Gavin no longer existed. And this Gavin who stood before her nearly broke her heart. He stood slightly stooped and offered only a sad half-smile. His close-cropped salt-and-pepper hair, his sickly jail-house gray skin, spoke to the ordeal of his years of incarceration. But what was far worse was the dull emptiness that filled his faded brown eyes. Lindsey could see no life, no energy behind them.

He pulled a chair out from a small oval table and, after brushing it carefully with his hand to remove any food scraps or other unwanted debris, he motioned her to sit. Taking the only other chair at the table, he sat across from her and folded his hands, waiting for her to begin.

"I—I wrote you Gavin, several times . . ."

"Yah, well . . ." he shrugged, offering no explanation.

"I was afraid you wouldn't want to see me, but the deputy—he told me you have pictures, a scrapbook."

Gavin dragged a hand down his face to cover his embarrassment. "That wasn't for you to know," he said crossly. "Stupid screw!"

"I'm glad he mentioned it, Gavin. It gives me the courage to ask you . . . to talk about why I'm here." He crossed his arms and lowered his head, giving no indication as to whether he was interested or not in what she had to say. "I want to start with an apology." His head snapped up at her words, and she saw she now had his full attention. "I was so naïve, Gavin, when I was your p.o. I held out a better life for you like a carrot on a stick. But I had no understanding how impossible it would be for you to attain it."

The wall of ice he had put between them began to melt away. "You? I should be the one—" His voice was husky as he choked out his words. "I really let you down. You saw something in me no one else did, and I trashed it." As if this emotional confession had exhausted him, he shut down just as suddenly as he'd come to life and grew silent again.

Once it was clear he'd said about all he was going to, she continued, hoping to break through to him. "But my expectations were unrealistic, Gavin. I'm not stupid enough to think that's why you did what you did; that was bound to happen with all the outside pressures piling up on you. But I know it made things a lot harder on you when you were arrested and realized you were facing prison instead of college. He made no comment, and his continued silence began to unnerve her. She gave a nervous laugh. "You know, Gavin, I remember when I could hardly get a word in edgewise during our meetings at probation. You were so full of enthusiasm, so excited about everything going on around you . . ."

He raised his eyes and looked at her searchingly; then, as if reaching a difficult decision, Gavin spoke again. "Yah, well. I tried to keep my head on straight when I first got here. The warden let me take some classes on-line, college classes. I did okay, but after awhile I realized there wasn't much point. What was I going to do with a degree in social work, locked up in here? So now I guess I'm at the point of no return. I've come too far to go back to what I was, but don't have enough juice to keep on going. This place—it sucks it all out of you." He looked her straight in the eye. "I wish you could understand what it's like in here, especially at night— the damn loneliness, and knowing there'll never be an end to it."

Lindsey sensed the barrier between them had now fully dissolved. "My girl?" he continued. "I know she had to go on without me since I'm in here maybe forever. But, she should've come here to tell me that she was getting married, or at least sent a damn letter—but it's like I'm already dead to her. And Dad and Mom? They come every so often . . . it's such a long drive, they say, and it's pretty tough on them since Dad had to go to work, and Mom too, and since they lost the house . . . they go on and on like that. They can't hide the resentment in their eyes." He shrugged resignedly. "They might not come back—last time they were here and grumbling about hard times, I lost it. Told Dad maybe he should get his ass out on the streets like I did and try dealing for a living."

"You know I'd never touch that shit!"

"That's what he yelled at me, and Mom looked like I'd told him to go make friends with the devil."

Lindsey reached for him across the small table, taking his hand firmly in hers before he could pull away. "Gavin, I'm so sorry. But—I'm hoping you won't be in here much longer. I have an idea that I want to discuss with Judge Bates, the man who sentenced you. It may not work, so I need your okay. I don't want this to be another carrot on a stick."

"But I was told there's no way around a mandatory sentence for three-time losers like me, Ms. Delaware. Twenty years to life! Let's face it. I'm stuck here for a long time."

Lindsey shook her head in disagreement. "I checked your rap sheet, Gavin. Three-strike laws are aimed at violent offenders. I don't think the prosecutor should have hung that mandatory sentence on you, and I'll tell you why. Your first conviction was for drug trafficking, and you got off easy because you had no priors. Then you had a pretty good lawyer for your second trafficking offense, because he got it plea-bargained down to a drug abuse charge. That's how I got you on probation and why you had to convince me that you were a dealer, not a user."

"Yah, and why I had to drop urines and go to Cocaine Anonymous meetings," he grumbled. Then he shot her a quick look and added, "I learned a lot of good stuff in those meetings, though—like dealers are just as addicted to the power of drugs as users are."

She nodded in agreement, then looked at him earnestly, getting back to her reasoning. "Your third offense, Gavin, was once again for drug trafficking, and they made that one stick big time . . . as they should have with all those kilos of coke in the trunk of your car. But by my way of counting, even though drug trafficking is considered a violent offense, which is highly arguable in your case since you weren't carrying a weapon and weren't dealing within 300 feet of a school or park, drug *abuse* certainly isn't." She smiled brightly. "You were *never* convicted of three violent offenses, Gavin, because one of those convictions was bumped down to drug abuse—so no mandatory sentence, right?"

He looked skeptical. "I don't know—that's kind of stretching the point, isn't it? And you have a reputation for not playing around with the law—are you sure this mandatory sentencing thing is three convictions for a *violent* offense, not just any three felonies?"

"I'm trying to follow the 'letter of the law here,' Gavin, if not the spirit, and I'm ready to argue it out with Judge Bates if you give me the go ahead."

"Do you really think we have a chance?"

She nodded enthusiastically. "We have three things going for us, Gavin. If the judge buys my argument that you don't meet the criteria for a three-time violent offender, I'm going to ask that you be paroled into my custody for the remainder of your sentence. And since the state won't have to feed and house you for endless more years, that's going to save the taxpayers a bundle of money, at least $30,000 a year. Then there's the fact that I'm a Congresswoman with some voting clout as to how many tax dollars get relegated every year to the Department of Corrections. And finally . . . I'm a Delaware. I've never before used my name to gain favors, Gavin, but this time I think it's justified."

He looked at her in awe. "You're really going to try this, aren't you?" She nodded, then looking at him sternly, started to caution him. He held up a hand to stop her. "You don't have to say it. If I mess up this time, I'm taking you down with me."

"You won't mess up, Gavin." She stood to leave, then walked around the table and gave him a hard hug; this gave the correction officers behind the one-way glass something to speculate about. "Just don't get your hopes up until after we hear back from Judge Bates. I think he's going to want to do this, but it may take him some time to reach a decision—and to smooth things over with the prosecutor."

"Ms. Lindsey—I mean, Ms. Delaware . . ."

"I like 'Lindsey' better, Gavin," she reassured him.

"Okay—Ms. Lindsey . . . would you thank your dad for me?" He spoke in a nervous whisper, glancing at the mirrored window.

"Dad? Well, sure . . . but what exactly am I thanking him for?"

Gavin smiled sheepishly. "I was pretty sure you didn't know. He put in a good word for me with the warden when I first got here. Said he had a personal interest in my welfare. So no one, none of the cons or the screws have messed with ·me . . . well, you know what I mean."

Lindsey was all too sure she knew what he meant, and she could have kissed her father for trying to spare Gavin that additional torture of incarceration. "I remember telling Dad how worried I was about you, and how rotten I felt about trying to push you into something so unrealistic—but he never mentioned speaking to the warden about you."

"Well, like father like daughter . . . and you're both pretty special in my book. Ms. Del—Lindsey, if this doesn't work out, at least you've given me some excitement for the next few weeks."

And as she left, despite her cautioning him against it, she thought she saw a small spark of hope glimmer in his eyes.

*   *   *

The wedding announcement hit Wednesday's society page with a spectacular splash. Fortunately, it was not the one Lindsey had been dreading. Instead, it announced the impending June 6th 2009 marriage of Julie Lynn Trent and Dover's well-known psychologist, Dr. Lyle Grey, to be held in three weeks time at St. Patrick's Cathedral. They were in Lyle's kitchen, having coffee and making plans for the reception that would be held in Lindsey's elegant Dover home following the wedding.

As they watched Julie carefully preparing her coffee, Lindsey and Lyle began giggling at how her cup was practically overflowing with heavy doses of sugar. "Come on, you two," she argued. "How else is a recovering addict supposed to satisfy her sugar cravings? And who'd have guessed there was so much of the darn stuff in all that alcohol I drank?" She frowned a moment, then said resolutely, "Well, I gave up drugs and I gave up alcohol, but never will I give up sugar!" Then she added with a smile, "Now that that's settled, can we talk about the wedding?"

Although Julie had stubbornly tried to hold out for a small, inconspicuous ceremony, she and Lyle had so many friends between them that keeping it small had become an impossible task. "Besides, it's your first and last wedding, sweetheart," Lyle told her. "We have to make it memorable." He knew much of her reservation came from the fact that neither of her parents would attend the ceremony, but mostly it was the fear that Jonas, an ever-present evil playing havoc with her peace of mind, would somehow take out his sworn revenge on their wedding day. "We can't live out our life together in fear, Jules," Lyle said softly without mentioning Jonas. He knew just the sound of Jonas' name was enough to make her shudder and break out in a sweat.

Partly to distract her from thoughts of Jonas, but mostly because he meant every word, Lyle swooped Julie from her chair and held her high overhead. "How did I get so lucky, Lindsey?" he asked impishly. "She's simply gorgeous, and look at me. I'm too tall and scrawny to even be seen with the likes of her, not to mention my crooked teeth and busted nose."

As he set her back down, Julie laughed and wrapped her arms around his neck. "And when I look at you," she breathed, "all I see is perfection. You're wonderfully tall and lean with a sweet crooked smile and a nose with character. *I'm* the one that got lucky."

"Stop it, you two," Lindsey interjected. "You're making me cry."

Lyle sighed contentedly, wrapping his long arms around Julie's waist. "Well, at least when we adopt our kids, we won't have to worry about them growing up to look like me."

Julie looked anxiously at Lindsey, unsure how Lyle's offhand remark would affect her. "Isn't life crazy, Lyle," Lindsey simply said. "You two are so looking forward to that, and the thought of adoption just makes me sad."

"I guess it's the difference between having the choice to adopt, or having it forced on you, Lins, and that's a pretty critical difference."

Julie looked at him proudly, then whispered lovingly in his ear. "Babe, you always know just what to say. That's another reason I'm so lucky—and why I'd jump your bones right here, right now if we were alone."

Lindsey watched Lyle's face turn bright red and figured she was probably better off not knowing what Julie had just whispered to him—and also that it was time to give them some space. "I'm going home to fill Dad in on our plans for the wedding reception. He likes to feel involved . . ." *probably because he's given up on me,* she added silently, then chuckled as, before she was halfway out of the kitchen, she saw Jules pulling Lyle's shirt out of his pants and going for the buttons. Neither of them thought to say goodbye.

On the short drive home, Lindsey hummed happily. Every aspect of her life, save one, was remarkably more satisfying than she'd ever hoped for. The early months of her career as a Congresswoman had been beyond exciting, and she had plans to make them even more so. Julie had graduated from Harvard, finally, and had begun work on an advanced psychology degree while joining Lyle in his practice. Gavin had been paroled from prison and was now working as a counselor under Lyle's supervision, as well as volunteering at the ARC and continuing toward his degree in social work at a local college. Lyle was excited about bringing Gavin into his practice, as he'd never before had a trainee who was interested in working with recovering drug dealers as well as with addicts. Even Jonas had cooperated in making her life nearly picture perfect. True to Brian's prediction, a recent surprise raid on Jonas' Cambridge home had produced a stash of drugs large enough to level aggravated drug trafficking charges against him. Despite being free on bail at the moment, it looked like Jonas would soon be hit with a stiff prison sentence.

Damn! Lindsey said morosely as she pulled into the circular drive of her estate. Life would be so great—if I'd never met Brian. Or if I could at least get the jerk out of my head!

THIRTEEN

Just after dawn, Brian stumbled his way downstairs to Adriane's kitchen, desperate for coffee. After dumping yesterday's grounds down the disposal, he rinsed the filter, packed it firmly with Baby's Breakfast Roast, then watched impatiently as Mr. Coffee slowly dripped its fragrant brew into a darkly stained carafe. *God, didn't Adriane ever wash the darn thing?* he wondered. *Humph, silly question,* he answered himself. *She considers herself far too important to wash anything besides her own beautifully pampered body.*

Brian had learned early on that Adriane possessed an inborn sense of entitlement bordering on the obscene, and he had finally had enough of watching her ride roughshod over people she considered beneath her. Born into society's upper atmosphere, she now wielded the additional power conceded to major news media personalities—and her arrogance knew no bounds. He had concluded months ago that things weren't going to work out for them, but getting free of her was turning out to be as sticky as a bug trying to pry loose from flypaper.

Mr. Coffee finally offered up enough caffeine-laden liquid to fill one cup, and Brian took what he hoped was a clean mug from the cupboard, filling it to the brim. As he sat peacefully alone, he began reflecting on his own shortcomings as well as Adriane's. Thanks to her, he'd learned a thing or two about Brian Winchester's arrogance. By encountering her displays of overbearing haughtiness so frequently, he had come to recognize his periodic episodes of smugness. And now he had to admit that his belief in his ability to outsmart nearly everyone, and therefore get what he wanted, was based on his own brand of conceit. And he had no doubt his arrogance was just as reprehensible as Adriane's. Brian sighed deeply. He'd never get Lindsey back if he insisted on acting like a headstrong bulldozer. Lindsey had tried to warn him, but he'd just brushed her feelings aside, riding roughshod over her objections, intent only on winning every argument.

How often had he and Adriane bumped heads because of it? But with her, he usually acquiesced, leading her to believe it was because he cared deeply for her, when actually it was because he simply didn't care whether he won or lost their disagreements. Without Lindsey, nothing in his personal life mattered that much . . . damn, sometimes he thought he'd be better off if he'd never met the woman!

He swallowed the last drop of coffee in his mug and got up to pour another, wondering how he'd let his life descend into such a mess. He'd moved some of his things into Adriane's Washington townhouse six months ago, but when she started hinting at marriage, he'd let her know none too subtly that marriage simply wasn't in the cards. She'd thrown him out, stormed for three days, then changed tactics and begged him to come back. He still wasn't exactly sure why he had; except shit, she was a damn attractive woman and the sex she offered was pretty remarkable.

And now, out of desperation, she was constantly pushing herself at him. The more obvious it became that he was really on his way out of the relationship, the more aggressively provocative she became in their bedroom . . . but he had to admit, whenever he had sex with Adriane, always—always it was Lindsey he dreamed of.

*　　　*　　　*

Lindsey hurried down the wide marble steps of Delaware's state capitol building to her reconditioned silver Sebring she'd left hours ago in the congressional parking lot. Her father had arranged to have it completely refurbished after Jonas had marred the silver finish with his hateful words. And now, because of its advancing years and gleaming condition it was fast becoming a classic.

It was growing dark, and she breezed past the lone man seated on the park bench at the edge of the lawn. "Lindsey?" She stopped in her tracks but didn't turn as the man approached her from behind. "Lindsey," he said again, his voice soft and low and hauntingly familiar. He placed a hand on her shoulder, but still she didn't turn to face him. "Lindsey, look at me . . . please."

"Brian," she moaned. "Don't do this. Leave me alone."

"I can't, sweetheart. We can't leave things like this."

She whirled around to face him now, anger firing in her eyes. "Oh, I bet Adriane would disagree, Brian. Why don't we check with her?"

"There is no Adriane, Lindsey. Whether you and I can put this thing back together or not, *she* and I are history." He said it emphatically, with conviction.

The anger spread from her eyes and raced across her face. "And just how am I supposed to believe that, Brian, with all those photos and juicy tidbits about you and Adriane displayed in every conceivable gossip magazine and D.C.'s society pages?"

He placed both hands on her shoulders and looked deeply into her eyes. "There'll be no more, I promise. And despite what you think of me, Lindsey, I've never lied to you."

Desperation rang in his husky, baritone voice while his intense blue eyes bore down on her—and just that easily the white-hot need that only he could arouse tugged at her very core. "Brian!" She caught her breath and shakily pushed him away. "Don't do this to me again!"

Using a gentle hand, he tilted her chin up and stared imploringly into her ambivalent gray eyes. "I miss the music, Lindsey," he breathed. "All these long, lonely months, I've wanted only you. Come with me—" She backed away. "I—I don't mean *with* me, Lins. Not yet anyway. Just some place quiet where we can talk." She shook her head but he continued pleading. "Let me explain, Lins . . . God, I'm so sorry for the way I've treated you. It's been me all along who was out of line. I *know* you'd never try to deceive me about something so important . . . hell, you'd never deliberately deceive me about anything!"

His words were those she thought she'd never hear, and now they washed over her pain like the coolness of spring rain calming a burning desert. But the raging heat for what they once shared could not be calmed with mere words, and against her better judgment she allowed him to steer her toward his car, then drive to a quiet restaurant in the heart of town. She hadn't eaten since breakfast, but despite being famished, she was too anxious to eat more than a few bites of her meal. She avoided looking into Brian's eyes whenever he spoke to her, fearful that he would read the desire that coursed through her, see the sweat beaded on her brow. *My God, I'm like a bitch in heat,* she thought with panic. *I've got to get out of here!*

But when he reached across the table and took her hand in his, all thoughts of fleeing disappeared. "I'm so desperately sorry, Lindsey. I acted like an ass. Worse, a conceited ass. Can you forgive me?"

She raised eyes brimming with tears and looked at him longingly while trying to hold on to some semblance of common sense. "It's not a matter of forgiveness, Brian; it's a matter of trust." He took the pad of his thumb to wipe away a tear that trailed down her cheek.

"You *can* trust me, Lins, I swear. Just give me a chance to prove it . . . I won't hurt you again, darling—please, you've got to believe me or we'll both go crazy. We . . . I can't be separated from you when all I want is to be with you—to love you!"

Drawing a deep breath, she made a decision she prayed she'd not regret. "Where are you staying, Brian?"

His eyes lit with hopeful surprise. "I have a room at the Dover Arms . . . will you stay the night with me, Lins? It's been so long, sweetheart." At her slight nod of agreement, he quickly rose from the table, threw some money down and rushed her from the restaurant.

Within minutes, he had her back in his room and was holding her in his arms as if he'd never again let her go. He covered her face, the softness of her neck with kisses, then loosened her long ashen hair to let it fall around her face and onto her shoulders. A familiar spiral of heat twisted in him, setting him on fire. With a groan, he picked her up and carried her to his bed where he lowered her gently onto the covers. Placing her hands above her head, he pushed them into the soft pillow. Restraining his burning need to take her immediately, he slowly began undressing her, savoring each moment, and when he finally slipped her bra from her smooth white shoulders and placed the fullness of her breasts in his hands, he reveled in the tautness of desire he found there. A trace of moonlight slipped into the room, illuminating the length of her nakedness; her long, slender legs, the tempting darkness of her femininity, the firmness of her stomach, the perfection of her naked breasts. He drew a sharp breath. "Lindsey, my God, I'd forgotten just how beautiful you are."

Entranced, he ran his hands lightly across her stomach and breasts, caressing her as if she were a treasured goddess. Then he took the sweetness of a breast in his mouth and teased her gently with his tongue as he slid a hand between her legs and began stroking her erotically.

Soon she was sobbing and whispering his name. He could hear her raw hunger as her breath came fast and hard. Unable to wait another moment, she wrapped her arms around his neck and pulled his body down to hers, urgently pressing her hips against his hardness. "Oh, God, Brian, please. Please darling. Love me—love me now!"

He eased his way into her tight, throbbing heat, then thrust deeply into her, bringing a soft groan to her lips. He moved slowly, then with growing urgency as she met each rapid thrust with one of her own. Her response to him was wild, driven, and he realized with guilt that while he had indulged his sexual needs with Adriane, Lindsey had closed herself off and—and what? Waited for him? God, he hoped so. Well, he would make it up to her starting now. As he felt her shudder and stiffen in a long, satisfying release, he used every ounce of restraint to hold onto his emotions, then began slowly stroking her once again with the hardness of his erection, edging her toward what he hoped would be another joyful, shattering climax.

Lindsey cried out for him again as he teasingly brought her desire to yet another peak. This time he joined the thrill of her climax, filling her with the flowing heat of his passion. They held each other tightly, then gasped for breath as his hot, sweaty body covered her own. *It feels so right, so good*, she thought. *Surely I haven't made another mistake.* This time they would make it work, she was certain—but as wonderful as tonight had been, their love had to hold more than great sex. Because if it didn't, this time she was not at all sure she would survive.

"Oh, Bri, I've missed you so," she said into the gray light of morning as he lay beside her, propped up on his elbow, trailing his fingers through the long softness of her hair. "This is forever, right? You're not going to revert to some 'Lord and Master Attorney,' now are you?"

"I swear that's not how I want to be with you, sweetheart. Believe me when I tell you some good came out of all those rotten months I spent with Adriane, because watching her, I realized I had never learned how to *listen* to what you needed. I've always gotten what I want from people through clever persuasion and crafty lawyer tactics. I hate that about myself, and I'm asking you to help me, Lins. Show me the way through these damn murky waters of our relationship. Is that possible, do you think?"

She reached up to fill her hands with his thick, golden hair, pulling his face close to hers. "As long as your rudder's not broken, it's possible," she said with a smile. He raised a brow and looked at her quizzically. "You're like a great three-masted ship, Brian, so large it takes a strong wind to drive it. But it's guided by a very small rudder. Are you asking me to guide you, Bri?"

"Wow! That's really profound, and, and poetic." He looked at her admiringly.

She giggled. "I always thought so—it's from the book of James in the New Testament. But it really works here, don't you think?"

"Absolutely. And yes, I want you to guide me whenever I get off course. *And,*" he looked at her playfully, "I want you to know I too have the heart of a poet buried somewhere deep inside. And that heart is telling me that no matter what, I will come to you and be with you if you but call my name."

She laughed more loudly now. "Maybe, just maybe, Brian, you're not as big a jerk as I thought."

With an excitement she hadn't felt in far too long, Lindsey called Julie and told her she was bringing Brian when they met later that morning at Lyle's for their usual Saturday brunch.

"I don't think I heard you right, Lins. Must be something wrong with this phone. I thought you said you were bringing Brian—as in Brian *Winchester*?"

"I did, silly. Don't you think it's about time you met the love of my life?"

"Are you serious? I mean, is this for real? You two are *really* back together? Whatever happened to the 'oh-so-bad-but-beautiful' Adriane Woodridge?"

Lindsey laughed gaily. "I'll tell you all about it later. You just be on your good behavior when you meet him." She paused, then said seriously, "Jules, if I can forgive him, you'll have to too."

"Yah? Well, if you insist. I'll bury the hatchet—but not so deep that I can't dig it up again if he reverts to his old behavior."

Both Julie and Lyle were charmed by Brian's wit and good humor. He seemed genuinely pleased to be included in their small group and listened attentively as they finalized their wedding plans, all the while casting loving glances at Lindsey and reaching to touch her hand or rub her arm affectionately every few minutes as if to reassure himself she was really there. He even volunteered to help Lyle clean up the remains of their brunch while the women made numerous phone calls to the caterer, the florist, and David's Bridal Salon. The wedding would take place in two short weeks, and it seemed there was a myriad of details needing their attention during the next few days.

Half-an-hour later, as the four of them gathered in Lyle's cozy living room, Brian could tell that his new friends were bogged down in the muddy waters of anxiety, worrying over the number of things that remained to be done, and letting the unfinished details of the wedding consume their time and energies. Wanting to be helpful, he offered what he thought were some fairly simple solutions. When no one voiced an objection, he nodded his head sagely and said he'd make arrangements with his secretary first thing Monday to put his ideas into play. "Then we can all just sit back, relax, and enjoy the big day," he smiled with assurance, filled with a sense of accomplishment and feeling good about settling matters for Julie and Lyle. But when he was met with a room full of silence and three pairs of staring eyes, he realized something was awry. "And I just blew off course into some very murky waters, didn't I? Lindsey, will you help me out here?"

They were sitting together comfortably on a small couch, and she took his hand to pat it reassuringly. "We'll just back up and pretend the last few minutes never happened, sweetheart," she said softly. "Getting nervous and fretting over every possible aspect of the wedding is all part of the fun."

"It is?" Julie asked incredulously.

Lindsey laughed easily. "Don't worry, Jules. We have plenty of time to take care of all the loose ends. From here on out, it'll be easy."

"Easy . . . I like easy."

Brian hesitated, then joined in their laughter, relieved that they had so easily overlooked his momentary backslide into hot-shot attorney mode.

After a final cup of coffee, along with a slice of the best lemon cake Brian had ever tasted, he and Lindsey left with plans for the four to meet again for dinner the following evening at Chris's Steak House. "My treat, man," Brian had remarked to Lyle, "as long as you bring me the recipe for that cake of yours."

After settling Lindsey in his gleaming, black sports car, he turned to her. "Did I do okay, sweetheart, except for that one glitch?"

"You did great, lover boy," she laughed. "But Julie and Lyle are easy. Now comes the hard part—meeting Dad."

"Humph. I'm like Julie. I'd rather stick with easy."

Lindsey's phone call had been unsettling. James knew how badly she'd been hurt by Winchester, had watched with a heavy heart as she tried to regain some semblance of happiness. As the black Jaguar came to stop in his circular driveway, he left his rose garden and walked toward them, wiping the grime from his hands on a small towel he carried in a back pocket of his blue work pants. *Well, the man certainly is tall—and good looking,* he admitted grudgingly to himself as Brian unfolded his long legs from the Jag's sculptured bucket seat. *Damned if I can't see why Lins is so attracted to him.*

Brian helped Lindsey from the passenger seat, then straightened and with an arm around her waist, cast a warm smile in James's direction. As Lindsey introduced him to her father, Brian held out a hand in greeting. "I'm very glad to meet you, sir. James Delaware is a name highly respected in both Washington and your home state."

James eyed him warily. "You can call me Senator," he said briskly, ignoring Brian's outstretched hand as he continued wiping his own on the towel.

"Dad," Lindsey said in a warning tone. "Don't you think you could be a little more cordial toward your future son-in-law?"

"Son—! That happened pretty quickly, didn't it?"

"I'm sorry, sir . . . Senator. I'm sure it seems sudden to you, but Lindsey and I have wasted far too much time already." And with that, he smiled lovingly into her crystal gray eyes. "With your blessing, we hope to marry within a month, two at the most."

James let his eyes travel slowly from Brian's carefully styled hair all the way down to his chic leather loafers, then brought his hard eyes back to study his face—which was now sporting a less than hopeful expression. "I assume there'll be a wedding with or without my blessing?" James growled.

"There will, Dad," Lindsey interjected firmly. Then her tone softened. "But once you get to know him, I'm certain you'll be happy to welcome Brian into our small family." Hooking an arm in each of theirs, she led them resolutely toward the house. "And we're going to start that process right now!"

*   *   *

May had been an unusually cold and rainy month, but Julie was cheered by the warm June sunshine that greeted the city of Dover. It was a dazzling bright Sunday morning, one week before her wedding. "If this weather holds through Saturday, everything will be perfect," she sighed dreamily. All the pesky wedding details had finally fallen into place, and she and Lyle had just finished admiring the large ballroom in James's colonial estate where the reception was to be held. The happy couple were actually relaxing and looking forward to the big day.

The Senator could be heard humming happily in his kitchen, busily preparing a hearty breakfast of blueberry pancakes with eggs over easy, home fries, and country sausage for Lindsey and her friends. This morning the group included not only Julie and Lyle, but also Gavin, who was to be Lyle's best man, and Brian, who had quite willingly agreed to serve as head usher.

Knowing Julie's concern about Jonas possibly showing up to disrupt the wedding despite his current legal problems, Lyle had obtained a mug shot taken at the time of his arrest and given a copy to both Gavin and Brian. "If you spot this dumb ass at the church or here at the reception, I want you to forcibly escort him to a remote room and keep him under lock and key until I can get my hands on him. Jonas is a misfit without a moral compass and there's no telling what he might try." Then he gave Julie a reassuring smile. "And I don't want him anywhere near enough to frighten my lovely bride."

Julie, who was sitting next to Lyle at the highly polished antique plank table in James's family dining room, took his hand in hers and gave it an appreciative squeeze. "As long as I'm with you, sweetheart, I can put Jonas out of my mind." She looked at him lovingly with tawny brown eyes. "I have so much less to fear—to dread since you came into my life. Actually, I guess I inserted myself into yours; but either way, you're stuck with me now."

"Funny, I don't feel stuck at all, just damned lucky."

"Enough already!" Gavin interjected as he passed a huge stack of pancakes to Brian. "You're getting embarrassingly mushy here, and our breakfast is getting cold."

After stuffing themselves on far too many pancakes floating in way too much maple syrup, James proudly entered the dining room to present his guests with a cold dish of locally grown sweet cantaloupe and honeydew melon, insisting that they finish off their meal with a few bites of the tempting fruit. One never said "no" to the Senator, so they all dug in heartily and polished off the entire dish.

Sometime later, as each leaned back and groaned over how much they had eaten, Brian reached into the pocket of his khaki trousers and pulled out several glassine baggies, laying them on the table. Each sealed baggy contained two small pieces of bright orange sponge. Three pairs of puzzled eyes stared at them while Lyle snatched one up eagerly. "Ear plugs!" he exclaimed. "Brian, does this mean what I think it does?"

Brian smiled at him. "Yep, we're going to *The Monster Mile* this afternoon—" he gave a quick glance in Lindsey's direction, "if everyone is in agreement, that is."

Lindsey crossed her arms and looked at him from under raised brows. "Maybe we'll agree if you tell us exactly what we're letting ourselves in for."

"Hey! I know," Gavin answered. "I've never been there, but I always wanted to see it . . . Dover International Speedway—they have NASCAR races there, and if you're fantastically rich they'll even let you get behind the wheel of a genuine stock car and drive around the track at a couple-hundred miles an hour!"

"I think you'd have to be both rich *and* stupid to try that," Julie commented.

"You really have tickets, Brian?" Lyle asked eagerly. "Just to see the race, I mean; not to drive the track, although that would be way cool despite what Jules might think."

"I prefer getting my highs in other ways, thank you," she quipped.

The group of five laughed happily, then after helping James clean up, Lyle loaded them all in his Jeep for the short ride to US 13 and the race track. When they arrived, Lindsey and Julie could hardly believe the size of the 135,000 seat facility and the looming, forty-six-foot sculpture of the ferocious looking "Miles the Monster" who greeted them at the entrance. "Wow—this is bigger than pro football!" Julie exclaimed as Brian escorted them to their seats. "I'm really impressed."

"Wait until the race starts," Lyle told her. "*Then* you'll be impressed. Dover's *Monster Mile* is billed as the fastest one-mile track in the world!"

Brian added that every year NASCAR held three national touring events on the high-banked, concrete oval, but before he could go into any more detail, the loudspeaker bellowed, "Gentlemen, start your engines," and Brian quickly motioned them to put in their ear plugs.

Lindsey, Julie, and Gavin were stunned at the explosive burst of noise that greeted them, while Brian and Lyle, old-timers to the race scene, thoroughly enjoyed watching their awed expressions. They were sitting on bleacher seats close to the foot of the track, and as the cars shot forward and quickly gathered speed, the rush of wind they generated was almost frightening. They watched the beginning of the race as if spell-bound, unable to say a word to one another because of the thunderous roar of thirty-five high-powered engines.

After the first ten laps, Brian stood and motioned them to follow as he left his seat. He led them up the steep bank of bleachers toward the "Monster Bridge," a fifty-six seat, glass-enclosed structure that was suspended over the track at turn three.

"I wanted you to see up close what the race is really like," he told them as he ushered them inside, "but we can get a fantastic view of the rest of the race from here and talk to one another at the same time." They all nodded in agreement, watching the flash of brilliant color circling the track, but not missing the voracious wind or noise that swirled below them.

"It seems like we've just left the storm of the century and stepped into a peaceful glass sanctuary," Lindsey said in awe. "Brian, what a wonderful day you've given us." She reached up and planted a smacking kiss on his smiling lips. "I might just have to marry you some day."

He wrapped his arms around her and grinned. "Someday soon, you mean? Like tomorrow?"

"What? And miss all the fun Jules and Lyle are having planning a big wedding?"

"Yah, that's kinda what I meant. Otherwise we can wait and throw what would no doubt be Washington's social event of the season."

"Just think of it," Julie sighed. "Senator Delaware's daughter, a Congresswoman in her own right, and D.C.'s famous attorney, Brian Winchester . . . gee, can I come?"

"Can you come? You'd be in it, silly, as my matron of honor. But it's not going to happen, Jules. Brian and I have decided to forego all the hoopla and are having a quiet ceremony at the house in a few weeks . . . and yes, you and Lyle can come, and you too, Gavin. But other than Dad, that will pretty much be it."

"Great," Lyle said as he sank comfortably into one of the plushy cushioned seats overlooking the track. "Glad we got that settled. Now, can we please just watch the race?"

*   *   *

The newly finished décor of Lindsey's Congressional office in D.C. reflected her personal taste, and had the additional advantage of being only a few minutes from Brian's law offices. Lindsey turned from her desk to gaze out the tall, wide window bringing warm July sunshine into the room. She was near enough to the Capitol to afford her a breathtaking view of the magnificent, domed structure, and had taken time to brush up on its long, eventful history. She learned that the construction of the U.S. Capitol, beginning in 1793, spanned nearly forty-three years. British troops had set fire to the building during the War of 1812, and had it not been for a torrential rainstorm, the Capitol would have been reduced to rubble.

Over the years it underwent several design revisions, and renovations including the addition of gas heat, electric lighting, fireproofing, and a new dome. Today, it housed both legislative branches of government, with the Senate in the north wing and the House of Representatives in the south. A few Congressional offices, such as those for the majority and minority leaders, were housed in the Capitol itself, but most, like Lindsey's, were spread out among other buildings situated nearby.

Breaking into her reverie, Beverly breezed into the office, crossing the thick blue carpeting to drop a sheaf of bound papers onto Lindsey's desk. "Happy reading, Congresswoman," Beverly grinned. "Just because your bill made it out of committee doesn't mean your work is over. It's scheduled to come before the House next session."

Lindsey looked at the proposed bill lying on her desk with no small amount of satisfaction. It would provide much needed funding to subsidize quality child care facilities nationally, greatly expanding their numbers and reducing the cost for working, low-and-middle-income parents. The astronomical fees for day-care had become so prohibitive that many young parents were unable to enter the work force, leading to reduced incomes and too often, a great deal of frustration. During her first few months in office, Lindsey had co-authored the bill with a fellow Congresswoman from Connecticut, and had her fingers crossed that they had enough votes to pass it through the House and send it on to the Senate.

Lindsey could hardly believe how smoothly things were going, both in her political career and in her personal life. Julie's June wedding had been a fairy-tail affair with no interruption from Jonas whose trial was still pending, and she and Lyle were now on a three-week honeymoon in Hawaii—with a little financial help from Lindsey's father. Lyle had at first been reluctant to accept such a large sum of money, but seeing Julie's wistful glance, relented with a promise to repay the Senator. But James simply chuckled and insisted it was his wedding gift to the two of them with no strings attached, other than they enjoy every last minute of their trip. "Get used to it, Babe," Julie had announced emotionally. "The Senator has always enjoyed spoiling me as much as he does Lindsey."

As she settled back in her contoured leather chair to review the changes that had been made by the committee, she heard Brian's sexy, resonant voice speaking to Beverly in the reception room. As he came into her office, she greeted him with a happy smile. "Darling! What a pleasant surprise. I was on the phone with my pastor in Dover just a few minutes ago. He'll be more than happy to officiate at our wedding next week."

As she stood from her desk to give him an emotional hug, Brian stopped her abruptly. "Don't! Don't get up, Lins. Just stay there—please." She slowly lowered herself back into her chair, puzzled by the stress in his voice and the strange look on his drawn face. It was obvious something was terribly wrong. He began pacing in front of her, his hands jammed in his pockets. "You've got to let me explain this, Lindsey—Jesus! I know what I have to do, but it's the last thing I want!"

Now she was becoming frightened. "Does—does it have something to do with us, Brian?" He stopped pacing and she probed the dark blue eyes that met hers. "Something with Adriane?" she asked, her heart in her throat.

His face was like chiseled stone, confirming her fears. She gave a weak laugh. "Well, you're not going back to her, so what can she hope to—" His silent stare was as loud as a thunder clap. She clutched the arms of her chair with a white-knuckled grasp. "Dear God, Brian, what's going on?"

"You've got to hear me out, Lins," he pleaded. She stared at him wordlessly as he slumped into the chair beside her, just an arm's length away, but the distance grew with every word he spoke.

"Several months ago, I told Adriane that she and I were finished. When I couldn't give her a concrete reason other than that things just weren't working between us, she pleaded with me, begged me to give it just a little more time. I stuck it out for a while longer, only because she was trying so hard to be the woman she thought I wanted. She was—I don't know, softer, I guess. She stopped being so pushy, seemed genuinely concerned about me instead of everything being all about her. And the sex!" He stared at the floor, knowing how badly he was hurting Lindsey. "She just couldn't seem to get enough of me. Twice a day at least, sometimes three or four. God, I'm such a selfish bastard, Lindsey. I took what she gave and I have to admit it was hard to walk away from all that, even though I had no real feelings for her—nothing like I have for you."

"Anyway," he said with head bowed, as he scrubbed his hands over his face. "She called me this morning and insisted I come by to see her on my way to the office. She said she had something of mine that I'd left behind. Whatever it was, I told her just to keep it, but she sounded a little hysterical, which is out of character for her, so I finally agreed. She met me at the door of her condo with a seductive kiss, wearing nothing more than a slinky piece of black lace, and when I pushed her away she let out an ugly little laugh. Then she asked if I was over my little fling with you, and was I ready to come back to her—and our son."

It took a moment for the words to sink in, then Lindsey's heart slammed to a stop. "Your son!" she gasped.

He looked at her bleakly. "That was my reaction exactly. And when I asked her how the hell that could be when she'd been on birth control she shrugged, then admitted she'd gone off the pill as soon as I threatened to leave her. That's what all the sex was about, Lindsey. She was going to keep her claws in me by getting pregnant and dammit, it worked. She knew she was pregnant when I left weeks ago, but she waited until she had a damn sonogram as proof before she hit me with the news."

"Oh my God, Brian, what a mess!" Lindsey brushed at the line of tears that were streaming down her face, looking at him helplessly. Whatever was to happen next was completely up to him.

"I was so pissed, Lindsey. She was actually gloating about what she'd done, and all I could think of was using my bare hands to beat that arrogant smile off her fucking face—then she shoved the sonogram at me. 'Meet your son,' she sneered. I could only stare at it, Lins, as she pointed out his small head, his arms, his legs. Then she said in a taunting voice, 'What shall we name him, I wonder . . . Brian Jr.?'

"It was right then I realized how much I wanted him. This would be the child you and I could never have. All I could think of was doing everything dads do with their kids, you know? And I knew you'd be wonderful with him, Lins—a far better mother than Adriane could ever be. I told her I wanted shared custody and she could name however much damn child support she wanted, as long as he spent half his time with me."

His next words caught in his throat. "She just laughed that wicked laugh of hers that I'd come to despise when we were living together. And this is where it really gets ugly, Lindsey." His face was raw with emotion and she braced herself for what was coming next. "She's scheduled an abortion."

"An abortion! Brian, why on earth—?"

"Extortion . . . if I don't marry her, she's going through with it. She doesn't give a damn about the baby, Lindsey. She just wants my ring on her finger and the prestige of being Mrs. Brian Winchester . . . and the satisfaction of winning out over you."

Lindsey was numb, unaware of the tears trailing down her face and spilling onto her blue silk shirt. "You don't have a choice, do you Brian," she said dully. "You can't let her destroy your child. Even if you could somehow get an injunction to stop her, if she wants to abort the baby she'll find a way to do it."

He looked at her bleakly, clasping his hands between his knees. "But Lins, I can't bear the thought of losing you again . . . would you—would you consider still being a part of my life? Mine and my son's?" He hurried on before she could answer. "We'd have to be careful, I know, but we could work it out. We could spend time away together—"

"Don't you dare suggest that, Brian!" Lindsey's eyes fired, then she moaned and shook her head. "You have to make a safe, loving home for him . . . with his mother. And you're dreaming if you think no one would find out about us. Adriane will be watching us like an angry tigress protecting her territory." Lindsey was struck by a sudden thought. "Brian—does she know you're here?"

He nodded, then said with a deep sigh, "After I made her promise not to hurt the baby, I told her I had to see you to tell you in person that—that I couldn't marry you. The bitch actually gave me her permission. Her exact words to me were, 'That's fine, lover. And why don't you give her one last fuck for old times' sake? Tell her it's a gift from me.'"

Lindsey looked at him through sad tears. "So we can't even have that, can we Brian? One last time together? Because she'd be the one who sanctioned it. It would feel as if Adriane was right there with us." There was a long silence as her somber gray eyes looked away from him. "You have to promise to stay out of my life now, Brian. I have to find a way to go on without you."

He couldn't take any more. "Aww, Lins, don't ask me that." Then with the desperate sound of a dying man he sank to his knees and pressed his head into her lap, wrapping his arms tightly around her waist.

Brokenhearted, she choked back a sob as she ran her fingers lightly through his smooth, copper hair. "Promise me, Brian . . . please."

Standing, he pulled her into his arms, crushing her against him. But she was wasted, drained of all emotion and after a long unresponsive moment he stood back and said, "All right, dammit! I promise. But don't ever doubt how much I love you, Lins, how much I want you. And I swear to you, I'll never make love to that woman. Even if I have to appease her with sex, that's all it will be—it will never be an act of love." He settled Lindsey back into her chair and brushed his hand lovingly over her pale, drawn face. "I know you're right, Sweetheart. I can't ask you to wait for me . . ." he laughed lightly, "but you know how terribly selfish I am." His voice broke and he couldn't go on. With a deep shudder he turned and left her sitting motionless in her chair.

As he reached Beverly's desk, he forced his words through his constricted, burning throat. "Call Lindsey's minister, Beverly, and tell him she's cancelled the wedding—then call Julie. Tell her—tell her Lindsey needs her."

Beverly glanced through the open door of Lindsey's office. She was wiping her eyes with the heel of her hand

and staring blankly into space as if she'd just been given a death sentence. Beverly glared at Brian. "You sonofabitch!"

He winced. "Make that *stupid* sonofabitch, Beverly, and I'll agree with you."

She couldn't imagine Adriane being so cruel as to sacrifice her unborn child just to get her way. She couldn't imagine *any* woman being so cruel! But Brian was convinced Adriane would follow through on her murderous threat, and neither he nor Lindsey was willing to risk his son's life by challenging her. Lindsey clenched her jaw with a grimace. Until now, there had been only two people in her world that she could say with absolute certainty she hated— the drunk who had taken her mother's life and Jonas, who had nearly destroyed Julie's. Now she added a third. She not only hated how Adriane had invaded her life, she hated the woman herself to her very core.

Still sitting at her desk, she stared now with vacant eyes, envisioning Brian's torn features as he left her moments ago. Once again she'd allowed him to force his way into her heart, only to have him push it to the breaking point. And this time Lindsey didn't think it could possibly heal.

FOURTEEN

Even though Lindsey had assured him repeatedly that she was okay with it, Lyle felt a smudge of disloyalty whenever he and Brian got together; this was quite often, as the poor guy was clearly suffering and had no one else to dump his troubles on. Except for Lyle, Julie, Gavin—and Lindsey of course, everyone in Dover and D.C. thought Brian had the world by the tail; a highly sought after attorney married to a gorgeous, high-society newscaster and, as of January 2010, the father of a newborn son. Who could ask for more, right? *Well*, Lyle thought sadly, *anyone who saw the poor man's eyes welling up with tears every time he reminisced about Lindsey and the life he'd lost with her would know better.*

While Lindsey did nothing to interfere with the two men's continuing friendship, she frequently voiced her fear that she would unexpectedly run into Brian, and cautioned Lyle and Julie to help her avoid that possibility at all costs. So even though Lyle personally thought that it would be the best possible thing that could happen for the two star-crossed lovers, he and Julie carefully arranged their calendar to ensure that Lindsey's and Brian's paths would not cross whenever Lyle cooked one of his large homey meals for a gathering of friends.

Of course, as with all carefully laid plans, there was one momentous occasion at a black-tie fundraiser in the Capitol

Ballroom in D.C. where everything went wrong. Knowing that Congresswoman Delaware and attorney Brian Winchester were often invited to the same functions, Lindsey routinely had Beverly check the guest lists for each invitation she received, and would agree to attend only after getting Beverly's all-clear. During the early months following their final heart-rending breakup, these precautions had helped her avoid all close encounters. But this evening, while casually listening to the soothing music of a string quartet and enjoying a crystal clear glass of Dom Perignon, Lindsey looked over the rim straight into the surprised blue eyes of Brian Winchester.

The air was charged as they stared at one another—whether for five seconds or five minutes, neither knew. Lindsey's hand moved nervously to her throat—Brian's twitched restlessly at his sides. It was obvious to those who knew them that they longed to reach out and touch, but were restrained by an invisible barrier. When the initial shock passed, Lindsey choked back a broken breath and then, without wavering, acknowledged Brian with a brief nod. Her face looked calm and detached, but Brian could see the pain etched deeply in her eyes. How he longed to take away her pain, to fist his hands in her hair, put his mouth on hers, feel her breasts pushing against him. His body tightened and with a pleading look, he reached out to take her hand in his.

Adriane was at his side in an instant. Giving Lindsey a withering look, she hooked her arm possessively through Brian's. "My, how nice to see you, Lindsey. It's been a long time—hasn't it, Brian?" She cast an innocent look at him, then offered Lindsey a smug smile. "I persuaded my handsome husband to come this evening at the very last minute, or we would have missed you altogether." Her message was pointed, letting Lindsey know she had intentionally maneuvered this "chance" meeting. "You really should drop by sometime and meet our little boy . . . you do know we have a child—Brian Jr.?" Her shrewd eyes taunted Lindsey.

Without wavering, Lindsey lifted her chin and met the woman's hateful gaze. "I'm well aware of that fact," she replied evenly. "And I know how relieved Brian was that his son was born healthy and sound." Adriane scowled at Lindsey's subtle reference to the threatened abortion. "Now, if you'll excuse me," Lindsey said with a sculptured smile, "I see Senator Barrett across the room and I must speak with him." She made a graceful escape without looking back.

Although the encounter had happened more than a week earlier, Lindsey was still agitated beyond all reason. She paced her bedroom floor in the early morning light as she relived the event for possibly the hundredth time, anger spilling through her. *Get a grip*, she told herself disgustedly, and turned her attention to getting dressed. So what if her heart was broken? She was a Delaware, wasn't she? She wasn't going to let something as trivial as a broken heart stand in the way of what she hoped to accomplish with the rest of her life!

*　　*　　*

By November 2010, Lindsey was nearing the end of her first term in Congress and had begun making her mark. She knew how to work both sides of the aisle, and when that didn't work she took her case directly to the people. Fighting for what she considered long overdue political reform caused her congressional colleagues, both conservative and liberal, to quickly became disgruntled with her actions—but her constituents loved her. After running the idea past her father, she had created a modern version of Franklin D. Roosevelt's fireside chats. During the early days of radio, beginning with the Great Depression of the 1930's and continuing through the war years of the 1940's, Roosevelt had broadcast a weekly message to the entire nation, and the public welcomed him into their homes and their hearts as they listened to his strong, resonating voice.

Following FDR's lead, Lindsey developed a weekly TV chat of her own, broadcast every Sunday evening from the quiet warmth of her living room. The live feed was carried on a local Dover station but was quickly picked up by C-SPAN as her ratings skyrocketed. Rather than answering questions fired at her from a raucous group of reporters during random press conferences, she responded to the many e-mails she had received from her constituents. By going past the media directly to the general population, Lindsey was able to get her message out. Her demeanor was reassuring and unpretentious while her sincerity spoke of trust and truthfulness. The public was enamored, and gave her their overwhelming support.

Because Lindsey took care that the legislative changes she proposed were not only fully understood by her viewers, but made common sense as well, few members of Congress dared to stand against her. And when taking a stand on important issues, Lindsey didn't hesitate to expose politicians who had blocked change for their own personal gain.

One of Lindsey's major legislative efforts halted the age-old practice of the American taxpayer continuing to shoulder the burden for the full pension and health benefits of Congressional bureaucrats after they left office. Although her bill was only reluctantly passed by the House and Senate, it was applauded by every voting citizen—excepting, of course, the men and women holding Congressional offices. They had fully expected the largesse to follow them ad infinitum, all the way to the grave.

A second coup initiated by Lindsey required all government employees to pay into the same Social Security and

Medicare system as do ordinary Americans. *And,* it did away with the automatic pay raises that Congress had surreptitiously granted itself in late 2009.

"Ladies and gentlemen," Lindsey pointed out during one of her weekly TV chats, "were you aware that those of us in the U.S. House and Senate recently granted ourselves $10,000 in pay increases while we simultaneously vetoed a cost-of-living increase for our senior citizens living on Social Security? Somehow, we managed to rush the measure through, practically unnoticed, while the rest of our country struggles in the throes of a major recession."

She went on to reveal that because Congress wanted to avoid public attention and the animosity engendered by bringing their frequent salary increases to a vote, it quietly slid through legislation that would allow them to sit back and let their pre-established monetary gains glide silently into their bank accounts. Shortly after Lindsey cried "foul," the measure was promptly rescinded.

The popularity Lindsey gained with Delawareans during her first term as their at large Congressional representative led overwhelmingly to her reelection in 2012. It was then that she dropped yet another bombshell that rocked the House and Senate to its core. If passed, her bill would impose strict term limits on *all* elected officials. The outcry from Congress was deafening, as every career politician raged against her naivete. "Are you overlooking all the years your own father has served as a U.S. Senator, Ms. Delaware?" they challenged. "Would you have us lose all the experience and political know-how of our long-term, learned statesmen?"

"And we'll gain instead the dedication, talent, and abilities of those men and women who simply want to serve their country," she responded. "We are long overdue for

Capitol Hill to be filled with those who willing serve this country out of a sense of duty and with joy, rather than a sense of power and entitlement."

The fact was, even though she was convinced that term limits would benefit the country, Lindsey was not looking forward to her father's reaction. She was even more apprehensive when Delilah, his personal secretary for over thirty years, called her office. "The Senator would like to see you in his Dover law office as soon as you can arrange it, Lindsey." Delilah had known her since she was a small child and was therefore disinclined to use Lindsey's formal Congressional title.

When they met three days later, James locked her in their customary embrace before seating her across from him in a soft leather chair the color of browned butter. He chuckled as he read the apprehension in her eyes and reached out for her hand. "You can stop worrying, Congresswoman. You've put into action something that should have happened years ago. I've thought of advocating for term limits myself many times, but shame on me, I was never quite ready to give up the excitement and prestige of being a Senator. And of course, I was always able to convince myself that no one could do the job quite as proficiently as I, so . . ."

"Dad," she interrupted, "I'm not sure anyone could have done more for Delaware—or the country for that matter, than you have. And I know there are career politicians who are just as dedicated as you, but—"

"But long-termers like me need to move over for young-sters like you, for the fresh ideas you bring . . . and that's why I'm leaving the Senate at the end of this term, Lins."

"Oh, Dad! Are you sure? Did I push you into this?"

"Well, kinda," he laughed. "But it's the right decision at the right time—because I want you to run for my seat when I leave."

"The Senate? But, but I've barely settled into my second term in the House!" He nodded at her with a pleased grin. "But the U.S. Senate, Dad. I don't know if I'm ready for that."

"You're ready, Lindsey, trust me—I checked with Delilah just to be safe." That made Lindsey laugh along with her father. "By the time you run for the Senate you'll have completed four very successful years in the U.S. House of Representatives.. You must know that you're tremendously popular with Delawareans because of the job you're doing for them, sweetheart. You'll win my seat hands down over anyone foolish enough to run against you.

"But I have to caution you, Lindsey. You've come on like gangbusters in the House and have ruffled a lot of feathers. Creating a lot of animosity is not how you survive on Capitol Hill." He looked at her intently. "Not all politicians are demons, you know."

"Oh, Dad, I'm aware of that. Fortunately, the majority of them are as honest and dedicated as you. But it seems too many are out to feather their own nests at the expense of the country, and I can't abide them. Their greed and pomposity set my teeth on edge. I refuse to work with them when the only bills they're interested in passing are loaded with the kind of pork that will get them reelected."

She looked at James with a sudden glint in her eye. "Gosh, Dad, as Senator Delaware I could ruffle even more of their feathers, couldn't I?" She smiled thoughtfully. "Maybe I'm more ready than I thought."

FIFTEEN

When Julie and Lyle learned of the Senate plans James was mapping out for Lindsey, their enthusiasm more than matched her apprehension. Gavin was so excited he immediately volunteered to work on her campaign and suggested they use Lyle's rehab center in Dover as campaign headquarters. Lyle was thrilled with the idea, as it would underscore Lindsey's commitment to helping addicts as opposed to incarcerating them. But as the two men headed for Lyle's study to work on designing space at the Center, Lindsey noticed a look of concern on Julie's face.

Pulling her into the kitchen away from Lyle and Gavin, Lindsey studied her friend, who was staring morosely at the floor. "What is it, Jules? Do you think I'm rushing this? It certainly feels that way to me."

Julie quickly raised her head and focused her sharp brown eyes on Lindsey. "Of course you're ready! I don't know of anyone more qualified than you—it's just that . . ."

"What, Julie? Something about it is clearly bothering you."

"Oh, Lins. It's me! My sorry past! Everyone at New Beginnings and the ARC know about the awful things I've done and how close you and I are. Before long some eager, evil reporter like Adriane is going to sniff it out. I'm amazed the media haven't dug up all the dirt about me, your best friend, long before this."

"For Pete's sake, Julie! You make it sound like our friendship is something we should be ashamed of!"

"Think about it, Lins. How's it going to read when Adriane publicizes the fact that the long-time best friend of the would-be Senator from Delaware is a druggie and a whore?" She hugged her arms and lowered her head in shame. "Dear God, Lins! The horrible places I've been, the things I've done—"

Lindsey wanted to shake her. "Jules, stop it! That's *not* who you are . . . that was *never* you! You got caught up in all that ugliness because of how your father and Jonas used you."

Julie looked at her with soulful eyes. "But I *never* should have . . . do you think I'm going to hell for screwing up my life, Lins?"

Lindsey wrapped her arms around her friend as they both started to cry. She knew Julie's spiritual faith was the cornerstone of her recovery, and she desperately needed to reassure her. "You're the kindest, most honest person I know, Julie Trent. You'd never harm another soul, and if anyone tries to hurt you because of your past, they'll have *me* to deal with. And believe me; no one wants to mess with an angry Congresswoman—or Senator!" She stepped back and wiped the tears from Julie's troubled face. "Besides, girlfriend, you've left all that hell behind you, so if you get to heaven before me, just be sure to save me a spot, okay?"

With a sudden twinkle in her eye and her sweet pixie smile Julie asked, "Do you think heaven is like being high?" She laughed playfully as Lindsey sank onto a kitchen chair, shaking her head, then sighed and joined in her laughter. But after a moment, Julie became serious again. "You're right, I guess, about me not being totally abhorrent; because no matter what Jonas forced me into, I refused to sell drugs—or myself—to kids, Lins, not ever." She shuddered, trying to lock away the horrors of her old life, then looked at Lindsey with concern. "But it's not really me I'm worried about, Lindsey. It's *you* the press would go after."

"Well, we'll deal with them if and when the time comes, okay? But for right now, how about a hot cup of chamomile tea? This conversation has been pretty heavy-duty, and we need something to help us calm down."

Julie nodded in agreement and headed for the small teapot on the back of her stove, then stopped midway as she turned and faced her friend. "Okay, Lins, but—you have to promise me one thing. You can *never* let anyone know that you used drugs with me and Jonas that night at the frat house. I know it was only one joint of marijuana, but someone like Adriane would revel in using it to destroy your career. Promise me, Lins. Promise you'll carry that secret to heaven when you come to join me."

*　　*　　*

Julie's fears about her dark past providing Adriane with ammunition to go after Lindsey were unfounded. Throughout the remainder of her Congressional term and during her campaign for the U.S. Senate, Lindsey made it clear that she would be advocating for major changes in how drug addicts and dealers were dealt with, but nothing came to light about her and Julie's close association.

It was a mild January afternoon as Julie hurried down the busy city street, carrying a large turquoise bag from Dover's famed Nuevo Fashion Shoppe. It held the soft yellow sequined gown that the clerk, with a knowing nod, had said was just perfect for her. Julie had to agree. With a matching sequined bag, strappy high heels, and long white gloves, it would compliment her dark brown curls and the lush figure that had blossomed since she'd stopped abusing her body with drugs. It was perfect for the ball she and Lyle would be attending Saturday evening, in celebration of Lindsey's recent election to the U.S. Senate.

Senator Lindsey Delaware, Julie thought dreamily. *And she's still the same wonderful, unpretentious friend I've known since our days at Harvard.* A frown crossed Julie's brow as she thought of Brian and how that had gone so wrong. They both deserved better. Julie spent much of her time puzzling over how to extricate Adriane from Brian's life so he and Lins could finally and *permanently* have a life together. There was little doubt they could give Chip a far happier home than he had now. Julie smiled over the nickname Gavin had bestowed on Brian Jr. He looked so much like his father; the same light, copper-colored hair, bright blue eyes, and a heart-warming, captivating smile. "A chip off the old block," Gavin had declared when the little tyke was just a few months old, and despite Adriane's objections, the name had stuck.

. As Julie climbed the parking garage stairs to her small red Saturn on the third level, she pictured Chip and his endearing three-year-old antics. You couldn't ask for a sweeter kid, Julie thought, but Adrianne seemed to have little interest in the boy. She traveled frequently in her role as a roving reporter, and even though she frowned on Julie and Lyle with deep disdain, she was more than willing to let them care for Chip whenever it was convenient for her. And whenever he stayed with them he became more entwined in their hearts—convincing her and Lyle that they were ready to adopt a child of their own. She hummed happily as, keys at the ready, she unlocked the trunk of her car and carefully deposited her package.

Jonas moved silently, swiftly; a sleek, dangerous predator. Julie was completely unaware as he closed the distance between them—until he rammed her hard, face down, into the open trunk. Covering her body with his, he grabbed a wrist and turned it palm up. "Don't move, Jules," he warned as he pushed back the sleeve of her coat and slid the needle into an exposed vein. She cried out in protest only once, until the familiar jolt of heroin hit and spread its enticing warmth through her body. "Enjoy the trip, Babe," Jonas chuckled as he snatched up her keys and pushed her dazed body fully into the shallow trunk. Slamming it shut, he slipped the empty syringe in his jacket pocket, then wiped his sweaty hands on his jeans. A quick glance around convinced him that no one had witnessed what had taken him only seconds to accomplish. "And now for the rest of the story," he sneered through gritted teeth as he climbed into Julie's Saturn and headed for the secluded back streets of Dover.

*   *   *

"I'm going to wear a hole in this damn carpet if we don't hear something soon," Lyle raged. Lindsey and Gavin watched him pace his living room as relentlessly as the lead car in a NASCAR race. Initially, the Dover police had refused to put out an APB for Julie, saying she had to be missing for forty-eight hours. But when there had been no word from her by midnight on the day of her disappearance, James Delaware had intervened, convincing them that Julie's disappearance may well have been connected to his daughter's status as a newly elected Senator.

Within half-an-hour, the police found Julie's Saturn on the back street of a drug-infested neighborhood. It had been stripped bare; tires, engine, stereo, then torched to a crisp. That had been hours before, but there was no further word of Julie's whereabouts. Lindsey was practically numb with fear. All the memories of Julie's sudden disappearances from years ago came flooding back. But she refused to believe that

Julie had relapsed. She had as much faith in Julie's sobriety as did Lyle and Gavin.

"There's no way—just no way that she's relapsed," Lyle fumed when the detective assigned to Julie's case questioned them about her drug-addicted past.

"If there's one thing I know, it's addiction," Gavin added heatedly. "And Julie had none of the signs of a 'dry drunk'; no sign of someone about to lose their sobriety."

"We would have known," Lindsey agreed. "One of the three of us would have known!"

*   *   *

He'd had her for three days, held captive in the small dark room he'd found abandoned over an old garage. He smirked as Julie begged him over and over to let her go. "Please, Jonas. I'll give you whatever you want."

His eyes hardened as his smirk settled into a hateful grimace. "How much, Jules? How much you gonna pay me for the house I lost? And my car! My bank accounts! 'Ill-gotten gains,' they said. Asshole cops claimed everything I had came from drug money, so they took it all. And how about the three years I spent in the can?" he raged. "You gonna pay me for all that?" He glared at her. "Well, I'm back now, Jules, and finished my year of parole, so no one's watching over my shoulder. I can leave the state and start over—after I settle things with you and your high and mighty friends. I wonder how they're gonna feel when they find you all shot up with dope?"

"Damn you to hell, Jonas!"

He shrugged nonchalantly. "Fine, as long as they grow weed there." Julie watched helplessly from a filthy, narrow bed, too drugged to move, as he refilled the syringe with yet another dose of heroin. "Don't do this," she pleaded weakly as he leaned over her, his face sliding into an intimidating blur. "Jonas, it's too much. I—I can't take any more."

"Ahh, Baby, you know you want it. Let's see," he mused. "Where should we put this one? We have a nice set of tracks on both arms now. How about that vein in your pretty little neck? You'll get a fantastic rush from that."

Hours later, Jonas slapped her back into consciousness. "Wake up, bitch! Party's over. Time to send you back to dear Lins and your goody-two-shoes hubby."

"You're—you're letting me go?" She wanted so badly to believe him. Once she was safely back in Lyle's arms he'd help her through the excruciating pain of heroin withdrawal. She was ready to deal with that. She'd do *anything* to be safe and clean again. She could barely make out Jonas's dark form hovering over her in the dim room, the winter sun providing the only light through a cracked, narrow window. He reached down and gently put an arm under her shoulders, helping her to a sitting position on the edge of the bed. She shook her head slowly, struggling to fight back the dizziness and clear away the fog he'd kept her in.

"Almost over now, Jules," he crooned. "Just one more fix for the road, okay?" He held the needle out to her casually, as if it were an old friend. "Just a little shot of liquid coke this time. Coke *and* heroin—when they find you, we want everyone to know just how badly you relapsed." He slid the needle into her wrist and laughed as she cried out helplessly.

"No more Jonas, please!" she pleaded, even as the drug began lifting her to a place of peaceful serenity. He laughed and hummed contentedly as he sat beside her on the bed, rocking her soothingly. When he was certain the cocaine had flooded her system, he reached for the glass bottle sitting next to him on the floor.

"My, my, look what we have here, Jules," he said in mock surprise.

Even in her drugged state, Julie cried out in terror as she saw the quart of cheap whiskey he held out to her. Alcohol along with cocaine and heroin—every addict knew it was a lethal combination. "Jonas! No!"

"Ahh, come on, cry for me, Jules. Let me see those tears . . . then you're going to be a good little girl and drink this."

Holding her tightly, he grabbed a fistful of hair and jerked her head back, then covered her nose to close off her airway. His lips tightened into a sadistic snarl as he shoved the bottle into her mouth and began forcing the fiery liquid down her throat. Julie clawed desperately at his hands to no avail; she hadn't the strength to stop him. Unable to breathe, she choked as the whiskey spilled down her throat and out of her mouth, drenching her with whatever she didn't swallow. Jonas continued to pour the poison into her relentlessly until the bottle was empty. Fear hit her with an icy fist as her chest tightened in dire warning. Jonas wasn't letting her go—dear God, he was killing her!

*   *   *

Acting on an anonymous two a.m. phone call, the police found Julie sprawled behind a dumpster in a secluded alley. Barely breathing, she was rushed to Dover General where a frantic Lyle met the ambulance. Grabbing her hand, he followed the stretcher into the ER then stepped back, refusing to leave the room as they worked to revive her. Minutes later he collapsed to his knees with a moan as he took in their string of ominous words: "smells like a brewery—drug overdose—massive heart attack."

As soon as she received Lyle's nearly incoherent call, Lindsey rushed through nearly deserted, snow-laden streets to the hospital. He met her outside Julie's private room, hugging her in a tearful embrace. "Lins!" he cried, "They're telling me there's no hope! They say she overdosed—that there's terrible damage to her heart! All they're doing is keeping her comfortable. I—I just can't believe it." He sobbed deeply. "I begged them to try to find a donor—a new heart, but they said she's—she's not strong enough for a transplant. Jesus, Lindsey, they told me that she's in such bad shape, I should put her on a damn DNR code!" Straightening, he shook his head as if he could rid himself of the nightmare, then took Lindsey's hand and led her into the darkened room. "She's asking for you," he said tiredly, "whenever she wakes up. She's been drifting in and out. They're keeping her on intravenous painkillers, enough to control the worst of her pain, but she's still lucid."

Lindsey moved to Julie's side, where she lay as lifeless and pale as someone who had already left the living. The heart monitor by her bed recorded weak, erratic beeps that offered little encouragement. As if sensing her presence, Julie's eyes slowly opened. "You came," she breathed weakly, reaching for Lindsey's hand. Her eyes traveled to Lyle standing at the foot of her bed. Swallowing hard, she spoke softly through dry parched lips, her words barely audible as oxygen pumped into her lungs through a small nasal tube. "I . . . I really did it this time, Lins," she rasped. "They say I blew my heart out." Taking several shallow breaths, she continued. "'Sokay, though. Don't think I have another detox in me—and since I'm checking out, they're keeping me high. See?" Her eyes moved to the clear plastic bag suspended at the side of her bed. "Morphine drip—every addict's dream."

Lyle couldn't listen to another word. "Damn you, Julie!" he cried as he tore from the room.

When Julie heard the swooshing of the closing door, she clutched Lindsey's hand as hard as her weakened condition would allow. She spoke quickly, her disjointed words a hoarse whisper. "Lins, listen now. It was Jonas—he followed me—took me—did this to me."

Lindsey cried out in anger. "Dear God, Jules, I should have known he was behind this—but what you just said! You made Lyle think you had intentionally relapsed—why on earth?"

". . . can't let Lyle know," Julie begged. Lindsey shook her head, shocked. "He'd kill Jonas," she panted. "You. . . know he would. Lyle and Gavin . . . they'd track him down—make him pay . . . destroy their own lives. I can't let that happen—I won't!" she declared with a surge of energy.

Reaching out to calm her friend, Lindsey placed a hand on Julie's colorless face. Her skin was cold to the touch. Lindsey could barely see through her tears as she said, "I hear you Jules—but it's so unfair. You can't ask me to let Jonas get away with this . . ."

Julie gave a short shake of her head, her face as pale as winter. "No . . . you'll find a way . . . to bring him to justice—know you will. Too bad I won't . . . be here to see you pull it off." She choked back a sob, then gathered what remained of her ebbing strength. "I love you guys so much, . . . and you'll let Lyle know . . . the truth—when it's safe. And how much," she sobbed deeply now, "how much it hurt me to keep this from him—to make him believe that I'd done this to myself—to him. Promise me now. Promise that you'll do this, Lins!" She drew several short rapid breaths before she could continue. "Promise me before he comes back in here—to tell me he forgives me." She laughed weakly. "And you know he will . . . I could murder my parents and bury them in our back yard, and he'd still forgive me." Then she blessed Lindsey with a remnant of the pixie smile that was so endearing to those who loved her.

But Lindsey remained adamant. "Jules, you're asking too much! How can I live with this . . . pretend that it was all you're doing? I can't . . . I just can't!"

"You can't—but you will, Lins." Silence filled the room, broken only by the intermittent beeps of the heart monitor and the hissing of oxygen. "I know what I'm asking," she pleaded. "And it's okay if you have to share this with someone you can trust. Someone who won't go off after Jonas half-cocked. . . someone you can talk to, like your dad—or Brian."

"Brian!" Lindsey gasped just as Lyle re-entered the room.

"He's on his way with Gavin," Lyle said quietly. "I knew they'd want to be here." He was clearly still shaken, his pallor gray, as he stepped to Julie's bedside. Taking her thin hand in his, he leaned down and planted a soft kiss on her forehead. "Hey, Babe. Sorry I overreacted. Look, I don't care what happened out there—I just need you to pull through this, okay?"

Julie gave Lindsey a weak "I told you so" smile as she squeezed Lyle's hand. "Do you have any idea how much I love you, Lyle? How much you mean to me?"

Not hearing the response he wanted, he continued to plead with her. "You can beat this, Jules, I know you can. Just don't give up—don't!"

But even as he spoke, Julie's body stiffened. Overpowering the morphine, a tremendous shock of pain surged through her small chest. "Lyle," she gasped, her voice heavy and achingly slow. "It's time to let go . . . time for you—and Lins, to get on with . . . with what you have to do." Lyle sobbed as he laid his head next to her cheek. She ran her hand through his hair lovingly even as her eyes explored Lindsey's grieving face, waiting for a reply. Lindsey gave a reluctant nod of acceptance and Julie silently mouthed her thanks.

As her body tensed once again she cried out, then sighed deeply as her violet lids lowered against white cheeks. The monitor flipped to a frightening wail, bringing an elderly nurse, incongruously dressed in bright pink scrubs, hurrying into the room. They stood back anxiously as the RN took note of the DNR placard posted above the bed. With a frown, she placed her stethoscope to Julie's shallow chest and listened silently, then placed two fingers alongside her neck, searching for a pulse. After long agonizing moments, she shook her head. Lyle and Lindsey watched in stunned silence as death's cold sullen storm swept their loved one away, her life dissolving like snow in the warming sun—a life gone far too soon.

Three days later, shaken and devastated, Brian and Gavin stood in the bitter February wind, huddled with Lyle and Lindsey at the freezing gravesite. A soft pillow of snow blanketed the grounds except for the stark gaping hole waiting to receive Julie's casket. Lyle was inconsolable. He'd made it this far only with the help of his three friends. Taking turns, they'd made certain he was never left alone, but now they were beside themselves with worry. What would happen once they returned to their normal daily routines? Lindsey knew their lives would never be normal again.

SIXTEEN

Lindsey threw herself into her work, becoming even more dedicated as a Senator than she had been as a Congresswoman, hoping she could somehow ignore the choking loneliness of her life left by the loss of Julie and Brian. Whenever she reached the point of exhaustion, unable to deal with one more item on her political plate, her mind turned to Jonas. Every day he existed as a free man was torturous for her. She craved spending what little free time she had with Lyle and Gavin, sharing golden memories of Julie, but she couldn't bear to look them in the eye. Lyle wore a look of perpetual puzzled betrayal and Gavin told her it was beginning to affect his work at the ARC. "Both of us, I guess," he admitted with a grimace. "If we couldn't trust Julie after all those years of hard-fought sobriety, who can we? And how can we convince users there's a better life waiting for them if they commit to honesty and sobriety when it didn't work for Julie?"

She had told James the truth behind Julie's death immediately, and even though he was as angered and dismayed as she, he couldn't come up with a workable solution. "We have no witnesses, Lindsey, and when you try to repeat Julie's words on the stand, it will simply be ruled as hearsay. Even worse, it's well documented that there was no love lost between Julie and Jonas, so her statement will be highly suspect, especially since she didn't bother to tell her own husband. Jonas's attorney would make mincemeat of the prosecutor's case—if you could even convince him to take it on."

"Well, I *can't* let Jonas get away with what he did, Dad, and I *won't* turn Lyle and Gavin loose on him! Julie trusted me to make things right and by God I will . . . even if I have to tie the law in a knot, I'll bring that man to justice."

Lindsey fumed, plotted, and discarded one possibility after another, and over time the murky shadows of retribution began to form. It would be duplicitous, underhanded, and possibly deadly . . . just what Jonas deserved. Once she had finalized each step in her mind, she grew eager to put her plot into action. But being her father's daughter, Lindsey was wise enough to take a step back and question her objectivity. She desperately needed to run her intentions past James, but knowing he would frown on her involvement in anything that could possibly reflect on her stellar reputation, she reluctantly ruled him out. And that left? "No one!" she told herself sternly, as Brian's image ran fleetingly through her mind. "I refuse to even consider that possibility!" She went to bed that night in turmoil, but determined to find a solution to this new dilemma. There had to be *someone* she could talk to.

Knowing she was on break from the Senate, Lyle called the next morning to invite her to dinner. "Gavin's bringing his homemade ribs, I'm making Julie's favorite potato salad, and if you bring your great lemon pie we'll be all set. Oh, and your favorite film, *Marnie*, is on HBO tonight, so what do you say?"

Having seen it several times, Lindsey knew they'd pay little attention to Hitchcock's psychological thriller, and would choose instead to reminisce about golden times with

Julie. "Count me in," she said, then cautioned herself sternly. Even though she longed to reveal Julie's secret and how she planned to make Jonas pay, the truth would instantly send the two men off on a revengeful rampage.

Since her aging Sebring had been acting up lately, Lindsey called Gavin and asked if he could pick her up on his way to Lyle's. When she climbed into his SUV, the heady aroma of barbecued ribs immediately assaulted her taste buds. "Man, does it smell good in here," she practically drooled, then the two of them did what they always did when they got together; they rummaged through old memories of Gavin's probation days and Lindsey's inept attempts as his p.o. to turn his life around. "I'll tell you one thing, Gav, your ribs smell a whole lot better than that awful fried bologna they dished up in the county jail every day," Lindsey laughed. "Whenever I think of my days as a probation officer, that's the first thing that comes to mind."

They were still laughing when Lyle opened his door. "Hey, settle down, guys. No fair starting the fun without me." After giving each of them a welcoming hug, he took Gavin's tray of hot ribs and Lindsey's pie and ushered them into the kitchen.

An hour later, the dishes done and the kitchen restored to order, they settled into Lyle's den. Lindsey had just kicked off her loafers and curled her long legs onto the sofa when the front door burst open. A loud voice called from the hallway, "Hey Lyle, you home, man?" Lindsey gasped as Brian entered the room, led by a charming golden- haired little boy. "I'm sorry to dump on you again, but Adriane just informed me she's heading out on another one of her four-day trips and I—" he stopped abruptly as he saw Lindsey staring at him from across the room. "Oh, shit!" he said softly. "Lins . . . I—I'm sorry. I didn't think—I didn't see your car."

"Not s'posed to say shit, Dad," Chip admonished with innocent blue eyes, clearly happy that he could safely say the forbidden word himself.

Brian was dressed in a dark blue tux, obviously on his way to some formal affair, but he couldn't take his eyes off Lindsey. His son was oblivious to the heated emotion radiating between his father and the pretty woman across the room, and went directly to Lyle. Tugging on his pant leg, he looked at him hopefully. "Julie?" he asked softly.

Lyle went down on his knees and wrapped him in a hug. "No Chipper, you know Julie's gone," he choked.

Unable to take his eyes off Lindsey, Brian explained to her, "Even after all these months, Chip still expects Julie to be here when we come. She was more of a mother to him these past four years than Adrianne ever could be."

Chip freed himself from Lyle and looked to the pretty woman sitting nearby. Enticed by her nice smile, he went to her and placed a small hand on her knee. "Julie here?"

Lindsey wanted to wrap him in her arms and take away the hurt he was feeling; but being a stranger, she didn't want to frighten him. She put her hand on his small cheek instead and said, "You miss Julie, don't you Chip . . . we all do. Julie was my very best friend."

This seemed to satisfy him for the moment and he nodded in agreement, giving Lindsey a sweet, bright smile. "Julie my best friend, too." He then went to Gavin, who greeted him with a high five as they settled on the floor.

"How's Goldie doing, Chipper?" Gavin asked.

Chip shrugged. "Okay . . . but he's only a fish, you know." His large blue eyes met Gavin's sympathetic gaze. "Mommy . . . I mean Mother," he corrected, "says we can't have a puppy. She says she won't tol . . . tolrate no dirty animals in her house." He drew in a sad breath. "Are puppies really dirty, Unca' Gav?"

Lindsey's heart went out to the small child, unable to imagine what his life must be like with Adriane as a mother. No matter how hard Brian tried, Lindsey doubted he'd ever be able to counter Adriane's cruel self-centeredness.

As Lyle assured a relieved Brian that he'd be happy to have Chip spend the night, Lindsey reached a sudden, albeit reluctant, decision. Throwing caution to the wind, she slowly rose from the couch and walked toward Brian.

He stood speechless as she drew near, close enough for him to inhale her alluring scent. He studied her peaches-and-cream skin, the soft graceful lines of her throat. Unsure of her intentions, he fought the urge to take her in his arms and waited for her to speak.

"Brian, I have to see you," she said in a hushed voice. His heart skipped a beat. "Can you come to my office here in Dover sometime tomorrow?"

Disappointment registered on his face. "Sure, but— could we maybe meet for lunch? There's this new place near the docks . . ."

She put up a hand to stop him. "And how quickly would that juicy little tidbit reach Adriane, do you suppose? No, my office . . . please, Brian?"

Brian arrived early the next morning to find a disgruntled Beverly at her desk and Lindsey in her spacious law office, waiting for his arrival. "Leave the door open, Brian, if you would . . . someone might get the wrong impression."

He slumped sullenly into one of her soft leather chairs. "So what is it, Lins? Are we on again or off again? I'm getting dizzy here. We have to get off this break-up/make-up merry-go-round." Her silence offered him no encouragement. "What are you trying to do, Lins? Torture me? I—I dreamed about you last night . . . about us." His face took on a deep frown. "But what the hell, that's nothing new."

"I didn't ask you here to talk about us, Brian. It's about Julie—"

"Julie? Lins, you've got to let go of that. I know it's hard, but Julie's been dead for months now."

"Not dead, Brian—murdered."

"Murdered?" He half rose from his chair, then sank back. "You're grasping at straws, Lins. The autopsy—her system was polluted with drugs and alcohol, for God's sake, needle tracks all over her body." He shook his head. "You have to accept what she did, Lindsey, and go on with your life."

"Brian, do you honestly think I'd risk asking you here if I wasn't absolutely certain about this? Julie didn't kill herself. It was Jonas, Brian! Jonas!"

Brian sat spellbound while Lindsey revealed the truth behind Julie's tragic death. Once he grasped the reality of what Jonas had done, he erupted with rage. His loud, angry voice immediately brought a protective Beverly, glasses askew atop her head and a raised ruler at the ready, rushing into the room. But when Lindsey nodded at her reassuringly, she shrugged reluctantly, gave Brian one last scowl, and returned to her desk.

Once Beverly was out of hearing, Lindsey looked at Brian with misting gray eyes. "Oh, Brian, you don't know what a relief it is to be able to talk about this. Dad knows, but he gets upset with me now when I try to talk to him about it. He just wants me to put it to rest. And of course, Julie made me swear not to tell Lyle or Gavin."

"Makes sense why she didn't want them to know. Hell, Lins! I'm fighting the urge to find the bastard and wrap my hands around his skinny little neck myself. God, if he'd done that to you, nothing would hold me back."

He paused, then looked at her questioningly. "But I know you too well, Lins—you're not going to just let this go, are you?"

She shook her head emphatically. "Never!"

"Of course Jonas has to be held accountable, Lindsey, but what exactly are you looking for? Justice—or revenge?"

"Yes!" she replied without hesitation, "on both counts!"

"And that's why James gets so upset with you?"

She nodded glumly. "And that's why I asked you here, Brian. I think I've devised a way to make Jonas pay for what he did, but I need you to tell me if I'm off the mark."

He settled back and listened intently as she outlined, step-by-step, just how she hoped to deal with Jonas. He nodded in agreement at each twist and turn, but stopped her when she mentioned her own involvement. "You can't go there, Lindsey. What you're doing borders on the illegal. You've got to keep your distance from this or your opponents in the Senate will use it to bring you down, no matter how good your intentions."

She thought carefully about his concerns, then reluctantly agreed. "Okay, if we—if *I* can pull this off without bringing myself into the spotlight, I will . . . but if necessary I won't hesitate to use my influence."

"*We'll* pull it off, Lins. I want you to keep me in the loop. Lyle and Gavin have to be kept in the dark until this is resolved, and you may need more from me than just my advice. How soon are you going to put this into action?"

She drew a deep breath, wanting nothing so much as to reach out and embrace him for his willingness to help her. "Now! Today! While Jonas is still in Dover. I made a few phone calls last week and learned that his parole had been transferred from Cambridge to Dover, per his request, as soon as he was released from prison. His parole officer here said Jonas convinced the board that he'd have a better chance of staying out of trouble if he moved away from Harvard and all his old connections there."

"Makes sense," Brian said, "but it also put him in a perfect position to grab Julie."

"And I nearly lost him, Brian! If I have the timeline right, Jonas had already completed his term of parole when he took her. He was free to leave Dover as soon as—as he was finished with her. But ironically, the same night Julie was found in that alley, Jonas got into serious trouble. Seems he was celebrating in a late-night bar when a fight broke out and he was booked on a drunk and disorderly charge. His parole officer got a real kick out of telling me this next part. It seems the parole board hadn't yet signed the final termination papers, so Jonas was still technically on parole! Of course, they didn't know anything about Julie, but the D&D charge was enough to slap him with another year of parole. He's stuck here in Dover for several months yet, unless he violates the terms of his parole by leaving the state, and I doubt that he's going to do that."

"So the sooner we do this the better, right?"

She nodded her head emphatically. "I'll call Gavin right now and see if he can meet me tonight. Then it's up to the laws of fairness and probability to see if we're lucky enough to pull this off." She hesitated. "It was so good being able to talk to you about this, Bri. I didn't realize how much I depended on Julie just to listen and help me see things more clearly. God, I miss her so much!"

Brian nodded sadly, then looked at her longingly. "Please, Lins, before I leave, can I just hold you . . . just for a minute?"

She shook her head fiercely, backing away. We're not going there, Brian."

He gave her a hard look. "You're either very cold-hearted, Lindsey, or you don't care about us as much as I do."

"Either way we lose, don't we, Brian?" she said flatly as he turned and left her standing alone. But the real problem was that she wasn't coldhearted and that she did care . . . and that tonight would be just one more night when she cried herself to sleep.

SEVENTEEN

"I'm about to ask you for a huge favor, Gavin." Lindsey placed her hand on his arm, looking seriously into his dark eyes. They were sitting in a crowded, downtown diner where people paid little attention to the blonde-haired woman interacting with the young black male. Even if recognized as the new, young Senator from their state, it was not uncommon for Lindsey to be out and about in Dover, so as a rule people rarely bothered her.

Gavin took a big bite of his reuben, then washed it down with a giant swallow of Pepsi. "Ask away, Lins. There's not much I wouldn't do for you—short of going back to prison." He gave her a wink. "Not much chance of that, is there?"

He nearly choked when she replied, "I—I hope not, Gav. At least I don't think so."

"Holy crap, Lins! What—you're kidding right? This is some kind of test?"

"Not a test, Gav. It's deadly serious. And the worst part is, if you agree to help me you'll be doing it blindly. I can't let you know what's going on until it's all over."

"Well, shit! How fair is that? This isn't like you, Lindsey."

"No, it's not. And believe me, I have serious misgivings about the whole thing. But even knowing it can end up as a total disaster, I have to go ahead. I know I'm expecting an awful lot, Gav, but I'm counting on you to trust me—to help me with no questions asked."

He stared at her for several long seconds, studying her serious expression. Then he spoke with a decisive voice. "You know I'd trust you with my life, Lindsey Delaware, so of course, I have to say yes . . . now just what the hell is it you want me to do that may or may not land me back in jail?"

Lindsey looked around nervously, not wanting to be overheard. "Gavin, I want you to start spreading the word that there's an undercover informant—a snitch, who's about to name Dover's big-time drug lords—you know, the respected businessmen who put up the money to bring drugs into the city, then rake in the profits while keeping their hands clean?"

"The white-collar guys, one step above the boys wearing gold chains—yah, I know. Man, Lindsey, I wouldn't want to be him—the snitch. His life won't be worth a rat's ass! Who the heck is it, and why are you going to cause him such grief?"

She shook her head. "That's what I can't tell you, Gavin. I just need you to start circulating the—the rumor, at New Beginnings and the ARC. It should spread into the streets like wildfire from there. And if it doesn't, I'll mention it during one of my TV chats." Remembering Brian's caution she added, "But I'll only go public with the story if I absolutely have to."

Gavin's brown eyes studied her. "It's Jonas, isn't it? You want to pay him back for getting Julie hooked on drugs all those years ago. But Jesus, Lins—that's like giving the guy a death sentence!"

Lindsey shielded her eyes with her hand as she shook her head, dismayed at his perceptiveness. "Damn, Gavin, don't ask me that. For right now, you don't know who the snitch is, okay? Can you do that for me? I want the drug community to get really hyped about this before we drop the name."

Gavin leaned back in his chair. "You know, if this 'snitch' ends up dead you and I could go to prison for a long time, Lindsey. The law frowns on setting up nasty little games that lead to someone getting whacked—even scum like Jonas. What's it called—malicious intent? You can't stir up that kind of dirt without some of it getting on your own hands, Lins."

Lindsey flinched at his words. The actual legal term was callous disregard for human life that results in death, and it aptly described what she was about to put into play. "I know, Gavin, I know. But it may not go that far. Once he knows he's the target he'll probably run, leave the state. That would be his second parole violation, and would land him back in prison for several more years . . ."

Gavin gave her a hard look. "Or maybe he'll turn up very dead. Can you live with that, Lindsey?"

"I've thought long and hard about this, Gavin. And I honestly think I can. The only question now is, can you?"

"Well, Senator," he sighed heavily. "As much as I dislike that scumbag, there's no way I want to be responsible for his death . . . but for you, Lindsey, I guess I can."

Lindsey's eyes misted as she reached for Gavin's hand and clasped it tightly. She had just set something horrible in motion, and it was being done with the clear intent to cause harm. That made her culpable—and Gavin, as a co-conspirator.

Alone in her room that night, Lindsey stared longingly at the small night stand that held her phone. She so badly wanted to call Brian . . . but she had no way of knowing if Adriane would be the one to answer. Just as she decided to try to calm herself with a scalding hot shower the phone rang, startling her.

"It's me," Brian said softly. "I've been thinking about you and Gav all day. How'd it go?"

Lindsey inhaled a shuddering sob. "Depending on how you look at it, it went well, I guess—he agreed to do it."

"It sounds as if you're having second thoughts, Lins."

"Brian, what if I'm wrong? Julie was so strung out . . . what if she hallucinated the whole thing about Jonas? She could have relapsed on her own—or with him, but what if he didn't force her? Dear God, Brian, what if?"

"It's been bothering me too, Lins. We need to rethink this. No harm will come to Jonas until we point the finger in his direction. But maybe we don't have to go that far. Maybe we can stir things up just enough to make him talk."

"Admit to what he did? He'd never do that!"

"Oh, I think he will, Lins. I very much think he will."

It took three days to set things up and rehearse the parts they intended to play. Clearing their schedules, Brian met with Lindsey in her law office several hours each day, away from Adriane's watchful eye, but always under Beverly's stern supervision. During that time the news about an informant on the streets spread wildly through Dover's drug community.

A worried Gavin checked in by phone every morning to ask Lindsey if she still wanted him to go on with the ruse. "The word is definitely out, Lins. There are people coming to *me* now, asking if I've heard about it. And Lyle says it's the first topic of conversation in every one of his group meetings at the treatment center. Looks like we're in the clear as to who actually started the whole thing . . . Lyle certainly has no idea."

Lindsey told Gavin to sit tight and not name Jonas as the snitch until she gave him the go-ahead. She hated the position she'd put him in. "Dear Lord, Brian," she groaned after hanging up the phone. "As much as he hates this, he's willing to do it. And he's doing it for *me* without even knowing why. He has no idea of the hand we suspect Jonas played in Julie's death."

"It'll be over soon, Lins. I just left Jonas's parole officer, a big redheaded Scotsman named MacGuffie. Once I convinced him Jonas was responsible for Julie's death, he agreed to back us up and gave me Jonas's address. Are you ready to make the move tonight?"

She didn't hesitate. "The sooner we do this, the better. I just pray it works."

Brian smiled at her. "Well, to quote someone I know quite well, if there's any justice in the world, it will!"

* * *

The room was cramped and musty, reeking of stale cigarettes and fried grease; nothing like his river house in Cambridge. With disgust, Jonas threw a slice of half-eaten pizza back in its box, sitting on the ring-stained coffee table. Some damn pig was living in his Cambridge house now, or more likely, a crooked judge. Even though he'd settled the score with Julie, the anger still rankled. He pushed up from the ratty old couch where he'd been eating his pizza and took three short steps to a discolored, narrow window. Hooking a finger into the blinds, he looked out into the evening darkness.

The string of old apartment buildings lining the street was just far enough away from the "hood" to mollify Mac, his parole officer. *Stupid ex-cop Irishman!* He'd been a detective with the Dover police for many years until a bum knee forced him out. Because the work was less physically demanding, and because he was too young to retire, he had made the shift from police officer to parole officer. Now he was stalking Jonas like a vindictive jungle cat, waiting to pounce on him if he took one more misstep. *He wants to haul my ass back to the big house so bad; he's practically drooling.* Jonas's eyes scanned the streets below. *Nothing but stupid Polacks and Jews! No action around here—if I was still dealing,* he snickered.

After his parole violation, MacGuffie had forced him to take a demeaning minimum wage job in a Walmart gas station. And even though Jonas worked the thirty hours a week required by the parole board, he could barely pay his rent and feed himself. Once he was finally off paper he would be heading to Chicago, but he had to stash away a substantial nest egg to get there and get set up. Then he'd get in tight with the right people and be back to where he was before he lost everything. So Jonas was being real careful now. He did business only with pushers and users he'd known for years. Especially now that there was word out on the streets about some undercover—

A sharp rap at his door startled him. *Who the hell?* He didn't know anyone in the building and he didn't deal out of his apartment. He groaned. *Probably that dick of a p.o. comin' to drag me downtown for another piss test. Dumb ass knows I don't use. He just likes jerking me around.* Two more raps had him calling out heatedly, "Yah? Who's there?"

"It's Lindsey. I have to talk to you, Jonas."

"Lindsey! What the shit! What the hell do you think you're doing here?" His thick wooden door had a deadlock, two sliding bolts, and a chain, but the landlord had been too cheap to install peep holes, so he had no idea what was waiting for him on the other side.

"There's something we . . . please, Jonas, just let me in."

He undid the locks but kept the chain on. Peering through the small opening, he saw her standing, arms crossed as if she were freezing. He looked her up and down. As much as he hated the woman, he had to admit she was still a knockout. He undid the chain and peered out into the dank, dimly lit hallway. Seeing no one except Lindsey, he held the door back for her to enter.

"Don't lock it," she insisted. "I won't be staying long."

"What's the matter? Our big-shot Senator scared of Big Bad Jonas?"

She gave him a cold glare, standing her ground. "That's exactly why I'm here, Jonas. I'll make this short—Julie was still alive when you dumped her in that alley. She told me what you did." She stared him down with such intensity that he began to squirm.

"I got no idea what you're talking about," he said sullenly. But he had kicked himself a thousand times for not checking for a pulse more thoroughly. She had looked so wasted, so gone, he just wanted to get rid of the body. But when he learned that Julie had hung on for a time in the hospital his first instinct was to run; then he rationalized it would just be her word against his. Running would only confirm his guilt. And after her death, as the weeks and months went by, he assumed she'd never regained consciousness to rat on him and he was in the clear.

"Did you hear me?" Lindsey screamed at him. "She *told* me. She *told* me, Jonas!"

"Yah? Then why didn't you come after me before this? She's been buried in that cold grave of hers a long time, Lindsey. If you had anything on me, why wait 'til now?"

Lindsey choked back her anger. "She made me promise, you bastard—not to let anyone know. Because Lyle and Gavin would have put you in your own cold grave, and she didn't want them to pay for settling the score."

He grinned cruelly. "So where does that leave you, pretty lady? All you have are the dying words of a dead addict. There's no proof—so what's the point of all this?"

"I . . . I can't stand it any longer, Jonas. You *know* she didn't relapse. You have to admit to what you did. Show some remorse, for God's sake."

"Remorse? After what that bitch cost me?" He stopped suddenly and looked at her suspiciously. "Are you wearing a wire? Is that what this is all about, a setup?"

She let out a tired sigh. "No, Jonas, I'm not wired. You can search me if you want, but I promise I'll vomit in your ugly face the minute your filthy hands touch me."

He laughed wickedly. "Just like the first time we met, huh Lins?" He thought a moment, then nodded. "Okay, if that's how you wanna play it." He felt a rush of excitement, finally able to gloat about what he had pulled off. "No harm done telling you, 'cause there's no proof that Julie and I were together when she died. I was real careful about not leaving any of my DNA behind."

Lindsey drew in a shuddering sob as Jonas began to reveal what he'd done to her dear friend. She listened silently until he finished, then said incredulously, "And you blame *her* for everything you lost? It was *you,* Jonas. *You're* responsible for what happened to you—and for what you did to her."

"That's crap, Lindsey. But it was a great plan, don't you think? I got away with killing her and destroyed a piece of you at the same time. Revenge is sweet, Lindsey. You should try it some time." He snickered evilly.

Suddenly the door burst opened. Brian strode in and wrapped a sobbing Lindsey in his arms.

"What the fuck!" Jonas screamed. "What's going on? Get your ass out of here, Winchester. Both of you!" Jonas's face was a pulsing beet red as he stepped menacingly toward them. "I don't know what you think you heard just now, asshole, but I do know it's not admissible in court!"

Brian let go of Lindsey and faced him, holding his arms in the air to indicate he meant no harm. "Lindsey came here to clear up some things, Jonas, and I came along to keep an eye on her, understand?"

"Yah, right! So—things are cleared up now. So get outta here."

They turned to leave, Brian's arm protectively around Lindsey's shoulders. But as they reached the door, Brian stopped and turned, eyeing Jonas as if he were a bug to be stepped on. "One last thing, Jonas—just a heads-up. The rumors circulating on the street? They're all about you."

"What the hell you talkin' about?" He backed away, his face losing its color.

"You're the snitch, Jonas! And tomorrow's the day everyone will know. You'll be famous . . . for as long as you live."

"That's a lie!" He backed into the couch and sank down, reality punching him in the gut. "You—you set me up!"

"Like you said, man, revenge is sweet. We couldn't think of a better way to make you pay for what you did to

Julie. We'll let the pushers take you out instead of Lyle and Gavin."

Jonas leaped from the couch and rushed for the door, but Brian stood in his way. "You can't run fast enough or far enough to escape this, Jonas. I just wish I could watch what they're going to do to you . . . on second thought, maybe I don't."

Jonas began crying, terrified of what was about to happen. He looked at Lindsey pleadingly. "I—I'm sorry for what I did . . . I swear! Just don't do this, okay? You can stop this, right?"

Lindsey watched him sweat through his tears as she stared at him unfeelingly. A big part of her wanted to turn loose the blind justice he so richly deserved. But there was a better way, a legal way that Brian had helped her find. "You haven't named Jonas as the undercover informant yet, have you, Brian?" Jonas turned to look at him hopefully.

"Not yet; first thing in the morning, though."

She spoke to Jonas then, stone-faced. "All right, Jonas, how's this? We won't go ahead with this if you admit to what you did to Julie."

"Whaddah ya mean? I just did."

"But like you said, it doesn't count. It's not admissible unless you're Marandized and give a statement to the authorities."

He stared at her in disbelief. "You gotta be out of your fuckin' mind, lady!"

"Never more serious, Jonas. Think about it. If you confess, you know you won't get the death penalty in this state—but if you don't, and we name you as the snitch, the death penalty is exactly what you'll get when the drug dealers in this town get their hands on you."

His eyes flew wildly around the room, searching for an answer that was just out of reach. Finally, he sank back onto the couch and lowered his head in his hands. "No, there's no way I'll give myself up to the cops."

"Face it, Jonas. There's no one to help you out of this. You're no friend of the druggies on the street, and the big money men won't have anything to do with you. To them you're just a nuisance—small-time competition. If I name you as the snitch, they'll be only too glad to have someone take you out." Brian laughed derisively. "The truth is, the only place you fit in is with the prison population. They're the only ones who give drug-dealing murderers like you any respect."

Brian reached into his jacket pocket and drew out a cell phone. "What's it going to be, Jonas, the cops or the drug crowd?" He flipped the phone open and chuckled. "Well, would you look at that. I have the number right here on speed dial. If I call my friend he'll rat you out as soon as the sun rises—there'll be no way to stop it, Jonas."

Jonas watched with horror as Brian's thumb made a move over the key pad. "No! Wait . . . okay, okay . . . I'll talk, dammit—I'll talk to the fuckin' cops."

Brian walked to the door and opened it wide, signaling Jonas's parole officer to come in. "He says he's ready to talk, Mac."

As the oversized Scotsman entered the room, Jonas stared at Lindsey and Brian with hatred. "You filthy rich bastards—'the high and the mighty.' You always know how to play things out so you end up the big winner."

Mac motioned Jonas to stand and slid a pair of cuffs onto his wrists, ratcheting them tightly, then shoved him back onto the couch. "I think you've got that wrong, Boyo," he said. "It's scum like you who play things out so you always end up the big *loser*."

Pushing the pizza box aside, Mac set a small tape recorder on the coffee table and turned it on. After clearing his throat, he stated the date, time, and names of everyone present, then read Jonas his rights. "All right, Laddy. Let's hear what you've got to say before you change your mind." He shook his shaggy head and chuckled. "Whenever you open your mouth, Jonas, I never know what's going to spill out."

Jonas haltingly related the events that led to Julie's death—abducting her in the parking garage, holding her captive for days, pumping her full of drugs and alcohol. His face was grim as he spoke, pale with the dread of confession. "I—I think her heart gave out then . . . she, she was yelling, you know, about the pain." He looked at Lindsey imploringly. "It got pretty scary—I thought about getting her some help. But I was too far into it by then. It was too late. When she passed out, I thought that was it. Shit, I never saw her take another breath. I cleaned her up, wrapped her in a blanket, and dumped her in that alley."

Standing together, Brian held Lindsey, rubbing her back comfortingly while Jonas described the ugliness of her friend's death. Mac hovered over him, nodding whenever he paused, encouraging Jonas to continue to the end. "And where did all this happen, Boyo?"

"What? Here—here in Dover . . . I don't know; some-where in the hood." Jonas shivered. He couldn't—*couldn't* let them know where. That was his ace in the hole. With none of his DNA on Julie's body and a good attorney he was pretty sure he could beat the murder rap. He would say he was coerced into giving the confession and there would be nothing to prove otherwise. But the room where he'd kept her—he never figured they'd find it, so he hadn't bothered to clean it up. The bed—the bathroom, there would be all kinds of incriminating garbage he'd left behind. The liquor bottle! He'd watched it roll under the bed. It would be loaded with his prints, but none of Julie's. The needles . . . the baggies . . . all with his prints. And traces of Julie's blood from the injections!

"Where in the hood?" Mac persisted.

Jonas shook his head wildly. "Can't . . .can't remember." He watched with trepidation as Brian flipped open his cell phone and held it up for him to see. Hanging his head in defeat, he choked out the address.

He was sobbing uncontrollably as Mac hauled him off the couch. "That should do it for now, you piece of shit," he growled. "I'm taking you downtown where you can go over the whole thing again with your lawyer and the Dover detectives."

"Brian, we have to—"

"I know, sweetheart. I'm calling Lyle and Gavin right now to tell them to meet us at the station. Even though it's nearly midnight, it's past time they know the truth." He eyed Jonas with hatred. "They don't have to be kept in the dark any longer, and they'll want to watch how Jonas sweats this out."

The exhausted foursome sat around Lyle's kitchen table. They were drinking strong black coffee, trying to recover from the night's long ordeal. Lyle was still terribly shaken and angry with Lindsey. "You knew what Jonas had done to her all along!" he said accusingly. "How could you?" How could you do that to me, Lindsey, and to Gav?"

Brian reached out and placed a calming hand on his arm. "Think about it, Lyle. What would you have done if you'd known?" Lyle shook his head in dark silence. "You would have done exactly what Julie feared most. You and Gavin would have hunted him down and beat the last living breath out of him. You two would be heading to prison right now instead of him."

Gavin nodded his head. "You know he's right, man."

Lyle raised his head and looked at Lindsey with tear-filled eyes. "It's not just that, Lindsey. It's all the terrible thoughts I've had about Julie since it happened. I blamed her! I cursed her every day for what she did to our lives! And all the time she was innocent. How do I live with myself after that? I'll *never* forgive myself."

"You have to, Lyle. This is the way Julie hoped things would turn out. She knew how angry you'd be with her, but she also knew you'd never stop loving her." Lindsey rose from her chair and went to him, wrapping her arms around his shoulders and hugging him tightly. "Please, Lyle. Forgiving yourself means you're also forgiving Julie, and me for deceiving you. Can you do that?"

He buried his head in her arms and cried deeply, as if cleansing his heart and mind. After several long heartbreaking minutes, he raised his head and choked out, "I'll try, Lins. For Julie's sake, I'll try." He heaved a deep sigh. "And she was right. I would have killed the bastard with my own bare hands . . . because all of you know prison's too damn good for him."

"It is, Lyle." Brian agreed. "But don't worry. What I neglected to mention to Jonas was that Delaware's state pen is filled with addicts who knew Julie. She and Lyle tried to help many of them when they were trying to stay clean. They knew her and they cared about her . . . Jonas won't last long in that environment, and they'll make life pure hell for him until the end."

EIGHTEEN

The Senate was about to reconvene. The morning after Jonas's arrest, Lindsey slept in until nearly 10 a.m., then spent the rest of the morning packing for the drive back to D.C. Now that she and Brian had dealt the firm hand of justice to Jonas that he so richly deserved, she prayed she could find some solace. She wanted only to cling to golden memories of Julie and prayed the distance of time would leave the sad memories buried in shadow.

She was surprised when James called up the stairs to tell her Brian was waiting in the study to see her. Puzzled, she came down to meet him. They had clearly said their goodbyes in the early morning hours at Lyle's, and she had not been expecting to see him again.

She found him talking to himself as he paced the floor in her father's study, clearly practicing whatever he intended to say. He looked up and smiled at her nervously as she walked into the room. "Lindsey?" He approached her and took both her hands in his. "I want you to hear me out. No interruptions, okay?"

She looked at him questioningly. Taking a deep breath, he plunged in. "I want you to share your life with me, Lins. I need you . . . Chip needs you. Adriane is no kind of mother to him and since he's lost Julie, he's lost part of himself. These last few days with you—can't you see we were meant to be together? We can't keep letting outside forces get in the way."

"Are you finished now?" she asked coolly. When he nodded she said, "I didn't hear any mention of a divorce, Brian—"

"Lindsey! You know Adriane would fight me tooth and nail for Chip just out of spite. I can't risk that!"

"So—you would have me sneak around, putting my reputation at risk, my career?"

He looked at her longingly. "Yes, dammit! I know it's not fair, Lins, but yes, I'm asking you to do that."

"Oh, Brian." Tears spilled from her eyes. "You know I'd give it all up if we could be together—but you're *married*, Brian. I can't get around that. Adriane would always be there, between us. If we met somewhere for a quiet, romantic dinner, her presence would be at the table, and if we were together making love," she drew a deep breath and shuddered, "she'd be with us there, too. I'd never be able to give myself to you fully."

Brian grabbed her and held her achingly against the tightness of his body. "None of that matters, Lins. If I can't have all of you, whatever part you *can* give, Chip and I will take it."

She freed herself from his arms, stepped back and placed her hands lovingly on each side of his face. "Listen to me now. Before Chip was born, you chose your son over me. And you *had* to, Brian. It was absolutely the right thing to do! And I love you all the more for it. You're a wonderful father, and just like my dad, you'll make a good life for Chip without the help of his mother."

She took him by the hand and led him from the study to the front door. "You're not only a wonderful father, Brian, you're a terrific lawyer. And if I do say so myself, I'm a darned good Senator. We can love one another from afar, Bri, but your son and our careers will have to be enough."

As he walked to his car, head bowed, Lindsey knew he was crying. *Dear God,* she wondered, *how am I going to go on? I've lost them all—Mom, Jules, Brian, Chip*—her eyes and throat burned, but no tears would come. She'd cried them all away.

*   *   *

As in the past, Lindsey found the answer to loneliness in her work. She discounted the accolades she received, knowing much of her stalwart dedication was due to purely selfish motives—survival being uppermost. Her worst fear was that at some unguarded moment she would be pulled into the dangerous torrent of memories past, and drown there. So she worked at a frenetic pace, ensuring that when her head hit the pillow at night, she would be too exhausted to think. And even though she couldn't stop Brian and Julie from slipping into her dreams, she left them behind the moment her eyes opened in the morning.

Her first term in the Senate ended swiftly, and between her ongoing TV chats and her reputation for intelligent decisions and always treating others with fairness and equity, she easily won a second. But she was filled with trepidation as she wondered what on earth she would do when her second term as a U.S. Senator came to a close. Standing by her belief in two-term limits, she would not run for a third. James was disappointed that she would be leaving politics, but was also looking forward to her returning full-time to their law practice. Lindsey was doubtful, however, that the practice of law would fill the void in her life. Could it possibly compensate for the loss of her best friend, for never having a marriage with Brian, or children of her own?

Beverly interrupted Lindsey's dismal train of thought as she rushed into her office and stammered breathlessly, "Lins—Lindsey . . . it's John Hayes on the phone . . . for you!"

Lindsey pushed the flashing button on her desk phone, amused at Beverly's excitement and curious as to why the governor of Florida, the Republicans' best hope to regain control of the presidency in the upcoming 2016 election, would be calling her. They had worked together over a year ago on a special committee appointed by the Senate. Lindsey had enjoyed tremendously the time they spent formulating new immigration policies, trying among other things to find a solution to the 130 year waiting list for Mexicans trying to enter the U.S. legally. Even so, their efforts had ended up trashed on the Senate floor. But during that time she and John Hayes found they shared common ideological ground. Lindsey had developed great respect for the governor, but hadn't heard from him for several months.

"Governor Hayes," she said into the phone with enthusiasm. "It's a pleasure to hear from you, sir. Is there something I can do for you?"

"You most certainly can, Lindsey." He cleared his throat. "This is an official call, Senator Delaware. While I know it's unusual for a presidential aspirant to seek a running mate before being nominated, it's not unheard of. So I'm asking if you would consider being my vice-presidential running mate for the GOP nomination this fall." He waited through the stunned silence on her end of the line, then laughed, "You still there, Lindsey?"

Lindsey was conflicted—elated one moment and frightened the next. She had entered politics barely eight years earlier, and now she'd been asked to run for the vice presidency? She was only thirty-five, for heaven's sake . . .

an infant in a world dominated by men—much older men. Julie's voice rang loudly in her mind. *Impossible, Lins! Impossible, but awesome!* Lindsey smiled. There was no doubt Julie would have pushed her forward, just as James was trying to do now. But as much as she idolized her father, she could not trust his judgment in this. Heck, he'd push her into becoming the first Pope of the U.S. if the opportunity arose, and she wasn't even Catholic! The problem was, there were few others she could turn to for advice. John Hayes had cautioned her to not let the cat out of the bag until he was certain he had enough delegates to win the Republican nomination. Only then would he announce his vice-presidential selection.

"There'll be a lot of speculation until then, Lindsey, with a lot of names being thrown around—it'll keep my campaign in the forefront of the news media."

So Lindsey sought out only those she believed were knowledgeable enough to give her sound advice, as well as being trustworthy enough to remain silent. And without reservation, the few friends and co-workers she polled encouraged her to step into the race. She saved her two most critical resources for last: Royce White, who still directed RCAP, and Brian. Royce was delighted with her news and insistent that she accept the governor's offer. "I've met a lot of good and bad actors in my time, Lindsey, and even though you and I worked together just a few short months, I'd have to say there's no one I know of who could do a better job."

She thanked him profusely, swore him to secrecy, then took a deep breath and dialed Brian's cell phone. He'd given her the number when they were collaborating on Jonas's downfall, and she had committed it to memory.

He listened to her carefully while, unknown to her, he brushed tears from the corner of his eyes. "You really want my truthful opinion. Lindsey?"

"Of course, Brian! I expect you to be brutally honest. I mean, I know I'm too young, too inexperienced, perhaps a tad too naïve, and female . . . but other than that, is there any reason I shouldn't run?"

"You *know* you should run, Lindsey, and you don't need me to tell you that. Gawd," he choked out, "I'm so proud of you. You go for it, sweetheart, and know I'm right behind you. Count on me for *anything* I can do to help. I'll have to stay in the background, Lins, but I'll be pulling for you. And let me be the first to contribute to your campaign. It's going to take a shit-load of money to get you and John Hayes elected—even more than the Delaware family coffers are reputed to contain."

"Brian, the governor and I haven't even won the nomination yet! There's no guarantee—"

"You're a shoo-in, Lindsey, not only for the nomination, but for the general election. And believe me, between you and John Hayes the country couldn't be in better hands."

She thanked Brian for his encouragement, then before losing her courage, she asked Beverly to place a call to the Florida governor. Minutes later, she gave her acceptance to his offer, then qualified it by asking if he was certain.

"Of course I'm certain. You meet all the criteria. Under the Constitution the vice president must be a native-born citizen, at least thirty-five years of age, and must have resided in the U.S. for at least fourteen years. That's all there is to it," he laughed, then grew more serious. "Look, Lindsey, I've already had you vetted, and we've uncovered nothing that would stand in the way of you being my running mate. You're a brilliant young woman with an impeccable record in both the House and the Senate. Heavens, you even pay your taxes on time! That's more than can be said for some of our esteemed brethren," he grumbled.

She hesitated, than voiced her largest concern. "Sir, I believe you'll easily win both the Republican nomination and the presidential election, but I also believe that having a female running mate might cause irreparable damage to your campaign."

"Now don't go worrying about the gender issue, young woman. My dear wife, Sheila, continually reminds me that our country is long overdue for a female leader, and I happen to agree with her. The future is now, Lindsey, and you and I going to make it happen."

Lindsey wondered how many Americans agreed with the governor. Both Hillary Clinton and Sarah Palin had made a strong run in 2008; Hillary for the presidency and Sarah for the vice-presidential spot. But Lindsey's father had had little confidence in either woman overcoming the strong odds against them. "Lindsey," he had said, shaking his mane of white hair, "this country just isn't ready for a female president. Mark my words. We'll elect a black man to that office before we'll ever elect a woman." Shortly after his prediction, James was proven right. Much to the chagrin of the Clintons, the powerful Kennedy clan withdrew its support from Hillary and threw its weight into the Obama campaign. With their endorsement, the Democratic nomination went to America's first man of color, Barack Obama, who, with the help of a friendly media, went on to win the 2008 presidential election.

Although they'd been defeated in their bids, many believed that Hillary and Sarah had paved the way for a woman to command the country. And even though they couldn't have been more different, Hillary being all about politics while Sarah was all about faith and family, between the two they had shown that a woman could be an adept leader, no matter what the arena. "The path will be a little easier the next time," Hillary had predicted, and Lindsey hoped to prove her right.

The news lit up the media like an exploding meteor. John Hayes made his announcement from the steps of the Florida Capitol Building a month before the Republican National Convention, with Lindsey and his wife, Sheila, at his side. Spontaneously, reporters and commentators fought amongst themselves to be first to get to Lindsey. Refusing all interviews, she flew back to Washington to continue her work in the Senate. Lindsey felt strongly that the governor was the one who should be in the spotlight, and she intended to keep her availability at a minimum.

"Well, I'll be damned!" Beverly exclaimed from the next room as she slammed down her phone. Lindsey found this alarming, as Beverly was not one to use profanity.

"What on earth?" she called to her. "Who did you just hang up on, Bev?"

"Adriane! And I didn't hang up on her. I transferred her to your line." Lindsey eyed the flashing light on her desk phone with distaste. "She assured me that, since you and she are such *close* friends, she's certain you'd want to take her call *personally*. Sorry, Lins, I was bubbling with anger at her conceit and just wasn't thinking. I transferred the call to you before I told her what I *really* think of her. I can pick it up and tell her you're not available."

"No, she won't give up. It'll save us both a lot of grief if I deal with it now."

Adriane's voice was sugar sweet as she tried to lure Lindsey into a one-on-one interview, then grew catty as she realized her efforts were in vain. "You know, darling, I have a world of influence in this town and I can do you a lot of . . . good. No one has a greater interest in seeing you win this election. Why, Brian and I are just thrilled about the whole thing . . . or has he told you that already?"

Ignoring her probing question, Lindsey responded, "I'm certain you could provide me with a lot of exposure, Adriane, so I'll let you be the first to know. I'm holding a press conference here in the Senate Office Building tomorrow at ten a.m. I'll look forward to seeing you there." She disconnected before Adriane could reply, then glumly placed a call to Tallahassee to fill the governor in.

"Now, Lindsey, don't fret," he assured her. "Actually, the more attention you get up there in D.C., the better it will be for us come November."

The sun was shining brightly the next day, its strong rays warming the August air as a swarm of reporters and TV cameras crowded into Lindsey's air-conditioned Senate office. After apologizing for the close quarters and giving a short political statement, Lindsey turned the meeting over to reporters for questions. Not surprisingly, Adriane's hand was the first to shoot up. "Senator Delaware," she said in a commanding voice, silencing the rest of the group.

"Well, I'm glad to see you made it, Adriane," Lindsey smiled resignedly. "You have at least one question, I'm sure."

Adriane waited until she was certain the cameras were focused on her. No TV journalist had perfected their on-camera technique better than she, and she was adept at always positioning herself in the best light. "Senator, let me be the first to congratulate you on your amazing accomplishment. My, my, who would have thought our own little Lindsey Delaware could possibly become our next vice president?"

Lindsey bristled at Adriane's lack of respect for a U.S. Senator and her taunting words, but held her tongue. Adriane continued. "I'm sure you're familiar, Senator, with the old adage that the vice president is only a heartbeat away from the presidency. If that regrettable event were to occur, how do you think the country would respond if you, a young female, rose to the presidency—then became pregnant while in office?" Several loud gasps could be heard in the room, along with a spattering of cuss words. Adriane continued unheeded, "A pregnant United States president—now that would be a history making event, wouldn't it? But shouldn't you be concerned about how much time a nine-month pregnancy would absent you from your presidential duties? To say nothing of the possible risks involved to your health during the delivery."

As Adriane concluded her inflammatory remarks, the relentless eyes of the TV cameras refocused on Lindsey, waiting for her response. Through gritted teeth she answered with as much calm as she could muster. "Adriane—you are either remarkably uninformed or remarkably cruel, neither of which speaks well for your integrity. But be that as it may, while there is no possibility of my having a child while in or out of office, I speak from my heart to the American people. Whenever that blessed event does occur in the presidency, it will be considered just that, a blessed event. And no more time would be lost nurturing that child than with a male president raising a young family."

*   *   *

It was a 2016 landslide election. Looking back, President-elect Hayes often surmised that Adriane's cruel remarks and the stately, composed way Lindsey handled the woman, was the watershed event that had put him and Lindsey into the White House—that, and an unprecedented hiccup in history. It seemed the country believed it had performed its egalitarian duty by putting a black man into the presidency, and it was now time to "return to normalcy" by electing a man who was reassuringly conservative, elderly, and white. "I'm ashamed to admit that got us a lot of votes, Lindsey," John Hayes confided immediately after the election. "So we have an obligation, I think, to select a good number of qualified minorities to serve in our administration."

Lindsey nodded. "I agree, Mr. President-elect. Our choices have to be more than a token effort to balance the scales and an attempt to create good will. Actually, I already have several people in mind."

Hayes smiled approvingly. "I knew that you would, Madam Vice President-elect.

Although she had anticipated a strenuous adjustment from her role as Senator to that of vice president, Lindsey found it to be a fairly easy transition. As the office of the vice presidency had few formal duties, it required no more hours on the job than she was used to as a Senator. However, John Hayes had assured her from day one that she would never be relegated to being just a pretty face in his administration; he expected her to have an active, hands-on role. But any free time she could carve out of her schedule could be devoted to projects of her own choosing. And Lindsey knew exactly what those choices would be!

The dust had settled in her personal life, namely regarding Jonas and Adriane. On a cold January morning shortly before she was sworn into office, Jonas had been convicted of murder one and given a life sentence. Four months later on a sunny day in May, Lindsey learned Jonas was having difficulty withstanding the brutality of prison life and had been placed on suicide watch. Exhibiting signs of extreme paranoia, he had been given heavy doses of psychotropic meds, but his mental state continued to deteriorate. By the high heat of August, he was transferred to a forensic prison for the criminally insane where he was to live out the rest of his miserable existence.

Adriane had earned the wrath of her network and the entire press corps for her cruel on-camera comments. She was summarily fired and blackballed by the media. Despite her parents' considerable wealth, they couldn't—or wouldn't bail her out. They had never approved of her common performance as a news reporter, and her days as a TV journalist were over.

This was followed by frequent rumors in the gossip magazines, predicting a Brian/Adriane breakup, but Lindsey knew Brian would do everything he could to protect Brian Jr. from further notoriety. Besides, Lindsey was certain there would be no divorce until Chip was old enough to decide which parent he wanted to live with. As for now, if Lindsey kept her thoughts away from Brian, she could devote all her time and energy to her political goals . . . and she intended to enact a gigantic slice of justice for those living with the disease Julie had endured throughout years of addiction.

Following the election, Lindsey had set about the work of vacating her local office in Dover and assembling her new vice-presidential staff in Washington. Her first conversation was with Beverly. "Bev, how do you feel about leaving the golden dome of the Capitol Building here in Dover to continue as my administrative assistant in Washington? I've relied on you keeping me on track for years, and I can't imagine running my new D.C. office without you."

Beverly raised a hand from behind her back, showing crossed fingers. "Lindsey, I've been walking around like this for days now, hoping you'd ask. Of course my answer is yes! I'd be honored to continue working with you, Madam Vice President." She gave her a sly wink. "Actually, I've been packed for days!"

Lindsey's next call was to Royce White. He was flabbergasted at her offer to serve as an advisor on her personal staff. "Madam Vice President, I'm no good at politics," he argued. "They'd eat me alive."

"Royce, you've been fighting off vultures for years. You just don't realize how good you are at it. And I need your insight. That, and I don't know of many others I can trust for straightforward advice as I do you."

As much as Lindsey wanted Lyle and Gavin to join her staff, she knew she'd be exposing herself to accusations of cronyism, so she contented herself with knowing they would always be in her corner, along with Brian. She could call them at anytime for opinions and advice.

But a part of her staff that would take getting used to was that of a personal bodyguard. She'd never needed one before, not even as a Senator; but now, as Vice President Delaware, it was required. The Secret Service had a select group of men that she was to choose from. Actually, she knew the choice was ultimately theirs, but they were providing her with the illusion that she would make the final decision.

After interviewing several serious, stone-cold automatons, all of whom seemed identical in every way from their underwear on up, a less severe-looking young man by the name of Kris Andrews sat across from her in her office. He was tall and trim with the narrow-hipped body of a runner. His thick, closely-cropped hair glistened with streaks of gold and brown. Kris looked to be about her age, much younger than the others had been, and he was certainly more open in his demeanor. He gave her a cheerful smile backed up by warm blue eyes, and she felt immediately at ease with him.

"Are you the one I'm supposed to choose, Agent Andrews?" she joked.

"I'm certainly hoping you do, Ma'am. But it's entirely up to you—within certain restrictions, of course," he joked in return.

After several minutes of routine questioning, Lindsey asked the one question that was most critical to her. "Kris,

I've asked this of everyone on my staff . . . it's a deal breaker. How knowledgeable are you about drug addiction, and how tough do you think we should be on users and dealers?"

Kris's face grew dark as he crossed his arms defensively. "I figured that would come up." She looked at him questioningly. "So my brother Mike was an addict. So he OD'd on coke. So what?"

Lindsey was surprised by his revelation, but continued on. "Ever use yourself, Agent?"

He rose slowly from his chair and gave her a steel-laced stare. "It took years to get around what happened to Mike— to earn back the respect of the Service, and you expect me to put all that on the line by admitting I used? *If* I used."

"Would you be shocked if I said I didn't care, as long as you're clean now?" She glanced at the weapon strapped to his belt. "And steady as a rock with that thing."

"You won't find anyone better than me, Ma'am . . . so," he studied her cautiously, "the business with my brother, that doesn't rule me out?"

"On the contrary, Kris, that definitely rules you in."

With the move to her new office and Lindsey's staff selections barely in place, President Hayes arranged twice-weekly early-morning briefings with Lindsey in the Oval Office. In her role as president of the Senate, Lindsey collaborated closely with him, keeping him informed as to what that illustrious body was up to. "I have to confess, Mr. President, the first time I picked up that gavel and called the Senate to order, I felt a little like Peter Pan flying off to Never-Never Land."

"The butterflies will settle soon, Lindsey," he chuckled. "Just give it time."

A lot of time, she thought. *Heck, I'm still in awe of* you!

"You know, Lindsey," he continued, pushing aside her trepidation, "you and I have been handed a tremendous opportunity. At this moment in history, the United States is not engaged in active warfare anywhere on the planet, and I intend to keep it that way. And even though we still have a serious debt problem, we're slowly regaining a sound financial footing. Just think of what we can accomplish if we can get our politicians to pull together . . . and the media, of course."

"You're well liked, Mr. President, by both parties—that is rare, isn't it?"

"Practically unheard of in my lifetime, Madam Vice President, so let's get a move on and get as much done as we can before someone upsets our apple cart!"

NINETEEN

Eight months into office, coinciding with the time Jonas was transferred to Delaware's state forensic prison, Lindsey decided she had her v.p. duties well enough in hand to begin working on her political dream. Using Beverly's D.C. apartment for maximum privacy, she invited three male colleagues to join her for a covert meeting. All three, Lyle, Gavin, and Brian, responded immediately to her call.

Agent Kris Andrews drove Lindsey to Beverly's apartment where he carefully scanned each room, then stationed himself in the hallway, guarding the area against uninvited intruders. Primarily, he kept an eye out for any nosy reporters, with their supersonic audio equipment and intrusive, long-range cameras.

The small group gathered in Beverly's spotless, nothing-out-of-place living room where she served them coffee and homemade brownies, then discreetly retired to her kitchen. Lindsey began the meeting formally. "Gentlemen, I'm relying on your personal expertise to predict what will occur if I'm successful in initiating a new federal drug-enforcement policy." They listened intently during the next twenty minutes as she went into detail. "So gentlemen, summing it all up, the federal policy would mandate harsher penalties for offenses committed while under the influence of drugs, and against aggravated drug trafficking, especially the selling or providing of drugs to children."

After several moments of silence, Brian was the first to comment. "You realize this will put an even heavier burden on our state prison systems. They're already bursting at the seams with drug offenders."

"I realize that, Brian. Right now, it's probable that somewhere between seventy and eighty percent of prisoners incarcerated in the U.S. are there because of drug-related charges. This new law will keep them incarcerated much longer. That's why this legislation will also provide federal funds to help the states get onboard with this."

"But you're not coming down harder on the addicts, Ma'am, if I heard you right," Gavin said. "Only if they commit a crime while using?"

"You heard correctly, Gavin. No increase in the penalty for drug abuse. Where's the wisdom in punishing addicts when they're already punishing their own bodies? That's why I also intend to provide federal funding for detox and recovery clinics."

Lyle looked at Lindsey with tear-filled eyes. "You're doing this for Julie, aren't you, Madam Vice President?"

Lindsey dropped all pretenses at formality and grinned broadly. "You bet your *bong*, Lyle!" When the laughter died down, Lindsey added, "And I understand you have quite a collection. Julie told me whenever your clients turn over a new leaf they turn over their bongs, too."

He nodded with a measure of pride. "They fill several display cases—safely locked, by the way. Some of them are quite elaborate . . . real waste of money, actually."

"Well, let's hope the day will soon come when their popularity will diminish. But for now, gentlemen, hearing no objections, I'll proceed with running this by the president."

Lindsey longed to reveal the second, far more dangerous part of her drug reform initiative, but knew to the man they would argue vehemently against it. They had enough hands-on experience with the drug world to know that she would be putting herself in extreme jeopardy when she proposed the final step of her legislation. And she was wise enough to know she would also be putting anyone at risk close to her. The drug kingdom would do whatever it needed to stop her, no holds barred. So it was a blessing in disguise that she was unmarried and without children. With Julie gone there was only her father to worry about, and she prayed the Secret Service would protect him well.

Brian held back when Lyle and Gavin asked for permission to give their favorite vice president a goodbye hug. Lindsey happily obliged and walked them arm in arm to the door. As they left, she looked questioningly at Brian, who seemed intent on staying behind. "I need a minute, Lindsey—I mean Ma'am, if you can spare me the time?"

Lindsey hesitated, worried about any possible improprieties, then acquiesced. "Of course, Brian. And please, you can drop the formalities when we're alone . . . up to a point," she added quickly as he stepped closer and flashed his handsome grin.

"Oh, Lins, I don't think a simple hug is going to do it for me . . . you don't know how badly I want to wrap you in my arms right now." She took a step back, putting her hands up in warning. "It's okay, Lins. I have something to tell you that's going to make all the difference for us—Adriane's gone!"

"Gone? Gone where?" she asked with confusion.

"Gone wherever cheating little wives go—she's left me, Lindsey. And she left Chip behind."

Lindsey sank into the nearest available chair. "Brian! I can't believe it!"

"Me neither, but it's true, Lins. When Adriane's career tanked, she got bored real fast with being just the mother of a seven-year-old kid and the wife of an attorney who could no longer stand the sight of her. She hooked up with some multi-millionaire playboy, and they're off on a whirlwind cruise at this very moment."

"Well I'll be damned!" Lindsey cupped a hand to her mouth. "Sorry, some of my old probation language slipping out."

"My sentiments exactly, Lins, but get this. Adriane and her new squeeze are hot to get married, so I agreed to a quickie divorce, provided she relinquishes full custody of Brian Jr." He smiled broadly. "It's what we've been praying for, sweetheart. I can't wait to tell Chip you're going to be his new mom. I'll have to tie him down to keep him from running through the neighborhood, shouting out the good news."

Brian pulled her from her chair and began waltzing her around the room, humming happily in her ear. "Remember the night we first met, Lindsey? Hah, once I started dancing with you, I refused to let you go." He stopped abruptly, puzzled at her lack of enthusiasm. "Lindsey? Is something wrong? We're going to be together now, right?"

Leave it to Brian to ask the difficult questions. She shook her head and backed out of his arms. "Brian—I can't. Not now. Everything's changed."

"What? . . . you don't love me anymore? Don't want me? Jesus, Lindsey, my body aches for you every minute I breathe—you can't say you don't feel the same way."

"Brian, please don't put me in this position . . . you know I still want to be with you more than anything, but—oh shit, as usual the timing's all wrong."

Brian was livid. "Timing? No! It's you that's got it all wrong, *Ms. Vice President*. I'm not good enough for you anymore, is that it? Chip and I just won't fit into the White House scene, right? Well, excuse me while I get out of your way." He strode to the door and jerked it open, brushing past Agent Andrews, then stopped suddenly and turned back to face her. His eyes were hard, but at the same time sad. "I never would have thought it of you. I—"

Lindsey slowly closed the door and pressed her head against its coldness. She wanted to scream out to Brian that he had it all wrong. That she wanted nothing so much as to be with him, but that being together was too dangerous. That if he married her, Brian Jr. would become an instant target. And if the unthinkable were to happen—*No. it's better to end it here and now,* she told herself. *What's the point in letting Brian back into my life when he'll only end up hating me?. . . more than he already does.*

Royce White listened attentively as he sat in the vice-presidential office. "I've already run this by several other knowledgeable people, Royce, but I need you to tell me if I'm way off base before I approach the president. I know of no one who has had more encounters with addicts, dealers, and the court system than you."

Royce steepled his fingers under his chin and replied thoughtfully. "When John Hayes picked you as his running mate, Lindsey, he knew exactly where you stood on drug reform. We can't continue to withstand the damage drugs are doing to our country, both in wasted lives and wasted resources. I'd surmise that he's waiting for you to bring him your ideas on the issue, and what you're proposing looks good to me. I especially like the funneling of federal funds into recovery programs on an equal status with what's being spent on state incarceration. It's long overdue, to my way of thinking."

Once again, Lindsey had to bite her tongue before divulging her full intentions. She sensed that now was not the time, but she prayed she'd have Royce's full support once the time arrived.

Lindsey dressed with extra care for her morning briefing with the president. She had a lot riding on this. Examining herself critically in her bedroom's full-length mirror, she stepped closer to view the lines of fatigue around her eyes. Sleep was so hard to come by. Being vice president of this great country was demanding and exciting, but what robbed her of peaceful, restful nights were the relentless memories of loss—her mother, Julie, Brian. She sighed deeply as she brushed her hair into a twist, then ran a hand down her matching pinstripe jacket and skirt to erase any wrinkles. *Erasing the lines on my face should be so easy,* she scoffed. As she stepped to the door she paused and set about the day's first order of business—to silence the sorrow in her heart.

"I like it, Madam Vice President!" John Hayes exclaimed.

Lindsey exhaled a deep breath. *He liked it!*

Waving the papers in the air that contained her proposed legislation, he continued, "I can't think of any other issue that's more urgent than drug reform, and right now we have the resources to do something about it. I agree wholeheartedly that we should be putting as much effort and money into rehabilitation as we do incarceration."

Lindsey looked at the president with a mixture of excitement and relief. "Dr. Lyle Grey and others like him have put to rest the long-held theory that nothing works when trying to rehabilitate addicts, Mr. President. His success rate is impressive and he's shown that rehabilitation is seven times more effective than incarceration in getting people off drugs. If our county mental-health agencies across the country were to duplicate his program with the help of federal funding, I'm certain that thousands of lives will be turned around."

"And most of those lives are attached to families who will also benefit. Let's get the ball rolling, Lindsey. I'd like you to draft a 'Federal Drug Enforcement Policy' to present to Congress ASAP!"

Lindsey, Royce and the rest of her staff worked tirelessly on the bill. It reached Congress in record time where it encountered little opposition. Democrats applauded the creation of a worthwhile, big-budget federal program while Republicans were enamored by the stiff penalties for drug crimes, and the idea that in the long run, each addict was to be held accountable for his or her own recovery.

The day after the bill's passage, Lindsey called Royce into her office. He was exuberant over their success and reached across the desk to shake her hand. "Only a year in office, and look what you've accomplished. You must be so pleased, Madam Vice President."

"Lindsey, please, Royce. And we're not about to rest on our laurels. If you'll have a seat, I want to discuss a major follow-up which will have a more far-reaching effect then the legislation we just passed."

"Whew, and I assumed you asked me in to celebrate." He smiled at her broadly with crinkling brown eyes. "What exactly do you have up your sleeve now, young woman?"

"What I have up my sleeve, Royce, is a dramatic piece of legislation that, if enacted, will change our legal system and the entire civic life of our nation as nothing before, at least not in our lifetime."

Royce's demeanor grew seriously alert. "This sounds like something that could be alarmingly controversial, Lindsey."

"You're very perceptive, Royce, and I'm going to need your full support if there's a chance in hell of getting it past the president's desk."

Lindsey closed her eyes and drew a deep breath. *Here goes,* she thought. *The first time Julie's law will be spoken aloud.* "Although it's likely to be earth shattering to friend and foe alike, I'll make it short and sweet, Royce—the 'Trent Mandate,' that's the title I've chosen, will decriminalize the use of illegal drugs."

Royce shot out of his chair. "My God, Lindsey, do you know what you're suggesting? The far-reaching impact a law like that would have? It's not only controversial, it's dangerous!"

"It's the best and only solution to the mess our drug culture has us mired in, Royce, and you can't tell me you haven't reached the same conclusion, after all that you've seen in the world of drugs and criminal justice!"

Royce brushed a hand through his short, gray hair, showing his frustration. "Of course, Lindsey, but saying it and dealing with the practicality of it is like the difference between day and night. Things look very different in the light than they do in the dark. First off, everyone will think you're legalizing drugs—"

"Which I'm not, Royce! Decriminalizing drugs and legalizing them are two very different things."

"I know that and you know that, but that's not the message people will hear." He sank back into his chair. "Lindsey, you can't put yourself in the line of fire over this. Everyone, and I mean *everyone,* who makes money off illegal drugs will be out to stop you. It's a forty-billion-dollar-a-year enterprise, for God's sake. You have to realize that!"

"I'm well aware of that, Royce. But when you look at the difference it will make for hundreds of thousands of people, it has to be worth the risk."

Lindsey received the same sharp, negative reaction from Lyle and Gavin, and taking her idea to Brian was out of the question, since they were no longer on speaking terms. However, she gained confidence from knowing that Royce, Lyle, and Gavin all agreed, albeit reluctantly, that decriminalizing drugs was likely to be highly beneficial in the long run.

Using the privacy of Beverly's apartment once again, Lindsey convinced Royce, Lyle, and Gavin to meet with her to strategize her presentation to the president. Beverly plied the small group with coffee and fresh-baked oatmeal raisin cookies from her kitchen, then left them to their work. Lindsey insisted that they begin by listing all the likely benefits that would come about if the Trent Mandate were put into action—this is what she would present to the president. Whenever they voiced concerns over probable dangerous consequences, she brushed them aside, saying they'd get to the negatives later.

"Okay," Lyle said reluctantly after they had made a sizable list. "So, that's the good part, but just how do you see this all playing out? You're going to set up, what . . . distribution centers? A junkie can just walk in and get a joint? Or an ounce of coke? Holy shit! They'll be lined up like starving refugees in a war zone!"

Lindsey didn't let his sarcasm faze her. "We'll use our state liquor stores, Lyle, only now they'll be handling both alcohol *and* controlled substances like marijuana and cocaine. Only the cost of a joint or an ounce of cocaine will be minuscule compared to what the pushers are getting on the street. Good Lord, it's so unbelievably stupid that we didn't learn our lesson from the days of Prohibition! All the racketeering and loss of lives because the government tried to outlaw alcohol. And it was an absolute waste of effort.

"Then we turned around and did the same thing with drugs, because drug abuse is so much more frightening than alcohol abuse. But believe it or not, the British found that alcohol is *more* dangerous than heroin or crack, because it's just as addictive and far more socially debilitating. It's alcohol that puts a drunk behind the wheel of a speeding, two-ton automobile. What's the old beer slogan? 'Say no to drugs so you'll have more time to drink.'" She looked them in the eye. "Don't you think it's time for our government to legally take control of the distribution of *all* addictive drugs, gentlemen, not just alcohol?"

But Lyle wasn't ready to concede. "Lindsey, what if this goes into effect and it turns out to be a complete failure? Can't you see what a mess you'll have created?"

"It *will* work, Lyle, and I'll hang my hat on that, because . . . because it has to!"

"Your hat and your political career, Madam Vice President," Royce reminded her. "And I'm curious. Did you ever have this discussion with your friend Julie Trent?"

Lyle and Gavin turned as one and gave her a questioning look. Lindsey nodded reluctantly. "Oh, yah. She agreed with me that prosecuting . . . mmm, I think she said *persecuting* drug users was a monumental waste of time. The gist of her conversation went something like, "Keeping drugs away from an addict is like working with quicksilver. Once you think you've got it cornered, it slides off in another direction. If the DEA were ever successful in shutting down the drug trade, keeping weed and crack off the streets, we'd just find something else to take its place. Hell, when I was using I would have sniffed bicycle seats if I thought it would give me a high!"

The three men laughed in sober agreement. "She was right about that," Gavin said.

"But I have to be totally honest," Lindsey continued. "Julie went on to say, 'I have years of being clean and sober behind me now, Lindsey, but the thought of having that kind of easy access . . . it scares the hell out of me.'"

"Well, there's your answer, then," Lyle said definitively, his voice cracking with emotion.

"But she was wrong, Lyle," Lindsey insisted. "I don't care how accessible drugs were, Julie had hit her bottom and would never have relapsed."

"She's right, Lyle," Gavin said. "The fear of that kind of accessibility would just have driven her deeper into her sobriety."

Lindsey slapped her hands on her knees and stood, bringing the meeting to a close. "Well, it's settled then. Royce and I will meet with the president as soon as he's available and present this to him formally."

"Lindsey, wait!" Lyle begged. "Before you get any deeper into this, Gavin and I want to run it by Brian. You know how his legal mind works, and he may have some insights that we've missed. Are you okay with that?"

Lindsey's shoulders stiffened. "I really don't think that's necessary, Lyle."

"Yes it is, Lindsey," Gavin said quietly. "For our own piece of mind . . . it is."

She shrugged in irritation. "Go ahead then. But swear him to secrecy first—and know this, gentlemen; I'm not interested in knowing one word of what he has to say."

*　　　*　　　*

"Lindsey! What the hell is this?" The president put a hand on his chest while a scowl formed on his face. "You're giving me heartburn!" The Oval Office reverberated with the president's harsh words, his normally welcoming eyes snapping with disapproval. "Legalize street drugs?" John Hayes rose from behind his desk and glared at both her and Royce with disbelief. "I expect more out of the two of you—not this naïve, prep-school, pie-in-the-sky kind of reasoning. We have more important business to attend to." He put a hand up and began counting off. "One, our immigration problem is still a mess! Two, we badly need a national mass transportation system. Three, the terrorists are being held at bay only because the past administration effectively severed our ties with Israel, but that could change at any moment. We'll have to come to Israel's defense if the Arab nations decide to go ahead with their threats to wipe them off the map . . . there's no way we're going to let them be annihilated, like the Nazis tried to do in the 1930s and '40s—"

"Excuse me, Mr. President," Lindsey interrupted, "but we wouldn't actually be legalizing street drugs, just . . . regulating them . . . legally. And you yourself said there was nothing more urgent than solving our nation's drug problem—umm, sir."

The president's face flushed a deep red as he raised questioning white brows. He was not used to Lindsey disagreeing with him. "And didn't we just do that, young lady? Because of your initiative, we're pouring bushels of federal tax dollars into rehab clinics in every county of every state!"

"And that's exactly what will be needed if the Trent Mandate becomes law, Mr. President. Please, just hear us out

. . . and try to relax, sir, you're hyperventilating and it's scaring me."

He sank back into his heavy leather chair with a thunk and waved an angry hand at her. "Okay, go ahead. I'm listening, but this better be damn good."

Lindsey glanced at Royce and then proceeded with what she thought of as her list of "good news."

"Well, first of course, it would put the drug dealers out of business. People would be able to obtain regulated, recreational drugs from state operated stores, just as we purchase alcohol from state liquor stores—only at a cost of two cents on the dollar versus what they're currently paying on the street. And since the drugs would be controlled and packaged by the state, people wouldn't be buying cocaine laced with rat poison and other dangerous substances dealers use to cut back on drug purity.

"Then, with the business of selling drugs taken off the streets, the crime rate in every city across the country would drop precipitously. In turn, this would drain our national prison population down to a fraction of what it is now. Our courts and prisons would finally be free to deal with truly dangerous criminals like child molesters and sociopaths—the thirty percent or so of current inmates who should be locked up to keep our cities safe."

"And what about our kids, Lindsey?" the president practically roared. "With recreational drugs being that available—"

"That's exactly why it was so important that our recent drug enforcement policy be enacted as a first step, sir," Lindsey interrupted. "The penalty for providing drugs to kids is now so stiff, it acts as a powerful deterrent to anyone even tempted to give or sell marijuana or cocaine to anyone under age.

"And this additional step, sir," Lindsey continued, "will insure that when users reach that point in their addiction where it is destroying their health, their careers, and their relationships—and that will happen, just as it does with alcoholics—they'll have immediate access to rehabilitation clinics. Of course, we'll have to launch an ongoing media campaign, spelling out the downside of using drugs, just as we did with tobacco. Even though the government will be selling the stuff, we want to paint an accurate, horrendously ugly picture of where drugs can take a person if they become addicted."

The president heaved a deep sigh. "Okay, okay. Let's say you're right—that this great idea of yours is what's needed to get drugs off the street and addicts into recovery. Have you even thought about the big guns? The ones on both sides of the drug world who'll be coming after you? If this mandate becomes law, it will effectively put the DEA out of business right along with the dealers. You'll be putting thousands of police officers and prison personnel out of work. And all the big banks who make a fortune laundering the money funneled to them by drug lords—good Lord, Lindsey, they'll all be out for blood the instant you suggest legalizing . . . damn, *decriminalizing*, drugs!"

"It's all I do think about; yes, sir. And I know you would be putting yourself at great risk with this—"

"Stop right there, Miss!" John Hayes raised his hand in objection. "If, and I do mean *if* this thing goes forward, it will be *your* doing. I'll agree to stand aside and not block your efforts, but it will be on your doorstep, not mine." He shook his head as if warding off a swarm of bugs. "But I need some time to think this over, *Ms. Vice President*. As you know, I'm leaving for Camp David this afternoon for some peace and quiet and a much needed rest. I'll let you know my decision when I return." He glared at her accusingly. "Darn, Lindsey, until you hit me with your cockeyed idea I was really looking forward to this getaway—except for that damnable seventy-mile flight in the Marine One Helicopter. Lord, how I hate those things."

Lindsey and Royce were nearly out of the Oval Office before the president's voice stopped them. "Tell me one thing, Lindsey. How did the apple of my eye suddenly become a thorn in my side?"

TWENTY

It was so tempting to pick up the phone and place a call to the president at Camp David, knowing she would be put through immediately. Lindsey caught herself for the umpteenth time, being about to do just that. *Give the man some peace,* she told herself. *He'll be back in three-days time and then you'll know. At least he hasn't sent word that he's completely ruled out the idea.*

It was after seven in the evening, and having put in a good number of desk hours for the day, Lindsey decided she was in dire need of a strenuous workout. How she missed her long walks with Julie. But walking in a D.C. city park was out of the question. Agent Kris Andrews' heart skipped a beat each time she suggested it. "Impossible to keep you safe," he argued. "Too many nooks and crannies in those places for sickos to hide in." So Kris made arrangements for her to workout in the D.C. gym reserved specifically for Secret Service agents, which left her little to complain about. Equipped with a jogging track, mats, machines, and weights, she could exercise away the stress that built up from one hectic day to the next.

Although it was late when Lindsey and Kris arrived, the gym was filled with the grunts and groans of the agents who were working out. Heading for the women's locker room, she quickly changed into the old tank top and shorts she kept there, then climbed the stairs to the gym floor. Spotting a circle of women off to one side, Lindsey pulled a mat in their direction and joined in their efforts to strengthen abs, thighs, and calf muscles. She dropped out after thirty-five repetitions of sit-ups, and rested while the group of female agents fought to reach a hundred. There was no way she would ever reach their level of fitness, but what she accomplished made her feel good, and the results brought a smile to her physician's face during her physical.

The women had just started a series of deep-knee squats, not one of Lindsey's favorites, when Kris took her urgently by the shoulder. "We've got to get back to the White House immediately, Madam Vice President." His voice was strained and formal. "There's been an accident."

A feeling of dread filled Lindsey. She knew even before she asked. "The president, Kris! What's happened? Is he all right?" The agent was silent, his face grim. "Oh God, Kris," she demanded. "Tell me he's all right!"

"He left Camp David earlier than planned and was on his way back to D.C." Kris's voice was flat, devoid of emotion. "Ground control lost contact with Marine One somewhere over the Catoctin Mountains in Maryland. They searched for several hours, Ma'am, and finally located it torn to pieces at the bottom of a steep precipice. The chopper was nearly disintegrated and there . . . there were no survivors."

His words hit Lindsey like a fist in the gut. Every bit of air left her lungs, and she could barely breathe around the pain. "Oh God, oh God, oh God," she moaned.

Sheila Hayes met Lindsey in the drawing room of the West Wing. The president's wife fought for composure even as the shock of her husband's death rocked her to the core. "Madam President." Sheila reached to Lindsey with outstretched hands, then pulled her into an embrace as

Lindsey's face crumpled into a tearful mess. "Hush, don't cry," Sheila soothed her. We'll get through this together."

Lindsey pulled back. "Sheila, I should be comforting you!"

"You *are* a comfort to me, just knowing how much you loved him. But right now, John would want you to carry on with the important business of running this country. As our new president, you know what must be done."

The words that had been added to the Constitution rang through Lindsey's mind: *". . . the vice president shall be empowered to assume the president's duties in the event of absence, illness, or death."* Lindsey shuddered, then said, "I asked Royce to call the chief justice to administer the oath of office, Sheila. But since the oath can be performed by any judge or public official, Royce suggested calling my father instead. Fortunately, he's in D.C. on business and will be arriving here within the next few minutes."

"Of course," Sheila said, wiping her tears aside. "Under these stressful circumstances, I know you'll find some solace in assuming the presidency with James Delaware at your side."

The brief ceremony was held at ten p.m. in the Oval Office, with draped flags and a subdued group of witnesses gathered around the Seal of the Republic woven into the blue-carpeted floor. Of those few present, it was impossible to know who shed the most tears as James spoke the solemn words that shifted the immense burden of power and responsibility as the nation's commander in chief onto Lindsey's small shoulders. She was a reluctant leader at that moment, but she stood tall and determined as she placed her hand on what had been her mother's family Bible and pledged to uphold the Constitution of the country she so dearly loved.

Hours later Lindsey sat alone in her office, a small lamp illuminating the desk she had used so briefly as vice president. She had insisted that Sheila remain in the private living quarters of the White House for as long as needed before vacating them.

Lindsey fell into bed well after midnight. She slept poorly and for only a few hours before rising at 4:30. The blank screen of her PC stared back at her as she struggled to find the words needed to reassure a suffering nation. She had always written her own speeches, but never one as critical as this, and it had to be completed quickly. Her first presidential address had been scheduled for later that evening.

Lindsey was startled when at six a.m. the phone shrilled loudly in the quiet of her office. Answering it, she was surprised but relieved to hear Beverly's voice. "Bev, what on earth are you doing here so early? You didn't have to—"

"Yes I did. I've made a pot of strong coffee, the kind that makes your spoon stand at attention, and some fresh breakfast rolls. If I know you, you haven't bothered to eat since long ago yesterday . . . oh, and Senator Shakett called just now. He asked if he and speaker of the house Billings could see you first thing this morning. He insisted that it's extremely urgent, Lindsey—I mean, Madam President." Her voice caught as she spoke.

"Gawd, Beverly, I can't get used to it either. President? I keep hoping I'll wake up and find things just as they were before I left my office yesterday. But—okay, we'll do this one step at a time. Call the Senator and tell him 11 a.m. in the Oval Office. I should have this speech written by then and will have met with all the powers that be who need to bring me up to speed on everything President Hayes was involved in."

Lindsey was deeply engrossed in her speech when her cell phone chirped its soft tone. Only four people had the number, and she'd already spoken to Beverly, Lyle, and Gavin. She quickly flipped the phone open and asked hopefully, "Brian?"

"Hi," he answered. "I—I wasn't sure you'd want me to use this number any longer."

"Always," she replied softly.

"I don't know what to say, Lindsey . . . John Hayes, he was an amazing man. I can't believe—oh Lord, life can be so shitty." There was a long pause before the connection ended.

Senator Roger Shakett and Congressman Benjamin Billings arrived promptly for their eleven o'clock meeting. Lindsey rose from behind the antique desk in the Oval Office and extended her hand to each of them. After offering their condolences, Senator Shakett gave her a friendly grin that flashed in the sunlight streaming into the office. Lindsey had never cared for either man, both of whom she considered consummate politicians, all flair without much substance. *Two peas in a pod,* Lindsey thought as they settled into armchairs across from her, *except for their personal appearances.* Congressman Billings was short and rotund. His expensive cologne and heavily gelled hair did little to compensate for his bulbous nose and pale complexion, the consistency of skim milk. Senator Shakett, on the other hand, was tall, thin, and well-tanned with disturbing, penetrating eyes and a nose that cut down the center of his face like the blade of a knife.

Billings gave Lindsey a reluctant smile as Shakett got straight to the point. "The Speaker and I want to congratulate you on the impressive work you accomplished as vice president, Madam President, but," he cleared his throat before continuing, "even though President Hayes thought very highly of you, you must know that he and the members of his Cabinet never expected you to follow him into the presidency. The Speaker and I are here to make you aware of their misgivings."

His brutal remarks stunned Lindsey. "Certainly no one expected a tragedy of this magnitude, Senator, but—"

"I'm not talking about these circumstances. You were never intended to ascend to the office of the presidency under *any* circumstances!"

Lindsey rarely lost her temper, but it shot immediately to the boiling point in reaction to his insolence. Rising from her chair, she stared the man down. "*Mister* Shakett! How dare you? You and your—your cohort here may have a problem with me ascending to the presidency, but this is neither the time nor the place to voice such vitriolic misgivings."

"They are more than misgivings, Lindsey. They are John Hayes's own words, and we are duty bound to make you aware of them. You must step down, Madam, and immediately, before things get even more out of hand."

With an eager nod, Billings chimed in. "President Hayes often commented about how having you on the ticket helped him win the presidency, but that you didn't have what it takes to be the leader of a country the size of ours. It was common knowledge among his staff and close associates, Madam President.

"Look," Shakett added before she could reply. "If you were *James* Delaware, things would be different. Your father would certainly be highly qualified as the president. But you, Lindsey? Face it, you can try to imitate your father, but you'll never *be* him! And this isn't a sexist thing. There are some women who are strong enough, tough enough to lead this country. But you're not one of them—you'll be seen as insignificant compared to other world leaders."

The two men, like sharks with gapping mouths and shining teeth, were sitting on the edge of their seats, eyeing her carefully, waiting for her reply. Stunned, but determined to not let them see how shaken she was, Lindsey squared her shoulders and spoke loudly enough to startle Agent Andrews on the other side of the door. "I may be insignificant, gentlemen, but I'm capable of seeing the enormity of things. The urgency of this moment demands stability. You are proposing that I step aside and throw the presidency up for grabs, but nothing could be more damaging to this country, and *I will not allow it!"* She leveled a sharp look at Shakett. "I'm not a fool, Senator." She said it quietly but absolutely— and his silence proved he got the point. "And now, as my first official act as president, I am ordering you two rouges to vacate this office—immediately!" She hit the black button on her desk that brought Kris into the room before she'd finished speaking. "Agent Andrews will see you out."

Shakett paused at the door and clipped his words. "When this is over, Madam President, you're going to feel like you got hit by a Mack truck."

Old memories of a renegade car slamming into her and her mother rushed into her mind. She tapped down her anger and gave Shakett a hard look. "Wrong choice of metaphors, Senator. Now kindly leave this office. Its use is meant for far better men than either of you."

Lindsey was still standing at her desk, visibly upset, when Beverly came into the room, a puzzled look on her face. "I thought—the Senator and Speaker Billings, didn't they ask you to lunch after your meeting?"

"No, they had *me* for lunch, Beverly."

Fortunately, Lindsey had finished writing her address to the nation shortly before her visitors had delivered their horrible revelation. She felt physically ill after they left— sick to her stomach at the thought of President Hayes' death, coupled with what might have been his dire estimation of her abilities. *It can't be true,* she told herself. *I couldn't have misread him all these months.* There was only one person she would trust to verify or disavow what she'd just been told. And right now Sheila Hayes had the burden of grief and a national funeral to deal with. There was no way Lindsey could approach her with her concerns until after John Hayes was laid to rest. And that meant she had to face the House and Senate tonight and convince everyone that the country was in good hands. How could she do that now with the crushing uncertainty the two men had dumped on her? President Delaware lowered herself into her chair and felt her courage and determination slowly ebbing away.

There was a light tap at her door, then Beverly stepped into the office. "Forgive me for interrupting, Madam President, but the former First Lady is here and would like a word with you, if possible." Lindsey nodded, and Beverly ushered Sheila into the room.

Always the First Lady, Sheila was impeccably dressed in a soft blue, linen dress that accentuated her kind blue eyes and went so well with her white, shortly coiffed hair. But her drawn face and the dark circles under her eyes made it apparent she'd slept very little, if at all. She spoke softly. "I was wondering, Madam President, if you could possibly join me for lunch. Chef Rupert has prepared a wonderful luncheon for me, and I do think I'd enjoy it a great deal more if you and I could share it. Are you free?"

Lindsey brightened and walked over to embrace her. "I'd love to join you, Sheila. You know, that's something else I'm going to miss terribly. It was always such a pleasure when you and the president invited me to dine with you in the West Wing. It felt like we were family, not just politicians."

They were halfway through their lunch when Sheila placed her hand on Lindsey's arm and looked at her questioningly. "What is it, Madam President? There is something terribly wrong—it's more than John's death. You seem so . . . so distant, as if you'd simply like to disappear."

The tears formed before Lindsey could stop them. "Oh, Sheila. I can't—I didn't want to face you with this until you've had some time to recover."

"Humph, I doubt that I'll *ever* recover from the loss of my husband, Madam President, so why don't you just come out with it?"

Reluctantly, Lindsey began relating, piece by piece, the conversation she'd had with Shakett and Billings. By the time she'd finished, Sheila could barely contain her anger. "Why the nerve of those two, two . . . I have no words adequate to describe them. They are absolutely despicable!"

"But were they being bluntly honest, Sheila, or bold-faced liars? I can't imagine they fabricated the entire thing. They had to know they'd be found out if none of the filth they spewed was true."

"No doubt they hoped their ploy would cause you to immediately resign before their trickery was discovered. By then, it would be too late . . . and with Billings as Speaker of the House, he would be in line to ascend to the presidency."

Lindsey looked at Sheila imploringly. "It's—it's not true, then? The president thought I . . ."

"Lindsey, listen to me, now!" In her urgency, Sheila neglected to use Lindsey's title. "John and I were never blessed with children, but he said on many occasions that he thought of you as his own daughter. We both did, and I still do! And as for your competency, he had great faith in your abilities, and became excited when he thought about all that you would accomplish if you followed him into the presidency. He was dead certain—oh dear, what a horrible choice of words." She drew a deep breath and collected herself. "But regardless, he was positive you would be the next president of the United States, Lindsey, and quite likely one of the greatest; after him, of course. Why, I can't tell you how many times he remarked how pleased he was that he'd chosen you as his vice president. He admired you, Lindsey. He said he was as proud of you as your own father must be."

"Then Shakett and Billings, they were outright lying to me!" She felt as if she were drowning in a sea of confusion. "Dear God, Sheila, how on earth will I know who to trust?"

"It's called political hardball, Lindsey. Just count this as a lesson well learned. John's first rule was to surround himself with people he could trust absolutely. Everyone else was suspect."

Later that afternoon, while sitting alone in the small study next to the Oval Office and reviewing the message she wanted to impart to the American people, Lindsey thought long and hard about Sheila's warning. It made perfect sense, but unfortunately Lindsey could count on one hand the people she really trusted—her father, Beverly, Royce, Lyle, and Gavin . . . and Brian, of course, but what use was he when she couldn't even talk to him? As for her father, she and James had made a tacit agreement that he be kept out of the presidential loop as much as possible. In that way she would be less vulnerable to accusations that her father was running the country while she merely served as a glittery show piece.

Twenty-four hours following the announcement of the president's death, Lindsey stood before the joint branches of Congress, blinking uncomfortably in an effort to adjust to the blinding lights surrounding her. Wearing a stylish gray sheath and a matching jacket that hung nearly to the hem of her dress, she faced cameras that momentarily would broadcast her image across the nation and to the world. A small prayer and a deep breath steadied her as she received the signal to begin.

Her message was composed of two critical parts. One spelled out what she hoped to accomplish while in office, and the other how it was to be done. But first, Lindsey had to impart her own deep sense of sorrow over John Hayes's death, before asking for the nation's trust and support as their new president. She was unashamed of the tears that filled her eyes as she began by speaking of John and Sheila's lifetime contributions and the loss the nation had suffered with his passing. As she put into words the grief shared by so many, even hard-line members of the media who crammed onto the floor of the Senate reached for handkerchiefs to wipe their faces and stifle choking coughs.

Lindsey then gathered herself and launched into the substance of her message of reassurance to the nation. Leveling a silver gaze into the nearest camera, she began:

"President John Hayes and I shared a dream. A dream that one day our nation would speak with one voice. Far too long our country has been ripped apart by our own warring parties. Depending on who holds power, we've been pulled to the far left, the far right, and back to the middle of the road—all leading to years of failure. And even though we are well into a new century, that failure has kept us entrenched in the past. It's time our legislators in the House and Senate lived as though they love this country more than their party. Time for them to come together to forge a visionary future that will take us fully into the 21st century.

"Our country is not about intellectual discourse and heated debates, it's about doing! It's time for action, ladies and gentlemen, and I can absolutely promise you this," her voice rang with sincerity. *"As we take the steps to begin anew, to forge ahead in a new direction, I will* always *put my country ahead of what's best for my party or what's best for*

me politically. With your help it can *happen, it* should *happen, and it* will *happen!"*

Applause thundered within the historic room, but many legislators in attendance looked at one another skeptically. A long-term Senator nudged Senator Shakett in the ribs and whispered, "Wow! What a line, 'putting the country ahead of her party'. She really hooked them with that one."

"Shakett glared at him. "Yah. But there's one little problem—she really means it!"

As the applause died down, Lindsey continued. *"So I am now calling for the immediate actions that Congress must take. First and foremost, we must build a mass transportation system that will stretch across the entire nation."* Lindsey raised a determined chin. *"It's a hundred years overdue, ladies and gentlemen. Our railroad system is in shambles, the cost of air travel is prohibitive despite government subsidies, and our automobiles have caused a glut of traffic on major highways along with a congested, unhealthy environment in every large city across this nation.*

"But I am not suggesting that we sacrifice the luxury of our personal autos until there is something better— something more 21st century to replace them. For a country of our great size, a practical answer lies in the development of high-speed bullet trains—individual turbo-driven cars varying in capacity from two to twenty-six passengers. Multiple tracks running east and west, north and south will move each bullet at a speed of 220 mph, with their destinations programmed by computer. They will exit at full speed onto spurs that will slow the bullets to a stop, where they will be met by electric transportation that delivers passengers to their final destinations. Oh, and by the way," Lindsey smiled broadly at this point, *"the interior of the bullet cars will be organically disinfected after each occupancy. How's that for living in the 21st century?"*

Lindsey's smile changed to an expression of stern determination. *"And now a warning to the leaders of our bureaucracy. If you can't work together to accomplish this in a timely manner, then with the backing of the American people I will create a mass transportation team that* will *make it happen—and I personally will walk the needed legislation through both houses. If this sounds like a threat, Senators and members of the House, be assured that it is!"*

Lindsey concluded this part of her speech by stressing the long overdue need for rebuilding the national infrastructure, and for increasing the use of wind turbines, solar energy, and all other means of clean alternative energy that would reduce the country's dependence on foreign oil. Then she assumed a dramatic change of tenor, intending to close with what would be the heart of her message.

"If I sound overconfident that we can attain these lofty goals, let me proclaim how it will be done—through our faith and through our adherence to the American Constitution. These two remarkable forces shaped and continue to bind our country together. I need to remind our national leaders that while the Constitution demands separation of church and state, I do not believe it suggests that we keep God out of our politics. How can we forget that our country was founded on freedom of *religion, not freedom* from *religion? The founders of this country were men and women of great faith. They established this nation on the cornerstone of religious faith and religious liberty. The Constitution puts great restraints on our government to ensure that citizens will be allowed to practice their religion in whatever form they wish. Today, however, we have bureaucrats leading the charge in hostility toward religion instead of allowing faith to flourish on its own. They have created a poisonous atmosphere where division and skepticism flourish.*

"But I can promise you this. While I am in office, the White House will ring aloud with my prayers for this

wondrous nation, and I ask for your prayerful support in return. How can this be unethical, or dangerous, or unwise when one of our most respected forefathers, Patrick Henry, thought otherwise? In his last will and testament, after disposing of all his property, he concluded with the hope that he had given his family what he deemed to be the most important gift of all, faith in God. He wrote that if they had that, and he had not given them one shilling, they would still be rich; and if they did not have faith, and he had given them all the world, they would be poor.

"So dear people of all religious beliefs in our great country, I ask that you pray. Pray that our leaders now move forward in unison to make at long last a visionary mark upon history. And I ask you to support, to serve, and to pray with me for God's continued blessings on the United States of America."

Lindsey's speech garnered unequivocal favorable reviews. Networks and newspapers, from left and right alike, gave her a resounding congratulatory ovation, praising her strong yet reassuringly calm message. But Lindsey had little time to rest on her laurels. She had only the remaining two years of John Hayes' term to serve before she would have to stand for election in her own right.

Her first order of business was to select Cabinet members quickly but carefully. She asked Royce to join her in the West Wing study and sounded him out. "Mainly, Royce, I'm going to ask current Cabinet members to stand with me. If John Hayes trusted them, I'm confident I can do the same." He nodded in quiet agreement.

"I am going to make one important change, however. You will no longer be my chief White House advisor, Royce—I want you to serve instead as Secretary of State."

His eyes widened in alarm. "You can't be serious, Madam President! Thomas Roget has an excellent record as Secretary of State, while I—I can't imagine taking on that job."

"But I can, Royce," Lindsey said resolutely. "With your sense of diplomacy and the ability to work with all sides to reach equitable resolutions, you were made for it."

"But—but what about Roget? Won't he be . . . excuse me, Ma'am, but won't he be royally pissed?"

"I think not, as I've already asked him to step up to serve as our new vice president. His knowledge will be critically helpful to me in so many ways, Royce." She laughed at the blank expression on his face. "Admit it. I have you over a barrel because there is no better solution."

He eyed her thoughtfully for a moment, then said, "Here's the deal, Madam President. If you assure me you won't try to enact that Trent Mandate of yours, I'll serve as your Secretary of State. There's no way I want to deal with all the fallout from that bombshell."

Lindsey laughed. "Rest assured, Royce. I've put my dream of national drug reform aside for now. My presidency and the stability of the country are too uncertain to risk any additional turmoil."

Lindsey's cabinet selections had barely been announced before Senator Shakett demanded to see her. He stormed into her office, then sank into the visitor's chair facing her desk. Looking not at all apologetic, he grumbled, "Look, I know you and I got off on the wrong foot, but you have to understand that Congressman Billings and I were voicing the opinion of many of our top legislators." Getting no response, he continued. "And what the hell's going on, anyway? You know you have to clear the decisions you've been making with ranking members of Congress. We understand how things work up here. And believe me, we're prepared to take a stand against Royce White. There is no way that man is qualified to be Secretary of State! For Chrissake, everyone knows you want him appointed just because he's black."

A thin smile played across Lindsey's lips. "And I'm old enough to remember a time when Royce *wouldn't* have been appointed for the very same reason. The racism shoe really pinches when it's on the other foot, doesn't it, Senator?"

"Dammit! You're talking ancient history here. I had nothing to do with whatever happened in the past. I've never discriminated against a black man, and I'm not a racist!"

"It's a matter of physics, Shakett—for every action there's an equal and opposite reaction. Our lily-white ancestors pushed the pendulum too far, and now it's swinging back with an attitude."

"That doesn't make it right. And for God's sake, you don't have to make that n—that nut case Secretary of State."

"Why? So you or your good buddy Billings could be appointed instead? Tell me, Shakett, have you no ethical code? How do you live with yourself?"

He answered her in a tone laced with sarcasm. "I have a clear conscience, Madam President. Believe me, I sleep well at night."

"A clear conscience, Senator, or no conscience whatsoever?"

Seeing he was getting nowhere, Shakett slapped his hand against the arm of his chair and rose to leave without bothering to ask if the meeting was over.

Lindsey stopped him at the door. "Senator! Let's get one thing straight—no, two things. One, Royce *is* qualified and two, you *are* a racist. And by the way, I have consent from more than enough fair-minded people eager to approve

Royce's appointment. Now, you can get your narrow-minded, puritanical ass out of my office."

Stiff-spined, he studied her with an expression of intense dislike, then turned and exited the room. Instantly, Lindsey pressed the intercom button on her desk. "Beverly, I need to see Secretary-designate White."

"Yes, Madam President. He rearranged his schedule after you announced his appointment, and he's set for nine a.m. tomorrow."

"Not soon enough, Beverly. I have to see him today."

"Today! But Lindsey," she sputtered, forgetting protocol in her frustration, "you're booked solid. I could barely work him in tomorrow."

"Today, Beverly," Lindsey insisted as she ended the conversation. Now her briefing with Royce would include a strong warning about Shakett. Not only did Royce have to prove himself as a competent secretary of state, he would have to watch out for Shakett and his kind; the power brokers who would be working feverishly behind the scenes to bring him down. "But he knows that already," she sighed. "I'll just be preaching to the choir . . . ."

They met over an evening pizza in her private office, a luxury that rarely fit into their hectic schedules. Royce smiled knowingly as Lindsey recounted her run-in with the man she described as Senator "Snake-in-the-Grass" Shakett. "I expected nothing less, Madame President," Royce assured her. "Every time I make a mistake as your Secretary of State, it won't be because I'm still at the low end of the learning curve and don't quite get it yet. It will be because I'm black and never *will* get it. And you're correct. Long ago I developed my own sense of radar that warns me when a friendly smile hides a malicious intent."

"I could certainly use some of that radar myself, Royce." She shook her head in discouragement as she spoke over the aroma of pepperoni and mushrooms. "How am I ever going to be tough enough for this job?"

Royce looked at her in surprise. "But you *know* how to be tough, Lindsey. As a probation officer, you had over 130 felons to supervise at any given time. In comparison, this job is a piece of cake!" She looked at him with skepticism. "Well, almost," he corrected.

Lindsey decided to continue the TV Chats she had held during her days in Congress. She had learned that once-a-month personal conversations with the American people were far more honest and effective than monthly press conferences, where her words would be instantly reinterpreted and misconstrued by the panic mongers in the press corps. She settled comfortably into an overstuffed chair in the drawing room of the West Wing and acclimated herself to the glaring lights of the cameras. Her approval rating at this moment was as high as that enjoyed by John Hayes, and she fully intended to strike while she was still in the country's good graces.

After greeting her audience, Lindsey wasted no time getting straight to the point.

"As you know, my work in the House and Senate often focused on leveling the playing field so that no one in government received preferential treatment over any other citizen. I can't say I was always successful. Perhaps as your president, and with the power of your vote, we'll now get that job done. So this evening, I am proposing some dramatic changes in how our government works. The referendums will appear on the ballot at next November's election and will be enforced if approved by a majority of you, the American voters.

"First, we've made some progress in setting term limits, but more needs to be done. After all, our founding fathers envisioned citizen legislators who regarded serving in Congress as an honor, not a career. I therefore propose that all elected officials serve a limit of two terms in any one office and, if elected to other offices, no more than twelve years overall.

"I also propose that Congressmen and Congresswomen abide by all laws they impose on the American people. That means they'll get more than a stern reprimand if they fail to pay their taxes or misuse public funds. Being chastised by one's colleagues on the floor of the House or Senate is embarrassing, but nowhere nearly as devastating as the penalties inflicted on the common citizen for the same misdeeds.

"In the same vein, if any government official sexually compromises a young page or intern, that official will be subject to immediate dismissal and possible imprisonment, just as in the outside world. No blaming the youngster!

"I don't know about you, ladies and gentlemen, but these measures seem like straight common sense to me, along with a good dose of fairness and justice. Your letters and emails regarding tonight's TV Chat will be read and categorized by my staff, so I look forward to learning where you stand. And as always, I ask for God's blessings and your prayerful support for the work carried out by your elected officials. Goodnight, one and all."

It was no surprise to Lindsey when Beverly buzzed her in the Oval Office at six a.m. the next morning. "Madam President," she said with exasperation, "there's a group—a delegation of Republican Senators here who want a word with you. I explained that you are already heavily scheduled, but . . ."

"It's all right Beverly. I've been expecting them. Send them in."

It was also no surprise that the group of eight impeccably dressed elderly gentlemen was led into the room by Senator Shakett. As was his style, he started off with a slick comment to catch her off guard. "Amazing messages you've been sending out to the public, Madam President. And what a line from last evening: 'legislators should regard serving in Congress as an honor, not a career.' I'm sure your listeners ate it up."

"Was I believable, Senator?"

"Entirely! You're no JFK, but you're very good at delivering a speech."

"Well, often when someone is believable, Mr. Shakett, it's because they speak what they truly believe." Then she added, "And I do my own writing, by the way, whereas John Kennedy's great speeches were written primarily by Ted Sorensen from the time Kennedy was a freshman Senator."

"That's bullshit!" Senator Creigher, a big bull of a man, roared from the back of the room as his face grew dangerously red. "And if you think for one minute you're going to get away with enforcing those term limits—"

"How long have you been a senator, Mr. Creigher?"

"I'm proud to say I've served for over thirty-five years, and I assure you, no one from my district could do it better!"

"Oh, I rather doubt that, Senator. This country is blessed with an abundance of bright, richly talented young men and women. When given the opportunity, I think we'll be amazed at what they accomplish."

A loud, disgusted snort drew everyone's attention as a tall angry man, Senator Thompson, pushed his way to the front of the group. Lindsey knew him to be one of the more vociferous Republican leaders. He peered down at her. "You're no Republican, Lindsey Delaware. You're a Goddamn Libertarian. You don't get to do whatever you want. And if you think you can get reelected without the support of our party, you don't have the brains of a skeleton."

"You seem to be forgetting yourself, Senator Thompson." There was an edge to her voice. "I'm not a Goddamn anything! I'm president of the United States." His tongue twisted in knots as he struggled to hold back the scurrilous words he wanted to spew. "And it's not the support of the party that I care about. It's the support of the American people that's important to me, and they'll let me know if I go too far astray from their standards." Her eyes cut across the men who stood before her. "And even if I don't fit your definition of a Republican, Senators, I am genuinely American."

"Shit! You're a one-woman wrecking crew, that's what you are!" Shakett hurled at her, then stormed out of the room, followed by the rest of his grumbling, disgruntled cronies.

TWENTY-ONE

With newly appointed Secretary of State Royce White and Vice President Tom Roget at her side and her father looking on from the wings, Lindsey sailed through the first few months of her inherited presidency with little opposition. All three of her proposed government reforms were endorsed overwhelmingly at the November election, despite loud rumblings from Congress. Giant strides were made in the development of the mass transportation system she had envisioned, and the use of clean energy was on the rise.

Lindsey went on to complete the two remaining years of John Hayes' presidency with what was described by the media as substance and style. But she gave much of the credit to the two men who became her most valued political assets: Royce had stepped into the role of Secretary of State as if he had been born to the position, and she found Tom Roget to be indispensable as her second in command. Tom was a stalwart man in his mid-sixties who stood ready to back her in every circumstance. Just as importantly, he was an expert at navigating the muddy waters of double-dealing politics and helped her steer clear of potentially dangerous entrapments.

When the general election was held in November 2020, Lindsey stood for the presidency in her own right, winning by a huge margin. No longer an accidental president,

Lindsey was again sworn into the highest office of the land, this time by Chief Justice Elena Kagan.

All the pieces were in place now. President Delaware had the confidence and support of the American people, and had surrounded herself with a staff that would follow wherever she led—it was time. Drug reform had been her major campaign issue and those politicians who support her drug initiatives were swept into office with her. *It's now or never, Jules,* she mused as she gazed out the Oval Office window, lost in the expansive view of the White House lawn. But before announcing her intentions, she had to speak to Sheila. Lindsey knew President Hayes had been struggling with his decision over the Trent Mandate while at Camp David two years earlier, and as was his custom, had likely discussed his quandary with his wife.

Lindsey called Sheila personally and asked if she'd mind coming to visit her in the West Wing whenever she was free. "Why, I'd be delighted, Madam President," she responded. "I love the home John and I shared here in Virginia, but it gets a little lonely wandering around these large rooms all on my own."

They sat together now, enjoying tea and the homemade biscuits Beverly had smuggled in without Chef Rupert's approval. Sheila eyed the small drawing room approvingly. "I see you haven't made many changes in the décor. This was always one of my favorite rooms."

"I haven't made *any* changes, Sheila. You did such a beautiful job decorating these rooms; I see no need to try my hand at it." Lindsey paused, then said, "I'm sure you know I had a reason to ask you here, Sheila, other than that I miss seeing you."

Sheila reached over and patted her hand reassuringly. "Of course you do, dear, so why don't you just come out with it?"

"This is difficult, Sheila, but I have to ask you . . . just before President Hayes left Camp David that last time, did he say anything to you about having to make a decision about a radical drug-reform program I'd proposed?"

"Oh my, yes. I remember it clearly. It was so obvious that he was having a dreadful time with it. I told him he might just as well give up and let me in on whatever was bothering him so." Her eyes widened. "I must admit I was quite surprised—well, shocked actually, when he told me of your idea. He was so worried about all the upheaval it would cause."

Lindsey heaved a heavy sigh. "He—he had decided against it, then?"

"He believed *you* were right, Madam President. A monumental change is needed to end the terrible things that drugs are doing to us. But he also knew *he* was right in that your idea would open a door that might best remain closed. I think he likened it to Truman having to make the decision whether or not to drop the atom bomb on Hiroshima.

"After watching him agonize over it for days, I finally said, 'You and Lindsey are *both* right, John, but it's a question of whose right carries the most weight.' He said something like, 'I have to admit Lindsey's right outweighs mine, and even though it feels like I'm stepping into a pile of shit, in all likelihood it's the right thing to do.'"

Lindsey's face brightened even as tears of relief pooled in her eyes. "Oh, Sheila! He was going to approve it, then? He was going to do it?"

Sheila cleared her throat. "Well, actually, I think he was going to have *you* go ahead with it while he remained in the background. But he was going to support you, yes."

Lindsey came out of her chair and gave Sheila a delighted hug. "You never said anything. I wasn't sure—"

"Oh, I was just waiting to see what you would do. I didn't want to encourage you until you were certain you wanted to proceed with it. It's going to be an extreme challenge, but I have a feeling you'll handle it beautifully."

"I've prayed over the wisdom of going ahead with this for a long time, Sheila."

"You needn't have waited, Madam President. Sometimes God simply says, *'It's your move.'*"

*   *   *

Lindsey stood at the podium on the steps of the White House and looked out over the large crowd gathered there on an unusually warm sunny day in January, 2021. *Well, this is it,* she told herself. Her first political speech since being soundly elected in her own right, and the moment she'd chosen to announce the Trent Mandate. Life had given her this chance to make a difference. She wasn't going to blow it!

To strengthen her resolve, Lindsey mentally reran the terrifying scene that Julie had described to her in full detail—Julie's near-death experience in a Cambridge crack house, sucking on the muzzle of a Colt .45 while a slimy drug dealer towered over her, laughing his head off. With effort, Lindsey shook the memory aside.

"My fellow countrymen and women," she began, her voice ringing strongly and clearly in the cold air, *"although this moment is one of the most joyous I've ever known, I speak to you today with a heavy heart. Despite remarkable progress, our nation remains devastated by the illicit power of drugs. Illegal drugs have claimed the right to annihilate our major cities and millions of our youth. The greed they engender is bankrupting the moral fiber of our country, our families, and our future. And the sad truth is that no matter*

how many drug battles we win, the war is already lost. Despite all our efforts, the demand for drugs in the U.S. is not diminishing, and the crime rate associated with gangs and drugs has grown into a chaos of violence. At this very moment we have drug smugglers living in caves in Arizona, whose only purpose is to feed the multi-billion dollar appetite Americans have for drugs. And we have drug cartels in 200 American cities pumping our money and guns back into Mexico.

"Are you aware that 70% of our street-level crime is committed by addicts to obtain the funds needed to support their habits? Were you angry when CNN announced the theft of 2000 presents from 'Toys for Tots' in Toledo, Ohio, toys that were then sold for drugs? Do you know that our federal government spends $20 billion a year of your tax money on the war against narcotics, and that doesn't include what's spent at state and local levels? But our dilemma is almost laughable when compared to the viciousness engendered by drugs just across our border with Mexico.

"We have been so focused on Iraq, Iran, and Afghanistan, we've lost sight of what's happening in our own backyard. How can we ignore the drug-cartel wars in Tijuana, where two million people have been decapitated or had their tongues cut out? There are so many drug-related deaths there, the medical examiner often runs out of supplies. In Juarez, gunmen broke into a drug rehab center, lined everyone against a wall and murdered them execution style, evidently in retribution for the police seizing their cache of drugs. And in Cancun innocent people were killed when a gasoline bomb exploded in a bar after a drug deal went bad. In Northwest Mexico thousands of people are slaughtered by drug cartels every year. There are 500 drug-related deaths each week in Mexico, where the level of violence has became an accepted way of life. And that violence has taken root and spread into our own cities.

"Our DEA is trying to fight this violence by using superior *violence, but is failing. Billions of dollars worth of cocaine and marijuana are smuggled from Mexico into our country every year, some of it in privately owned drug-cartel submarines.*

"I'm convinced you're as sick of this as I am. Richard Nixon declared a 'War on Drugs' over fifty years ago, and it has failed miserably. I stand here today to proclaim that we are starting a new war on drugs. This time with a workable solution designed to finally end the horror of drugs in our country. I've recently met with President Cortez of Mexico and Prime Minister McAllister of Canada to inform them of what is about to happen, as our solution will greatly affect each of their countries. And that solution, ladies and gentlemen, is what I bring to you today. As of this moment, we are waging a new war on drugs, a dramatic tactic worthy of the 21st Century."

Lindsey took a deep breath and steeled herself before continuing. If the media and the American people could not accept what she was about to do, if they turned on her, it would be the beginning of the end of her presidency—and in all likelihood her very life, but she had to push on.

"Why did we think that criminalizing drugs would be any more successful than criminalizing alcohol during the years of Prohibition? Our society found it couldn't stop people from drinking by making alcohol illegal, just because some people act stupid when they drink. The only thing Prohibition accomplished was to put money in the pockets of gangsters while breeding deception, crime, and death. Where was the wisdom in that?

"Ted Koppel, a renowned newsman, advocated for the rehabilitation of addicts rather than incarceration. We took an important first step in that direction when our government enacted a drug policy that provided federally-funded

rehabilitation programs across the country. But today we will take rehabilitation a step farther."

She raised her voice to a near shout. *"By Presidential Executive Order our new war on drugs, to be known as the Trent Mandate, will* decriminalize *all illegal substances."* She paused as shocked gasps and loud rumblings surged through the crowd. She held up her hands for silence. *"Please understand that drugs like cocaine and marijuana will not be* legalized, *but will be* regulated *just as we regulate the use of alcohol. All of you are aware that we have stiff penalties in place for those who commit crimes while high on drugs or alcohol. And these laws will continue to be strongly enforced. But please believe this, it's not* doing *drugs that makes them so dangerous—it's not* having *them that makes addicts desperate enough to commit crimes."*

Lindsey ended her speech on that note, sensing that her message needed to be absorbed and deliberated upon before the nation could deal with further information. She relaxed in her bedroom now, too tired to think. She had just pulled her covers up to her chin when her cell phone buzzed. She had already talked to Lyle and Gavin, both of whom had congratulated her enthusiastically, and she doubted Beverly would be calling her this late. That left only . . .

"Brian?" she asked as she put the phone to her ear.

"Hi," he said softly. "That was quite some speech you hit us with today."

"Yah, well, what can I say? Never a dull moment at the White House. What—what did you think?" she asked, eager for his opinion.

"What do I think? I think I know now why you pushed me away two years ago when you took over the presidency.

You knew even then, didn't you, Lindsey? You knew what you were going to do—and how dangerous it would be."

"Brian, I—"

"Don't deny it, Lindsey. You sent me away because you didn't want me and Chip in the line of fire. I'm not stupid, Lindsey. Anyone close to you right now is in imminent danger. But you had no right, Lindsey. No right to make that decision for me and Chip. He's not a little kid anymore, Lins, and he and I had the right to decide whether having you in our life was worth the risk."

"But *I* can't risk it, Brian. I've already lost Julie. I couldn't exist if I were responsible for the death of either you or your son. It's hard enough worrying about Dad. He's fully protected day and night, but I hate that I've put him in such jeopardy."

"And there is no one else, is there? You've cut yourself off from everyone, other than Lyle and Gavin, and few people know about your friendship with them . . . but is this what Julie would have wanted, Lins?"

"It's what *I* want, Brian." Blood throbbing at her temples, Lindsey closed her eyes and said softly, "Please take care of yourself. And tell Chip I have his school newspaper mailed to me so I can keep up with all his activities. You must be so proud—" With a heavy heart she ended the call, not able to go on.

Brian was right. She had intentionally created an isolated existence. Her life was challenging, exciting, stimulating—but it had been a long time since she knew what happiness was.

With a great sense of relief, Lindsey read in depth the article in *American Republic* that focused on the radical drug-reform mandate she had announced the previous day.

AmRep was a powerful, ultra-conservative newspaper without whose support the Trent Mandate would surely meet an early death, along with the effectiveness of the remaining years of her presidency. The news article was couched in words of obvious approval while on the Op Ed page; the editor-in-chief gave her a rousing go ahead. He called it "a daring but long overdue move rarely seen in the cover-your-butt world of politics."

Lindsey smiled broadly. The far right-wingers in her party would have a difficult time bucking her now, even though, if left to their own devices, they would have shot her down without a second thought. And those on the left could hardly go against something so clearly left-wing.

Finishing her coffee and the small plate of fresh fry cakes Beverly had covertly placed on her bedside table, Lindsey quickly dressed in her sweats and climbed the private White House stairs to the workout room on the third floor. She was fighting hard to reach fifty stomach crunchers, designed to either strengthen her abs or kill her, when Beverly interrupted her count from the overhead intercom. "I hate to bother you up there, Madame President, but Agent Andrews would like a word with you."

"Bless you, Beverly. You just gave me the excuse I needed to quit this torture. Send him up here, would you? Along with more of those sinful fry cakes you made. I polished off the ones you left in my room, and I bet Kris would enjoy a few along with some coffee." Beverly beamed with pleasure as she nodded an okay to the agent and loaded him up with goodies before sending him on his way.

As Andrews entered the workout room carrying a thermos of hot coffee and a small plate of four greasy fry cakes, Lindsey patted the floor mat beside her, inviting him to sit.

"Take your jacket off, Agent Andrews. Might as well be comfortable when you can. Business suits aren't exactly in style up here," she smiled.

Handing her the coffee and fry cakes, he tugged off his jacket, folded it carefully, and placed it on the floor beside him, exposing the brown leather shoulder holster and small handgun that Lindsey believed were permanently attached to his body. But at this moment he was grinning from ear to ear, his usually formal demeanor nowhere to be seen. "Wow, Madame President," he said as he squatted down Indian style on the mat. "I think you knocked their socks off with that one—the Trent Mandate. I admire your courage, Ma'am. I— I just wonder if things would have turned out differently for my brother Tommy if the mandate had been in place before he went off the deep end and OD'd."

Lindsey leaned forward with a look of concern. "You were very close to him, Kris. What do you think—would it have helped him?"

The agent thought long and hard before answering. "I'd have to say it could have gone either way for him, Ma'am. With drugs being so easily available, he might have done himself in even sooner, but on the other hand, maybe not. It was some really bad shit that killed him, cocaine laced with ketamine, the medical examiner said—a horse tranquilizer that's supposed to intensify the high." He shrugged. "Tommy had tried several times to get into rehab, but without any money or insurance it never worked out for him. Today . . . maybe he'd have had a chance."

Kris grimaced, then shifted to what had brought him to the president, his voice low, concerned. "But I want to fill you in on what we do expect to happen as a result of the drug mandate, Ma'am. When you first took on the presidency, the Secret Service was worried about all the crazy male supremacists out there. They've been ranting and raving about the travesty of having a female president, and bragging about how they're going to bring you down—but the Service isn't focused on them at the moment. It's the guerillas from the drug cartels that've got us on our toes, because you've just destroyed their golden calf."

Lindsey nodded in agreement. "We've just pulled the trillion-dollar plug on some of the world's most violent, ruthless, and utterly vicious monsters." She looked at him intently. "But that's only part of it, Kris. You'll have to keep an eye on the fat cats in the banking industry who've made billions laundering money for those same drug cartels. And then there's the big business execs who'll try to take me out because that laundered money will no longer be diverted into their coffers. The drying up of huge profits they make from the constant flow of drug money is likely to lead to a sudden financial crash in the market.

"And, of course, I'll be hated by the thousands of police and corrections officers who will lose their jobs because most of our non-violent drug offenders will be diverted into treatment centers instead of prisons. Our U.S. prison population is about to shrink by more than half, Agent Andrews. And isn't it ironic that the fact of addicts going into treatment to dry out will lead to the drying up of all the entities that fed off them?" Lindsey reached over and placed a hand on his arm. "And, Kris, it may even be some renegade DEA agent from our own government who'll come after me. After all, I'll be destroying the mission those men and women worked so hard to accomplish over the years, many losing their lives in the process." She watched Kris's face darken as the reality of her words sunk in.

She shrugged dejectedly, then said, "And possibly the biggest threat of all will come from some distraught parent. From here on out, I'll be blamed by every mother in the country who loses a child to drugs. I pray every waking moment that our rehab centers will be equal to the task. Quite a change from all the legal entities who've been persecuting the victims of addiction while needing them to keep their own jobs."

The silence in the large workout room settled heavily on Kris's shoulders as he considered the crushing demands that would be made on him as Lindsey's personal bodyguard in the coming months. He rose slowly from the mat and helped his president to her feet. Squaring his shoulders, he said, "It took a lot of guts for you to put yourself on the line like this. And I can promise you, Madame President; I'll never allow you to be placed in a situation where I can't protect you, and I swear I'll keep you safe from any of those idiots out there that come after you."

After Kris left, Lindsey decided she'd had enough physical exertion for the day. She grabbed a quick shower and had just finished dressing when her cell phone beeped. Her heart skipped a beat, hoping as always that the call would be from Brian. But it was Beverly, who rarely called on her cell unless it was something urgent. "What is it Bev? I'm on my way down."

"I just wanted to warn you, Madam President," she said in a hushed voice. "There's another, uh—delegation waiting for you in my office."

"I'm not surprised," Lindsey sighed. "But if they're in your office, where are you calling from?"

"From behind the coffee machine. I don't want them to know I'm alerting you. I'm afraid they're waiting to pounce on you, Lindsey."

Minutes later, Lindsey strode into Beverly's office, a large smile on her face. "Good morning, everyone. Did we have a meeting scheduled?"

"This won't take long, Madam President." Not surprisingly, it was Shakett who spoke up from the group of at least twelve Congressmen and Senators who had crowded into Beverly's office. Shakett moved to the door of the Oval Office and swung it open, motioning Lindsey to enter. "After you, Lindsey—er, Madam President. We just want a word with you."

Lindsey scowled at him. "I think not, Senator. I don't particularly feel like being ganged up on this morning. But I'll gladly meet with a representative from each party. I'm certain any two of you can speak for your entire delegations." Amid the rumblings of dissension Lindsey said firmly, "Congresswoman Sanchez," and nodded toward an angry, red-faced woman wearing a charcoal skirt and black blazer. This immediately quieted the Democrats, as Roberta Sanchez was one of Lindsey's strongest opponents and would voice her party's displeasure with authority.

Senator Shakett cleared his voice loudly. "I'll represent our fellow Republicans," he proclaimed. "I believe I'm best suited to speak for them."

Deliberately ignoring him, she motioned to a slightly stooped elderly man dressed, as always, in a rumpled black suit and a string tie. "Senator Crowell," she asked with affection, "would you be so kind as to join me and Ms. Sanchez?"

The Senator was well known for vociferously speaking his mind no matter who it offended, and for this reason and for this particular issue, he was highly acceptable to both parties. Crowell looked at her from under shaggy white eyebrows with skepticism. "Now don't you think I'll go easy on you just because your father and I are lifelong friends. I happen to disagree with this crazy drug scheme of yours, and like everyone else in this room, I'm here to stop you."

Lindsey acknowledged his proclamation with a small smile, then addressed her assistant. "We'll want to record this, Beverly. Please engage the remote cameras in the Oval Office."

"Yes, Madam President." She was so proud of Lindsey, she practically saluted. As far as Beverly was concerned, her boss had handled this potentially explosive situation as well as any politician she knew could have done—and she knew a slew of them. Beverly pushed a series of buttons on her console. "I have the video cams in record mode now." She looked at the remaining men and women still standing in her office. "Now then, can I get coffee for anyone before you leave? It's my own special blend."

As Lindsey entered the Oval Office, she invited her two visitors to sit on one of the soft, blue sofas in the center of the room. Returning their brisk handshakes, she joined them on the other. Despite her gracious manner, the stern expressions facing her left little doubt that she was in for a rough time. Undaunted, she began. "I intend to use the recording of this discussion for this evening's TV Chat. I know you're going to hit me with all the difficult questions everyone in the country wants answered."

Roberta Sanchez glared at her with smoldering rage. "Let's get real here, Madam President. You'll edit out everything that makes you look bad."

"Uncut and unedited," Lindsey said, "including your opening statement, Roberta. You have my word on it."

Senator Samuel Crowell, his craggy face locked in a scowl of determination, leaned forward and spoke in his rich stentorian voice. "Do you have any idea what you're doing, Madam President? You are about to throw our nation into chaos and economic crisis! You must listen to reason."

"I fear the voice of reason is rarely found in politics, Senator," she answered, then added reluctantly, "but you're right. There *will* be an initial increase in crime, as those who have been making their living off illegal drugs will find themselves without a product to sell. Pockets once lined with hundred-dollar bills will suddenly be empty. Our law-enforcement people are already gearing up to deal with that."

"And what about all those addicts who are about to go ballistic using your oh-so-easily-obtained drugs?" Roberta jumped in. "And everyone else who never used but will be tempted to give it a try now that the drugs will be legally available?"

"If you recall, Roberta, during the Obama era your own party entertained the idea of legalizing marijuana, not to put drug dealers out of business but primarily to strengthen the floundering economy and create jobs. And to answer your question, if those who use drugs are adults, they are responsible for putting those substances in their bodies. And if they commit a crime while doing it, they'll be prosecuted to the full extent of the law, which you know is now quite severe. But we'll no longer be sending our citizens to jail for simply using drugs. If they don't sell to kids, don't rob or steal from anyone—who are they hurting other than themselves?"

"Who are they hurting?" Senator Crowell roared. "They're keeping the Goddamn drug dealers in business!"

"No, Sam—*we're* keeping them in business, but no longer. Not with the enactment of the Trent Mandate."

"Ahh, yes," he said derisively, staring holes in her. "Lindsey Delaware, the lone voice of wisdom crying out for justice. Tell me, who made you the savior of the world?"

Seeing Lindsey's stunned silence, Roberta rejoined the battle. "For heaven's sake, Madam President, why this grand plan? Why aren't you simply continuing to go after the drug dealers who get people hooked on that trash in the first place?"

Lindsey managed to stop before her voice shook. Nothing she said seemed to be getting through. Gathering herself, she tried again. "If a drug dealer is responsible for hooking people on drugs, then are state governments responsible for hooking people on gambling? How many state-operated lotteries and casinos are there, Roberta? And how many people lose everything they own because they become addicted to gambling? A gambling addiction is no different than a drug addiction. But we don't incarcerate gambling addicts."

"No, it's not the same," the Senator argued. "Most people don't commit crimes to support their gambling habits, but most drug addicts do."

"Because casinos are freely available to them, Sam. That's my point exactly. And besides, if you're going to gamble, you're going to find a way—whether there are casinos available or not. The same is true for drug addictions." She probed the icy blue eyes that met hers, hoping for understanding.

He made a tsking sound. "I'm amazed at your talent for self-deception, President Delaware. And you've deceived us as well. How were we to know? You blinded us with all your rhetoric about being tough on drug crime, and we failed to see what you really intended."

Her smoke-gray eyes turned to slate. "When we shine the light of judgment on others, the glare tends to blind us, Senator. But if I've truly deceived myself as well as my country, there is a simple solution—I'll stand for impeachment."

"Just as well," he snarled, "because you're no Republican, Lindsey. You're a Goddamned Federalist, taking control out of the people's hands and turning the entire drug mess over to big government."

"Wrong! I advocate for the smallest government possible, Senator. I wholeheartedly agree with Thomas Jefferson, who said, 'government is best when it does the least.' And I adhere to Ronald Reagan's Republican mantra that a government big enough to give us everything we want is big enough to take everything we have' . . . but in this case, yes. I believe our government has to be in charge of regulating the distribution of drugs. Oh, and by the way, I've recently been accused of being a Goddamn Libertarian, so I wish someone could tell me where I really fit in here before I have an identity crisis."

Roberta Sanchez raised her hands in the air. "Enough of this bickering! I just want to know one thing, Madam President. How do you see all this ending?"

There was a long pause before Lindsey answered. "I'm unsure, Roberta. I'm acting by faith—not by sight."

The truth confounded the Congresswoman. "In other words, you have no idea!" Lindsey nodded without smiling. "Well, this is really going to play well on your TV Chat this evening, Madam President. I trust you'll stick by your word to air this entire debacle." The Congresswoman laughed, but it was low, mean, and dangerous.

The pale blue dress of linen was simply styled and fell appealingly over Lindsey's slender figure. She had chosen the peaceful Lincoln Sitting Room for her evening broadcast, and settled into one of the room's antique brocade chairs. Then she steeled herself for the onslaught of glaring lights and the fallout that was to follow. Not everyone is going to love you, Lindsey, her father had warned when she first entered politics. But she had been loved and respected by many—and she needed that to continue if she was going to make this work.

Lindsey could not remember a time when she had been so completely exhausted. Using only a touch of makeup, she now worried that the unforgiving lights would reveal her fatigue. From the back of the room, Lindsey heard, "We're live on the count of five, Madam President." She waited until she spotted the red eye over the camera, then nodded and began her broadcast.

Lindsey told her viewers that this evening's TV Chat would begin with a video that had been taped in the Oval Office earlier in the day. She explained the circumstances of the meeting, then waited until the video ended. "The harsh tone and remarks made during that meeting were unquestioningly as upsetting to you as they were to me," she said. "But they clarify the doubts that accompany the Trent Mandate and troubling questions that need answers.

"I can only reiterate what I've already stressed. The purpose of the mandate is *not* to encourage increased drug abuse. Nor does it tolerate crimes associated with drugs or alcohol. It doesn't matter whether people are aware of what they're doing when they are in a drunken stupor or a narcotic haze. They must be held accountable for their criminal actions whenever they choose to put those mind-altering substances into their bodies.

"Yes, the drugs of cannabis, heroin, and cocaine will be available in state stores, right along with alcohol. Drugs that are already available on our city streets but at a terrible cost, both financially and to human life. It's time we stopped punishing the victims and provided them rehabilitation instead. Do you recall the Lefever conviction in Michigan? As a young woman she was promised a light sentence for her first offense of cocaine possession if she admitted her guilt, then was unfairly sentenced to twenty years. After several months in prison she managed to escape and fled to California where she lived a productive, drug-free life. Her husband, children, friends, had no idea of her past until years later she was rearrested and taken back to Michigan to complete her sentence. Fortunately, after several more months of incarceration, the state came to its senses and let her return to her family rather than keeping her in prison at a cost of over $30,000 a year.

"This is only one example of thousands that cry out for justice. The next several months will be difficult while our nation adjusts to the radical changes the Trent Mandate will bring about—but it will all be in the cause of justice."

As Agent Andrews walked her back to her private rooms, Lindsey made a sudden decision. "Kris, I want to spend a few days with my father in Dover. Can you arrange things with security?"

"Of course, Madam President. How soon do you want to leave?"

"Tomorrow morning," she responded without hesitation.

"I'm afraid it will take a little longer than that to get everyone in place, Ma'am. We'll have to recon the area around your estate and—"

"Tomorrow morning, Kris. I'm serious. I'm calling Dad tonight to let him know."

After speaking with her father, Lindsey toyed with her cell phone. She so badly needed Brian, to hear his voice. But it would be selfish to let him back into her life; the simple truth was that Lindsey did not expect to survive her presidency.

Brian picked up on the second ring. "Lindsey?" He spoke into the silence that followed. "Hi, sweetheart. I, I guess things are pretty tough right now . . . but you're doing the right thing, Lindsey." His voice was low and rough. Lindsey could hear the desire he was holding back, and she began crying softly. "Aw, don't cry, Baby. Just talk to me, okay? Talk to me, Lindsey . . . Lindsey?" She felt as if her heart was being ripped away, but she couldn't say the words he longed to hear. Tearfully, she ended the call. Brian cradled his phone in the palm of his hand long after it went dead.

After a restless night, Lindsey ate a hurried, solitary breakfast in the small dining room off the Oval Office, then found Beverly at her desk. "Sorry to throw you a curve, Bev, but you'll have to rearrange my schedule. I'm going to spend several hopefully restful days with my father. I'll check in with you every few hours, but of course I want you to call me right away if anything urgent comes up."

Beverly gave her a hard hug. "It's been too long since you've taken a break, Madam President. You're long overdue. Then reluctantly she handed Lindsey a stack of several newspapers. "This morning's news. I've highlighted the articles you'll want to read on your way to Dover."

Agent Andrews escorted Lindsey to the underground garage. The presidential limo stood waiting. "We have a small contingency of agents already in place at your father's estate, Ma'am. We don't want to draw too much attention, so we'll have just your car on the drive there with two motorcycles in the lead and two more following. We should make it in a couple of hours, easy." He eased her into the spacious back seat of the limo, then climbed into the front passenger's seat. He motioned the driver to proceed as the cycles fell into place in the small motorcade.

Fighting her fatigue, Lindsey settled into the comfortable seat and began reading highlighted sections of the newspapers Beverly had given her. Her pallid face and deeply shadowed eyes spoke to her exhaustion. After a few minutes she dozed off, the papers falling to the floor at her feet.

TWENTY-TWO

Terror struck at their hearts. The men had dismounted their motorcycles in the Senator's driveway when they heard the first shot ring out. A heartbeat later, it was followed by a second. Their terror morphed to anguish when they saw the fallen bodies of their president and fellow agent. Two of the men threw themselves over the president, shielding her and Agent Andrews while the other two knelt, prepared to take aim at anything that moved. Seconds later, three more Secret Service agents burst from the house, weapons in hand, and ran to the limo.

"Were they hit?" shouted one.

"God, are they okay?" cried another.

Agent Andrews lay white and still on the hard floor of the foyer where his men had carried him, waiting for the ambulance. He was unconscious, but breathing. Lindsey sat above him on a settee, willing him to regain consciousness, with James at her side.

"What the hell happened?" snarled Agent Young, who was in charge. "We have an agent down and a nearly dead president. Didn't any of you assholes see anything?" He was clearly shaken. "Don't everyone speak up at once, for Chrissake!"

It was clear no one had observed the frightening incident. As if in a trance, Lindsey spoke. "Kris—Agent Andrews was helping me from the car. He, he was leaning over and just as he straightened I heard an awful thudding sound. He fell at my feet, but managed to wrap an arm around my legs to pull me down just as the second shot was fired." Tears slid down her face. "Where—where was he hit?"

"In his Kevlar vest, thank God," Young answered. "The bullet was fired from a high-powered rifle and hit his metal jacket square in the back. He must have felt like a cement truck slammed into him. Knocked all the air out of his lungs, but somehow he managed to get you down before he lost consciousness. Good thing. The sniper used a long-range scope and was clearly an expert. Both bullets could have been kill shots if Agent Andrews hadn't stood up when he did to block the target—that would be you, Ma'am. His actions clearly saved your life. He's going to have one hell of a bruised back, but he should be able to return to duty in a few days."

Even so, when the ambulance arrived Lindsey insisted on accompanying her agent to the hospital. She had to be the first to talk to him when he regained consciousness. His playful behavior as her knight in shining armor had turned out to be a lifesaving gesture, and would make for an exciting entry in the history books. But for the sake of Kris's career, Lindsey would make certain no one would know how things had actually played out that fateful day.

James was waiting impatiently for Lindsey to return from the hospital. When she finally arrived, accompanied by an entourage of special agents, he gave her a welcoming hug, then pulled her into his study for privacy. "I see they finally have all kinds of protection for you," he said disgustedly.

"Typical; now that the horse is gone, they lock the barn door."

"Dad, be fair. They had very little notice that I would be coming here. They usually insist on days to prepare when I travel, but I gave them no choice. The real question is how on earth the sniper knew of my plans to visit you. Whoever put him in place either had our house already staked out, knowing I'd come here sooner or later, or they have a way to track my every move. What's most maddening is it's unlikely we'll ever know who was responsible."

The Secret Service had scoured the grounds but came up empty—not a shell casing, cigarette butt, or footprint had been left behind. The agents could only surmise that the sniper had been concealed in one of the tall oaks surrounding the house, or on the rooftop of one of the numerous out-buildings on the property.

"Wouldn't surprise me if that old reprobate Sam Cro-well was behind it," James growled. "He told me all about the rough time he and Roberta Sanchez gave you."

Lindsey laughed. "The Senator? That's highly unlikely, Dad. I think he was just doing everything he could think of to scare me off and get me to change my mind about the mandate. He even called me a Libertarian, for heaven's sake."

"A 'Goddamn Libertarian' is what he told me," James said with a chuckle. "And you're right. He has no faith in what you've put into action, and believes it will irreparably damage the country."

"And you, Dad? Do you still support me?"

"Lindsey, you managed to convince me long ago that decriminalization was the only hope for resolving the mess that drugs have created. And the fact that John Hayes was behind you, even though reluctantly, spoke volumes. But," he put his hands on her shoulders and looked at her imploringly, "God help me Lins, after today's attack . . . you're my *child*, Lindsey."

"Dad! What about the thousands of innocent children who have been killed in Mexican drug violence, and thousands more right here in America? Who is going to stop this insanity? We can't back out now. Look, we knew the chances were high—probable, that assassination attempts would be made." He nodded his head slowly and dropped his arms in resignation.

"I can only look ahead, Dad," she went on. "I have face-to-face meetings scheduled with every world leader whose country is going to be impacted by the step we've just taken. In fact, I'm flying to Mexico City in a few days to meet with several of them. The first item on my agenda will be to assure them that the dirt-poor peasants who grow cocaine in the jungles of South America will not be left to starve. Right now they are lucky if they make $5,000 a year off their hard labor, while the drug kingpins make a thousand times that. We will agree to pay those laborers a fair price for their work. In return we will be assured of a clean product that we'll package and distribute through state stores."

James gave her a slow smile. "Can't we just convince them to grow tobacco instead?"

"Tobacco?" Lindsey laughed. "You mean that cancer-causing agent that our government continues to denounce while raking in the tons of taxes it imposes on every pack of cigarettes? That's exactly what we'll be doing with street drugs—except all the tax money will be going back into drug education and treatment."

"Okay, okay. You win, Lindsey. I always said it was useless to argue with you once you've made your mind up about something." There was a twinkle in his eye as he added, "But sometimes, young lady, you're too smart for your own good."

"Can't help it, Dad. It's the way I was raised."

Minutes later, Lindsey was upstairs in her bedroom preparing to retire early. She had explained to her father that she left Washington at daybreak that morning feeling absolutely exhausted, and that the day's events had only added to her fatigue. She stripped out of the gray Calvin Klein suit she'd worn all day and shook her head. It was one of her favorites and had been like new when she donned it earlier, but now it was rumpled and stained. Her headlong fall onto her father's driveway had nearly ruined it. Tossing it aside, she took a steaming hot shower, then slid into her favorite pair of plain cotton pajamas. She'd managed to find them in the bottom drawer of her dresser, neatly folded along with several other pieces of old clothing she'd left behind.

Plumping up her pillows, she sat back and, barely managing to keep her eyes open, retrieved messages from her cell phone. The first call had been from Beverly. Lindsey regretted the sound of barely controlled panic in her friend's voice. Beverly had left the message as soon as she heard that shots had been fired at the James Delaware estate. Lindsey had already called Beverly from Kris's bedside in Dover Hospital to assure her she was unharmed, so she deleted the message. The next two were from Lyle and Gavin. Calling Lyle first, she found that Gavin was waiting with him for Lindsey's call and they put her on speaker phone.

"Dammit, Lindsey—I mean dammit, Madame President, this is exactly what Gavin and I predicted would happen," Lyle bellowed. "You've got to back off. Julie would never have wanted this."

Lindsey spent time talking with the two men, trying to calm their fears. "You can yell at me all you want, gentlemen, but I know full well that if either of you were in my shoes, you'd see this through to the end."

The last call was from Brian, as she'd expected. She hesitated before playing it back. Her emotions were in such turmoil she didn't think she could withstand the bittersweet pain of hearing his voice. With a heavy sigh she closed the cell without playing his message, turned off the bedside lamp, and reached for her covers—just as her father's insistent voice rang from the bottom of the stairs.

"Lindsey, come down here," he demanded. "There's something in my study I want you to see."

Wearily, she threw back the covers. Sliding out of bed, she padded in bare feet and pajamas across her darkened room and down the carpeted stairs. *I will get some sleep, I will, I will, I will,* she promised herself. Reaching the study, she saw her father gazing out the window on the far side of the room and went to him. "Dad, you have something to show me?"

He turned and smiled broadly, then motioned behind her. "I'm afraid it's someone, not something, Lindsey. *Two* someones, actually."

Lindsey turned slowly and locked into the cerulean blue of Brian's eyes. A smartly dressed boy stood with him; an eleven-year-old, nearly five-foot-tall version of Brian who could only be Brian's son. At the moment, Chip was staring at Lindsey as if she were an apparition.

"Brian? Chip? What on earth are you doing here? And how did you get past all the security?"

"I'm afraid I imposed on the good graces of your father, Madam President. The Secret Service has this place barricaded like a fortress. I—I wasn't sure you'd give us clearance, so I called James and pleaded with him to have the agents pass us through." His gaze traveled the length of her homey, well-worn pajamas. "I guess you weren't expecting company," he smiled.

Chip spoke up. "Dad made me wear this darn ole' suit and tie, but—gosh, you look just like everybody else!"

Lindsey laughed appreciatively. "That's the best compliment anyone's given me in a long time, Chip," she said. "And please forgive my bad manners. It's wonderful to have you here."

She extended a hand to him but he paused to look questioningly at his father. "Am I supposed to salute, Dad?" he whispered.

Now it was Brian's turn to laugh. "I think shaking her hand would be proper protocol, son," he said, patting him on the shoulder and giving him a gentle shove in Lindsey's direction.

But instead of a handshake, when he reached Lindsey she extended her arms and gave him a hard hug. "I've known you since you were a little boy, Chip, so I hope you don't mind if I break protocol and give you a hug instead of a handshake." As Chip tried to recover from his embarrassment, Lindsey's eyes shifted to Brian. "I know we have to talk, Brian, but I am so tired right now, I can't think straight. Can you and Chip stay the night and we'll talk in the morning?" He nodded briefly and she looked again at Chip. "We have a spare room that Julie used whenever she was here. Would that be okay?"

"Julie? It was her room? Sure, I'd like that a lot." He looked at Brian. "So we're staying, Dad? It's the weekend, so I won't be missing school—and my friends are *not* going to believe this," he added.

After getting their guests settled in, which included a trip to the kitchen for hot chocolate followed by a search for new toothbrushes, Lindsey once again crawled into bed.

Within moments she fell into a heavy, welcoming sleep, only to be awakened a few minutes later by a light tapping on her door.

"Dad? Now what," she grumbled sleepily. "Can't it wait 'til morning?"

Her door opened quietly. From the dim hall light she glimpsed Brian slipping into her room, dressed only in T-shirt and boxers. "*I* can't wait 'till morning, sweetheart. We've got to get this settled." He slid under the covers and snuggled against her. "Like your pajamas," he breathed softly, "but they might get in the way."

"Brian! We can't do this—what about Chip? My father?"

"I think they'd approve . . . I can go ask them if you like." But he wrapped his arms around her instead and leaned in, finding her lips with his. He had waited far too long for this: to once again fist his hands in the thickness of her hair, to put his mouth on the softness of her lips, to feel her firm breasts pushing against him.

It was a long slow kiss that warmed Lindsey to her toes and threatened to set her on fire. She tried to pull away. "Brian, please. I can't *think* like this!"

"I don't want you think, Lindsey. I just want you to *feel*." He stroked her breasts possessively as he buried his face in her tumble of hair, breathing in her essence. "You can't tell me you don't want this—need this, as badly as I do." Her deep, desperate moan reassured him and he tightened with desire.

"God, Lindsey, I was so frightened when I heard about the assassination attempt. And then, once I knew you were safe, I was angry. All I could think of was all the wasted years. Years we should have been together. But no more, Lindsey! No more! I swear from now on I'll overcome every barrier that comes between us, and Lord knows there've been enough of them—my selfish reaction to our inability to have kids, my stupid involvement with Adriane, your rocketing career to the presidency, and your fear that something bad might happen to me or Chip."

"It still could, Brian," she cried, struggling to hold back her fear. "It still could."

"Hush." He kissed the tears from her cheeks. Then looking into her eyes, he drew a deep breath and spoke her name. "Lindsey . . . I knew, Lindsey. The minute you announced your decision to decriminalize drugs, I knew. *That* was the reason you pushed me away after Adriane left. Not because the presidency had gone to your head, but because that drug mandate has made you and everyone close to you a multinational target."

"Brian," she cried, "how can you even consider putting Chip at such great risk?" She tried once again to escape his embrace but he held her wrists firmly, refusing to let her go. "We can't do this anymore, Brian. How many times have we gotten our hopes up, only to have them taken away? I've been hopeless for a long time, but that hurts less than having our expectations dashed repeatedly."

"Listen to me now, Lindsey. After the shooting Chip and I had a long conversation. Actually, I was agonizing aloud about our situation and the danger involved. Finally, Chip got in my face and said no way was he going be the one to stand in the way of you and me being together. He *wants* this for us, Lindsey, as much as I do. And if you're honest, as much as you do."

"But he's a child, Brian. You can't let him decide—"

"He's a pretty gutsy kid, Lindsey, and darned smart for his age. He understands the danger, especially after today, but figures being the stepson of the U.S. president is worth the risk. Besides, he loves you, Lins. He remembers you and

Julie from his early childhood. He's followed your career every step of the way, and he's treasured every gift, every letter you've sent him. Please don't sell him short—and don't let him be a barrier any longer . . . and if you don't agree to have sex with me right this minute, woman, I'm going to explode."

He was right, she knew. They had wasted far too many precious moments, too many years. It was time they left behind what lay in the past and reach out for what lay ahead. She placed her lips to his ear and whispered softly, "But, Bri, I think you're forgetting the most daunting barrier of all."

"What! What is it? I'll fix it, I swear."

"Dad and Chip, right across the hall."

"Aww, heck, that's easy. We'll just make love silently."

"Can we do that?"

"You bet, sweetheart. Long, slow, and very quietly."

For Lindsey, it was long, slow, and beautiful. She had forgotten how it felt to wrap herself around Brian's strong, muscular torso. To feel the ecstasy of his hard heat deep within her. The wonder of her body becoming one with the only man she'd ever loved.

Minutes later they lay side by side, holding hands and reveling in the glory of being together again. They were panting from their nearly frantic sexual reunion and from trying to muffle the sounds of their lovemaking.

They listened for a time to the loud snoring of James and the stillness coming from Chip's room. Relieved they had not disturbed anyone, Brian spoke huskily into the darkness. "From now on we'll be completely one, Lins—you in me and me in you."

"Is that a promise, counselor?"

"Never would I try to deceive the president of my country, especially after that spectacular round of lovemaking."

"Well, you know what they say about spectacular lovemaking—once is never enough."

Lindsey lost count after the next several spectacular rounds, then fell into a restful sleep entwined in Brian's arms. They awoke at dawn and spoke in whispered tones of their plans for the future—what role Brian would play as the first gentleman of the country, where Chip would go to school, where they would live when Lindsey left the White House. To their amazement, they agreed on everything.

"Guess we've grown up, Lindsey. I want whatever you want—nothing is as important as our being together."

"Oh, Brian, we're finally going to make it, aren't we? After all the sadness, the agony of being apart." Magically her mood changed, and she rolled playfully on top of him, planting a kiss on his smiling lips. "Have you ever proposed to the president of the United States before, Brian?"

"Am I about to?"

"I think so, yes."

"And will I be turned down?"

"I don't think so, no."

"Lindsey Delaware! I've proposed to you a hundred times over the years. A man can only take so much rejection." He studied her still smiling face. "Well, what the heck, maybe a hundred-and-one will be the lucky charm. So will you, dear Madam President? Will you marry me?"

Lindsey answered dreamily, "My sweet, sweet, Brian. After all these lonely years you've turned my darkness into dancing. How could I not marry you? That's a yes, by the way. Now," she said, giving him a final kiss on his forehead, "don't you think you should slip back into your room before Chip goes looking for you?'

"Don't think so. He's the one who sent me."

"What?"

'It's true. He practically pushed me out of my room last night saying, 'Don't you think you should fix things with Lindsey before she gets away again, Dad?' I wanted to hug him, but he decided a while back that he's too old for that."

"Well, *I'm* going to hug him, a lot, and he's just going to have to get used to it."

"My guess is he won't mind it at all coming from you."

As Lindsey and James, Brian and Chip gathered at the breakfast table that morning, James asked them to join hands while he gave a heartfelt prayer of thanks. Following the "Amen," Brian beamed at Chip and James, then made the announcement. "Lindsey and I decided . . . the four of us? We're a family now. We want you to help us plan where and when the wedding will take place and a whole lot of other things."

Lindsey didn't have to worry about Chip not wanting her hugs. He jumped up from the table and ran to wrap his arms around her. "This is too cool, Lindsey—I mean Mrs. President."

Lindsey hugged him back and smiled happily. "Chip, would you feel okay calling me 'Mom?' Your dad and I talked about this and I want to adopt you, if you're all right with that."

"Sure! You were *supposed* to be my mom, anyway." Brian coughed loudly into his napkin, but Chip continued undaunted. "You know it's true, Dad. Whenever Mother got angry at us"—he looked at Lindsey, "and that happened a lot, she always yelled that you wished Lindsey was my mom and she did too. I think she said it to hurt us, but really, it made me feel pretty good—knowing you wanted me even if Mother thought I was a nuisance."

"Oh, Chip," Lindsey said. "You're such a great kid. I can't imagine anyone thinking of you as a nuisance. I lost my mother when I was a teenager, but she was a wonderful mom, and I promise that's what I'll be for you." She gave Brian the full benefit of her gray eyes. "And a wonderful wife for you, Brian."

"Well, if promises are in order," said James, "then I promise to be a wonderful grandfather. That will be so easy. But as for being a wonderful father-in-law—?"

"You'll be great," Brian laughed, "as long as I'm a wonderful husband to your wonderful daughter, right?"

The private wedding in the Lincoln Room was small but elegant. Chip, cutting a striking appearance in his black and gray tux, proudly served as Brian's best man while James presented his daughter to her husband-to-be. Lindsey's satin gown of pearls and creamy lace brought Beverly to tears and made Brian's heart thud with pride and desire. Lyle and Gavin, along with the minister from Lindsey's church completed the wedding party.

Scattered around the room were a handful of very special guests including Secretary of State Royce White, Vice President Roget, and Agent Kris Andrews with his new young wife, Kathy. A cotillion of Secret Service agents stood stiffly at the edge of the room, their faces watchful and expressionless. A lone photographer filmed the ceremony for posterity.

Kris patted his wife's hand as they listened to the vows being spoken. The bond that had formed between him and his president had grown even stronger following the near assassination. Initially, he had been ridden with guilt and was determined to resign the agency. But the president had sat with him tirelessly in the hospital, finally convincing him that if he hadn't done exactly what he'd done that day, the sniper would in all likelihood have succeeded. Lindsey insisted she would not consider any other agent as his replacement, and added with a smile that she was making that a presidential order.

The previous month he had once again tested the president's decision to keep him on by handing her his and Kathy's wedding announcement. Lindsey had looked at him with surprise. "Congratulations, Kris. I'm very happy for you . . . but sad, too. You know I make it a practice to use only unmarried agents for my personal security. I hate the thought of losing you."

"Yes, ma'am. Some of the men think it's because you're concerned we'll be too distracted by our family responsibilities to put ourselves in the line of fire. But I know that because of the danger involved, you don't want us to leave families behind, right?"

Lindsey brushed that aside. "But, Kris, you know the rules."

He shook his head. "If you fire me, ma'am, I'll have to sue for marriage discrimination."

"There is no such thing, Kris," she laughed.

He beamed at her, "There will be if you fire me for marrying Kathy!" With a chuckle, the president gave in and agreed to keep him on as her personal bodyguard.

Immediately following the wedding, a large reception was held in the diplomatic reception room on the ground floor of the White House. Hundreds of guests were in attendance, comprised of old school friends, business associates, politicians, news media, and of course every possible lobbyist who could wrangle an invitation.

Brian had left her side to greet an old friend, then returned several minutes later with a scowl on his face. "Listen to this, Lins." He placed a small hand-held recorder in her palm, laughing at her puzzled expression. "I always carry this with me. It's come in handy quite a few times."

As she hit the "play" button, Lindsey listened with growing agitation to the smooth voice of Senator Roger Shakett speaking over the loud noise of the wedding reception. Evidently, he was being questioned by a group of news reporters.

"How are you feeling at this point about decriminalization, Senator?" one of them asked. "It's been in effect several months now. Do you see any progress?"

Shakett gave a snort of laughter. "Hell, it's obvious that the country is pretty much a mess since President Delaware's mandate went into effect. There's been a dramatic rise in drug use and as a result, hundreds of deaths from overdoses. The stock market's taken a terrible hit and unemployment's gone through the roof." He shook his head in disgust. "I don't care if she is a member of my own party. We need a new, strong leader to get us out of this predicament, gentlemen, and you can quote me on that!"

Lindsey stopped the tape and looked at Brian in exasperation. He nodded his head and said, "I figured he was up to no good when I saw him jawing away with those reporters. That jerk is nothing but a publicity whore—but that's what gets him reelected! Anyway, unbeknownst to him I stood directly behind him while I taped this. I figured you'd want to know ahead of time what's going to be on the morning news."

Although Lindsey had promised herself she would not talk politics at the wedding reception, it seemed she had little choice. It was time for some serious damage control! Taking Brian's arm, they walked onstage to the emcee. Brian asked for the microphone and, after getting the crowds' attention, announced that his new bride had been asked to comment on what seemed to be the hottest topic of the century.

Taking the mike, she first thanked everyone for coming then said, "I know you are wondering if I still believe we made the right decision in decriminalizing drugs. I can honestly tell you that my son Chip seems to think so. He's told me there are no more drug dealers hanging around his school, and no more bullies in the bathroom trying to intimidate the younger kids into using. The legal ramifications for that just don't make it worth their while. The rest of the good news is that there are signs that drug abuse is beginning to taper off, the market has stabilized and is starting a slow upward climb, and the unemployment rate is about to take a serious tumble as we're putting a lot of money into retraining those who lost their jobs in the field of criminal justice. And what's most exciting is that the rehab centers across the country are showing encouraging results. They're exceedingly busy but not turning anyone away, and their recovery rate, based on the number of people successfully completing treatment and remaining drug free for a significant period of time, is remarkable."

"Oh, and I am meeting with the Canadian prime minister and his staff next week. They are seriously considering decriminalization, since much of our drug trade and its associated crime has migrated across their borders. I'll go into detail with them about all the pieces we put into place before the mandate was enacted in our country, and I believe it will reassure them.

"Now, I hope you enjoy the rest of the evening, because the White House staff has gone to considerable lengths to make this an historic occasion. Personally, I think they've done a miraculous job." Then, with a warm smile she handed the mike back to the emcee.

But now that they had her, reporters in attendance were not about to let her go. They began throwing out a barrage of questions. Seeing her dilemma, Brian took her arm and stared down at the reporters who had gathered at the foot of the stage. "Gentlemen, if you'll excuse us, I'd like to get my wife back to being the beautiful bride at this celebration instead of the president. Why don't you give us a little break here?"

As Lindsey and Brian left the stage, the sound of the orchestra filled the room with a beautiful waltz. "It's our dance, Lins, remember? That first night at Harvard? I knew when I held you that I wanted you in my life forever . . . I just didn't know how difficult it would be."

Lindsey sighed as she put her head against Brian's shoulder and swayed with him to the music. "It's been quite a dance, hasn't it, Bri? But no more changing partners or unhappy arias. I'm staying in your arms until the music ends."

EPILOGUE

Winter blew off the Atlantic to cover Dover with a blanket of ice and snow; making each day seem colder than the last. Whenever she was in Dover, Lindsey kept a low profile, attracting as little attention as possible. No motorcades with only Secret Service agents stationed surreptitiously along the route and Agent Andrews serving as her driver. Today they had taken the well-fortified black sedan to her doctor's office for her annual checkup. Lindsey sat on the examining table clad only in a thin gown. Despite the coldness of the room she was comfortable with her newly appointed physician, Monica West, who was at this moment checking Lindsey's blood pressure.

"Steady as a rock," the middle-aged doctor proclaimed, blowing back loose strands of gray hair that had fallen into her face. "I don't know how you can be so calm with everything going on in your life."

"And I'm about to add more, Monica," Lindsey confided happily. "Brian and I have decided to adopt a child. If your examination shows that I'm as healthy as I think I am, there shouldn't be any more obstacles in our way."

Her doctor looked at her with raised brows. "I'm very surprised that you and your husband aren't interested in trying for a child of your own. Even though you're approaching forty, you're healthy enough that age shouldn't be a problem."

Lindsey stared at her with hurt and anger. "Surely you're familiar with my medical history, Monica. You know I can't. The hysterectomy—"

"Dear God in Heaven!" Dr. West looked at Lindsey very much like a teacher lecturing her favorite student. "Tell me, Madam President, what types of cancer are you routinely screened for?"

"I don't know . . .breast cancer, lung cancer, colon cancer—"

"And ovarian cancer. That drunk driver delivered a terrible blow to your insides. Took out your spleen, broke both pelvic bones, and the surgeon had to remove your uterus to stop the hemorrhaging. But you still have your ovaries, Madam President."

"So—so you're saying . . .?"

"You have eggs, Brian has sperm, and science has the Petri dish. With a little help from ART, you should do just fine."

"Art? Who the heck is Art?"

"Assisted Reproductive Technology. The only other thing you need is a healthy, surrogate mom who is willing to carry and deliver your child. You know, Madam President, giving birth makes you a mother only in the technical sense. The woman who raises the child, loves and cares for the child, is its mother in the true sense of the word. And this child will have your and Brian's DNA. So yes, you *can* try for a child of your own."

Impatient to reach home, Lindsey urged Kris to navigate the snow-covered streets as rapidly as possible. Brian would be ecstatic! She kept going over the last conversation they'd had before making the final decision to adopt.

"Are you absolutely sure you can't conceive, Lindsey? There've been so many medical advances since your accident."

"Brian, stop! You know I'm missing some very necessary parts. So giving you a son or daughter just isn't in the cards."

"I'm . . . I'm sorry, Lins. I keep expecting some kind of miracle."

She laughed aloud and Kris gave her a questioning glance. "I'm about to give my husband the 'some kind of miracle' he's been praying for, Kris. We're going to make a baby!"

"Really? That's great, Madam President." He didn't ask for details. As far as Kris was concerned, his president was capable of accomplishing anything she put her mind to. He brought the car to a smooth stop in her father's circular driveway as Lindsey quickly unbuckled her seat belt and opened her door. "Wait!" Kris shouted. "No more ignoring protocol, Madam President. You wait until I'm sure all the ground security is in place before I come around to let you out."

Waiting impatiently, Lindsey stopped herself from bolting to the front door, allowing Kris to help her from the car and shield her with his body until she was safely in the house.

"Brian!" she called loudly from the foyer. "Brian, where are you?" James came briskly out of his study while Brian and Chip scurried out of the den where they'd been sword fighting on their *Wii*. She laughed at the worried expressions on their faces, as it was unusual for her to make such a ruckus. Tucking her arm in Brian's she said, "Let's go in the study, everyone. I have some news."

"Your doctor's appointment—everything's okay, isn't it, Lins?" Brian's voice was alarmed.

"What is it, Lindsey?" her father joined in Brian's concern as he closed the study door.

Picking up on their worried expressions, Chip kicked his foot into the carpeted floor. "Darn! I knew everything was going too good to be true."

"No, no, everyone," Lindsey laughed. "It's good news. Actually, it's wonderful news! We all have to pitch in and get the nursery ready. I'm pretty sure there'll soon be five of us."

"You found a baby already?" Chip said excitedly.

"No, it will be *our* baby, Chip, your father's and mine." She quickly explained the procedure Dr. West had described. Chip's eyes grew large with wonder while Brian's and James's grew moist with happiness. Then Brian pulled her into his arms and held her, not wanting to let go.

"Well. I'll be darned," James said, shaking his head as if in shock.

"Me, too," Chip said, imitating his grandfather.

Lindsey slid her arm around Brian's waist and smiled. "We have just two things to decide," she said. "Who will carry our baby for nine months, and who gets to tell Beverly, Lyle and Gavin?"

Chip said thoughtfully, "I'll bet Julie would want to be the pregnant mom if she were here, wouldn't she?"

Lindsey reached over and ruffled his hair. "Absolutely, Chip, but we'll do the next best thing by naming the baby after Julie if it's a girl. Now, I'm going to call Beverly on my cell. Brian, would you call the guys? Then we're going to have to look for that 'pregnant mom' that Chip so aptly described."

As if in a race, Beverly, Lyle, and Gavin simultaneously pulled into the Delaware circular driveway and slammed on their brakes. Lindsey greeted them at the door and escorted them into the kitchen where Brian, James, and Chip were already celebrating with leftover pizza. "I've ordered some fresh," Brian said, working his mouth around a large bite dripping with sauce. "It'll be here in a minute."

"Hey, Chip. I'll arm wrestle you for the first hot piece," Gavin said, pulling him to a corner of the table. "One of these days you might actually beat me."

"Never mind the pizza, Beverly said excitedly. I want to hear about the baby."

"It's going to be a DNA kid, right Dad? Yours, mine, and Mom's. I think that's what you said." Lindsey laughed and, giving Chip a wink as he settled into serious arm wrestling business with Gavin, she went into more detail.

When she finished, Lyle spoke up. "I have a brilliant idea, guys. I've kept in touch with a cousin of Julie's, Sandy Benson. She and Julie hung out together in high school and were pretty close friends. Anyway, Sandy has four children and would love to have another, but her husband, Ken, says, 'no way.' They just can't afford another kid. But I bet Sandy would love being pregnant again, *and* carrying the president's baby. I don't think Ken would object as long as you two are picking up the tab."

Later that night, after a hurried call to Sandy and Ken Benson who gave an eager acceptance, Lindsey and Brian celebrated with a glass of sparkling wine in their bedroom. Brian clicked his glass against Lindsey's. "Alone at last,

Lins. You and I have so little time together. I treasure every minute."

"It truly is a life to be treasured. I think I've finally come to terms Julie's death, Jonas is rotting away in that forensic prison, and after all those wasted years you and I are together and expecting our own child. With Chip and the baby, we'll have the family I could only dream of. It's all falling into place, isn't it, Brian?"

"Our personal life, yes. But what about your political life, Lins? Are all those pieces falling into place?"

"Absolutely, Bri, because by the end of this term, I won't have a political life."

His eyes widened in disbelief. "You mean . . . quit the presidency?"

Lindsey nodded. "I've already informed the chair of the RNC so the party will have time to consider future nominees.

"But the people still love you, Lindsey, despite all the turmoil we're in right now! There's no doubt you'll be reelected to serve your last four years. Look, if it's about the baby, I know you. You can have this kid and run the country at the same time—blindfolded if necessary."

Lindsey shook her head. "At the end of this term, Brian, I'll have been in the political arena for twelve straight years, six in the presidency. I've loved every minute of it, but you know how strongly I feel about term limits, and I don't believe anyone should serve longer than I already have. I know it may look as if I'm turning tail and running away from a difficult situation of my own making, but I'm truly not. Things *are* improving rapidly now, and whoever takes over will have some fresh ideas about decriminalization and everything it entails." She laughed. "I guess that was a long answer to a simple question, wasn't it?"

He gave a whispered sigh and, setting their wine glasses aside, pulled her into his arms. "But it's one I like, sweetheart. And I think Julie would agree. The Trent Mandate is helping people who wouldn't get help otherwise, and its brought justice to Julie's cause." He tipped her chin and looked into her eyes. "I know greatness isn't always measured by success, Lindsey. But when the pieces are all in place and the dust has settled, you'll be remembered as both. A *successful* president and a *great* president."

"Hmm, that's fine, Brian," she sighed as he held her. "As long as I'm best remembered as a successful wife and a great mom."